WAS

If her tale wa[s]... reason to feel ill at ease in his company.

"I'm not going to apologize, you know," Marcus remarked, dabbing at his mouth with his napkin to hide his satisfied smile. She was a magnificent creature, and so easy to goad.

"Apologize for what?" Celia wasn't even trying to dissemble. Her emerald-bright eyes glinted with anger, telling him she knew his meaning.

"Kissing you, of course. I enjoyed it immensely. Should we try it again?" For a moment he wondered if she were going to throw something at him—the cup and saucer, the teapot, the footman . . . ?

"Take a pair of stubborn, headstrong lovers, add a truly delightful cast of supporting characters, spice with some wonderfully inept rascals, and mix in a dash of danger."
—Kasey Michaels,
author of *The Secrets of the Heart*

CELEBRATE
101 Days of Romance with
HarperMonogram

FREE BOOK OFFER!

See back of book for details.

Harper Monogram

(signed: Sarah Eagle)

Lady Vengeance

⧁ SARAH EAGLE ⧁

HarperPaperbacks
A Division of HarperCollins Publishers

This is a work of fiction. The characters, incidents, and dialogues are products of the author's imagination and are not to be construed as real. Any resemblance to actual events or persons, living or dead, is entirely coincidental.

HarperPaperbacks   *A Division of* HarperCollins*Publishers*
10 East 53rd Street, New York, N.Y. 10022

Cover illustration by Bob Berran

First printing: August 1995

Printed in the United States of America

HarperPaperbacks, HarperMonogram, and colophon are trademarks of HarperCollins*Publishers*

❖ 10 9 8 7 6 5 4 3 2 1

To Eileen, in honor of wounded heroes
and too much champagne one fateful afternoon

Prologue

Celia Tregaron had never been more frightened or more annoyed in her entire twenty-two years of life. Shifting impatiently in the armchair by the dwindling fire, she adjusted her woolen cloak around her shoulders, then tightened her hold on the pistol in her right hand. The concealing shadows that surrounded her in the unfamiliar room were ideal for her purpose. After months of planning she was finally going to have her revenge—killing the earl of Ashmore, late of His Majesty's Navy.

He deserved to die after what he had done, she determined, wondering—not for the first time—how long it would be before her intended victim would finally return home. The case clock in the entry hall had struck half past two when she had warily made her entrance from the kitchen stairs of the Cumberland Square town house. Now its somber chimes were faintly sounding four o'clock. With each passing minute she became more uneasy. Not that she would lose her nerve, even if she had never killed anyone before tonight, or ever had the desire to do so. She had traveled too far and waited too long for this rendezvous to give up now.

If only the man would make an appearance before she was discovered lurking in his bedchamber. So far fortune had smiled on her. First by allowing her to maneuver the unknown streets of London without mishap, then by helping her break into Ashmore's home undetected. Her luck had continued to hold as she located the correct room after only one miscalculation. Fortunately, the lace-capped occupant had been sleeping peacefully.

Though Celia was disheartened to discover her prey missing when she entered the right chamber, she had settled into one of the comfortable winged armchairs arranged side by side before the fire. No servant had appeared to disturb her vigil, making her mistrust the efficiency of the man's household.

Everything lay in readiness for his lordship's return. A single candle burned in a candelabra on the night table beside the massive bedstead, which looked terribly inviting at the moment, since she was developing a cramp in her right leg. The bedclothes were turned back, the pillows plumped and fluffed to receive the tardy gentleman. His silk dressing gown, an extraordinary garment of scarlet and indigo, lay neatly arranged on the dark bedspread at the foot of the bed. The inviting picture was completed by a decanter of dark liquid sitting on the dressing table not far from the fireplace.

Celia considered sampling what was undoubtedly strong spirits, remembering her brother telling her about courage in a bottle. She resisted temptation, however, knowing that she must have a clear head for her mission. As it was, her imagination was playing havoc with her judgment. Was the room growing darker, more foreboding? Unfamiliar noises of the house settling shivered along her nerve endings and tripped down her spine. Then a creaking floorboard in the hallway brought her out of her self-induced panic.

This was not the time for missish games, she resolved, willing her fingers to stop trembling. The pistol was difficult enough to hold with her palm so moist. She tensed, trying to make her five-foot, six-inch frame as small as possible by pressing back against the upholstery of the armchair.

Then she waited for the overdue encounter with his lordship.

1

Marcus reached for the front door latch with his good hand, only to find himself clutching empty air seconds later instead of hard metal. The gleaming brass door ornament seemed to have moved the second his hand came within range. Taking a deep breath, he set his mind to the task once more—and failed to achieve his goal.

The simple chore of entering his own home in the wee hours of the morning was proving more difficult than he anticipated. Looking back over his shoulder, he was gratified to see that the hackney he had hired to return from his evening's entertainment had already moved on down the square. He didn't need a gaping jarvey witnessing this piece of work.

If he were a less considerate employer he could simply knock up Baskin, his majordomo, and be on his way to the comfort of his bed in a matter of minutes. He was, however, a very considerate man, if not somewhat stubborn, and insisted his servants should have a good night's sleep—even if he didn't. Swaying on his feet, he studied the problem with the same direct consideration he once regarded the enemy across the muddied battle-fields of the Peninsula. He was determined to overcome this obstacle on his own, if possible before anyone discovered him foolishly loitering on his own doorstep.

Resolute to succeed on his third attempt, he leaned his right shoulder against the doorframe to hold it in place. Then, for good measure, he pressed his cheek against the wooden panel, always keeping the recalci-trant door handle in sight. He thrust his left hand for-ward, bruising his knuckles without feeling the pain. He triumphed at last.

Almost too triumphant, he realized as the door swung open in response to the slightest touch of his hand on the well-oiled latch. Despite his finely honed reflexes, Marcus Knowles, Earl of Ashmore, almost measured his six foot frame on the inlaid wood entry hall floor as he stumbled inside. Muttering dark threats at the hapless door, he maintained his bal-ance, though his hat fell to the floor.

Fortunately, the dimly lit entry was deserted, as it should be at four o'clock in the morning. In his relief Marcus kicked the door shut, and cringed at the resounding thud that seemed to bounce off the paneled walls.

"Shhh," he hissed, raising his finger to his lips, checking once more for any sign of life in his immedi-ate vicinity. With a smile of satisfaction he leaned down to grab his headgear, and managed to snag it after only two stumbling steps. He placed his curled beaver top hat back on his head at a cocked angle and began his assault on the stairs.

He was in a splendid mood after an excursion to several gaming hells with his friends. His pockets were well lined with his winnings, and thanks to his slightly intoxicated state, he would surely sleep well. Once more he had eluded his mother's transparent machinations to rivet him to some idiot virgin bride. Not that he had anything against virgins, they had their place in society, but not next to him at the altar just yet.

As a practical man, he knew his greatest allure was an earl's coronet as well as twenty thousand pounds a year. Not overly vain, he acknowledged that his looks weren't a deterrent, having cut a dashing figure when still an ordinary major in His Majesty's Service and baronet's son. Several ladies had complimented his laughing green eyes and chestnut curls, but none had succeeded in capturing his interest beyond the moment. At two-and-thirty, he simply wasn't ready to wear the shackles of a husband.

The thought made him stumble up two stairs, making it necessary for him to firmly grasp the banister. Perhaps that was why he had enjoyed himself so thoroughly this evening, he conceded. Instead of being tortured by the musical talents of a nest of simpering ninnies that his mother, and most of the *ton*, considered eligible, he had spent the evening relaxing with his cronies. The inestimable Garth Cruthers, who had excelled as a scavenger during their service to king and country, claimed he had dire need of his former comrade-in-arms.

He smiled at the memory of their brilliant maneuver as he let himself into his room. This door was much more cooperative than the one downstairs, swinging open at the merest touch of his hand and quietly shutting again. As he walked by the matching brocade chairs next to the fire Marcus expertly flicked his left wrist and sent his hat spinning to land dead center on the seat of the one closest to the fire.

With his trusted Foster visiting his sick mother, Marcus chose to see to his own needs. Something that wasn't entirely foreign to him after so many occasions on the Peninsula. As he struggled to shrug out of his coat, he began humming the little ditty he had heard at the last, and most disreputable, of the establishments they had visited.

Only after managing to free his left arm did Marcus remember the sling that cradled his gloved right hand. Without hesitating, he slipped the black silk material off his arm. He then made short work of his cravat, waistcoat, and linen shirt, tossing them aside without the least regard for where they landed. During the past year he had become quite deft at undressing with only the use of one hand. Once he stripped to the waist he replaced the sling from habit, and frowned in concentration over his next move.

A slight turn of his head brought the decanter on the dressing table into his peripheral vision. Pausing for a moment by the bed, he lit the brace of candles from the almost-gutted one Baskin had left burning and sauntered in the direction of the dressing table. One last drink before retiring was just what he needed, he decided judiciously as he set down the candelabra and reached for the port.

"Please don't take your hand off the decanter," instructed a voice from the shadows as he grasped the neck of the cut crystal container. The voice was unknown to him and coming from the shadowed chair by the fire, four feet to his left. Marcus almost choked on the half-formed note of his song, something that had to do with the willingness of a winsome maid from Chester, and turned slowly to stare in amazement.

In a split second he forgot the song and lost most of the euphoria of his befuddled condition of the past few hours. There was nothing like a stranger sitting by the fire, holding a pistol trained directly at him, to clear his head, he decided, especially when that stranger was female. Apparently he was more than slightly tipsy not to have noticed his visitor, a more than sobering thought. He did exactly as she instructed; after all, she had said please.

"You *are* the earl of Ashmore?" Her second comment didn't put him any more at ease. Her voice wasn't much steadier than the tapered fingers holding the dueling pistol. She clasped the gun with both hands, her elbows resting on the arms of the chair as if the weight was too much for her slender wrists. At that moment she was aiming at a portion of his body that he didn't care to lose and a number of satisfied ladies were extremely fond of.

Always known for his agreeability, he saw no reason to change at that moment. He inclined his head in a slight nod. A sudden move might prove to be disastrous. Or at least he thought so until she spoke again.

"Good. I have come a long way to kill you and wouldn't want to shoot the wrong man." Suddenly her tone of voice was steady and uncompromising, convincing him that she was indeed serious. She leaned forward in her seat, allowing him his first glimpse of her face and startling him anew. He was being held at gunpoint by a schoolroom miss.

"May I ask, if it isn't too presumptuous, exactly why you want to shoot me?" If he could keep her from her purpose just a few minutes more, assuming she might be lucky in her shot, perhaps they could clear up this misunderstanding. He also needed a few more minutes to clear the last remnants of brandy fumes from his brain. Disarming her would take all the wits and skill he could muster. "I don't think we've met before this, have we? I have a lamentable memory for names at times. You are?"

"My name isn't important, sir. I've come to avenge my brother's death." For the first time he noticed there was a curious inflection to her speech. "Since Ethan is dead, I don't think it is fair that you should remain alive."

"I don't want to appear a complete nodcock, but I really don't think I know anyone named Ethan," he said as he calculated the steps between them. Really, the whole experience was rather intriguing. Women didn't usually threaten him when he entertained them in a bedchamber, except with pleasure. Cautiously he slid his foot to the right, careful to move only his lower body and praying the shadows behind him concealed his movement.

Assessing his opponent with the eye of a connoisseur, he determined that there were other activities he would much rather pursue with this young woman. She had straightened indignantly at his denial, giving him a better view of her face and upper body. His assailant also wasn't as young as he first thought, possibly in her early twenties. He had miscalculated her age, since only the innocent members of the *ton* didn't indulge in the artifice of cosmetics. This vengeful miss owed none of her appeal to the paintpots. Perhaps it was merely the influence of the liquor he had indulged in so liberally earlier, but she was a handsome piece, her rounded figure much more compelling than that of Louise, his recently discarded mistress.

Her sable hair fell in waves past her shoulders, shaping a pale oval face that was dominated by glittering eyes. He was not sure of the color of her almond-shaped eyes, but wagered to himself that they were dark brown. The candlelight and shadows clearly defined her cheekbones and straight nose above a wide, inviting pair of lips. Her skin was flawless, especially the provocative swell of her ample breasts so delightfully framed in the triangular opening of her cloak.

"Why should you remember Ethan? He was just a face among so many American sailors and so unimportant." Her bitter words stopped his speculation on how her soft body might feel pressed against him.

He realized two things with sudden clarity; he should be taking her threat more seriously, and her accent was from the former Colonies. Her inflection was similar to that of some Canadian soldiers he had encountered while serving in the Peninsula. Another fact he noted with regret, aside from her accent, was that she was well-spoken. With this thought in mind, he took a closer look at her clothing. As he suspected, her woolen cloak and what he could see of the gray dress beneath were quality goods. Whoever she was, she appeared to be a lady, so he quickly suppressed his amorous thoughts and returned to the matter at hand—disarming her. He slid forward another inch or so, making sure he had plenty of room to maneuver when the opportunity arose.

"So, I met this Ethan at sea? Exactly when did this momentous meeting take place, my dear?" The only time he had spent at sea had been on troop transports to and from Portugal.

"Your ship captured our vessel in the spring of

1813. I suppose you took so many prizes during the war, you've forgotten," she snapped, her knuckles turning white around the handle of the gun.

If he didn't disarm her quickly, she was likely to shoot in a fit of pique from his taunting, Marcus decided. He noted with interest her reference to *our vessel.* Although he wasn't sure exactly what that meant, he knew it was significant.

"I'm to understand that you and your brother are Colonials, then? I impressed your brother into the Royal Navy against his will," he stated without hesitation, casually shifting his weight to his left hip and leg. For good measure, he crossed his good arm over his sling, drawing her attention to his incapacitated right hand and forearm. The diversion worked. With her wide-eyed gaze riveted to his gloved hand, she seemed to relax as he intended, never realizing that he was within striking distance now.

"I'm an American, sir; we did win—"

"'Milord,'" he broke in gently to correct her form of address, adding a slight smile of condescension. "I realize things are a bit primitive where you come from, so I'll forgive your ignorance in polite matters. You should address me as 'milord,' not 'sir.' If I were a duke, you would say 'Your Grace.'"

"I beg your pardon?" Her outrage was magnificent, and it gave Marcus the opening he needed to make his move. He sprang across the short distance between them, quickly grasping the gun barrel and pulling her from the chair in one fluid movement. Her gasp of surprise made him smile in satisfaction. Clearly she had not guessed that he was left-handed. In her surprise she grasped the pistol in her weaker left hand, just as he had hoped. It took more than a little effort, however, to keep her wrist shackled in his grip. She wasn't going to give up without a struggle, and squirmed against him to raise the pistol he safely pointed at the floor. For a moment he thought it was a near thing before he managed to retain control.

Her slippered feet were no match against his well-muscled calves, though he flinched as she kicked him more than once. Marcus stopped that maneuver by trapping her ankles between his own while still keeping the pistol out of harm's way. Fortunately his right arm was incapacitated only from the elbow down, allowing him to secure her delicious body firmly against his own. In spite of the possibility of disaster, he was enjoying himself immensely. She was more than a match for Louise, he concluded, now that he held her soft curves against the full length of his body. Her height was another surprise, the crown of her head reaching his chin, what he would consider a perfect alignment given different circumstances.

The report of the pistol in their joint clasp brought the wrestling match to an abrupt end. His vixenish opponent gave a startled cry that mingled with his own curse before she slumped against him. He tossed the pistol across the room, then looked down at the smoldering hole in the Axminster carpet with a grimace and remarked, "Baskin isn't going to like that at all."

"What?" she asked, blinking up at him in total confusion, heedless of the uncertain temper of the ruler of the household.

Marcus dismissed his majordomo's displeasure under the spell of the most compelling pair of green eyes he had ever encountered. The vivid color circled by thick, sooty lashes reminded him of emerald gems laying on a bed of brown velvet. To break the spell he lowered his gaze to her parted lips. He was never sure if it was the last of the brandy asserting itself or the thought he might never have this opportunity again that prompted his next move. He deserved some reward for his bravery under duress. Almost to himself he murmured, "Why not?"

2

Sweet heaven, the man *is kissing me. How can this be happening?* Celia thought wildly, astonished at the firm, warm pressure of his lips against hers that effectively silenced any protest. Instinctively she flattened her hand against his chest to push him away, and was startled at the feel of his bare flesh against her palm. How had she forgotten that the man was half-naked? Hadn't he paraded himself in front of her shamelessly just moments before? In agitation she tried to move her hand, but discovered it imprisoned between their bodies, and she only succeeded in rubbing it against his hair-roughened skin once more.

Perhaps she had fallen asleep while waiting for her quarry. That would explain this bizarre state of affairs. If so, this was the strangest and most realistic dream she had ever had. Her sense of touch and smell were strangely heightened, adding to the fanciful quality of the situation. Her head was filled with the balm of tobacco, brandy, and cloves mingling to create a uniquely masculine scent. The demand of his mouth had begun light and teasing but changed when she didn't resist. Only belatedly as she felt the edge of his teeth and a curious suckling pressure on her bottom lip did she realize she should still be fighting him.

Her body, however, wouldn't cooperate. Though she felt the most extraordinary tingling sensation from head to toe, a curious lethargy overtook her limbs, making it impossible for her to move. No man had held her this close since Daniel's death. Even then she hadn't experienced this awareness of her femininity or a man's strength and power to bend her to his will. This, from the man she came to kill! She never once considered that she would be within touching distance, much less held close in his embrace.

She certainly shouldn't be clasped against his muscular body, his reaction to her nearness blatantly imprinted against her abdomen. Nor should his hand be wandering at will over the contours of her back, moving inexorably lower in an intimate caress that pressed her more completely into the cradle of his thighs. As his tongue sought entry between her lips Celia gasped, but not simply at the intrusion. His pillaging touch was only possible if he had released her left hand. Just as she managed this single rational thought, a pounding on the door distracted her attacker.

"I knew it couldn't last."

For a moment she didn't understand. Her gaze was riveted to the sight of her hand clutching his lean shoulder as if she didn't want to let him go. When the meaning of his words sank in, she came to life, pushing against the wall of his chest with all her strength. Her action wasn't a moment too soon as what seemed like an army of people burst through the doorway, everyone shouting at once. Light from a dozen or so candles flooded the room.

"Marcus, what is going on?" asked a matronly woman, drawing a floral print wrapper around her plump figure.

"Milord, I heard a shot," said a deep voice from behind her almost at the same moment.

"Really, Marcus, what have you done now?" followed from a tall young woman, who was grinning from ear to ear. "Or shouldn't I ask?"

The matron Celia recognized as the lace-capped occupant of the bedchamber she had blundered into while searching for Ashmore's room. This was clearly a relative due to the resemblance to her opponent, though the chestnut curls that peeked from beneath her lace cap were liberally intermixed with silver. Her eyes, however, were the same striking blue-green as the earl's. The girl next to her was close to Celia's age and had his curls, but her amused eyes were golden brown. Behind the pair of ladies were various servants, all in their nightclothes.

"Milord, we seem to have interrupted you at an inauspicious moment," the man declared, his disapproval more than apparent over his employer engaging in a dalliance in his own home—and being caught. "Forgive the intrusion, but we were misled by what seemed to be the sound of gunfire."

The spokesman was a tall, thin gentleman of undetermined years standing head and shoulders above the others. Even in his nightshirt he had an air of

authority, his tailcoat properly in place without looking the least bit absurd with his nightshirt and the tasseled nightcap that topped his grizzled head.

"Baskin, and my dear Sylvia, this is not a romantic
assignation, I assure you, so you both can come down
off your high horses," his lordship announced, sounding as though he was having difficulty with his
breathing just as Celia was. His voice seemed laced
with amusement as well, but she couldn't be sure,
since she was extremely busy studying the blue and
red pattern of the carpet.

From the corner of her eye she saw him turn
abruptly on his heel. He strolled to the bed and bent
to retrieve her discarded pistol from the floor. When
she took a step forward he merely cocked a solitary
eyebrow, which caused her to drop her gaze back to
his kneecap. Through lowered lashes she observed
that he carried the pistol between his forefinger and
thumb to Baskin.

"You will kindly take charge of this before anyone
gets hurt," he instructed succinctly, ignoring her murmur of protest, since it was drowned out by the astonished gasps of the observers. "This belongs to Miss . . ."

A pregnant silence hung in the air, forcing Celia to
raise her head once more. Everyone was staring at
her, undoubtedly following the questioning look he
had trained upon her. Under their regard she realized
she was standing there like a nitwit with her hand
over her mouth as if it had been branded by his kiss.
Hastily dropping her hand to her side, she opened her
mouth to speak, but her throat was suddenly dry, cutting off any sound. Taking a deep swallow she
squared her shoulders and tried again. "Tr-Tregaron."

"Ah! This is Miss Tregaron's property, Baskin.

Take good care of it, in spite of what she's done to the carpeting." With a wave of his hand he indicated the charred imprint near the armchair. At the scowl on his servant's angular face, he commented, "Yes, I should undoubtedly have thrown myself in front of the gun to save the furnishings, but my reflexes were off."

"Marcus, really, must you?"

"Mama, there's no need to scold. You know as well as I do that Baskin doesn't think I have the proper respect for my station or possessions."

Celia wished that he had the decency to cover himself. His sling did nothing to detract from his half-naked state. She lowered her eyes to the carpet once more to keep from remembering the feel of his skin under her hand. It was one thing to parade around while being held at gunpoint and quite another to show no modesty in front of spectators. "Isn't that right, Baskin?"

"Just so, milord," the man agreed, not looking the least perturbed by the question or his master's lack of dress.

"There you are, then. Now, if you would be so good as to take Miss Tregaron down to the library, I shall attempt to preserve my modesty."

At his words Celia forced herself to look directly at him. Still unperturbed, he waited for his audience to leave. His chestnut curls were in fashionable disarray, framing a narrow face that was more distinguished than handsome. Though his nose was slightly beaky, it complemented the strong character of his blunt cheekbones and high forehead.

Whatever caused his disability hadn't dampened his spirit. As his eyes met Celia's he grinned and winked broadly at her. The gesture was rude and suggestive, an audacious reminder of their intimate contact.

Her face hot with mortification, Celia tossed her hair and followed Baskin as he marched out the door and toward the stairs.

If she hadn't wanted to kill Ashmore before this, she had good cause now, she thought as she descended the stairs. He was even more abominable than she imagined, or else he was insane. Certainly no man in his right mind would kiss a woman who threatened to kill him, would he? Preoccupied by the question, she was startled to discover that they reached their destination. Baskin, however, was clearly waiting for her to precede him through the open door in front of her.

With her chin thrust upward at an exaggerated angle she walked past the grim-faced servant. The room she entered was impressive, but also reminiscent of her father's study at home. The massive walnut desk to one side was almost a twin to the one she'd left behind in Baltimore. Instead of green drapery, this room was dominated by royal blue. Apparently Ashmore had a penchant for the color, she decided, looking idly at the book-lined walls. She grimaced at the one glaring difference in the decor at the sight of the king's likeness above the mantel. Her father had given that place of honor in his house to a portrait of General Washington.

"If you'll make yourself comfortable, his lordship will join you in a few minutes," Baskin intoned from directly behind her. Fleetingly she wondered if he was going to scurry off and count the silver as soon as he left the room, just in case she had helped herself earlier. "Allow me to take your cloak so you won't be hampered by it during your interview, miss."

She was about to refuse his command, then changed

her mind at his implacable stare. While untying the laces she wondered if he would actually have wrested it from her if she had objected. "Thank you, Baskin. Would it be too much trouble to ask for a cup of tea?"

"Do Americans really drink tea? I thought they hated it." Both Baskin and Celia turned toward the doorway at the unexpected question. Sylvia, who Celia assumed was Ashmore's sister, stood hesitantly on the threshold, her expression part apprehension and part rampant curiosity. Somehow she had managed to change into a simple walking dress, though she was still awkwardly buttoning the bodice.

"Miss Sylvia, I'm sure his lordship would like to speak with Miss Tregaron privately."

"Well, he isn't here yet, and we must keep our guest entertained. You wouldn't want me to be impolite," the young woman said, seeming to gain courage from outsmarting the man. She grinned and looked pointedly at the top of his head. "I'm sure you'll want to change into something more appropriate before you bring Miss Tregaron her tea, won't you?"

Baskin looked as if he would like to deny her sweetly worded question, but the tassel of his nightcap suddenly dangled before his eyes. "Very well, Miss, I'll let his lordship handle the matter. He might think you should be wearing shoes when you receive visitors."

He marched out of the room with great dignity, despite having the tassel of his cap marking time with his footsteps. His errant mistress had the grace to blush, looking down at her bare toes peeking from beneath the hem of her gown. Then she directed a chagrined smile at her companion.

"You aren't going to get in trouble for being here,

are you?" Celia asked, feeling at ease with this young woman. Hadn't she been the subject of censure too many times to count from the three very autocratic males in her own household? Sylvia confounded her by breaking into laughter.

"I don't think anything is going to take Marcus's mind off that pistol shot long enough," she observed, giving Celia a frank stare. Inappropriate amusement seemed to be a family failing, since her expression held no hint of malice or dislike. "No one has shot at him since he sold out of the army last year, unless he has been fighting duels on the sly. Of course, he really doesn't have the temperament for dueling, always laughing off the merest slight. He very rarely takes anything seriously, even when he was fighting with Wellington—"

"Did you say the army?" Celia cut in ruthlessly to the seemingly endless monologue at the dread name of the English general. Surely she misunderstood the young woman's prattling. How could Ashmore have been in the army *and* the navy? Perhaps she *had* fallen asleep during her vigil after all.

"Miss Tregaron, are you all right? I think you should sit down before we continue," Sylvia said. She touched Celia's elbow and led her to a nearby medallion-backed chair. "You suddenly looked so pale, perhaps a reaction to all this excitement. Should I fetch Mama's sal volatile?"

"No, I'm quite all right, thank you. Please tell me what you meant by the army." Celia emphasized her urgency by grasping the girl's arm with both her hands. She noted that she was trembling. "I really must know."

"Marcus was a major in the dragoons until he injured his arm almost a year and a half ago now,"

Sylvia replied as she sank gracefully to her knees beside the chair, a concerned frown marring her forehead.

"Oh, dear." Though she had never fainted in her entire life, she thought she might at that moment as she slumped in her seat.

"What is it, Miss Tregaron? What have I said?" Her companion's urgent whisper didn't help her state of mind, nor did the chaffing of her hands. It did, however, keep her from losing consciousness altogether in the next few moments. "You look dreadful."

"Well she might, sister dear. She has just discovered that she almost killed the wrong man tonight."

If ever there was a time to faint, it was now, Celia decided, keeping her lashes lowered to mask her dismay at the interruption. Her tormentor's untimely entrance almost took away any remorse she felt over the error, but it did settle her equilibrium. Unfortunately, she never reacted exactly the way she was supposed to react, or so she had been told numerous times. That didn't mean she couldn't pretend to be overcome with emotion. Or could she? She watched Ashmore prop his shoulder against the door frame and clasp his injured elbow with his free hand. He finally had had the decency to put on a shirt, she noted, though it was open at the collar. His hair appeared to be damp from a recent scrubbing. None of this, however, relieved the taunting quality of his hooded look.

"Marcus, what a horrible thing to say," his sister said accusingly from her position by the chair. She retained her hold on Celia's hands in what appeared to be a show of support.

"Horrible, but true, little one. Or did you think she came to my bedchamber with a gun because I had dishonored her?"

"Really, Marcus, you know I loathe that lounging attitude of yours. Now, stand away from the door and remember that I did teach you decent posture." At his mother's imperious command, he moved immediately then clicked his heels and gave a smart salute. A spasm of some unidentified emotion crossed his face when Baskin followed in his mother's wake, a tea tray clasped in his hands.

"Oh, it only wanted for this—a predawn tea party. Miss Tregaron, I salute you as well," he pronounced, giving act to his words under Celia's amazed stare. She gave up all pretense of an emotional collapse, too amazed at the tableau before her. Perhaps she had mistaken her destination as well as her man; she was certain she was in the midst of a theater troupe or escaped lunatics. "You have managed to set this house completely on its ear. I suppose it won't do the least good if I order you upstairs, Mama, Sylvia?"

"Don't be silly, Marcus," his mother admonished him, directing Baskin to set the tray on the desk before he held a chair for her directly across from Celia. She had also managed to change rapidly from her night-clothes, something Celia began to think was a family talent before she realized the lady was still wearing her lace nightcap. The adornment didn't look terribly out of place with her lilac-colored gown, however.

"Somehow I knew that would be the answer," he murmured absently as he looked over the assembled group. "Baskin, just how did you manage to have tea ready so conveniently? Even someone of your perception couldn't have foreseen Miss Tregaron's clandestine arrival."

"Cook was already up, sir, and had the kettle on the boil," was Baskin's reply. He straightened to his full, imposing height, much more impressive now that he had shed his cap and gown for a regular suit of clothes. "Will you be needing anything else, milord?"

"Not at all, my good man. You can take up your post outside the door, so you may relate this merry tale we're about to hear in the servant's quarters," Ashmore remarked, sitting down in the oversized maroon leather chair behind the desk.

"Marcus, you can't accuse the servants of listening at the keyholes," his mother scolded, as she poured tea.

"Mama, you know very well that he does. Not that it's a crime; at least they get an accurate account and don't make up erroneous gossip."

She gave her son an exasperated look. "Well, of course he listens; you just aren't suppose to accuse him of it. He has his pride. Now, Miss Tregaron, do you take milk and sugar, or do you prefer lemon?"

All three family members turned to watch her as she made her reply, as if it was of tantamount importance. For a ludicrous moment she wondered if her answer would determine her fate. "Milk and sugar, please."

Once tea was dispensed, the silence that had fallen over the room continued. The ladies took turns sipping their beverage and surreptitiously glancing at the earl, who seemed preoccupied with stirring his brew. Celia's thoughts were in a turmoil over the news of her ghastly mistake. She knew the name was correct since she had seen it in print, but the man was clearly the wrong one. What did it mean? How was she going to find out what had happened to Ethan?

"Now that we have dispensed with the pleasantries, I think we should proceed with the matter at hand." Ashmore's calm statement made Celia start in surprise and nearly spill her tea in her lap. "First I think we should clear up our major problem. I must deduce from your comments about the navy that you intended to put a bullet in my cousin Ambrose, late of His Majesty's Navy as well as of this world."

"Of this world— He's dead." She didn't need the man's slight nod of agreement. Now she understood the mistaken identity. In spite of her cold feeling of dread, she forged ahead. "You apparently inherited the title from your cousin fairly recently."

"About six months ago. Until then I had been Sir Marcus Knowles, happily rusticating in the country with no thought of having to step into his shoes." He continued to stir his tea without looking up. "To prevent further confusion, let me present my mother, Lady Knowles, and my sister, Miss Sylvia Knowles. As you see, your journey from America and plans of revenge seem to have come to naught."

He looked directly at her then, and she knew he was wondering if she was revising her plans now to avenge his licentious behavior. Though she hadn't expected to be kissed so thoroughly by an attractive stranger when she set out this evening, she had other worries that took precedence.

Ethan's captor was the last person to see her brother alive, as far as she knew. What could she do now? Return home in defeat and join the rest of her family in mourning Ethan's death?

"Miss Tregaron, perhaps you might explain how you came to be here tonight," Lady Knowles prompted gently, removing the cup and saucer from Celia's hands. She smiled kindly, as if asking who her dressmaker could be. "Maybe we can help you with whatever is troubling you. Did Marcus say you came from America? How extraordinary. Your family must be worried sick about you."

"Yes, I'm a Tregaron of the Baltimore Tregarons. Our branch of the family is in shipping, while the Philadelphia branch is in banking." She concentrated on what she was saying, unwilling to give too much away. The lady's offer of help might be needed. What could she say that would continue to keep her in the older woman's sympathy? She had to be convincing and pitiful at the same, with the knowledge that she had never been a good liar.

"I'm an orphan, actually," she went on when she knew she couldn't remain silent without arousing further suspicions. She sat up straight in her seat, purposely not looking at the gentleman behind the desk. Perhaps if she kept to the truth as much as possible it would help. "My parents were killed ten years ago, so we were raised by two uncles, one from each side of the family." She paused for a second, then took a deep breath before she blurted out, "I'm all alone in the world now with Ethan gone."

"Oh, no, your uncles have passed away as well?"

"Yes, not long after we heard about Ethan being impressed into the British navy," she continued, giving what she hoped was another forlorn sigh. She also sent a prayer of forgiveness to her very-much-alive relatives, who had adamantly opposed her making this trip. "You see, Ethan went to sea in 1812 to learn the family business as an ordinary seaman. Even though war hadn't been declared, I thought it was too dangerous, but he wanted to do exactly what our father had done at the same age. Our ship was stopped on the way to the West Indies, and he was impressed into service. The British captain had insisted on taking him, even though Captain Vanderhoff protested that Ethan had never even seen England."

"And the captain was Cousin Ambrose. How absolutely dreadful." Sylvia squeezed her hand in sympathy and Celia gave her a brave, wan smile that wasn't all pretense. Relating the full story brought back bittersweet memories of her younger brother and his determination to go to sea and prove himself.

"Just how do you know that Ambrose was the captain?" asked the earl, his abrupt question breaking through Celia's wandering thoughts. She realized that she was going to have to keep her wits about her under his watchful eyes. The ladies were all kindness and approval, but she knew without looking that her former opponent was truly skeptical. From the corner of her eye she could see that he remained relaxed against the back of his chair, which fed her annoyance. He should by rights be out of sorts from their earlier confrontation, just as she was.

"The first news came when Captain Vanderhoff returned to port months later. He had gone on to Jamaica after the British confiscated his cargo, then made the return trip." She decided to finish the tale without embellishments to avoid further danger. They wouldn't be interested in her condemnation of Silas Vanderhoff for allowing her brother's impressment. "I received two letters from Ethan as well during the next year. He found a friend among the crew who smuggled the letters ashore so his family would know that he was alive. According to Ethan, the captain was a vile individual and a harsh disciplinarian. He seemed to single out Ethan for censure and punishment. I haven't received any word directly from my brother in over seven months."

"Here, my dear, another cup of tea should bolster your spirits," Lady Knowles said, handing her the cup without waiting for any comment. Apparently the unplanned catch in Celia's voice had been inspiring. "This is utterly fascinating, almost suitable for a tragic play."

"Isn't it though, Mama? You do have a fondness for sad tales of misfortune," her son commented dryly, still not moving from his comfortable pose. "Pray, Miss Tregaron, continue your tale. I'm anxious to learn how you came to be waiting in my bedchamber this evening."

Celia could feel a heated flush color her cheeks at his drawled command. And it was a command. Or was it a dare? She knew that she couldn't falter now. "News came that, er, your cousin's ship had been captured in battle. Unfortunately, another battle occurred the following day and the British were victorious, sinking the American ship. I don't know if Ethan survived either confrontation, so when the news of the peace treaty came in February I began making my plans to come to England."

She paused in her recital, under the pretense of taking a refreshing drink of tea. It wouldn't do at this stage to blurt out that she ran away from home to book passage from Philadelphia so her immediate family wouldn't stop her. Only she believed that Ethan could still be alive, no matter what the others said. She had to know if her brother was alive, somewhere.

"How very enterprising." Sylvia practically gushed her admiration and squeezed Celia's hand once more.

"Not an example to follow, my dear sister. Please, Miss Tregaron, continue."

"I traveled as a companion to a Mrs. Sanders and her two small children, since I couldn't bring my maid along. When I reached London I contacted our former shipping agent, Mr. Thomas Hampton, and have been staying with his family for the past week." Almost finished with her narrative, she dared to look directly at Marcus.

She regretted her bravado immediately. Marcus was smiling, and none too pleasantly. His expression was that of a superior being humoring a child or a half-wit. Wildly she wondered if he would rise from his chair and stroll around the desk to pat her on the head. If there was one thing she hated in the entire world, it was being patronized by an arrogant male. She had had too much experience with the breed in her own home. But Marcus simply raised an eyebrow.

"Mr. Hampton made several inquiries around the shipyards, but to no avail. I began to think everyone was right about Ethan's death. Then, while reading this morning's newspaper I discovered that Ashmore, at least the man I thought to be Ashmore, was in London. Someone's ball or rout was described, I think." Her voice took on a harsh tone as she related the day's events, her anger returning at the memory. If only she could muster the cold, clear anger she had felt earlier as she downed two glasses of Mr. Hampton's best brandy.

"The more I considered the injustice of such a person surviving and enjoying himself, the angrier I became. I sat alone in the parlor this evening after the Hamptons went to bed, and decided what I must do. I wanted to see justice served, and finally learn my brother's fate." Suddenly she felt very tired and alone. Looking into the countess's kindly blue-green eyes, she realized how long it had been since she knew the comfort of her own mother's tenderness. No pretense of dismay was needed as she declared, "Now I find that it has all been for naught. Ashmore is dead and taken his secrets to his grave. If Ethan is dead, I have no proof to take home with me. What am I going to do?"

"Why, 'tis very simple, my poor, dear Celia. You are going to stay right here with us," Lady Knowles stated firmly, rising to her feet. Then she clasped Celia's hands, pulled her to her feet, and enfolded her in a motherly embrace as if she had read her mind. "Our family is responsible for your brother's disappearance. Naturally, Marcus will do everything in his power to help you. He won't rest until he finds Ethan and restores the dear boy to the bosom of his family. I'm just as sure as you that the boy is alive. Fate wouldn't be so cruel after all your perils."

Celia was speechless at her astounding victory. She had hoped for the ladies' support in extricating herself from attempting to murder Marcus. Never once had she considered that she would be adopted by the family, almost like a stray pet. This was truly the most extraordinary group of people she had ever met. Before she could utter a word the older woman released her.

"Come, Sylvia, Celia needs her rest after such a harrowing adventure. We shall put her in the daffodil room next to yours," Lady Knowles ordered, purposefully herding both young ladies toward the door. She didn't seem to think her behavior was out of the ordinary, nor did she confer with her son on the matter. "I'm sure some of Sylvia's things might fit, even if you are slightly shorter."

Celia dared to peek over her shoulder as Lady Knowles chattered about alterations and fresh linens. Marcus looked as stunned as she felt. Or was he? For once he had lost the hooded look she had seen during the few hours of their acquaintance. In fact, she realized, he was glaring at her. Impishly she wondered what he would do if she blew him a kiss over her shoulder, though she didn't dare. Lady Knowles and Sylvia were championing her now, and there wasn't a blessed thing Marcus could do about it, she decided.

Unfortunately, she couldn't resist one small act of retaliation. Reverting to a childhood tormented by masculine siblings, she stuck out her tongue. The evil smile that Marcus gave her in response had her scurrying out the door under Lady Knowles' protective wing, wondering exactly what she had gotten herself into by coming to England.

"Oh, how lovely, now I have a companion to share the season. I just know we're going to become fast friends," Sylvia pronounced with irrepressible enthusiasm. Celia tried to smile as the young woman linked their arms and walked briskly toward the stairs. "We can drop all this Miss nonsense and be very cozy as Sylvia and Celia. We'll be just like family."

A shiver of some dark emotion shot through Celia as she turned to ascend the stairs. Her eyes were drawn inexorably to the light spilling from the open library door. There was one person in the household who certainly wasn't going to welcome her with open arms.

3

The sight that greeted Marcus as he entered the dining room some six hours later made him smile in pure pleasure for the first time since his mother had shepherded her new protégée from the library the previous night. He wondered if maybe it might have been better if the damsel had shot him. That would certainly have put him out of his misery, if misery was what he had been experiencing after a fitful night's sleep.

Her unexpected arrival and its aftermath kept him from his bed until past dawn. He had lain awake staring at the satin gathers of the canopy as two separate thoughts careened through his brain. First he wondered how he was going to determine if the little baggage was lying, as he suspected. Was there really a missing brother?

Second, and more worrisome: Was it simply wishful thinking on his part that she wasn't the innocent as she tried to appear?

He couldn't forget the feel of her lush body in his arms, nor the enchantment of her kiss.

Ruthlessly he dismissed the memory from his mind, as he decided that starting the day with a hearty breakfast was a good idea. Apparently his *guest* had the same thought, since she was busily checking under the chafing dishes on the sideboard. If he didn't know better, he would think she made a charming picture of guileless beauty at first glance.

Dressed in the blue and pink flowered muslin dress, she was the ideal of a chaste miss making her debut in town. Marcus was, with some annoyance, quickly reminded of his assessment of her attributes during their first meeting. Possibly the snug fit of the dress, no doubt borrowed from his sister's wardrobe, caused his thoughts to run in that direction. Celia's more rounded curves made the garment more provocative than virginal. With the thin material clinging in all the right places, he longed to run his hand over her firm buttocks as he had done once before. Her black tresses, gathered in a bow at the nape of her neck, hung down the length of her spine almost like an invitation for his touch.

"So you are an early riser, Miss Tregaron," he said more harshly than he intended, to keep his unruly imagination in check. Until he could prove or allay his suspicions he needed to think and act as if she were one of Sylvia's silly, unalluring friends. It didn't matter how his subconscious taunted him, awake or dreaming.

A silver lid went clattering onto the mahogany surface of the sideboard and his companion turned to glare at him. "Must you sneak into a room like that?"

"Apparently I'm acquiring some of your talent as a

cracksman," he returned, walking forward to save the lid from tumbling to the floor. Purposely he stopped within a foot of her, enjoying her disgruntlement as he put the lid back in place. "You must be rather proficient at stealth to gain entry into the house without detection. Will you tell me how you accomplished that? We didn't get much detail about that portion of your tale before Mama whisked you off to bed."

"Will your mother and sister be joining us for breakfast?" Her query might have sounded casual if she hadn't been looking anxiously over his shoulder, as though both ladies would appear at the next moment. She was also evading the issue at hand, but he would play along—for now.

"No, don't hesitate on their account. Mama has taught Sylvia to follow in her footsteps." He paused just to keep up her hopes for a moment longer. "Neither of them rise much before noon and undoubtedly will be later still after last night's interruption. So it will be just the two of us. I suggest we make our selections. I'm ravenous, but perhaps your appetite isn't quite so voracious."

He bent toward her as if he were sharing a secret, and she leaned backward. Her indignant expression almost made him grin, and for a moment he was tempted to kiss her parted lips. Instead he reached to the side and picked up a plate. "How can I serve you, Miss Tregaron? Some sausage, a kipper?"

"I don't seem to be as hungry as I first thought," she finally managed. She directed her gaze at the shoulder seam of his morning coat. The telltale flush of her cheek was another indication of her discomfort. "Perhaps I should wait for your mother in the sitting room."

"No, please, don't abandon me to a solitary meal," he cajoled, giving her his most ingratiating smile outside polite society. Whatever or whoever Celia Tregaron was, she was a tempting morsel, he acknowledged, unable to keep from wondering if she could be a castoff of his late cousin's. He considered offering her his protection, something much different from what his family had in mind. She certainly made it damned hard for him to concentrate on the matter at hand.

To insure her acceptance he set down his plate and pulled out a chair at his side. Since he stood between her and the door, she had no means of escape. Still she refused to look at him, keeping her lashes demurely lowered. He fixed his gaze on the expanse of flawless skin framed by her square-cut bodice when she slipped into the chair. He knew he was going to be hard-pressed to remember that his family considered this woman a young lady of quality.

"So, Miss Tregaron, how do you like your visit to London so far?" he asked once she was seated, acting as though he were concentrating on his breakfast selection. His military friends could have warned the young lady that Marcus Knowles was always most dangerous when he seemed completely distracted.

"I really haven't had a chance to see much of anything," she answered so quietly he almost didn't hear her.

"Ah, yes, this is your first visit and you've been staying with this shipping agent person . . . Hamilton?"

Though he kept his back to her, he knew that she was cautiously glancing over her shoulder. Occupied with the intricate transfer of a coddled egg nestled in a pastry shell and covered in cream sauce, he waited for her answer.

"Mr. Thomas Hampton," she snapped finally as if the silence was straining her nerves, just as he hoped.

"Yes, that's it, Hampton. I hope he isn't going to come bursting in here at any moment demanding to protect your honor," Marcus commented as he took his seat and opened his linen napkin with a snap. Hampton would be receiving a visit from him in the very near future.

"Why should he?"

"Why should he indeed?" he shot back, smiling across the table at her, appearing amazed at her question. "I can't say what the reaction of the trading class would be. If I were in his position I might consider the need, being that he was in your family's employ and all."

"I sent a message this morning relating your mother's kind offer." Her jaw was rigid as she seemed to be attempting to speak and clench her teeth at the same time. "Even if he were of a chivalrous nature, I'm sure Mrs. Hampton would remind him he has a wife and four children to feed. She has enough common sense to know your family can easily afford an unexpected guest."

"So true." He let the comment hang in the air and blessed the footman for entering at that moment with his morning coffee. As the young man bustled around the room Marcus dug into the assortment of food on his plate. He hadn't lied; he was ravenous. A good fight always made him appreciate his victuals. He maintained his silence some minutes after the footman departed to fetch a pot of tea. Calculating the time it would take to accomplish the errand, he continued with his meal.

His companion sat rigidly in her seat, no doubt bracing herself for his next move. That more than anything else made him suspicious of her motives. If her tale was the absolute truth she would have no reason to feel ill at ease in his company. At this moment she wouldn't be sitting with her hands folded primly, but tightly clenched together, on the tabletop. Except for the delightful rise and fall of her bosom, she might have been a statue.

"I'm not going to apologize, you know," he remarked, dabbing at his mouth with his napkin to hide his satisfied smile at her glare. She was a magnificent creature, and so easy to goad.

"Apologize for what?" She wasn't even trying to dissemble. Her emerald-bright eyes glinted with anger, telling him she knew his meaning.

"Kissing you, of course. I enjoyed it immensely. Should we try it again?" Right then the footman returned just as he had anticipated. For a moment Marcus wondered if she were going to throw something at him—the cup and saucer, the teapot, the footman? Her fair skin was now a brilliant red as she tried to contain her temper. With more than passing interest he noted the strain her breathing caused on the bodice of her borrowed dress.

"Oh, lovely, Celia has already come down for breakfast, Mama."

Marcus usually had an affection for his mother and sister, but at the moment he wanted to throttle both of them. Instead, he rose to his feet, but almost stumbled when he glanced at his companion. She was giving him the same look of relieved triumph that she had before she stuck out her tongue at him last night. Then, as now, his first response was to imagine teaching the young woman some other uses for that appendage besides childish antics.

"What the devil is this apparition? Can it be both my dear Mama and esteemed sister are awake and actually walking, not to mention talking, at this hour?"

"Stubble it, Marcus," his sister answered inelegantly, but gave him a kiss on the cheek in greeting. Her interest immediately riveted to the chafing dishes on the sideboard.

"Ah, now I understand—that militant gleam in your eye is for food. You're going shopping today and you need your strength," he remarked, seating his mother directly across from Celia. "Mama, let me select something for you before Sylvia devours it all. Sister dear, a young lady of quality does not stuff herself like some bran-faced urchin on the street."

"Marcus, you must stop this awful teasing," his mother chided with a loving smile. "You will give Celia the wrong impression of your character."

"Not at all, Mama. Miss Tregaron has a very good impression of my character by now," he murmured dryly before joining his sister at the sideboard.

"His teasing sounds remarkably like my own brothers'—"

"There you see, Marcus, you have upset her. Her hand is trembling."

"Miss Tregaron, I most humbly apologize." He set his mother's plate in front of her, all the while studying Celia's expression. Her green eyes were wide and her hand covering her mouth as if she were truly distressed. It couldn't be any of his foolishness. Could she really be upset over some childhood memories?

"Well, I think today's shopping expedition to Bond Street will do you a world of good, my dear," the older woman assured her guest with her panacea for settling an ill humor. "Although I'm not sure what colors will be right for you. Your coloring isn't quite right for pastels, which are so inevitable for young, unmarried ladies."

"And incredibly boring," Sylvia supplied, taking her seat next to her new friend, her plate mounded with food. She plucked at the puffed sleeve of her pale pink dress and grimaced. "I think Marcus should accept my first presentable offer, so I'll be allowed to wear a decent color."

"Hardly a reason to marry someone," Celia responded, taking the opportunity to turn away from Marcus. "Marriage is difficult enough, so make sure you are compatible with your partner."

Something in her tone bothered Marcus, but with his relatives present he couldn't pursue the matter. He should never have underestimated his mother's perseverance.

"Celia, how wise of you. Most young ladies your age only think of a handsome face and charming manner when they marry." The lady nodded in approval. "I think you're going to be a good influence on my scatterbrained daughter. We must discuss this at length."

"Thank you, Lady Knowles, you are too kind—"

"Nonsense, dear. A sensible outlook on life should never be taken lightly. Too many girls find themselves wrapped up in foolish daydreams about dashing young officers or trying to reform rakes."

"Mama, I think you're embarrassing Miss Tregaron," Marcus interrupted, knowing his mother could continue on this theme ad nauseam. Celia was looking decidedly uncomfortable, but he felt it was his prerogative to make her so.

"No, I think I am taking undue credit," Celia said hesitantly, keeping her eyes downcast as she ran her index finger around the rim of her cup. "I have been married, you see."

"You've been *what?*"

"There is no need to shout, Marcus," his mother chastised him, dismissing his rude outburst with a flick of her wrist.

He wasn't to be put off, however. He felt like that blasted horse had rolled over him again and didn't understand why. "Don't tell us, *Miss* Tregaron, this Ethan is your husband, not your brother."

"Good heavens, no. I've been a widow for over two years," she shot back, daring to look him directly in the eye once more. He didn't understand her defiant expression at his demand. "Daniel Sloane was killed at sea about eight months after we married. I took back my maiden name, since we weren't married very long, barely two months before his ship left."

"Well, how delightful."

"Mama!"

"Oh, how silly of me. I meant we won't have to be restricted to pastels for your wardrobe after all," the lady reasoned, with a benign smile. "Now, Marcus, you, of course, will be making inquiries about poor Ethan while we're out shopping. I expect a full report before we go to the theater this evening."

With that Marcus knew that he had been dismissed. His mother began expounding on the shops they would invade in the course of the morning. When he cast a final look at Miss Celia Tregaron, he was surprised to discover she seemed to be openly studying him. Rising to his feet and making his farewells, he decided to let her continue to wonder about his motives.

As he studied his image in the gilt-trimmed convex mirror near the front door, he wondered what other surprises his enigmatic guest had in store for him. While Baskin assisted him with his left glove, Marcus decided Mr. Thomas Hampton was his first matter of business. He wasn't about to go on a wild-goose chase after the mythical Ethan Tregaron until he had a few more facts at hand—facts that were supplied by someone else besides the deceptive sable-haired wench sitting in his dining room.

"I really don't know what else I can tell you, milord."

Marcus had the urge to shake the plump gentleman sitting behind the desk but maintained his affable smile. He forced himself to relax, stretching out his feet as if inspecting the polish on his tasseled Hessian boots. For good measure he pretended to remove a speck of lint from the knee of his tan pantaloons. In the hours since meeting Miss Celia Tregaron he had discovered a very cynical turn to his nature that had been deeply buried. Perhaps her influence was at work here as well.

She was certainly responsible for ruining what could have been a delightful afternoon at Tattersall inspecting horseflesh or placing odds in White's betting books on when Napoleon would confront Wellington. Instead he was sitting in an uncomfortably hot, unkempt room with the stench of the sea in his nostrils. The visit to Hampton wasn't going to be his only cross to bear, he acknowledged grimly, if it turned out she was telling the truth. His mother would see to it that he pursued the brother's trail until no stone lay unturned.

"So, your acquaintance with the Tregarons has been limited to correspondence, and you had heard nothing since the beginning of the Colonies' most recent uprising?" Marcus summed up the nature of their conversation neatly, picking up his cane from where it rested across his thighs. Toying with the polished blackthorn surface would keep his fingers from reaching for the man and shaking him. "You can't be certain that the young lady is actually a member of the family, then?"

"Good heaven, I never gave it a second thought," Hampton exclaimed, his eyes growing rounder as the idea took root. His double-chinned face was turning ruddier by the minute. "Are you suggesting that she might be an impostor? Why, she could have murdered us in our beds and robbed us blind. My wife said there was something havey-cavey about a woman traveling alone like that. Everyone knows that Ethan Tregaron was killed at sea during the war."

"Ethan Tregaron's death is common knowledge? How is that possible?" Mr. Garth Cruthers asked idly from his position at the dusty window overlooking the docks. Dressed in austere black that accentuated his fair complexion and golden curls, he looked even more out of place in the cluttered and cramped room than Marcus did. "I was out of the country during most of the hostilities, so I didn't realize the American casualties were posted by the Home Office."

"Of course they weren't, sir. The information came to me through a captain who once worked for the Tregarons," Hampton pronounced while mopping his receding hairline with his handkerchief. He seemed dashed uncomfortable for a man telling the truth, Marcus determined, though he knew the pointed blue gaze of his friend Garth could be damned uncomfortable. "Captain Mulkey mentioned the tale over drinks one evening not long after the news of the peace treaty with America was announced."

"Did the talkative captain remember anything else? Perhaps he gave you a fair description of young Ethan's sister?" He didn't bother to look up from the gold lion's head at the top of his cane. Hampton seemed to have a very inconvenient memory, one that worked only with some prodding—but not so much that it frightened him senseless. Marcus's apparent indifference would be a nice contrast to Cruthers's Inquisitor style.

"He did mention the girl had taken the news of Ethan's impressment very hard. Naturally she would, with her husband getting killed about the same time," Hampton volunteered almost unconsciously, as if he were talking to himself. The thought of this seemed to increase his need to fidget. "I had forgotten about her marriage; seems mighty strange that she introduced herself as Miss Tregaron. I would say you're right on the money about her being an impostor. She can't know the family very well if she didn't know about the marriage."

"So you didn't ask her about her late husband? What exactly did she offer in the way of credentials when she arrived on your doorstep?"

"Why, she had a letter from the family solicitor in Philadelphia, milord. I would never have let a stranger come in my house and endanger my family, even if she did look so forlorn and pitiful."

"You never mentioned the letter from the solicitor." Marcus could barely conceal his impatience with the nodcock; there wasn't anything forlorn or pitiful about the Miss Tregaron in his household. They had been wrangling for the past hour over the matter of Miss Celia Tregaron's identity. "You wouldn't by any chance still have the letter?"

"Oh, no, milord. I returned it to Miss Tregaron, or whoever she is, after I returned from the bank. . . ." His voice dwindled to a reedy whisper as he completed the sentence, fidgeting even more and twisting his handkerchief between his pudgy fingers.

"Did you procure funds for Miss Tregaron due to instructions from the letter?" prompted Cruthers. He leaned his shoulder against the windowsill and crossed his arms over his chest. A quirk of his eyebrow told Marcus he was equally annoyed with the fellow. They were using expert techniques of interrogation learned while on the Peninsula, but their subject was hardly worthy of their talents.

"Yes, there were some monies left on account when the embargoes first began. I was instructed to turn them over to a representative of the family at an opportune time," Hampton pronounced with a ring of self-righteousness in his quivering voice. He was, however, staring downward, not meeting either of his visitors' gaze for the first time since the beginning of the interview.

"How much was left in the account, Mr. Hampton? I would like to know the amount my guest has in funds during her visit." From the man's behavior the Tregaron account had undoubtedly been reduced over the past few years, and not by a member of the family. "Since Miss Tregaron has the proper credentials, it seems I was mistaken in my suspicions. If she is in need of my charity I shouldn't hesitate to come to her assistance."

"I gave her fifty pounds, but, er, there is a bit more left in the account in case of emergencies. I, er, wasn't sure how soon the Tregarons would be resuming business, you see."

"Oh, yes, I understand, Mr. Hampton." Marcus rose to his feet, tapping his cane on the wooden floor to keep from prodding the dolt in his overstuffed waistcoat. "If Miss Tregaron has additional expenses, I shall visit the bank myself. You won't have to worry your head over the matter another minute. I'm sure the young lady will contact you if she wishes to reinstate your services in the future."

With a curt nod he turned on his heels and walked toward the door. The sound of footsteps assured him that Cruthers was right behind him. Descending the narrow stairs demanded all his concentration, and Marcus welcomed the distraction. For a few moments his mind was free of the dangerous allure of Miss Celia Tregaron and her myriad problems. He still wasn't sure if she was an accomplished actress spinning a Banbury tale, or precisely what she claimed to be. The real problem was he didn't know which outcome he desired the most, but he was going to do his damndest to find the answer.

4

"I tell you, Garth, there's still something wrong with the jade's story."

Celia stopped abruptly in the middle of the hallway at Marcus's pronouncement. She hadn't realized he was in the house, or she never would have ventured anywhere near the library. Just a moment before she had been thankful for the absence of the seemingly ever-present footman in the hall. At home there had been only a housekeeper and cook, no army of servants constantly underfoot. If a servant had been present, he could have warned her.

With Sylvia and Lady Knowles paying calls, she had thought to occupy her time reading until dinner was announced. She wasn't prepared to match wits with the master of the house yet again. Her reluctance had nothing to do with her dreams last night where she found herself in Marcus's arms once more, only this time there had been no gunshot and no interruption.

"Really, Marcus, are you sure it isn't wounded vanity? No gentleman likes to admit that he has been held at gunpoint," stated an amused but unfamiliar masculine voice, "especially by a female. I only regret I wasn't there to witness the momentous occasion. It almost makes me sentimental about our harrowing days in the army. London has seemed decidedly flat of late."

"Your sense of humor is perverse as usual. I have yet to see any amusement in the situation and doubt if you would have been laughing if an angry woman was aiming at a most treasured portion of your anatomy."

Celia's face warmed momentarily. She didn't have time to dwell on her past indiscretions, however.

What had he discovered that made him distrust her? she wondered. She had been very careful in everything she'd said. Hadn't she? Where could she have made a mistake? Had she been too careful? Did he truly suspect she was being less than truthful? Perhaps he had learned something of her family from Hampton, for she knew Marcus had gone to visit the gentleman the previous afternoon. She'd purposely avoided her host's company since their encounter at breakfast yesterday for precisely that reason.

Short of visiting her in her room he couldn't have had a chance for a private conversation with her. His presence in her dreams had been disturbing enough. Despite a twinge of conscience, she had used Sylvia and Lady Knowles as a shield against him. She was aware of him in an unsettling manner that she couldn't understand. Why did this particular man affect her in this way?

Though he'd managed a few barbed comments at dinner the previous night, he had finally admitted defeat by leaving the house directly after the meal. With a keen sense of self-preservation, Celia had requested breakfast in her room this morning. Yesterday's encounter with Marcus had left her shaken, unable to understand why he alternately fascinated and infuriated her.

She hadn't left the sanctuary of her room until Sylvia came to fetch her. The lack of proper clothing had been a convenient excuse until just an hour ago. Unfortunately, to Celia's way of thinking, the modiste had been anxious to please her affluent and influential customers, undoubtedly working her seamstresses long into the night to complete two walking dresses.

"If you're so suspicious of the girl, why not confront her?"

The unknown man's question made her stiffen. Exactly what did Marcus suspect? She hadn't told the absolute truth, but that was her prerogative. Would anyone in her position be scrupulously honest? She was alone in a foreign county, a country that had been at war with her own until recently. Her host knew all that was necessary at the moment. He didn't always have to have the upper hand. The British need for control was what had caused her countrymen to rebel in the first place.

"Oh, how blessedly ignorant you are, my dear friend," Marcus responded in a lazy drawl. As she pictured it, for once someone else was on the receiving end of his unnerving, slumberous regard. A shiver went down her spine, not unlike her reaction in Marcus' presence. Why did she care what Marcus thought about her? She was here to find her brother, not to toady to some bored, arrogant earl.

"Something tells me you're about to enlighten me."

"Most assuredly. Ladies seem to have an aversion to being called liars, even the variety with the nerve to assault a gentleman in his bedchamber," Marcus answered smoothly. "I prefer to observe Miss Tregaron's movements during her visit. She will undoubtedly make a false step sooner or later, especially if her mind is so preoccupied she doesn't have time to work out her schemes properly. I plan to aggravate her into forgetting to guard her words, then I'll have her where I want her."

"An interesting choice of words, my friend, and you'll be only too willing to take advantage of any mistake. I'm in awe of your indulgence in this matter," his companion remarked, a thread of laughter in his words. "Though I have yet to clap eyes on this treacherous individual, should I hazard a guess that she's a comely wench? Anything less would lower my admiration of your skill and perception."

"If you didn't hold the secret of my injury, my dear friend, I might be tempted to eliminate you from my acquaintance. I should tell you that Miss Tregaron has a squint and a face that could stop a clock."

"But you won't, even without the threat of making public the secret of your noble wound. She must be an incomparable." His statement was punctuated by the chime of crystal against crystal, making Celia suppose the pair were indulging in spirits as well as sharpening their wits by shredding her reputation.

The sound of voices from beyond the front door and the ominous beat of footsteps ascending from belowstairs warned Celia that she wouldn't learn Marcus's answer. She wasn't interested in his opinion of her looks, she told herself vehemently, or what he thought of her character, for that matter. At the moment she had to avoid detection, but could find no means of escape. Her only chance lay in reaching the bottom of the stairs before anyone entered the hall.

Snatching up the skirt of her peach and azure striped gown, she scurried toward the stairs. She reached the bottom step with only a second to spare, managing to turn facing the proper direction as Baskin opened the door beneath the stairs. Slightly off balance, she clutched at the newel post and stretched a smile across her lips as she tried to catch her breath. The sound of her heart beating in her ears kept her from hearing Sylvia's first words as the young lady burst through the front door the minute Baskin opened it.

". . . is such a boor. I simply can't abide the woman, so why does—Mama, look, Celia is wearing one of her new dresses. How splendid."

"My dear, you look absolutely charming, just as I imagined," Lady Knowles pronounced, running a critical gaze from the top of her head to the tip of her toes. "Step down and turn for me, so I can inspect the entire garment. Of course, we'll have to do something about your hair soon. We can't have you running around like a little country cousin with it hanging down your back. Oh, well, Raphael will know exactly what is needed."

Celia did as she was instructed, pivoting and turning as her hostess rambled on about her hairstyle. It was useless to protest that she liked her hair as it was. She was already learning that Lady Knowles rarely heard other people's words unless it suited her purpose. The lady simply completed whatever she wanted to say before allowing anyone else to speak.

"Lovely, my dear, just lovely. I wish Marcus were home so we could show him the first of our acquisitions. He is always demanding to know how I can spend so much money. Now, when I have actual proof, he has disappeared. How utterly tiresome of him."

"Beg pardon, milady, but his lordship is in the library with Mr. Cruthers," Baskin expertly informed her as she took a deep breath to begin her next soliloquy. Celia groaned inwardly at the man's intervention. The last person she wanted to face at the moment was Marcus before she had a chance to mull over what she'd just heard.

"Excellent," Sylvia exclaimed, tossing her bonnet to the majordomo and grasping Celia's hand in one fluid movement.

"Really, Sylvia, I don't think we need to bother your brother over such a trifle," Celia said as she ran to keep up with her friend's longer stride. The men in her family were never enthusiastic about the latest fashion, nor did they encourage any interruption in their inner sanctum. Marcus was undoubtedly of the same mind. Though she had objected to such male arrogance countless times in the past, at that moment she began to think it had merit.

"Nonsense, Marcus and Garth are only discussing something trivial like the latest wager at White's or who they'll favor in the Derby," Slyvia assured her, as they reached the library door. "Besides, we need to ask Marcus if he will help you with your dancing steps. No matter what you learned in America, I'm sure you aren't conversant in the waltz. Some still think it is barely respectable in London."

"No, absolutely *not*," Celia snapped louder than she intended just as they crossed the threshold. Both gentlemen turned expectantly at their startling entrance. She was sure that she looked like a recalcitrant animal on a leash with Sylvia tugging on her sleeve.

"Is there a difference of opinion, ladies? Surely you aren't coming to seek my humble intellect to settle the matter?"

Celia had a sudden urge to throttle him for the ingratiating smile on his handsome face. She knew what he intended to do, but she hadn't had time to consider exactly how to counter his plan. Only one thing was clear: She would have to meet every one of his challenges head-on without hesitation.

"Don't be so buffle-headed, Marcus. We came to let you know Celia's wardrobe has begun to arrive," Sylvia said, unwittingly coming to Celia's rescue.

Celia felt her cheeks flush under the regard of her host, who remained seated behind his desk. She forced herself to remain still under his scrutiny, indignant that her fair skin was betraying her emotions. She was sure that he was memorizing the garment's every detail, from the lace-trimmed square neckline to the scalloped hem that brushed the tops of her slippers.

"Aren't you going to introduce me to your guest, Sylvia?"

The stranger's voice broke the spell that Marcus seemed to cast over her, allowing Celia to look toward the fireplace. "How silly of me, Garth. I didn't realize you hadn't already met Celia. Miss Celia Tregaron, may I present Mr. Garth Cruthers."

He walked across the room, never taking his gaze from her face. An affable smile played across his square-jawed face, but she suspected he was remembering his recent conversation with his friend. Celia started in surprise when he took her hand and formally bowed. His breath was warm against her knuckles, though his lips didn't touch her skin, as was proper for such an introduction. Unaccustomed to such gallantry, she stared at his golden curls, stepping back involuntarily when he raised his head again. His sky blue eyes had an unsettling directness at such close range, which was tempered by his amusement.

"Don't give the chit false hopes, Garth," Marcus drawled from his chair, only increasing the heat to Celia's flushed face, this time from annoyance more than anger. Why did she find him so fascinating even when his manners were abominable? "Tell her about the light of your life and have done."

"Not all of us have the manners of a half-pay officer, Marcus. I believe, Miss Tregaron, he is referring to my engagement to Miss Julia Abercrombie." He cast his friend a withering look, which made her wonder about his affections for the young woman in question.

"Don't take your frustrations out on me, old man. I can't help it if she's stuck in the country helping nurse her younger brothers," Marcus replied. "Now, to the matter at hand. What was it that caused such a vehement denial, Miss Tregaron? What has Sylvia done to earn your displeasure?"

"Nothing at all. Sylvia has been most helpful since my arrival, milord." She matched his winning smile with one of her own.

"Ah, I see. As the perfect guest who doesn't want to wear out her welcome, you aren't going to cast aspersions on your hostess's offspring." He twirled the stem of his glass between two fingers. This activity seemed to preoccupy him more than the conversation. Or so she thought. "Now, I wonder why you're looking so imploringly at my sister? Could it be that you have spoken out against me, your benevolent host?"

"Must you be so odious, Marcus?"

Sylvia stamped her foot and crossed her arms over

her chest. One look at her pouting expression made Celia vow never again to pull the same stunt. No wonder she had never gotten any satisfactory results in similar circumstances or when being severely lectured. She must tell her new friend about her discovery, in a diplomatic way. Preoccupied with this revelation, she missed part of Sylvia's petulant response.

"—and that is why. So it wasn't something I did, or Mama. You must have done something obnoxious to cause her refusal, Marcus." She smiled in simpering triumph at her brother, fully satisfied with her conclusion.

Her smile quickly turned to a frown as the silence lengthened after her speech. Marcus merely raised a single eyebrow as he centered his annoying regard on Celia again. She began a study of the scarlet and blue carpeting, thinking she would be an expert on the floor coverings of the Ashmore town house very quickly at this rate. The gentleman next to her cleared his throat, clearly masking a chuckle. She remained silent, not daring to say an incautious word at the moment.

"Well, isn't anyone going to say *anything?*" Sylvia demanded, causing Celia to look up.

"Apparently Miss Tregaron has heard of my lack of prowess in the ballroom, my dear."

"Not at all, milord," Celia answered, some of her ire tempered as Marcus unconsciously adjusted his black silk sling. He might be the most irritating man in the world, but he didn't deserve a slight due to his injured arm. "I simply felt you had more important tasks than playing at dance instructor. It is not my place to take up your valuable time. I'm sure you have exceptional skills in the ballroom."

"And he can also dance fairly well," Garth contributed, bringing a genuine grin to his friend's lips.

"Touché," Marcus murmured.

Celia tilted her chin upward, trying not to acknowledge that she understood the man's meaning. The glint in Marcus's eyes told her it was useless. Did he also realize her heart had begun beating erratically at the sight of his broad grin?

"I think it would be best if we used a traditional dance teacher." She directed the statement to Sylvia, not wanting to match wits with her host any longer.

"I see they have some civilization in the Colonies after all. How enlightening. Always spend money on the expert whenever possible." Though the words were fairly innocent, Celia detected an underlying cynicism.

He wasn't going to let her quit the battle so easily. Well, she wouldn't give him his pound of flesh without a fight, either. With a sweet smile she answered, "If your lordship can't meet the expense, I have some funds at my disposal."

"Yes, I know, my dear, but I won't ask you to make the sacrifice just yet. You may need your money for an emergency," *perhaps to escape from me with your sanity intact,* his expression seemed to say. "I'm not in dun territory yet and can afford a few frivolous expenditures. I've been remiss in complimenting you on your new gown, haven't I?"

If it were possible she would have ripped the dress off at the moment and flung it in his face. His knowing smile seemed to say he anticipated such a reaction.

"Your mother and sister have been most kind," she returned, controlling her voice. If she couldn't win this encounter it would at least be a draw, she determined. "I hope you haven't been too inconvenienced by your inquiries about my brother."

"Yes, Marcus, exactly what have you done? I

wouldn't have guessed you would be such a slow top about this," his sister put in readily, an unwitting ally in Celia's attempt to discomfort him.

"Now, really, Sylvia, this isn't something that can be solved in an afternoon—"

"Have you done *anything?*"

"Your brother is a very busy man—"

"Balderdash! I'll wager the two of you have spent most of your time at the White's or some place less respectable and haven't given a thought to poor Celia's troubles." This time she placed her hands on her hips and divided her scowl between the two gentlemen. They had the grace to look uncomfortable at what apparently was an accurate accusation.

"I realize that this is an impossible situation, milord. Your hospitality has been most welcome and unexpected," Celia spoke up, delighted with the unexpected advantage. "I can easily make inquiries on my own. There are funds available—"

"Miss Tregaron, my family would never forgive me if I allowed you to wander around London on your own. Your funds are limited, so please don't belabor the expense." Marcus rose to his feet finally, his expression void of any mockery for the first time that afternoon. "I have made some tentative inquiries at Whitehall and am waiting for some answers before beginning a heedless search. Does that meet with everyone's satisfaction?"

Celia could tell by his attitude that she had done something to annoy him. His stiff-shouldered posture was all too familiar to her from dealing with her male relatives. What she had done, however, was the mystery. She should be pleased, since he seemed bent on disconcerting her at every turn. Perhaps she could enjoy his aggravation if it had been caused by a ploy that she devised. How could she dare to match wits with the man if she didn't know his weaknesses?

"Thank you, milord. I appreciate your assistance," she murmured hastily as he rounded the end of the desk. What else could she do at the moment?

"Then, ladies, we shall take our leave." He nodded to her and Sylvia in a semblance of a bow and directed Mr. Cruthers to follow him with a barely discernable movement of his head. When he reached the door he turned back, almost as an afterthought. "Miss Tregaron, as I mentioned earlier, keep your fifty pounds for an emergency. We won't speak of the matter again." With that he turned on his heel and called to Baskin.

"How strange."

"W-what was that, Sylvia?" Celia was only half-aware of her words. Could Marcus be angry because she wanted to pay her way, or at least contribute what she could to the venture? Surely she was mistaken.

"I just thought it was strange that he didn't care about your money. If Mama or I spend one farthing more than he thinks we should, Marcus is outraged," his sister said thoughtfully, chewing on her nail as she looked at the open doorway. "Maybe he is feeling guilty about Cousin Ambrose impressing your brother. I'm sorry I took him to task that way."

"I really don't know what to say. As long as we discover what has happened to Ethan, I shall go along with your brother's wishes." She would never admit as much to the man himself. If he did find her brother she would owe him her gratitude, no matter how grudgingly given.

"Then let's see if Mama has rung for refreshments, shall we? The Wilkins's had the most dreadful weak tea and only bread and butter to eat. Can you imagine?"

Celia didn't bother to answer as the other young woman linked arms with her. As they went in search of Lady Knowles she wondered what it was about the man that roused such conflicting emotions. His friend Mr. Cruthers was an extremely attractive man, but he certainly didn't affect her in the same way. In fact she had barely been aware that he was in the room most of the time. He was actually more classically handsome than her tormentor, but aside from his startling blue eyes, she really found nothing that held her interest.

As she ascended the stairs toward Lady Knowles's sitting room, she decided that her dreams were disturbing enough without thinking about Marcus during her waking hours. She should be happy that she had averted the disaster of having him on hand for her instruction in the waltz. From what little she knew of the dance she realized that she would be much too close to the man. That was certainly something she wanted to avoid. Weren't those unsettling moments in his embrace that evening in his room the reason for her unease now?

Celia resolved that her only concern with Marcus should be his efforts to find her brother, nothing more. There was enough trouble in her life at the moment without bringing into play her inexplicable reaction to a man she had known less than three days. She had known her late husband Daniel most of her life and didn't remember thinking about him as much. So she was going to forget all about Marcus, except as the man who was going to find her brother. That was the only way she would be able to match wits with him on equal ground.

*   *   *

"Really, Celia, I don't think your mind is on what you're doing. You've stepped on the poor man again," Sylvia scolded from her place at the pianoforte. She emphasized her point by playing a fractured chord. They had taken over the parlor, pushing back chairs and rolling up the carpet to produce a makeshift dance floor. Lady Knowles had miraculously produced a dance instructor overnight. "I begin to think we'll have to pay Monsieur Claude triple or at least pay his doctor bills."

"I'm so sorry, but I'm having trouble counting and holding a conversation at the same time," she admitted, giving her companion an apologetic smile. The dance really wasn't that difficult, but she was distracted by the memory of her encounter with Marcus in his bedchamber. When was she going to be able to put him from her mind?

"Never mind, mademoiselle, we shall begin again. I have withstood much more suffering than the feather weight of your delicate toes," the elderly émigré assured her nobly before nodding to Sylvia to resume playing. He carefully positioned Celia's hand on his forearm, then looped his arm loosely around her waist and gathered her free hand in his. "Now we keep this distance between us, almost two inches, as is proper for all the young ladies, no closer. If such a gentleman tries, you are to snap your fan on his ear. You must remind him that you are a properly bred young lady."

Celia studied the seam of his morning coat, willing herself not to blush at the implication. She had been much closer to a man she barely knew, with incredible and unsettling results. How proper was that? He had taken her by surprise, but that didn't keep her from dreaming about the kiss they had shared.

As Monsieur Claude Davonette whirled her around the sitting room she glimpsed her figure, clad in rose-spotted cambric, in the rectangular mirror above the fireplace. She looked like the same young woman who had left Baltimore so many weeks ago, but she felt like a stranger. Who was this stranger who possessed her body and found the kiss of such an annoying, irritating, and totally infuriating man so unforgettable?

"Ah, mademoiselle is now learning, I think."

The words of praise cut into her thoughts and caused her to misstep once again. "Do I really need to learn this infernal dance? It isn't very well accepted at home, even if Mrs. Madison was reported to have introduced it at the White House."

"What is this White House?" Monsieur Claude asked, stepping back with a nod. He extended his hand to escort Celia to her seat. This she accomplished without mishap, since some of the rules of society were much the same here as at home.

"The White House is what they are calling the president's home now. They painted it white to cover the burn marks from the fire—" She broke off as she realized the direction of her statement. If Marcus had been there she would have continued for the sheer pleasure of annoying him, but she spared Monsieur Claude and Sylvia an account of the British troops' attempt to burn down half the capital city the previous year. "Anyway, Mrs. Madison is the president's wife and said to be the foremost hostess in the country."

"They may not find the waltz completely acceptable in the United States, but they do at Almack's. Lady Jersey was so kind to allow you a voucher when Mama asked," Sylvia announced while letting her fingers idly play over the keys. "Of course, you have to be properly presented to your partner by one of the patronesses before you can take the dance floor. It's so silly at times, being introduced to a gentleman you've known for weeks just to be able to dance a particular dance."

"Yes, I begin to wonder if I should bother to go with you to Almack's at all. It seems to have an incredible amount of nonsensical rules and regulations. I'm not going to be here long enough to learn them all."

Celia's statement was met by what could only be called an appalled silence. Both her companions were looking at her in openmouthed astonishment. She might just as well have told them about the dream she had about Marcus the night before, which shocked even her.

Why would she ever think of Marcus without his clothing, even in her sleep? During her brief marriage she had never even speculated about her husband in that manner. Intimate relations were a duty she was expected to perform; she had certainly never dreamed about the marriage act. Daniel had been her husband, usually a tardy one, but she had done what was expected of her. She had been somewhat fond of Daniel, and she certainly didn't have any finer feelings for Marcus. What did it mean? Why did her palm still tingle whenever she thought of the feel of Marcus's warm skin against her hand?

"Celia, where have you gone off to again? You must stop worrying about your brother and pay attention."

Sylvia's smile of sympathy made her feel like such a traitor, to her new friend and to her brother. Celia hadn't thought about Ethan once today; her mind was preoccupied by her frenetic emotions and chaotic thoughts. Dreaming about Marcus once might have been reasonable, a reaction to the actual events in his room, but three nights in a row was very disturbing. She didn't even trust the man, and he certainly didn't trust her. Hadn't he been telling his friend that only yesterday? Though she was still puzzled over what aroused his suspicions.

"I'm sorry, Sylvia, but I do wonder if your brother is doing anything to find Ethan. I've been here several days, and he has only said he made inquiries at Whitehall." She rose and curtsied to Monsieur Claude, signaling that she was ready to try again. If Marcus thought he was dealing with some illiterate Colonial miss, he was in for a surprise. There wasn't that much difference between London and Baltimore society, except some obnoxious rules.

"Ah, I see I have come at an opportune time. Sylvia, Miss Tregaron, how goes the lesson?"

Celia was relieved to see that Mr. Cruthers was the interloper and that he was alone. "I'm afraid Monsieur Claude is going to be soaking his very sore feet for hours tonight, Mr. Cruthers."

"I can't believe that is true. Is this right, Sylvia?" The gentleman advanced into the room, an ingratiating smile on his handsome face. Once again Celia wondered why such a good-looking gentleman didn't make her heart flutter in the least.

"Celia is exaggerating," she answered in loyal defense. The sharp look she gave Celia reminded her that a lady wasn't supposed to admit any shortcomings, at least not to a gentleman. "But what are you doing here in the middle of the day? And where is Marcus? You haven't pushed him into the Thames, have you?"

"You mustn't look so hopeful, my dear. A lady, even a relative, isn't supposed to be anxious to dispose of a gentleman," he chided, flicking the young woman's chin as he lounged against the pianoforte. "I had an appointment to meet him here at one. What has he done to earn your displeasure today? Refused an advance on next quarter's allowance?"

"Oh, pooh, of course not. He has suddenly been so disagreeable in the past few days. I don't really think he is actually looking for Celia's brother, either."

"'Tis not that he isn't trying, pet, but things never move very swiftly at Whitehall." His expression was thoughtful as he turned to Celia. "We learned that when we were waiting for supplies on the Peninsula, always getting blankets in the summer, you know."

"I'm not really complaining, since that means Celia will be with us longer. If she wasn't so worried about Ethan, I would tell Marcus to take forever."

"Sylvia, I can't stay here forever," Celia put in, laughing at her friend's compliment. "Your brother certainly doesn't want an uninvited guest for so long."

"Just give Marcus a chance, Celia. Once he gets over what is blue-deviling him, he can be very good company, even if he is my brother."

"High praise, I'm sure. Now, shall we put Miss Tregaron to the test with a new partner?" Garth asked, giving each of the young ladies a questioning look. "I put myself at your disposal to relieve Monsieur Claude's toes. He can check your form and precision from the sidelines."

"Oh, I wouldn't want to put you to the trouble," Celia protested, not sure she was ready to attempt another partner as yet. This was Marcus's closest friend, and she wasn't sure what she should do.

"I'm wearing boots, my dear, so you can't do much damage," he said, pointing out his shiny footgear with a flourish. "Besides, I never pass up an opportunity to hold a lovely woman in my arms, or get the march on my old friend Marcus. It will set his teeth on edge that I've succeeded where he has been refused."

Celia found that she was readily answering the gentleman's mischievous grin. The temptation to thwart Marcus, even in fun, was too great. She curtsied to her new partner, who bowed solemnly in return. To her surprise she was able to match Mr. Cruthers's steps with ease.

After a few experimental turns she found herself flying around the room, or so it seemed. Under his expert guidance she gave herself up to the dance, gliding and dipping with abandon. Now she understood why all the ladies were so anxious to learn the steps. It was like nothing she had ever experienced before, and she didn't want to stop.

When the music ended some minutes later she laughed out loud at her achievement. "How perfectly splendid. Mr. Cruthers, I thank you for your help. I had no idea that you were such an exceptional partner."

"Neither did I, Garth. That was quite a performance," came the dry comment from the doorway. Marcus was leaning against the wall, his buff kerseymere–encased legs crossed at the ankle, giving no indication of how long he had been there. Celia's breath caught in her throat.

"'Tis never difficult to overextend myself for the sake of a lovely lady. Miss Tregaron, I thank you for the dance." Mr. Cruthers bowed gracefully once more, a playful smile curving his lips. "Please save a waltz for me on the next Wednesday night, so we may do this again. Come now, Marcus, let's leave the ladies to their lesson while you tell me what has put that sour look on your face."

Celia wondered exactly the same thing. Was it something to do with Ethan? Whatever it was that had Marcus scowling, he wasn't going to disclose it to her. In fact, he barely looked in her direction before he aimed a curt nod at the room in general and turned on his heel. She watched the retreating backs of the two gentlemen in confusion. There was something going on here that she didn't understand.

At that moment she made up her mind that Marcus wasn't going to ignore her. At home she would never have stood for such treatment from her family. She was going to find out exactly what he knew about her brother. Ethan was her brother; she had a right to know. All she had to do was figure out how she was going to manage it.

5

"*Should I be writing Julia* a letter of condolence over her broken engagement in the near future?" Marcus inquired, unable to resist the gibe. He didn't bother looking up from the decanter of claret as he poured out two glasses.

"Whatever for?"

"Garth, don't bother to use that guileless tone. You're up to something, so don't try to fool me." He handed his friend one glass, while his humorless smile answered the other man's grin. Then he picked up his own glass and leaned back against the edge of his desk, making a pretense of inspecting the high polish of his Hessians as he waited for the answer.

The other gentleman took his time sampling his wine, as if it were the first time he had partaken of spirits from Ashmore's cellar. When his companion remained silent he gave a philosophical shrug. "You were so convinced the girl was a fraud I thought I would do a little investigating on my own."

"The last time you did *a little investigating* on your own the female in question was called Fernanda, I believe," Marcus reflected, half closing his eyes as he remembered the inauspicious event. Though he couldn't picture the woman, he did recall what had taken place. "I ended up losing my room at the inn when you and your friend commandeered it and had to sleep in a drafty stable."

"I think our latest subject is much more innocent than the lovely Fernanda."

"Innocent, but twice as clever. So, you were only getting better acquainted with the lady? Why do I believe only half of what you say?" For the life of him he couldn't understand his annoyance over Garth's attention to Celia.

"You've known me too long, I suppose, my dear Marcus, since we were in swaddling clothes, I daresay," he commented before dropping into one of the armchairs near the fireplace and propping his feet up on the lion-shaped andiron. "What other reason could I possibly have for the lady's company? She is dashed pretty, well-spoken, and dances like an angel. Hardly a thing to recommend her company except she doesn't seem to like you terribly well."

"Pardon?" Marcus was caught in a half-crouched position as he started to sit down. With a guarded look at his friend he sat down firmly in the chair, wondering why he had never noticed the man's annoying habits before this. In some thirty-two years he should have discovered that Garth Cruthers was incredibly galling when he was in high spirits.

"The minute you appeared on the scene she seemed very withdrawn. What have you been doing to the poor girl?"

"Dashed if I know," he replied, knowing full well that his lifelong friend wasn't going to be satisfied, but that was all he was going to say. Garth would be in whoops if Marcus admitted that he hated the sight of Celia in the other man's arms. He knew that was exactly what the other man wanted him to say, since he had been present when the chit denied needing any assistance from him to learn the waltz.

It wasn't what he was doing to her, more what she was doing to him. The tantalizing memory of this morning came back to bedevil him as it had at odd times during the day. All he had done was leave his room in search of Baskin for his assistance with his cravat. By some misfortune the maid left the door across the hall from his room ajar. An idle glance had left him feeling as if he had been poleaxed.

Standing clearly in line with his riveted gaze was an incredible vision of loveliness, a goddess of perfection in her natural glory. Then she was taken from his sight as the maid held up a towel and Celia had stepped from her bath. He had walked down the hallway without being aware of any movement. His over-stimulated mind was still preoccupied with the rounded curves of her hips and buttocks. Her raven locks had been secured at the top of her head, giving him an unrestricted view of every bedazzling inch of creamy flesh. Just as she had clasped the toweling to her body the hint of the lush curve of her breast had almost had him stepping forward into the room.

"Marcus, you must come clean. Are you in her black book because you haven't found hide or hair of her long-lost brother? Sylvia's convinced that you haven't done a thing about finding Ethan Tregaron," Garth informed him, a little too cheerfully for his way of thinking. "She isn't angry about it, since she wants Miss Tregaron to stay forever."

Marcus almost groaned aloud at the idea, riding so closely on his memories of that morning. Right now he wasn't sure if it was Celia's arousing presence that he dreaded most or the possibility of endless days of questioning idiot clerks about her brother. He needed to begin reinforcing his defenses against her, which had been of little avail thus far. "I'm beginning to think that her brother doesn't exist at all, and she is an accomplished trickster out to fleece me for every farthing I possess."

"Some wishful thinking on your part, possibly?"

"What do you mean?" he asked in mock innocence as expected by his friend's dry tone. The gentleman's train of thought wasn't that hard to follow. Hadn't he just been reinforcing his resolve against the lady's charms? As long as he regarded her with suspicion he could ignore the fact that she fascinated him more than any other woman he'd ever known, even on such a short acquaintance.

"I think, my friend, that it would suit your current frame of mind to discover that the lady wasn't all that respectable," Garth pronounced, then tossed back the remainder of his wine. "I might be tempted by such a lovely piece as that, especially if I came home one night and discovered her waiting in my bedchamber."

"Except for the existence of the comely Julia," Marcus put in, matching his companion's casual tone. Fortunately, he had had the good sense not to say a word about exactly what he did after he disarmed his lovely assailant that night.

"Yes, we should always make an exception for my

Julia," he returned. His look told Marcus that he shouldn't pursue that particular subject any further.

"Barring our friend Hampton, no one seems to know of the existence of one Ethan Tregaron, late of Baltimore, Maryland, and later still of His Majesty's Navy."

"You mean the girl could actually be an impostor? No wonder you haven't said anything to your family. What are you going to do now?"

"I'm giving her another week." *To discover her real identity or be taken away to Bedlam,* he added silently.

"Another week for what?"

"Another week of battling red tape at Whitehall, arguing with the imbeciles that pass themselves off as admiralty clerks, and visiting every shipping office on the London docks," he said, leaning his head back against the soft cushion of the embroidered headrest. She drove him to distraction now; what would happen if she was simply the innocent young woman she said she was? That was an avenue he refused to head down.

"You could have your solicitor or some other lackey handle the chore."

"Lord Ashmore, I wish to speak to you," a feminine voice demanded, saving him from admitting that what Garth said was true. The agitated female stalking toward him also saved him from coming up with a reasonable excuse, to his friend and himself, about why he didn't delegate the search for this Ethan person to someone else.

"So I see, Miss Tregaron. Is this how a lady handles such matters in the Colonies?" he inquired, not bothering to move. "Democracy is such an interesting form of government, but slightly ill-mannered, very untidy."

"Oh, stay seated, Mr. Cruthers. *He* isn't going to get up, so you might as well be comfortable." Celia gave the instruction with a wave of her hand, never taking her eyes off Marcus.

He was intrigued as well as amused by her defiant stance. For a moment he expected her to strike a pose similar to that of his sister in mutinous pout. She seemed about to, then changed her mind. Instead she took a deep breath and clasped her hands tightly in front of her. Once again he acknowledged that she was at her most magnificent when she was angry— discounting this morning's unexpected view.

Perhaps his strategy had worked after all, for she was every inch the daring lady who had invaded his home that first night. Except for her refusal to have him for a dance partner, Celia had been polite, ignoring his challenging statements whenever they met. Just as he began to wonder if he could irritate her into showing her true colors, she appeared with renewed vengeance.

"You wanted to say something to me, Miss Tregaron?"

"I demand to know what you have learned about my brother," she exclaimed, barely keeping from stamping her foot. He knew it took a real effort on her part to remain perfectly still.

"Ah, another democratic action, I see, ordering me to comply with your wishes," he murmured, taking a sip from his glass and taking his time doing it. He allowed the liquid to roll around on his tongue, savoring the flavor as well as the green fire sparkling in his opponent's eyes.

Then he noticed the way she clasped her fingers tightly together in front of her, the knuckles almost white at the pressure she exerted. If she was telling the truth, what little information he had gleaned might ease her anxiety. Setting his glass on the grate he rose and closed the distance between them. "Miss Tregaron, I can understand some of your frustration in the lack of news. I've spent two days now at the hands of half a dozen incompetents at Whitehall and was almost moved to violence on more than one occasion. Unfortunately, everyone is more concerned with matters on the Continent than a war that is old news."

"Yes, I can understand that," she answered softly. "Napoleon's escape must be very alarming to those who thought he was safely out of the way."

"You show much more perception over the problem than most." In spite of his doubts about her honesty, he knew she was intelligent and quick witted. "So you can understand why the fools have been able to discover only the location of the ship that may have brought your brother to England, which put into port for repairs last summer before being sent to the Mediterranean."

"Did they say anything about American prisoners on board?" She emphasized her urgency by clasping his glove encased hand with her own. "Oh, why didn't you tell me this sooner?"

Her entreating look was slightly marred by the beginning of a frown, but it was enough to break the spell she had temporarily cast over him. Marcus shook his head in denial of any softer feeling before he pronounced, "I learned of it only this morning. I didn't want to raise any false hopes, since the logbook showed only that prisoners were on board. They're still looking for a roster of the men put ashore."

Celia suddenly seemed to realize that she was holding his hand. She snatched hers away and placed it behind her back as if to keep from reaching out to him again. Her contrite look made him wonder, not for the first time, if she wasn't an accomplished actress. "I see. I suppose there isn't anything else to do but wait, is there? I apologize for thinking that you weren't actually looking for Ethan, but simply sitting at your club each afternoon."

Had she really meant to insult him with that apology? Marcus didn't care to reason it out, and fell back on disdain to save his pride and to keep his temper in check.

"How remiss of me. Garth, I have been neglecting my guest. How will I hold my head up at the club if this gets out?" Addressing his usually impassive friend was almost a disaster. The man was practically bursting to keep from laughing out loud, his hand over his mouth, his shoulders shaking uncontrollably. To keep from ruining his own arrogant portrayal he cupped her elbow in his hand and turned her toward the door. "Miss Tregaron, I offer you my most humble apology and shall do my best to adjust my behavior to meet with your rather bellicose democratic standards. I appreciate your bringing this flaw in my character to my attention, and for the sake of improved international understanding, don't hesitate to make your wishes known to me at any time."

All the while he lectured he moved steadily across the room. Celia was looking up at him in stunned silence, not even sputtering at his abrupt manner. Once he reached the hallway he released her arm and stepped back. "Now, my dear, for better relations between us, I have a word of advice."

Her eyes narrowed, but still she didn't speak. It was almost as if she didn't trust herself to utter a sound at the moment. She merely stood glaring at him.

"Always knock on the door and wait for someone

to give you permission to enter before you barge into a room." With that he shut the door firmly to ensure that he didn't slam it. A thump on the other side sounded less than a heartbeat later. That was followed by a purely feminine sound of disgust.

"I hope she didn't hurt herself. Do you really think she kicked the door?" Garth asked, peering around the high back of his chair.

"What odds do you give me it was her shoe?" he challenged with his hand resting on the doorknob. What he had just done was rude, but what else could he do when she had all but accused him of shirking his duty?

"Not even a pence from that glint in your eyes. Just be thankful it wasn't that jasper vase near the stairs."

Marcus didn't answer immediately. He was occupied opening the door and studying the polished floor of the hallway. When he bent over and retrieved a kid slipper from the tile his friend gave out a shout of laughter. "It amazes me, Garth, why our countrymen were so reluctant to relinquish that nest of hotheads across the ocean. Why did they need to rebel? Someone should have just let them go and good riddance."

"Oh, Marcus, at least admit that she is a damned attractive wench," Garth pleaded as his friend replenished their glasses.

"After all these years why would I be foolish enough to willingly provide you with fodder for that repulsive sense of humor of yours?" he asked as a means to prevaricate. Though he was his only true friend, Garth was the last person on earth to whom he would admit his unsettled feelings concerning Miss Celia Tregaron. Acknowledging that she had some strange power over him to himself was lowering enough. He wasn't about to add insult to injury.

6

"*Sylvia, quit picking* at your gloves," her mother instructed from her seat in the carriage that was heading for the Arbuthnot musicale. "Take Celia's example and sit quietly with your hands folded in your lap. One would think you came from the Colonies yourself."

"Mama, what a dreadful thing to say," her daughter said, continuing to fidget in her seat but placing her hands in her lap. "Celia has lovely manners."

"Of course she does, dear. Wasn't that what I just said?"

Celia bit back a laugh at her hostess's confusion. What would her hostess think if she knew the cause of Celia's perfect manners? Her hands were tightly clasped together to keep from strangling the gentleman lounging on the leather seat next to his sister. He was leaning back in the corner with his arm clasped over his sling, his top hat tilted forward covering the upper portion of his face.

If she did have the manners of a heathen, she would take her fist and slam it down on the crown of his hat. Since she was raised properly, she continued to quell the violent reaction his presence always seemed to evoke.

"It was so nice of his lordship to escort us this evening," she said sweetly instead, trying for some reaction from him, any reaction. Since yesterday's disastrous interview in the library he had been terribly polite on the two occasions they had met at meals. Ironically, she missed the excitement in their duel of words. Or was it the gleam in his blue-green eyes and his enticing half smile she wanted? Had her unintended insult caused this chilly stranger to appear? "Is there something special about tonight's entertainment that has granted us the unexpected pleasure of your company?"

"Besides your first presentation to polite society, not a thing," he answered lazily. "It should liven up a rather flat evening of cards and ceaseless chatter."

"Shall I bay at the moon, or simply stalk a few guests with a knife clenched between my teeth?" Not bothering to wait for a response, she continued, "Perhaps that would be too outrageous. Suppose I simply stride around the room with my mouth gaping open at all the unknown splendor surrounding me, such as tables and chairs. I could even pocket a trinket or two, just for good measure."

"Don't overplay your hand, Miss Tregaron," Marcus drawled, tipping his hat back in place with a nudge of his thumb. Even in the dim light of the coach his eyes seemed to glisten dangerously as he studied her. "Maybe you should simply remember to use utensils when you eat."

"Marcus, that is the limit. Celia can't know that you're a dreadful tease," his mother admonished, but

was forestalled from anything further as the coach
came to a standstill.

"He certainly can be dreadful," Celia agreed, ducking
her head to hide her smile, as Marcus preceded them out
of the coach. She didn't realize she had spoken aloud
until the gentleman's hand clasped hers longer than
necessary as he assisted her a few minutes later. When he
retained his hold on her fingers she looked up in surprise.

"Remember, my dear, that your current fate is in
my hands, dreadful or not." With a slight inclination
of his head he finally released her.

As he strolled forward to offer his arm to his
mother, Celia swallowed a retort. How could she
explain? How could Marcus understand when she
was perplexed by her own reactions? It was safer, for
her peace of mind, to consider that she had grown up
in a boisterous, somewhat argumentative family, so
that sparring with her host came naturally to her.

As the group ascended the stairs she realized with
surprising calm that she was about to attend her first
London entertainment. She hadn't had time to be
nervous because all her emotions had been centered
on Marcus until that moment.

If she had to keep smiling this way her face was going
to crack, Celia decided a few hours later, looking
around the room at the endless sea of unfamiliar
faces. So this is what society among the *ton* was like.
she mused, nodding at the young woman on her left
who didn't seem to know how to talk. Why was she
there if she wasn't going to talk? Were her feet as
tired from standing as Celia's? Maybe she had been
right earlier about chairs being a wondrous sight.

"Miss Tregaron, how enterprising of you to manage a voyage across the ocean," purred a tall, gaunt woman, who had just joined the group. The yellow plume fashioned in her blond hair bounced as she spoke. "How long will you be visiting in England?"

"I really can't say," Celia managed to reply. She had been about ready to yawn and still felt it threatening to overcome her. "So much depends on—"

"My brother is the only one who can answer that for now," Sylvia pronounced, surreptitiously pinching her friend just above the hem of her evening gloves. She gave a slight shake of her head when Celia frowned at her in question.

"Your brother, you say?" The woman repeated in a shrill voice.

"Did you have need of me, Sylvia?"

The woman's reaction to Marcus's sudden appearance was amazing. The hard, pinched look left her narrow face, replaced by an expression that made Celia feel queasy. The calculation in the woman's eyes and the ingratiating smile that she attempted made an ugly combination.

"Marcus, where did you spring from?" his sister asked, not hiding her annoyance. "I thought you were playing cards."

"Now, Miss Knowles, you mustn't tax your brother so," the woman chided, her eyes never leaving the subject of the discussion. She artfully fluttered her fan over her flat chest. "Your brother has been through so much. First his heroic wound, then poor, poor Ambrose's death. Oh, war is so cruel and tragic."

"A noble sentiment, Lady Frominster." Marcus's face was as expressionless as his voice.

"Why, everyone feels the same, I'm sure. Such

courage can only be admired and lauded, milord."
Slowly she moved her hand toward him, seeming
determined to touch him.

He moved his left arm to flip open his snuffbox
with his thumb. Raising his right elbow, he laid the
oval box on the back of his gloved right hand. Lady
Frominster stood motionless, her hand suspended in
midair as he took a pinch of snuff, then closed the box
and returned it to his pocket. "So many others were
less fortunate than I, milady. They didn't come home
to a loving family, but became permanent residents of
Spain. Now if you'll excuse me, I must see that my
mother doesn't fleece too many of the countess's
guests at whist. Ladies, until later."

"Miss Knowles, Miss Tregaron, good night," Lady
Frominster snapped before turning on her heel and
walking away. The bounce of her plume was quite
vigorous as she stalked across the room.

"Oh, I wish he wouldn't do that," Sylvia moaned,
pulling Celia away from the group that remained
watching the tableau in rapt silence.

"Do what? I have no idea what is going on here."
Celia was still shaken by what had taken place. "Am I
mistaken, or was your brother incredibly rude to that
woman? Just who is she? She seems to know your
family well."

"She would have been part of the family if she had
had her way. Rumor has it that she was planning to
snare Ambrose during his last leave," Sylvia explained,
a polite smile stretching across her face as two ladies
nodded in passing. "Ambrose apparently slipped
through her net and went back to sea a free man. She
married some old marquess to keep her creditors at
bay. At least that is what I've been able to glean from

the gossip. We were all rusticating at home when Marcus inherited the title. That was probably fortunate, or she would have undoubtedly set her cap at him."

"Good heavens, this could turn out better than a play," Celia mused, looking over the crowd with renewed interest. At home, social gatherings had simply been a chance to relax and enjoy their friends' company. Or had she missed the undercurrents there as well?

"Well, we're supposed to be too innocent to understand these things, but I think she might be considering taking a lover."

"What?" Celia couldn't contain her shock. That repellent woman was thinking of offering Marcus what her brother called a slip of the shoulder?

"Shh, we don't want the whole room to know." Sylvia looked around self-consciously, then seemed relieved that no one appeared to notice Celia's outburst. "She is always going on about his heroic actions, trying to touch him in a familiar manner and batting her eyelashes at him."

"So, that is why he was taking snuff," she murmured. Though Marcus had been coldly polite to her earlier in the day, it was nothing compared to the lethal manner he had presented to Lady Frominster. In fact, he had a special way of regarding her when he addressed her directly, similar to his manner toward his mother and sister. What was the difference? She wasn't sure she wanted to know the answer just yet.

"It was a capital touch, wasn't it? I was so irritated when he appeared, but that created a lovely diversion. Hopefully she'll look for fairer game from now on."

"Why were you irritated that Marcus joined the group?"

"Well, to be honest, I was about to tell a small lie. I

have never liked Sophie, so I was going to let her believe that you and Marcus were—"

"Sylvia, how could you? The last person on earth I want my name linked with is—"

"Celia, I had to do something. That woman actually asked him how he was wounded the last time she had him trapped in her clutches."

"What did he tell her?" She couldn't keep from asking the question. At home there were veterans of the War for Independence that were still bitter about the loss of a limb. In contrast, Marcus's attitude intrigued her. He didn't seem the least troubled. Had that been his purpose in the trick with the snuffbox, to test Lady Frominster's stamina by drawing attention to his hand?

"He hasn't told a soul, except Garth, that is. They were together when it happened, but neither of them will say a word about what occurred. Marcus simply showed up on the doorstep one day without so much as a letter announcing his arrival. Whatever happened he seems determined to keep to himself. The only change I've seen in him is that black sling and glove. He started wearing it when we came to town last year for the little season and only wears it when we are here."

"How odd." She didn't have time to comment further. A school friend of Sylvia's beckoned to her. As she followed her friend across the room Celia began to wonder if she would ever begin to understand Marcus's convoluted mind or the machinations of London society.

Everyone around her, with the exception of Sylvia and her mother, seemed to have an ulterior motive hidden behind a gracious smile and polite chatter. Had he discerned that she had been less than honest with his family, because he was accustomed to dealing with half-truths and prevarication at every turn?

With a discontented sigh, she wondered if she should ever have come to London. Immediately she regretted the thought. Finding Ethan was important, no matter what. If only she could remember to focus her thoughts on her main purpose for traveling so far from home instead of being distracted by her infuriating, but charming, host.

"Miss Sylvia will be down in a few moments, miss," Baskin announced the next afternoon as Celia reached the bottom of the stairs. "She requested the carriage at half past five."

"Yes, thank you, Baskin. I shall wait in the parlor," Celia said, then scurried across the hallway. The man still had the power to intimidate her with just a look, even after she'd been in residence almost a week. Whenever she saw him she was sure he was going to ask her to pay for the damaged carpeting in Marcus's room. She let out a relieved sigh when he closed the double doors behind her.

Feeling restless, she wandered around the room, gliding her hand over the back of the white and gold satin settee, then moving on to the embroidered fire-screen. Several more dresses had been delivered that morning, including the blue and white striped gown she now wore beneath a white satin spencer. A sudden wave of homesickness overtook her as she idly swung her poke bonnet by its blue ribbon from the handle of her striped parasol. At home she rarely needed to bother with all these trappings, except when she went into the city. In London she had to dress to the teeth from the moment she stepped out of bed.

The ormolu clock on the mantel struck the quarter

hour. In her haste to escape the confines of the house she had managed to be ready for their afternoon drive much too early. Lady Knowles had cautioned her that they must introduce her into society by subtle means, carefully selecting where she would appear in public. The Arbuthnot musicale had been her maiden venture. Celia simply wasn't accustomed to such limited activity.

Dropping her bonnet and parasol on the nearest chair, she continued to amble around the room. She began humming softly as she continued on her aimless stroll, idly examining a few of the porcelain birds that Lady Knowles collected. After a few minutes she realized that she was humming the waltz that Sylvia had been playing for her lessons for the past two days.

Smiling as she recalled Monsieur Claude's relief over her improved skill that morning, she began to practice her steps. The room was slightly confining with the furniture back in place, so she moved in a small circle, her eyes closed as she concentrated on her steps. When she was sixteen she had practiced for weeks before her first dance. She had gone over every step time and time again in her room, away from the teasing notice of her family.

"A lady should never have to dance alone."

She gasped at the sound of a voice so close at hand and opened her eyes to find Marcus standing only a few feet away. Before she could utter a word he stepped forward. Instead of the conventional dance position that Monsieur Claude used, Marcus bracketed her waist between his hands. Tiny sparks seemed to blossom through her body from the warmth of his touch.

"Unless you want to attempt to dance backward, we have to make certain concessions," he stated in answer to her questioning look. When she didn't protest he guided her into the first step.

"There isn't any music." She found herself whispering the words for no real reason. Perhaps it was the strange sensations that were coursing through her body at the moment. Or was it because for once Marcus wasn't looking at her in that cunning manner? His sea green eyes were smiling, and the ironic expression she had come to expect was absent.

"We'll just have to depend on my ability to count, or should we summon Sylvia to come and play for us?"

She shook her head in response, not wanting to break whatever spell that was cast over them. Marcus seemed to understand her meaning, since he didn't stop guiding her around the room. She shivered in response as he slipped his left hand into the hollow of her back, bringing her much closer to his muscular frame.

Staring straight ahead into the intricate folds of his cravat, she tried to ignore her reaction to the heat of his body and the tantalizing, spicy aroma of his pomade. Her hands tightened involuntarily where she clasped his upper arms. This was exactly what she had dreaded when learning the dance from Monsieur Claude, her reaction to being in such proximity to Marcus once more. Now she questioned her dread. Why wouldn't she anticipate such exotic, glorious feelings?

"Am I the dreadful partner that you feared?"

His question almost mirrored her thoughts. She knew that she had to assure him he danced beautifully, because the look in his eyes told her the answer was important. Nervously she wet her lips and swallowed while trying to form the necessary words. She wasn't prepared for his sudden groan before he lowered his head and captured her parted lips in a kiss.

Shivers of reaction coursed through her, intensifying the fire that seemed ready to consume her body.

Suddenly she realized she was experiencing passion for the first time in her life. Intrigued by this startling discovery she linked her arms around Marcus's neck, threading her hands through his silky chestnut curls.

She wanted to experience more, but wasn't really sure what she should do next. Tentatively she touched the tip of her tongue to his as he laved the corner of her mouth. The thrust of his tongue into her mouth frightened and aroused her at the same time. If this was her reaction to his kiss, how could she withstand anything more? A second later she whimpered in disappointment when he released her lips. Then she trembled and swallowed a moan of pleasure as he trailed kisses along her jaw to the underside of her neck.

"Celia, where have you disappeared to? The carriage is waiting at the door."

Sylvia's query from beyond the closed parlor door shook Celia from her passion-induced daze. She couldn't let her friend discover her like this in Marcus's arms. His sister already had too many strange notions about them to give her any ammunition. Until that moment she hadn't been thinking clearly, only reacting to the dictates of new feelings.

"Marcus, we can't be found—Good heavens, how did that happen?" she exclaimed, trying to scramble up from the couch, still not understanding how she came to be lying next to him. Could she really not have realized they were no longer standing? She had heard passion was a dangerous emotion, but only now began to realize the implications.

"Oh, sorry," she muttered, snatching her hand away from his gloved wrist. Instead of his body she used the back of the couch to push herself to her feet. As Sylvia called her name again she looked around for her bonnet and parasol, hastily checking her appearance in the mirror over the mantel.

"I'm sorry if you found the contact unsettling."

"What are you saying? There isn't time unless you want your sister to get some strange idea—" Celia broke off as she saw his reflection in the mirror. He was shoving his gloved hand in his trouser pocket as if to hide it from sight.

"Don't be a fool," she pronounced and spun around to face him. Without a second's hesitation she grasped his forearm and pulled his hand from his pocket. Holding his hand between her own she looked up at him, feeling both exasperated and surprised. "I didn't pull away because of your hand. I was trying to escape your sister finding us, er, well, finding us. Oh, never mind, she is calling again."

She grabbed her bonnet and pulled it on as she hurried to the door. Looking behind her, she almost screamed in frustration. He hadn't moved an inch, almost as if he didn't care his family knew they had been shut away together in the parlor. With a vexed sigh she slid open one panel door and slipped through, then firmly closed it again. One of them had to think clearly about the matter.

Her escape from the parlor was perfectly timed, since Sylvia was asking Baskin her whereabouts. For a moment she studied the majordomo's impassive face, trying to gauge what he knew. Apparently he had stepped out of the hall for a moment, and had not been available when Sylvia came down from her room, she decided while pulling on her gloves.

"Shall we go, Sylvia? I'm anxious to see how the fashionable folks promenade after your colorful descriptions," she stated, giving her friend her best smile. Right now she had a need for fresh air to clear her head. A ride in Hyde Park was just the thing to distract her.

Later she knew she would be haunted by her behavior with Marcus. Was it any wonder unmarried men and women weren't allowed alone together? How could she know that her dreams could be realized—or even surpassed? She was too shaken at the moment to know what she was to do next. Sylvia was an innocent ally, chattering away as they descended the front steps to the street. Only one thought disturbed Celia, making her awkward at the moment she was assisted into the open carriage: How was she suppose to greet Marcus when next they met?

As she crept down the stairs hours later in the dark of night, a single candle lighting her way, Celia couldn't help but shiver. The atmosphere was all too reminiscent of the night she had first entered the house. Tonight she had a candle, but the ominous silence around her was eerily familiar. If only she had been able to sleep. But sleep was elusive and the cure was simple. She needed something to read.

A book would be the ideal means of quieting her chaotic thoughts. The demon that kept her awake was the question of how to explain her response to Marcus's kisses, to herself and to him. She had not seen him since she had left him in the parlor. He had not been at dinner or returned home before she went to bed over an hour ago.

Not that she was complaining. She needed time to master her thoughts. Every time she closed her eyes she recalled the warm pressure of his lips against hers and the feelings engendered by his stroking hand moving over her body. That was why sleep had been so elusive.

As she reached the bottom of the steps she resolved to drive all thoughts of Marcus from her mind until morning. Why wasn't this a simple task? Why had she been asking herself the same question for the past few days, almost since meeting the man? She was no closer to answering the question as she entered the library.

She tiptoed across the room, refusing to look in the direction of the desk. Even though Marcus wasn't present—she wasn't even sure he was in the house— the desk and leather chair increased her sense of unease. Squaring her shoulders, she tightened her hold on the skirts of her wrapper and nightdress, keeping her gaze focused on the four rows of books directly in front of her.

Taking a few steps forward, she lifted her candlestick high enough to read the titles of the leatherbound volumes. Just as she reached for a likely selection a soft thud sounded behind her.

Barely repressing a scream in reaction, she turned automatically toward the sound. She relaxed, almost laughing at her own foolishness. There was no one there. Her over-stimulated nerves had her imaging a log settling in the fire was some sort of monster.

"Can I help you with your selection, my dear Celia? Or were you seeking something of better value?"

She whirled around in the opposite direction to face the desk, cursing her lack of perception a few minutes before. If there ever was a time to faint it was now, but she was mindful of the burning candle in her hand. Though at the moment burning the house down around them didn't seem like such a bad idea. Oh, why hadn't she stayed safely in her own room?

7

"*Any valuables are in a safe* in my bedchamber, my dear, including the family jewels," Marcus went on, not bothering to move from his favorite position, sprawled behind the desk. For a moment he wondered if he had conjured her presence from his fevered imagination. She was standing so still; he had to look closely to see if she was even breathing.

She was a fantasy come to life, and she brought his body to life as well. Her thin muslin nightgown did little to hide the delightful charms he had been imagining as he sat drinking himself into unconsciousness. When she had paused for a second in front of the desk he had wondered if it was by design or coincidence.

She had exquisite legs, or at least what he could judge from the ankle and calf she had accidentally uncovered. Or was it an accident? Fortunately, she had stepped out of the fire's betraying light, though the image was indelibly burned into his mind. "Are you going to speak, sweet apparition? Or are you simply going to stand there and torment me with your silence?"

She blinked at his harsh demands, then shook her head. The motion tossed her single braid from side to side. Was she answering him or refusing to believe his presence? He rose to his feet, regretting the abrupt movement immediately, but managed to maintain his balance. Just how much brandy had he consumed while trying to erase the jade from his mind? Eyeing the decanter, he calculated that approximately half the container had gone down his throat. "It wasn't enough, not nearly enough."

"What are you talking about, milord?" his tormentor inquired, making him realize he had spoken aloud. "What wasn't enough?"

"Never mind, my dear. Aren't we being a trifle formal for such an occasion?" he asked, setting down his glass. "Although I'm not sure what the occasion is."

"I came down to select a book," she replied, holding her candlestick in front of her, clasped in both hands. Was she thinking that was going to ward him off? he wondered as he moved from behind the desk.

"I couldn't sleep."

"Ah, neither could I. So we have something in common, don't we? Your means to aid slumber is much loftier than mine. I planned to drink until I blacked out. Not such a strain on one's brain, at least until morning. Would you care for some brandy?"

"No, thank you, milord. I think I'll return to my room." She was figuring the distance between them as well as how she could reach the door, he could tell.

"I think after all we've been to each other, you could call me Marcus. I plan to address you as Celia from this moment on," he said, wondering why he wasn't getting any closer. He was walking forward, wasn't he? He stopped and considered the matter. "You're moving, too!" he announced in triumph. With each step he took she made a counter step, always keeping the distance between them the same. He smiled as he realized he still had the advantage. Celia was avidly watching him, walking backward and sideways as he advanced. She couldn't see where she was going, but he could.

"Marcus, it's much too late for a row. We can talk in the morning."

His smile only seemed to add to her tension. "No, we can't. You'll hide yourself in your bedchamber or behind my mama's skirts." He knew he sounded like a sulky child over the matter, but she wasn't playing fair. Well, two could play in an underhanded manner. "I'm not going to hurt you."

"You don't like me."

Her challenge took him by surprise, but that wasn't what kept him silent or stopped him from stepping forward. Celia had relaxed her death grip on the candlestick, holding it lower, near her waist. She was unaware that her wrapper hung open, giving him a glorious, unrestricted view of her unbound breasts. The flickering candle created an arc of light that highlighted her satin skin, framed by the low gathered neckline of her now diaphanous nightdress.

As he had on the first night Marcus knew that he was being offered a glimpse of flawless beauty. Now he knew that her charms were not aided by any artifice. He swallowed a groan as his own body tightened in response.

"I don't dislike you, sweet Celia. At this moment I

can admit that dislike is the furthest thing from my mind." He knew he was taking unfair advantage as he stepped forward, but he had to touch her.

"Really, Marcus, this is ridicul—" She broke off as she came into contact with the edge of the desk. He had her exactly where he wanted her. She glared at him, anger warring with the suspicion in her shadowed gaze. "You aren't decently clothed."

"Ah, now I understand why you haven't been looking me directly in the eye. Perhaps your view has been impeded?" He reached up and deftly untied the knot of his sling. Until that moment he had forgotten that he'd torn off his cravat and unbuttoned his shirt before beginning his descent into brandy-induced oblivion. The gesture was to his advantage, and not in that it gave her a complete view of his chest—removing the sling gained him the limited mobility of his right arm.

Draping the limp material over his arm, he pulled the candlestick from her hand. She didn't protest, even when he blew out the flame and set the brass holder on the corner of the desk.

"What are you doing?" Her voice was barely a whisper as he stopped mere inches in front of her. The heat of her body reached out to him, continuing the siren songs he had been hearing since she entered the room.

He looped the black silk around her neck, drawing the ends together beneath her chin. "Do you like the feel of silk against your skin, my sweet? Silk sliding across silk," he murmured absently, bending closer until her scent filled his nostrils. Roses and lilacs were suddenly incredibly exciting.

"Marcus, I'm a guest in your home."

"That thought has been going around and around

in my brain for some time now. I've discovered I'm not strong enough to resist temptation, even if it is bad manners." With this he captured her lips, slipping his right arm securely around her waist. Her soft curves fit perfectly against his rigid frame. He closed his eyes to savor the moment, the feeling, the woman. The room seemed to spin around them.

Her lips were soft, challenging him to seek out more. He trailed his mouth across her cheek, seeking the delicate curve of her neck below her ear. At the same time he pulled the silk material across her nape, freeing her from the shackling hold and baring the tender skin of her neck to his lips.

"Please, Marcus," she whispered, her words thick and breathless.

"I am pleasing you, my sweet." He continued his exploration of her scented skin as he dropped the black silk on the floor. His hand wasn't empty for long. Almost greedily he reached for the material at her shoulder and slipped it down, exposing more creamy flesh as he trailed his hand along her arm. Her hand came up to stop his progress, but to no avail. He grasped her wrist and placed her hand against his feverish chest, showing her the slow caressing motion that he desired against his hair-roughened skin.

He inhaled sharply at the contact as her fingers trembled against his rib cage. His tongue delved into the valley between her breasts, knowing he was going to go mad at any moment from the myriad sensations chasing through his body. This mysterious woman had altered all his perceptions of passion in such a short space of time. He didn't know why; he only knew that he had to experience the madness.

A second later she moaned deep in her throat as he

dragged the thin material of her nightdress slowly over the engorged peak of her breast. He answered the sound as her lower body surged against his arousal, cradling him in the valley of her thighs. Like a starved man needing sustenance he suckled her breast, knowing he was beyond sanity. She moved restlessly against him, her small tantalizing sounds letting him know she found the same pleasure as he did. He almost shouted in triumph as her fingers threaded through his hair. A shudder of response seemed to travel from his body to hers.

He was aroused almost to the point of climax and could never remember being so dominated by his feelings with any other woman. How could she do this to him so quickly, so completely?

"Lord, but I want you, Celia. I've dreamed of having your raven hair blanketing our bodies as you twist and turn beneath me." He murmured the words against the shell of her ear. He could barely utter a sound the next moment as her bare breasts pressed against his chest. The cushioned softness against his sweat-slick skin broke through what little control he had left.

He bent her backward over the smooth surface of the desk, pressing his arousal into the warm juncture of her legs. Her legs parted readily against insistent movement. He cursed the material of his trousers and her nightdress that still separated them. Her back arched, presenting her golden skin to his heated gaze. Pressing heated kisses in the satin smooth valley between her luscious breasts, he demanded, "Tell me what you are thinking. Tell me now."

"It was never like this with Daniel." Her words were faint, broken bits of sound, but they acted like a douse of cold water on his befuddled senses.

"Daniel!" He spat out the name, abruptly standing straight. She had spoken the name only once before, but he knew who it was immediately. Unable to withstand the tantalizing sight of her half-clothed body, he turned away. While he had been buffeted by unfamiliar, intoxicating emotions, she was thinking of her dead husband.

He stumbled toward the fire and flung himself into a chair. Staring into the dying embers, he could hear her moving behind him. Neither of them spoke. What could he say to her? Madness and alcohol had robbed him of every rational thought and the dictates of polite society. It was a poor excuse, but that was all he had for his mortally wounded pride. Days of remembering the feel of her in his arms had led to this. Nothing had mattered.

When the door clicked shut in the deafening silence of the room Marcus finally looked up. His sling lying on the carpet was the only evidence of the impassioned moments that they had shared. If nothing else, he had the comfort of knowing she had been a participant. Had she been imagining he was her dead husband, or had she been responding to him in the present moment?

No matter how crazed he was from alcohol, he knew that given another chance he would act the same. Now he had more incentive than ever. He was going to discover exactly who Celia Tregaron was making love to tonight. More than his pride needed to know, but he didn't care to examine his full motives at present. It was enough that he had broken the social taboo of making love to a woman under his family's protection and that he still desired her as much as ever.

Rising wearily from the chair, he took himself off to bed, though he knew it was futile. He wouldn't sleep. Instead he would relive the exhilarating feel of having his raven-haired temptress in his arms. Was it a beautiful dream or a waking nightmare? Perhaps he had gone insane after all, he decided, bending to pick up his discarded sling from the floor. Or had Celia actually shot him that first evening, and he had finally made the journey to hell?

"Marcus, there you are, my dear, just when I need you. How fortunate."

His mother's usually pleasant tone grated on his raw nerves as he paused at the top of the stairs the next day. He gave her a bleary-eyed look, having finally emerged from his chamber well past noon. Since Foster still hadn't returned from the country, he had done without the cheerful man's morning elixir. His head was pounding, and he felt as if he would crawl out of his skin at any moment. Demon alcohol hadn't laid him this low since his days at university.

"Good morning, Mama," he managed with an effort. His tongue felt as if it were wrapped in cotton wool after growing three times its size.

"Oh, my dear, it is well past one o'clock," she returned cheerfully, seeming unaware that her son was out of curl at the moment. She linked her arm through his and practically dragged him back down the hallway. Since his brain was barely functioning, he didn't realize her intended direction until they reached the open doorway.

For a moment he considered using a favorite childhood trick, digging his heels into the carpet and refusing to budge an inch. Why was his mother leading him across the threshold of Celia's room? What had the chit said about last night's disgraceful encounter?

"Now, Marcus, we need a man's opinion." Lady Knowles's statement was answered by a sniff of outrage from a man standing by the fireplace. He was dressed in knee breeches and a smock in a hideous shade of chartreuse. "You really must tell us if Raphael is being obsequious, or if he has truly created a masterpiece."

Suddenly Marcus recognized the painfully thin gentleman as his mother's coiffeur. The overpriced idiot thought of himself as an artiste and dressed accordingly. With a growing sense of horror Marcus searched the room for Raphael's latest victim. He found her sitting quietly in the window seat, but he wouldn't have recognized her at any other time.

"Devil take it, what has he done to you?" he snapped, walking more swiftly across the room than he should. His head throbbed with every footstep.

Celia didn't flinch at his demand. She simply sat rigidly in position, her chin thrust forward as if to challenge anything he did or said. What held his horrified attention was her hair, or rather lack of it. Gone was the cascade of raven locks he remembered from their first meeting and dreamed about. Even having it clasped at the nape of her neck or last night's braid was preferable to this disgrace. Her dark hair clustered around her head in ringlets, barely longer than his own Brutus style.

"I heard the savages took scalps in the Colonies, but I hadn't realized that the custom had crossed the ocean," he bit out, barely managing to stop himself from reaching out to ruffle his fingers through her hair.

"I like it," she returned quietly, leveling a blazing green look that spoke volumes. This was her answer to his drunken advances last night. She'd allowed her beautiful hair to be destroyed because of his passion-induced words. Celia was having her revenge on him for his stupid blundering.

Marcus turned on his heel without a word. When he came abreast of the arrogant coiffeur, he stopped dead in his tracks. "Touch one more hair on her head, and I'll have you shaved from head to toe."

As he left the room he heard his mother declare, "How very odd. I suppose I should never try to talk rationally to Marcus too soon after he's been in his cups."

At the moment a drink didn't sound like a bad idea, but he had more important matters to take in hand. He was going to Whitehall to find out what anyone knew about one Ethan Tregaron. The sooner he discovered the boy's fate, the sooner that infuriating woman would be out of his house.

8

"*When is this wretched rain* going to stop?" Sylvia exclaimed from her sentry post at the parlor window that looked out on the damp, gray confines of Cumberland Square. Her usual cheerfulness seemed to have completely abandoned her. "This is the second day we'll be stuck at home. We were supposed to go to the Demerel's for an alfresco breakfast yesterday, and today was the ride to Tunbridge Wells."

"What was that, Sylvia?" Celia looked up from her seat at the Sheraton secretary where she was attempting to compose a letter to her relatives in Baltimore. After being in London for almost a week it was well past time that she informed them of her safe arrival in England, but she couldn't find the words. Even when she did, how was she going to have it sent? As far as anyone in London knew, she was an orphan.

"Oh, nothing, really, just wondering how I'm ever going to make an eligible connection if I'm house-bound forever." Her forlorn tone easily distracted her companion from her task. Under Celia's amused gaze Sylvia crossed the room and threw herself on the gold and green striped settee. Clasping her hands over the rolled, cushioned arm she propped her chin on her stacked fingers and sighed.

"Really, Sylvia, I don't think your hopes for marriage are going to be blighted so quickly." Celia couldn't hold back a chuckle. At times she felt years older than the English girl, she decided, running her fingers absently through her short curls.

"It is possible, since I've yet to meet anyone who is the least bit likely as a candidate. Of course, anyone I might find promising would undoubtedly be dismissed out of hand by Marcus." She sighed again, directing her soulful brown eyes at her friend. For the first time Celia began to wonder at this abject performance. "He'll marry me off to some toplofty blade who shall order me around from morning till night and make my life miserable. I'll have to retire to the country just to have my own way on occasion."

"You charlatan, you've been hoaxing me, haven't you?" Celia accused her, raising her feet for a closer look at Sylvia's expression. If she wasn't mistaken, there was suppressed amusement beneath all that pathos.

"Only a little. I do hate the rain," she responded and sat up with an unladylike bounce. Her unrepentant grin caused Celia to narrow her gaze as she walked closer to the settee. "You've been going about for the past two days tugging at your curls, alternately sighing and muttering to yourself. Something is bothering you, but you haven't had the good sense to confide your troubles in me. Aren't I your closest friend?"

Celia flinched slightly, not simply from the underlying hurt in her companion's words. What would

Sylvia, or her mother for that matter, say if she divulged that she had lain half-naked in Marcus's arms without protest? Or exactly why she had suddenly had her long black tresses shorn? How could she share those thoughts and images that she had suppressed so rigorously? In spite of her inner turmoil she smiled. "You are my *only* friend at the moment."

"And therefore I have a right to tax you about your problems," the girl concluded with a smug look.

"I just don't know how much longer I can stay here if your brother can't discover any news of Ethan's fate," she declared, hoping this would divert her friend. She couldn't tell her that she had been fearful every minute of actually finding herself in Marcus's company, then regretting that she hadn't. By concentrating on what was to come she could banish the memory of what caused her unease for now.

"What fustian! You can stay with us as long as you like. Marcus has taken ever so long over the matter," his sister admitted with a touch of sibling rancor. "To think that he used to be an exploring officer for Wellington's army. No wonder it took so long to get the French out of Spain."

"What's an exploring officer?" Celia latched onto the subject immediately. If she kept her mind filled with irrelevant details she wouldn't have to think about the tantalizing memories that were suddenly assailing her. Had she actually allowed him to press heated kisses against her bared skin, or was that memory from her disturbing recurring dreams?

"They ride forward toward the enemy lines and gather information for the army, at least that was Marcus's explanation."

"Like a spy?"

"Oh Lord, I wasn't supposed to tell. As far as anyone knows Garth and Marcus were still attached to their regiment. They'll skin me alive." Sylvia's distress was real as she clamped her hand over her mouth, then let her arm drop to her side with a sigh of resignation. "The one time he shares a secret with me, and I blurt it out without thinking. Besides, he wasn't a real spy since he always wore his uniform, or so he told me. You promise you won't tell? Cross your heart and spit on your palm."

"I never should have told you about that childish nonsense." Despite her chastening words, Celia went through the motions of the pledge from her adolescent days in Baltimore. Now, as a grown-up, however, she immediately pulled a handkerchief from the sleeve of her yellow and bronze floral round gown and scrubbed her palm. Her emotional turmoil from waiting for any news was suddenly too much. "So, if Marcus is so good at gathering information, why hasn't he been able to get those idiots at Whitehall to move faster? Perhaps I should go to the docks and look for the man that Mr. Hampton told me about to speed things along."

"You couldn't go to the docks alone. Could you?"

"I was resourceful enough to reach England on my own. Not only that, I managed to reach London and sneak into this house without anyone suspecting," Celia replied, not considering that she was boasting or extremely lucky in her journeying. She began pacing as she thought over the matter. Was a visit to the docks so outlandish? Perhaps if she could solve the mystery of her brother's whereabouts she could overcome Marcus's distrust. Or was the uncertainty over Ethan a safe haven that allowed her to keep from facing her actual feelings for her host?

"Just how would you go about finding this man?"

"Well, I would probably need to wear men's clothing. The docks undoubtedly aren't anyplace for a woman to be found alone. I always had an escort at home, even when visiting our own shipyard," she explained. She deliberated over the matter for a few more minutes. The idea began to look more feasible, especially since it would prove to a certain person that females were able to fend for themselves if need be. "I would also need transportation there and back. The man I'm looking for is the barkeep at a place called the Iron Fist, or so Mr. Hampton said. It's a tavern of some kind, so it would probably be best to go during the day to avoid the ruffians."

"Who is this man we're looking for?" Sylvia's breathless question stopped Celia in midstride. She turned cautiously to look at her companion, wondering if she had heard correctly in her distracted state. The rapturous expression on the young woman's face told her that her fears weren't unfounded.

"*We* aren't looking for anyone, but Mr. Hampton thought this man's brother was on Ethan's ship. Your family would kick me out into the street if they discovered I took you to the docks."

"Then I suppose I'll just have to tell Marcus that you've been withholding information from him." Sylvia jumped to her feet and crossed her arms over her chest in a militant pose. For a moment Celia wondered if she should just ignore the threat. "He probably would be extremely interested in why you haven't been completely honest with him."

She groaned over Sylvia's choice of words, so unwittingly on target. The man at the Iron Fist was the least of her omissions. She was trying to eliminate reasons for Marcus's distrust, not add to them. "If I take you with me you will do exactly as I say without hesitation or endless questions. Otherwise neither of us will set foot out of the house."

For a moment Sylvia grinned in satisfaction, then suddenly sobered. "How will we get out of the house? The first step we take toward the door will have Baskin wondering where we are going. Even if we weren't in disguise, he knows we've canceled our appointments."

"That's very simple. We'll go out the way I first came in, through the kitchen. Now where are we going to find clothing for our disguise?" If she was going to have a fellow traveler, she was going to put her to work. Was it possible that she was losing her wits to think of such a venture? she wondered for a brief moment. Celia couldn't deny that she was excited about the prospect of actively participating in the search for Ethan once more. The rigid structure of London society kept her inactive against her natural inclination, and the chance to prove herself to Marcus was more than tempting.

"The laundry, of course. I think we can find some of the footmen's things that won't be too large," Sylvia assured her, grasping her hand and pulling her toward the parlor door. "I'll bribe Tess with an extra half day off so she'll fetch what we need. While she is doing that I'll pin up my hair so it can be hidden beneath a hat. Isn't it fortunate that you had yours cut so short?"

Celia allowed the chattering girl to carry on, not wanting to think about the reason for her short curls. Where was the adventure going to lead her this time? Her last journey had landed her in a household that was decidedly eccentric, or was she the one who was out of step? She just prayed that Marcus would continue to be absent until she and Sylvia had returned from their errand.

Now was not the time for any confrontation with him. For some reason, success in finding the man at the Iron Fist was paramount to her. At least it gave her something to focus on besides her own inner turmoil, and she had come to England to find her brother, nothing else.

"And which docks would ya be wantin'?" the spindly little man asked from his perch on the hackney coach. He didn't seem pleased at the prospect of taking on two such strangely dressed passengers.

Celia stuck her chin in her hastily knotted cravat and made sure to keep her voice low. "The London docks, of course, my good man. There's an extra crown in it for you if you make the journey in good time."

Without another word she pushed Sylvia into the vehicle and scrambled up behind her. She closed the door with a snap and rapped on the roof with her umbrella for good measure. Did her show of bravado convince the man she knew what she was doing? Had she given him the right direction? The London docks were the right docks, weren't they? Absently she pushed back the sleeve of the coat that was two sizes too big, then shrugged the sagging shoulders back in place as best she could. If she was lucky, the second footman's shoes would stay on her feet for the next half hour. She had sacrificed one of her chemises, tearing it up to stuff into the toes of the shoes.

"Celia, this is incredible. I can't believe we've managed it," Sylvia whispered, apparently thinking that hushed tones were necessary for their venture. "How brilliant of you to remember the difference between the London docks and the others? We could have looked all over and never found this Iron Fist establishment."

Celia gave her companion a scathing look, wondering if she wasn't simply envious of the other woman. The two additional inches to Sylvia's height assured a better fit to her clothing. Her companion could have passed, without too close an inspection, as a young male on his half day ready to explore the city, while Celia at best looked like a child playing dress-up. Perhaps they should have waited until nightfall and allowed the cloak of darkness to aid their masquerade.

"I'm so glad Marcus is still out. Just think what would have happened if he had found us sneaking down the backstairs!"

A shiver went down Celia's spine at the thought of Marcus anywhere in the vicinity. This was one of true dread and not the ambiguous sense of anticipation she had experienced since his abrupt departure from her room yesterday morning. Without thinking, she reached up to touch the nape of her neck.

She really hadn't allowed her hair to be cut in anger. When Lady Knowles had roused her out of bed that morning, she had been confused and a little dazed over the events that had taken place the previous night. Raphael's suggestion for a shorter hairstyle had met with his patroness's approval, so in a moment of inattention Celia had agreed. She hadn't realized what the man was about until he had snipped off half a head of hair.

Marcus's accusing look a short time later gave her the first inkling of how her actions could be misinterpreted. How could she tell the man it wasn't in retaliation to his lovemaking, but rather a result of a moment's daydreaming about him? She was still trying

to determine how to explain her statement about
Daniel, or if she needed to explain at all. Marcus had
been drinking that night and undoubtedly didn't
know what he was doing. She didn't care to examine
her disappointment over the thought.

"Oh, Celia, we're here." Sylvia's voice was reed-thin,
but her grip on her companion's arm was like a vice.
Celia could feel Sylvia trembling against her as she
leaned forward to see exactly what "here" was. Or was
she the one who was trembling? What she saw didn't
raise her spirits. The hackney stopped at the mouth of a
wide opening between towering warehouses. Beyond
the gap was a seemingly endless forest of ships' masts
that almost blotted out the gray skies. This was nothing
like the Tregaron shipyards at home. The rain had
stopped, however. What kind of omen was that?

Sylvia stood half-crouched in the door opening.
Celia had to nudge her forward, sure they would be in
the carriage all day if she didn't. She jumped to the
ground with more spirit than she felt, shifting her
shoulders in the oversized coat once more. Was it her
imagination, or was everything around them dark and
sinister, even in the middle of the day?

"This be where ya wanted?" the little jarvey
snapped the second she looked up at him.

"Yes, my man, exactly. Here's your fare for your
trouble." With an expert flick of her thumb she sent
two coins sailing in the air. As he stretched to snatch at
them she inquired in her gruffest voice, "What's it
worth for you to wait until we conclude our business?"

The man tested the coins with his teeth and nodded before he answered. "I'll takes a guinea plus the
fare if yer back in less than an hour."

"Done," she replied, slapping her hand against the

round crown of her felt hat. The second she turned away she quickly suppressed a groan. In two shuffling steps she captured Sylvia's arm and dragged her along the grimy pathway toward the wharfs. "Keep your head down and your mouth closed. You look positively mutton-headed gaping at everything like that. Look down at your feet if you must, but don't keep staring."

"But, Celia, it is so filthy. There is garbage everywhere," Sylvia gasped, stumbling along beside her. "Lawks, that heap is a man lying against that barrel, at least I think that lump of rags is a man. And it smells!"

"Of course, it smells. It's dead fish," Celia muttered, hoping against hope that the shouts and chaos surrounding them muffled her companion's near-hysterical words. The air was thick with loud voices and ribald language as they turned to walk along the waterfront. Every man they passed seemed to be eight feet tall and more menacing than the last. How was she ever going to find the Iron Fist if she couldn't take a good look at the buildings? She dared not, however, in case she made eye contact with any of the unsavory humanity around her.

She didn't remember the place being so ominous the night she arrived. Of course, she had been under the escort of Mr. Sanders as he ushered his family to a waiting carriage. The darkness had hidden more than she realized, or had she been too preoccupied to notice? To her mind the docks here would be much the same as at home. Was she mistaken in that as well? Had she only been allowed in certain areas, closely chaperoned at all times?

"Hey, watch it, ya clumsy lobcock," snarled a voice at the same moment Sylvia's arm was jerked from her grasp. Celia instinctively reached in her pocket for her pistol, then remembered the only weapon she had was a blackjack. She wasn't sure the leather-covered bludgeon would even make a dent in the apparition in front of her.

"Whot has we here, my dears? Two young dandies come slummin', lookin' ta play a little pully hawly with ther whores." The man holding Sylvia's shoulder was the ugliest human being Celia had ever seen. Not only hadn't he bathed in days, maybe weeks, she was sure his face hadn't seen a razor in years. Two scars ran along his forehead and down his right cheek. His smile was all the more gruesome for the lack of most of his teeth.

"Apologize to the man, Sylvester, and we'll be on our way to the shipping office," she commanded her companion, who seemed to be imitating a stone statue. "We didn't mean any harm, just going to purchase tickets for a West Indies trip. Sylvester!" She squeezed Sylvia's arm to emphasize her point, and discover if her friend was still among the living.

"S-sorry, s-so s-sorry, r-really s-sorry, gr-greatly, s-sorry." She barely got out the words over her trembling, making Celia wonder if Sylvia was actually going to expire on the spot. Just in case she faltered she grabbed at her arm to pull her away from the repulsive giant of a man. That was a mistake. Sylvia tripped on the wood planking.

"Ho, mates, it ain't no spindle-shanked dapper come ta test the warmin' pans, but a dolly-mop lookin' for some sport." His shout could be heard ten leagues out to sea, Celia decided grimly, grabbing Sylvia's hat from the ground and shoving it back in place. "I be glad ta gives ya a taste of the whore's pipe."

"Sir, my sister and I are here to book passage to Jamaica," Celia gasped out as best she could while trying to keep Sylvia upright and maintaining her own masculine pose. "We don't want any trouble. Now she has apologized so we'll just be on our way."

To her amazement the man didn't say a word as she turned Sylvia back in the direction they came. They took two steps before he called after them. "Mayhap ole Squeezer needs ta come along with ya. Ya gots a long walk ta the West Indies docks from heres."

Celia didn't turn or acknowledge that she heard him. She stiffened her spine and began walking as fast as her oversized shoes would allow. "Sylvia, can you walk on your own, or actually run for the hackney?"

"Ohh," was the only reply she received as the slender body next to her seemed to suddenly weigh an additional twenty pounds.

"Don't you dare faint on me now," she gritted out between clenched teeth as she shook Sylvia, then pinched her for good measure. The action was partly to keep her friend conscious and partly to alleviate her own anger. A glance over her shoulder didn't help. Old Squeezer was still behind them, walking slowly, as if he had all the time in the world. "Sylvia, snap out of it. This is the adventure you expected, but you damned well better be awake to all suits."

"Celia, did you swear?" the girl asked in a semblance of her normal voice, to Celia's relief. Now she wouldn't have to try and escape while attempting to carry the dead weight of the other girl. "Marcus isn't going to like that."

"That will be the least of his worries, if we manage to get home," she remarked, her gaze straight ahead, trying to find something, anything that looked like it might be a safe haven. A cluster of men standing directly in their path looked to be less reprehensible than any she had seen so far. Their clothing was plain, not of high quality, but they were clean and respectable in appearance. Unfortunately Sylvia came to her senses at that moment. "Celia, he's right behind us. What are we going to do?"

Before she could answer, Sylvia pushed away from her grasp. Celia reached out on reflex, knowing they shouldn't be separated. A beefy hand closed over her forearm. "Old Squeezer weren't done talkin' yet."

Celia sensed movement from the group ahead of them, but knew she couldn't wait for possible assistance. Taking a deep breath, she turned to face her assailant and was almost sorry she had. He seemed to have gotten uglier in the past few minutes, and his fetid breath made her nauseous. Sylvia was babbling next to her, but she couldn't be bothered as she tried to remember what her brother had taught her. All her thoughts were on protecting Sylvia and herself.

Squeezer was startled that she took a step forward instead of moving away. With the advantage of his surprise Celia closed her eyes and jerked her leg upward at the same moment. The man gave a strange gasping sound when her knee connected with his body, squarely between his legs. She opened her eyes in time to see him begin to double over, his face contorted in pain.

Just as she looped her hand through the strap of her blackjack a male voice from behind her broke into her consciousness. "Here, what's going on?"

Celia was barely aware of the whimpering man falling to his knees on the wood planking. She spun around to meet the new, unexpected danger, knowing the worst moment of her life had arrived with a vengeance. "Oh, sweet heaven, it can't be!"

The sight before her made every muscle in Celia's body stop functioning, including her brain. She forgot about Old Squeezer, her stunned companion, or for that matter where she was. As the group of men she had spotted a few moments before converged on her, she stood stock-still in the middle of all the bustle and confusion.

"What are you doing, Celia, have you lost your mind? We have to get out of here, now. Celia, are you listening to me?" Sylvia's ability to speak returned in answer to her friend's shock, her voice rising to a high-pitched shriek, but nothing roused her companion. Even grabbing her shoulders and shaking her didn't bring her out of her dazed stare at the men no more than three feet in front of them. "Marcus is going to ring a peal over both of us for this. Celia, what is wrong with you?"

The last appeal was accompanied by another shake that managed to dislodge her hat at the same moment the tall man who caused her paralysis was less than a foot away.

"Good God Almighty." The oath rang out in an all-too-familiar voice.

"I can't believe this," the man bellowed, striding forward to stand directly in front of her. An older, white-haired man was right on his heels, hindered somewhat by the large, dark brown canine he held on a short lead. Chaos reigned in the next few minutes as Celia watched with seeming uninterest.

She could see and hear everything that was going on around her, but all other sensations abandoned her at the unexpected sight of the man in front of her. Sylvia squeaked in alarm as Old Squeezer attempted to stand upright, but the new arrival grabbed him by the front of his shirt. He effortlessly lifted the ruffian off his feet with one hand. Celia didn't join in her friend's cheer as the grimy miscreant went sailing into the water, undoubtedly his first acquaintance with water in years. Celia tried to swallow, tried to think of what to say, tried to make her brain function in some minor capacity, but couldn't seem to overcome her paralysis.

Just as the large man turned back to tower over her still figure, another assailant was upon them. Feelings and a myriad of emotions flowed back into her body as the short-haired retriever demanded her attention. With his large paws on her shoulders, he gave one deep-chested bark before covering her face with a wet kiss of his rough tongue. In spite of herself and her present dilemma, she giggled at the tickling sensation when he repeated the salute.

"See here, sir, do something before that beast hurts her," Sylvia ordered, her best lady-of-the-manor tone returning with the disappearance of Old Squeezer. "He is going to eat her face."

"Ma'am, he won't harm a hair on her head. She's spoiled that animal rotten from the day he was born," responded the large man, unimpressed by her imperious tone. "Now, young woman, explain yourself."

"Well, how uncivil. I've never been spoken to in such . . ." Sylvia sputtered at the rude demand while watching her friend gently pushed the compactly muscled dog to the ground.

"My dear Sylvia, he is talking to me," Celia declared, her tone resigned to her fate. She gave the man a calculating look as she made the inevitable introductions. "Miss Sylvia Knowles, may I present my brother, Mr. Zachary Tregaron, and my uncle, Mr. Thaddeus Abernathy, along with my brother's prize Chesapeake Bay retriever, Madison?"

"How extraordinary! I don't think I've ever been formally presented to a canine before this. Your American customs are so unusual, Celia," the lady murmured, not bothering to look at the animal in question. Instead she had turned a speculative eye on Zachary's six-foot, four-inch frame, topped by a rugged countenance and a thatch of dark brown hair.

"Madison is an exceptional animal, when he isn't influenced by bad company, ma'am," Zachary volunteered, giving his sister a scathing look before remembering to remove his cap. As she had hoped, he was diverted for the moment in talking about his prize possession. "I have the honor of owning one of the first of a true American breed of dog. He comes from the lineage of those two magnificent animals shipwrecked in 1807 . . ."

"Zachary, dear boy, I think we should discuss Madison's pedigree at another time. Perhaps in a less hazardous area than the waterfront? The ladies shouldn't be standing here in the chill air." Thaddeus Abernathy gave his niece and nephew an exasperated look before smiling in apology at the other lady present.

"The ladies shouldn't be here at all." Zachary narrowed his dark green eyes as he turned to his sister once more. He placed his hands on his hips, presenting an all-too-familiar imposing image to the young lady under his scrutiny. He knew that she had purposely tried to divert his wrath with her unorthodox presentation of his dog.

"Perhaps I should summon a carriage to take us . . . Oh, my, where will it take us?" Thaddeus's round face crumpled into a mass of worry lines as he considered the matter. He absently ran his finger under his collar, then fiddled with his watch chain.

"We have a hackney waiting, at least I think we do," Celia finished weakly when she realized she had no idea how much time had passed. "He said he would wait an hour."

"Then lead the way, my dear. I'm sure we'll be able to have a very easy conversation once we're all settled indoors before a warm fire with some spirits to refresh us." Her uncle beamed at the thought, his smile growing even wider as he offered Sylvia his arm. "Does your father keep a tolerable cellar here in town, Miss Knowles?"

"My brother does, Mr. Abernathy," the lady corrected and lead the way back toward the waiting hackney. She glanced back over her shoulder to see if the others were following as the older man extolled the virtue of a fine brandy on such a damp day.

Celia didn't bother to wait for her brother's escort, even if he had thought to offer his arm. Instead she stuffed her hands in her trouser pockets in an ungentlemanly manner and shuffled forward in her oversized shoes. She could hear Zachary muttering to Madison, but she moved forward without a word. How much misfortune was going to befall her? Not only hadn't she reached the Iron Fist, but she was returning to Cumberland Square escorted by relatives she had claimed didn't exist.

"Now, young lady, please explain exactly what is going on here," Zachary said, cutting through the silence Celia was praying would last until they reached their destination. Though she was pointedly looking out the window of the carriage, she knew that Zachary had been glaring at her since their journey began. Though normally an even-tempered man his anger was easily triggered by Celia's behavior.

She turned to give him her most ingenuous smile. "I'm looking for Ethan. I did leave you a letter—"

"Which was posted from Philadelphia a week after you left the country. Cousin Penelope has already been lectured about listening to any of your wild tales again." He crossed his arms over his broad chest, meeting her gaze with an uncompromising look, his impressive scowl drawing his straight, dark brows together over his imposing nose. At times like these he reminded her of a granite statue, hard and unfeeling. "That wasn't what I was asking, as you well know. I can guess most of your story until today's little adventure. What in the name of heaven possessed you to attire yourself in this idiotic manner and go posturing around the docks? Even someone with a small amount of common sense would have known better. But then, we both know you've never been long on common sense."

"Zachary, you must remember your sister has just had quite a shock."

Celia found her uncle's soothing words irritating along with his intervention. She had been dealing with her older brother's displeasure for years without needing anyone to champion her. Zachary was only seven years older than she, but he took his duties as her closest male relative much too seriously for her way of thinking. She was an adult now, and although he was concerned about her well-being, he shouldn't take her to task for every misdemeanor, real or imagined.

"This isn't just one of her harebrained notions of freeing someone's mistreated animal or forgetting her dignity in climbing a tree to rescue a distraught child, uncle," he declared, his gaze never wavering from the subject of the discussion. "This time she has put herself in real danger. I shudder to imagine what else we'll discover as we hear the details from the rest of her tale. See, look at the way she's blushing. It's a sure sign of guilt when she shows any discomfort."

Celia wanted to put her hat over her face to hide the betraying redness. Zachary couldn't know just how her mind reacted to his words. Not for anything must he discover what had taken place between her and Marcus. Celia knew that she had to keep even the merest hint of any intimacy between them a secret. That was something she must deal with in her own way and in her own time, when she was ready to face the memories.

"You have to admit that Ethan is gone, once and for all, Celia. We're going to collect your baggage, make our apologies and reparations to whomever you've inconvenienced, and head for home as soon as the *Aphrodite* is ready to sail," Zachary said. "When we get you home I'm tempted to send you off to Aunt Amelia's in Charleston, the next best thing to locking you away in a tower. You won't get into any mischief under her iron discipline."

Sylvia slipped her hand through her friend's arm and she murmured, "It could be worse. Marcus always says he'll send me into a convent."

"You haven't seen Aunt Amelia," Celia replied, knowing her brother was simply venting his emotions. He'd been threatening to send her to Aunt Amelia's for years now.

"Of course, I suppose I shouldn't be surprised that you've found a companion in idiocy here in England. I'm sure no properly brought-up lady would lend herself to such behavior in Baltimore," he continued, his eyes narrowing at the whispered exchange. "I've heard enough stories about the upper crust in this country not to wonder at your actions. You couldn't have gotten these disreputable clothes without some help, now could you?"

Celia gasped at his audacity, wondering if he realized that in his anger he was insulting her friend. She reached over to grasp Sylvia's hand in apology for her brother's loutish manners. The trembling of her friend's body told her that his hateful, and unnecessarily harsh, words had found their target.

Then she realized that Sylvia wasn't quaking in fear, but laughing. She clutched at her friend's hands, gasping out, "He's so ferocious, even worse than Marcus. How delightful."

After a week in the Knowles's household Celia didn't find this behavior unusual. She might have kept her composure if she hadn't looked across the coach at Zachary to explain. His face was now a ruddy hue, and it wasn't from anger. She knew the signs of anger all too well. Her brother was blushing.

Looking back at Sylvia, she started to comment, but found herself joining her in laughter instead. She wasn't entirely sure what was so amusing, but she needed an outlet to her pent-up emotions. It was either laugh or cry, she realized, looking down at her trembling hands, for she had just injured a man.

Within minutes she and Sylvia were clutching at each other to keep from tumbling onto the floor of the coach. Whenever they tried to stem their mirth, the dark mutterings from the large man seated across from them set them off again.

9

"*You look like you've just lost* a packet on the 'Change," Garth commented the moment he walked into the library past Baskin's disapproving figure. The sight of his gold-trimmed scarlet regimental dress uniform brought a look of surprise from his host.

"Not anything so drastic," Marcus replied. He was surprised to discover he had crumpled the piece of paper in his fist. Relaxing his grip, he looked over his friend's shoulder at his faithful, but scowling retainer. "Fetch my sister and Miss Tregaron, Baskin, and Lady Knowles, if she isn't resting."

"Miss Sylvia and Miss Tregaron aren't at home, milord."

"Very well, let me know when they return." He waved off the servant, though he could tell the man had something else to say before he turned abruptly on his heel and quit the room. "You really should let the old boy announce you properly, Garth. I think you're wearing on his nerves."

"Good, that was my purpose. An experiment to see if he has any nerves," his friend explained, helping himself to a glass of claret from the decanter set out near the fireplace, then pouring a glass and presenting it to his companion. "What the devil are Sylvia and Celia doing out on a day like today? A case of any discomfort is worth it for the sake of entertainment?"

"I shudder to think. I let Baskin worry about such trifling matters, knowing that he'll report any misdemeanor almost before it occurs." He laid the crumpled letter on the mahogany surface of his desk. "What brings you out in the driving rain? Fond memories of Portugal and Spain, perhaps, from the look of your attire?"

"Very close to the mark, actually," Garth answered, studying his drink with great interest. "I've been to Whitehall to see what's what with our fat little French gentleman."

"Not unlike our young ladies, you're looking for a way to alleviate your boredom with civilian life?" Marcus leaned back against the desk, carefully watching his friend's movements. That wasn't the only question Marcus wanted to ask, but knew it was the only one he would be allowed concerning the man's personal life.

"There is that, but I was summoned, actually. They're going to make up an intelligence unit this time, instead of gathering information piecemeal," Garth returned, not looking up from his glass, unaware that he was shifting his weight from foot to foot. "They wanted a list of likely candidates besides the obvious choice of Colquhoun Gordon, and I was in town, is all. Now tell me what has you out of sorts again, or should I hazard a guess?" He gestured with his glass toward the crumpled letter on the desk.

"Ah, I've discovered that there really is an Ethan Tregaron," he managed without grinding his teeth, though it was a near thing. He had enough on his conscience without any hard evidence that Celia Tregaron wasn't trying to play him false, at least not about her brother. Fortunately, Garth wasn't about to step over the line and question his innermost thoughts any more than he was. "It's possible he is being held at Dartmoor Prison, if the ship's cook can be believed. A rather enterprising clerk ran the man to earth in Cheapside."

"Still a prisoner of war? Are they planning to let them out now that the war is over?"

"There seems to be some trouble in sifting through the authentic Americans and common British riffraff, who claim an alternative nationality," Marcus explained. The point of view of Whitehall usually had nothing to do with the wants or needs of those actively involved with their machinations.

"And some simple bloody-mindedness on the part of the ministry no doubt. How has our Celia taken the glad tidings?"

Marcus took refuge in emptying his glass, then leaned his hips back against the edge of the desk. Studying the toe of his gleaming tasseled Hessian, he said, "I was just about to let her know. I thought I would ask you to accompany me on the journey west, but it seems you might be otherwise engaged."

The other man flinched at the last turn of phrase, but nodded with regret. "Nothing is definite, but I'm to be ready at a moment's notice." He drained his glass as well, walking purposefully over to the decanter to pour another round.

"Sorry, no more for me. I think I'm going to need my wits about me when I disclose this latest bit of news." *And finally come face to face with the lady after making a blasted fool out of myself, not once but twice,* he added silently. For the first time in his life he was purposely avoiding a confrontation, which in itself he found disconcerting. He'd managed to leave the house yesterday and this morning before anyone else stirred and return last night when they were in bed. At odd moments he wondered if it might be easier just to take rooms at the Albany until the Tregaron matter was settled.

So far his family hadn't questioned his movements, which was fortunate. A man couldn't admit that he desired a guest in the house or that he couldn't trust his own behavior, no matter how tempting the lady. He wasn't sure which was worse, however, the attempted seduction or the way it had ended. Marcus didn't think he could stand the sight of Celia's shorn hair until the moment was actually thrust upon him. Now the news of her brother had brought him to the point.

"Dealing with the female of the species can be absolute hell." The amount of feeling behind the statement brought Marcus out of his distraction. Garth's sudden challenging grin promptly put the barriers back in place. "This is going to be vastly entertaining. How are you going to keep the charming Celia from demanding on going along on this quest?"

"Good God, I hadn't even considered it." He knew his feelings were probably clearly written across his face at the other man's laughter. "Damn, how could I—What is that racket? It sounds like we're under siege."

Raised voices in the hallway turned both gentlemen's attention to the half-opened door. It did sound as if an entire battalion was charging the house. This army was like no other either had experienced, since feminine voices could be heard among the melee, and if Marcus wasn't mistaken, the occasional bark of a dog.

"You don't suppose Sylvia's tried to rescue a climbing boy again?" Garth inquired.

"Oh, Lord, that last crusade not only had me taking my seat in the House for the cause, but the annual expense of a home for the beggars and the salary for two of the most imposing women in London to maintain the establishment," Marcus muttered, straightening from his lounging position and striding toward the door. If this was one of his sister's causes it would at least act as a diversion, keeping his traitorous thoughts from remembering the enchanting feel of his houseguest in his arms.

Unfortunately, his first sight of the group in the entry hall was of Celia. Immediately, his temper, which had been easy to control until the week before, quickly came to the fore. The young lady was standing toe to toe with a giant of a man, clearly not intimidated by him. She was speaking rapidly without noticing her volume or that the man was talking equally loud at the same time. For some reason she seemed to be trying to shield Baskin from the ire of the oversized stranger. She held one arm out to the side as if to protect the butler from an assault while emphasizing her point by poking the colossus in the chest with her index finger.

"Here, what's this about?"

No one paid the least attention to Marcus's shouted question. He looked around him for a means to break into the cacophony. To his surprise there were only six people, counting the servants, creating the near-riot in his home. Everyone was speaking at once, but not necessarily to each other. An older gentleman was arguing with Sylvia and the footman over what appeared to be a brown-haired retriever. For a moment the unknown gentleman seemed in danger as his sister gestured wildly to stress her words.

"This should do the trick," Garth announced, needing to practically bellow in his ear. *This* was the silver tray Baskin seemed to have abandoned on the table near the door. Before Marcus could respond he dashed the tray against the shining inlaid wood flooring. If the deafening clang didn't stop the combatants, then Baskin's concern for the damage to his flooring would certainly draw him from the fray, Marcus decided, flinching against the echoing clatter.

The startled expressions on the half dozen faces before him almost made him laugh aloud. He noticed Garth had no compunction about guffawing at the silent group as Baskin bent, with a click of his tongue, to pick up the tray. Taking advantage of their surprise, Marcus focused on the one person in the group over whom he felt he held some measure of authority and ordered, "Sylvia, explain yourself at once."

"So, you're the man in charge of this madhouse, not this posturing stick," snarled Celia's Goliath as he turned to face him. Marcus noted rather grimly that she apparently didn't feel the need to protect him. Instead she took the opportunity to remove her hat. Only then did he notice the ladies' unconventional attire, but he didn't have time to dwell on the matter. "So, explain yourself to me, sir," the man went on. "Why is this pair out capering along the London docks, dressed in the most preposterous clothing? Is this the way you run things in this country? Letting your women do as they please, practically begging to be attacked by any rum gagger or swaddler that happens to pass by? Maybe if you weren't off fighting wars with countries that are none of your affair, you might have some concern about the harebrained, irresponsible members of your family!"

"Oh, bravo!" Sylvia exclaimed, ignoring the fact that the man was insulting her as well as Marcus. Both her brother and the ranting stranger turned to give her a quelling look which quickly erased the smile from her face.

"Who on earth are you?" Marcus managed to snap out as his opponent took a deep breath to continue. He hoped it wouldn't become a physical confrontation, since the man was a good four inches taller and outweighed him by two or three stone. "If you're going to assault me, I would at least like to know whom I'm fighting, if not why."

"That is a reasonable request, Zachary," the older man put in, though he looked contrite for having spoken. The animal next to him took the opportunity to punctuate the statement with a loud woof.

The massive individual only hesitated a moment. Then he planted his feet firmly apart and placed his beefy fists on his hips. "My name is Zachary Tregaron of Baltimore, Maryland, and I have come to take my sister home to the United States of America where she belongs. Is there something wrong with that, sir?"

"Milord," Celia corrected him.

Marcus looked away from the enraged man in front of him to stare at Celia. She appeared as startled as he by the interruption. He had never imagined that their next confrontation would come even close to resembling this altercation. There wasn't time to dwell on her sudden show of propriety over his title, however. He met the man's fiery green scowl and asked, "Zachary, not Ethan? How strange; I thought Miss Tregaron no longer had any family left."

"Celia, how could you?" squeaked the nervous man next to Sylvia. The young lady had the grace to look uncomfortable over his affront, making Marcus wonder yet again how much she hadn't told him about her life.

"Uncle Thaddeus, you know she hasn't a conscience when it comes to getting her own way," her brother declared. Unwittingly he confirmed Marcus's own thoughts on the lady's veracity. "That's not the point, however. I found them down on the docks not an hour ago about to be attacked by one of the scurviest looking individuals I've seen in all my years at sea. What would have happened to them if we hadn't had the good fortune to disembark today? Now explain that to me, sir. And what have you done to her hair?"

"I think you're putting the saddle on the wrong horse, old man," Garth broke in from where he lounged against the newel post, still not bothering to hide his amusement. "I think the ladies are the ones who should be questioned. It should be vastly entertaining to hear their rationale."

Both the young ladies broke into speech at once. "We needed to go. . . ." "I didn't think Marcus was doing anything. . . ." "How else could Celia find her brother . . .?" "There was a man at the Iron Fist. . . ." "Old Squeezer knocked my hat off or we would have . . ." "We went during the day to avoid any danger. . . ." "I made Celia take me. . . ."

None of the disjointed mutterings seemed to be leading to a coherent story. Marcus considered grabbing the silver tray that Baskin was now holding

protectively in his clasp. The solution of grabbing
Celia and kissing her speechless wasn't an alternative,
no matter how appealing the thought, he determined.

After a single day without a glimpse of her, he
wanted to feast on the sight of her lovely face, but
knew it was a ludicrous, if not a perilous, thought.
Even the slightest attention on his part would have her
bellicose brother grabbing for his throat. Since he had
no idea how to proceed with his emotional reaction to
the lady, he had best deal with the matter of the ladies'
bizarre state of dress and their trip to the docks. The
need was taken out of his hands a moment later.

"Oh, how delightful, we have guests!" announced
Lady Knowles from the top of the stairs. Her soft-
spoken statement had the same effect as the clanging
tray some minutes before; everyone was suddenly
mute. "Marcus, for heaven's sake, why are all these
people standing in the hallway? It is extremely bad
ton. I can't understand why Baskin has allowed this.
Bring them up, this instant."

Before he could respond his quick-witted sister
grabbed Celia's hand and led her up the stairs to the
sanctuary of her mother's company. With a sigh of
disgust at her ploy he motioned the Tregaron men to
precede him, ignoring Baskin's look of revulsion as
the older gentleman handed him the dog's leash. With
one foot on the stairs he paused to look at Garth. "I
suppose you're coming along as well?"

"Naturally I think you need at least one ally. The
women will all band together and the uncle is afraid
of his own shadow," Garth said as they climbed the
stairs together. "And I don't think I need to mention
that the brother isn't going to like the fact that you
even thought his sister was a handsome morsel."

Marcus stifled a groan. Her brother wouldn't even bother with pistols for breakfast; he would beat him to a pulp without a second's hesitation. Now more than ever he wished he knew what was going on beneath the bewitching raven tresses of the most dangerous woman he had ever met. She could well attain her vengeance against the earl of Ashmore by one incautious word, even if this one had nothing to do with her brother Ethan's disappearance.

"Now, isn't this so much better than standing in that drafty hallway?" Lady Knowles pronounced once everyone was behind the closed door of the sitting room. She sat in the center of the green damask settee, placing Celia and Sylvia on either side of her as if they were her ladies-in-waiting. "This way the servants won't have quite so much to report on their next half day. Won't you gentlemen take a seat?"

While Marcus took his customary place standing before the mantel he noted that Garth settled himself in the straight-backed chair closest to the ladies. Zachary Tregaron gave Marcus a challenging look, his hands linked behind his back. His stance dared anyone in the room to put him in a chair while his host was still on his feet. The other American gentleman had no such problem, scrambling to sit on the matching settee across from Lady Knowles.

"Marcus, *are* you going to introduce our new guests?" his mother prompted when the silence in the room lengthened beyond what was comfortable.

"I think you had best let Sylvia do the honors," he replied, taking his snuffbox from his pocket and placing it on his gloved hand. "I seem to be at the disadvantage of not being properly introduced to Miss Tregaron's relatives."

"Celia's relatives? How remarkable. Do proceed, Sylvia."

As his sister performed the task he kept his gaze trained on Celia in her masculine attire. Masculine was the last thing he would think of, he decided as he lingered over the supple line of her leg clearly outlined by her trousers, though the clothes had been baggy and oversized when she was standing. He clenched his fist as he remembered the feel of her hips and buttocks against his hand, only the thin material of her nightdress depriving him from the feel of her smooth skin.

"Marcus, are you paying attention at all? We simply can't let Mr. Tregaron drag our dear Celia away so soon," his mother declared, giving him an arch look that used to make him shiver with dread when he was seven years old. Now he found it amusing, but also hard to resist. "Do something, Marcus."

"Yes, Marcus, do something. The chap looks like he is about ready to drag her out of here by the scruff of her neck," Garth added. "Either that or he ate something that disagreed with his digestion."

He knew his friend's bantering tone was a sham, but did his bidding. Zachary Tregaron was looking daggers at his sister, which meant he hadn't noticed Marcus's preoccupation with the lady's state of dress. Marcus cleared his throat and looked pointedly at his mother. "Suppose we have the ladies, one at a time this time, please, tell us their version of what they were doing—" He broke off as the full import of Tregaron's earlier rantings broke through his preoccupied brain. "You were at the docks!"

"Oh, Marcus, you are so like your father. Control yourself, because we'll never get to the explanation if you have an apoplexy now." As if satisfied her words would magically ward off such a fate, she then turned to her daughter. "Sylvia, tell us about your little adventure."

"Hsst, close your snuffbox unless you want to dust the entire room with the stuff."

Garth's dire warning was true, Marcus realized as he looked down at his hand. The enameled box could slip to the floor at any moment due to the trembling of his body. Still maintaining rigid control on his anger, he reached up and snapped the lid shut, then shoved the box into his pocket.

". . . so Tess got us the footmen's clothing from the laundry. Once we got into our disguise, we went down the back stairs and out through the kitchen while the servants were having their tea. Marcus, did you know that was the way Celia got in that first night? The kitchen door goes out into the alley beside the garden."

"Fascinating."

"Yes, I thought it was. Celia was magnificent. I don't think the jarvey doubted for a moment that we were young gentlemen on a lark." Sylvia rewarded her friend's cleverness with a warm smile, apparently feeling much braver now that she was safely home. "I don't know what I would have done without her courage."

"Not gone?"

"Garth, please, this is *my* story."

"Forgive me, Sylvia, I don't know what I was thinking."

"Pure and simple logic," Marcus put in, noticing that Celia's back was becoming more rigid with each word.

"As I was saying, everything was fine until that horrid Old Squeezer person grabbed me and knocked my hat off. But for that he never would have known I was a girl. Fortunately, Celia did the most remarkable thing and disposed of the man, with some assistance from her brother. Our one turn of bad luck wasn't quite so bad since we were able to find Celia's family, was it?"

Strange murmuring sounds drew Marcus's gaze across the room. Tregaron was pacing along the edge of the carpet, muttering under his breath. Though he couldn't discern the words, Marcus was sure the man was pronouncing a litany that he clearly understood. For a moment he felt in complete harmony with the stranger.

"You still haven't told us the reason for this little foray, my dear," Garth prompted when Sylvia didn't continue.

"Oh, didn't I? We were going to a place called the Iron Glove, no, the Iron Fist. Someone there knew someone who had been on Ethan's ship," she concluded, her smile similar to the radiance she had when she finished performing on the pianoforte for guests. "Did I get that right, Celia?"

"Yes, Celia, tell us if Sylvia left out any details from her enlightening recital." Marcus's attempt at goading her to look at him wasn't rewarded.

"Ethan is dead, Celia. You have to accept that, just as I have," her brother said in a low voice. The remorseful look on his angular face took the sting out of his words. "Be done with this once and for all. You can't bring him back, and you have a life at home to get on with."

"Mr. Tregaron, I'm the last person in the world to raise false hopes, but there is a possibility your brother is alive." Marcus's words riveted everyone's attention

to his solitary figure in front of the fire. He continued
the explanation to only one person in the room. "It
seems that Ethan was indeed transported back to
England and is listed as an official prisoner of war."

"How marvelous! I knew that fate wouldn't be so
cruel." Lady Knowles clapped her hands in delight
and leaned over to kiss Celia on the cheek.

She barely seemed to notice, as her gaze was fixed
on Marcus's face. "There is more, isn't there?"

"Don't look so tragic, my dear. According to Cecil
Owens, apparently the only industrious clerk in our
government, your brother is at Dartmoor Prison." He
wanted to close the distance between them and take
her in his arms. Her eyes were moist with tears and
she held herself perfectly still, almost afraid to believe
what he was saying.

Then she turned away at a shout from her brother,
who bounded across the room and swept her onto her
feet. The pair was laughing and crying at the same
time, hugging each other over the news.

"Marcus, why didn't you tell us this?" Sylvia
demanded.

"I just did, Sylvia. If you hadn't gone haring off
without a word to anyone, you would have been here
when I received the message from Whitehall," he
responded in a tone much harsher than he intended.
"We will deal with that matter at another time,
strictly among the family. I'm sure Mr. Tregaron has a
few words to say to his sister about the matter when
they have some privacy."

"It's useless, you know." Tregaron looked over the
top of his sister's head, still holding her against his
chest. "No matter what I say, she'll challenge the next
hazard without a thought to her own safety, as long

as she thinks the cause is worthy. She came here, even though I did everything in my power to dissuade her, and it seems Ethan is alive."

"Oh, dear, Marcus, you must go to the prison at once. He could still be in grave danger."

"Mama, what are you talking about?" Marcus asked, wondering what had his mother so agitated. The others were all looking at her curiously as well, including Thaddeus Abernathy, who had finally seemed to lose his temerity.

"Dear lady, of course the boy isn't in the best hands in prison, but the war is over," he said soothingly, directing a reassuring smile at his niece and nephew. "Once we explain his situation to the authorities, I'm sure they'll release him, especially if Lord Ashmore lends his support."

"You don't understand—the riot." She threw up her hands in dismay, then fumbled at her wrist in search of her handkerchief. Over the lace-trimmed hem she directed her tearful gaze at her son.

"What are you going on about, Mama? I can't understand a word you're saying with that linen stuffed in your mouth."

"Zounds, the prison riot last week," Garth exclaimed, rising to his feet. "I had forgotten about it until now. The prisoners tried to break out and—"

"Were there any fatalities?" Abernathy asked, sitting forward in his seat.

Marcus couldn't believe the man's insensitivity, even if he was Ethan's uncle. Garth had at least had the good sense to stop before mentioning any tragic results.

"Yes, yes, there were. I saw a list of names in the newspaper myself!" cried Lady Knowles before burying her face in her handkerchief once more.

"Since when have you been reading the newspaper, Mama?" Marcus found himself asking, realizing at once it wasn't very relevant.

"It was an accident," she wailed as if to excuse some truant behavior. "I was looking for the announcement of the Aldershot girl's engagement. I forgot all about it the next day when Celia arrived. You have to find out what has happened, at once, Marcus."

"Lady Knowles, you mustn't be so upset. I'm sure Ethan is fine." Celia moved away from her brother to sit beside her ruffled hostess and comfort the older woman.

"Well, it looks like we're off to Whitehall again," Garth stated, his usual good cheer absent.

"I'm beginning to think I should just have them set up a cot in the corridor for me," Marcus said, assured that he was never going to be able to have a moment's peace. His household was beginning to look like a hostelry for visiting Americans. He promised himself that once he determined that Ethan wasn't on the casualty list he was going to have a long talk with Miss Celia Tregaron.

When he reached the doorway he glanced back over his shoulder. She should have appeared ridiculous in her footman's garb, but he was amazed how feminine and delicate she looked. At that moment she met his regard, then quickly lowered her gaze, her face turning a delicate pink. What did that portend?

Was she remembering their time together in the library, or did something else cause her unease? He realized until just that moment she had avoided looking at him until forced to. The most important fact he wanted to know was how she felt about her dead husband.

"Well, are we going to go, or aren't we?"

Zachary Tregaron's abrupt question brought Marcus to his senses, making him curse the woman who did this to him. The man clearly wasn't going to be left behind. If he had been in the same situation, he knew that he wouldn't stay cooling his heels if he could obtain the information firsthand.

"Onward, stalwart leader. Who knows what knowledge awaits us in the august halls of war?" Garth said, throwing open the door and leading the way. "Do you think they'll even let us cross the threshold with an American in tow?"

With a nod of his head Marcus signaled Zachary to precede him. As usual his inestimable friend had inspired him. Wouldn't Celia's brother know something about her marriage and the man she had been married to? The expedition to Whitehall took on a new light as he descended the stairs and called for Baskin. If he couldn't manage to gain the lady's confidence quite yet, he would arm himself with information from a secondary source.

Now, how the devil was he going to ask the man if his sister was still mourning her husband? He couldn't possibly tell him that she had cried out the man's name while they were making love.

His years spent on the Peninsula told him that there was more to this man than his blustering over the dock episode or his gruff indulgence toward his sister. How was he going to discover anything about the fascinating Celia without having her rather oversized brother asking him some uncomfortable questions? Those questions were ones he couldn't answer for himself. He only knew that he desired Celia Tregaron more than any other woman he had ever known.

10

"*Zachary Tregaron, you should* burn in the fires of Hades. No, you should be keelhauled until you beg for mercy, then fed live to the fishes," his loving sister muttered as she climbed the stairs to her bedchamber. Her progress was awkward, as she stumbled in an effort to keep the leashed Madison close to her side. She stopped to clutch the skirts of her dress and cloak firmly in her other hand once more and sighed. The animal butted against her just as the clock in the hall below chimed two o'clock.

"Curse him for a lily-livered coward," she added and continued the journey up the stairs, wondering if she was destined to continuously wander the halls in the dark of night. Zachary and Marcus had mysteriously disappeared after dinner. She wasn't sure if they were out together or alone, nor did she particularly care. Right now she wanted to teach the canine next to her the skill of savaging her brother when he returned. Perhaps he could have Marcus for dessert.

Only the fact that she was disobeying her brother at the moment gave her any cheer. He had sent her to her room without supper in a belated surge of authority, aided and abetted by his host, who dealt out similar treatment to his own sister. Marcus was already having a bad influence on Zachary, but of course, Zachary's behavior was worse, since he was unfamiliar with Lady Knowles. He didn't know that she would simply order trays of food to be served to both young ladies in their rooms as soon as the gentlemen were out the door.

"Come on, you miserable hound. I need to have my rest for the day to come," she ordered when she reached the top of the stairs. Then the dog broke loose from her relaxed grip and loped down the hallway dragging his leash. Zachary deserved everything she wished would rain down on his head. This had been her third trip to the garden with her brother's stupid pet, she thought with disgust as she followed him.

Halfway down the hallway Celia wanted to scream in vexation, just at the moment the idiot dog disappeared through a partially open door. She silently prayed that the room was empty as she followed. If she hadn't already been in disgrace for the afternoon's escapade, she would have left Madison exactly where he was. The disobedient canine was a fitting late-night companion for the master of the house.

She pushed opened the door very slowly, attempting to peer around it without actually entering the room. No one was in sight, although Tess had mentioned earlier that Marcus's valet, Foster, had returned from visiting his ailing mother. He could be the one who had left the door ajar. A snuffling noise from beyond her sight forced her to step into the room, which she had hoped to avoid. She had vowed never to cross the threshold after her first eventful night there.

Madison was sniffing at a door against the far wall. She began to relax. The room was deserted. Foster undoubtedly had left the candles burning for his absent master's return. Feeling more at ease, since she was sure Marcus was still out on the town, she went forward to retrieve the inquisitive dog. As she reached down to grab the leash the animal nosed himself through the door, inadvertently drawing her with him into the dressing room.

Celia wasn't sure who was more startled, she or the single occupant. She felt the paralysis from earlier that day return to her body, but this time it wasn't from anxiety, it was from seeing the man sitting on the low upholstered bench against the wall barely a foot in front of her. A single candle burned in the sconce above his head, clearly defining the muscles of his damp, naked chest. His only covering was a towel haphazardly thrown over his lap, leaving his long legs bare as well.

Neither spoke as they continued to stare at each other. Even if she had been able to master the power of speech, Celia wasn't sure what she could say. Marcus's regard was wary, almost defying her to comment on what he was doing. His arms were buckled into some sort of leather apparatus that looked like, of all things, a horse's harness with the reins attached to the wall above his head. His gloved hand was raised level with his shoulder, and his other hand was in a fist close to his knee.

"You seem to have me at a disadvantage." His husky words caught her by surprise after the protracted silence. When she still didn't speak a slight smile curved his lips. "You have an interesting sense of what is proper, my dear. You visit the library half-clothed and always come to my bedchamber fully dressed. The customs of the Colonies never cease to amaze me."

His half smile and goading words released her from her fascination with the corded muscles of his arms and the dusting of dark hair over his chest and flat stomach. Before she realized what she was doing she allowed her gaze to follow the dark arrow of hair to the edge of the towel. Her hands clenched into tight fists as she remembered the feel of his skin against her palm. She was also tempted to brush back the damp tendrils of hair that clung to his forehead and temples. All the memories she had managed to suppress came rushing back. Heat suffused her body as she began to tremble in reaction.

"I'm not practicing any dark pagan ritual, so you needn't look so apprehensive. This contraption is to exercise the remaining muscles that work in my arm." His tone was harsher than necessary for the candid explanation. Almost defiantly he kept his body in the position that she found him.

"It's ingenious," she finally managed, hastily directing her gaze to the floor just in front of his toes. Now she could speak, but she couldn't seem to move. "Most men wouldn't bother and prefer to use such an injury to their advantage."

"I'm not most men."

She knew that already. No other man of her acquaintance had ever made her feel this way. Never once during her marriage did she desire to run her hands and face over a man's body as she did now. The fever that assailed her the night she lay pressed against his body had returned tenfold. At this moment the sound of her erratic breathing seemed to echo off the walls. The growing heat in her abdomen confused her, as did the aching feeling in her breasts. Fully clothed Marcus was elegant and daring; stripped to his skin he was primitive and dangerous, making her feel extremely delicate and vulnerable.

"Did you love your husband, Celia?" he asked abruptly, his words hitting her like a douse of cold water. Had he been able to discern her thoughts that had so quickly dismissed the man in her past in his favor?

She slipped her hands behind her back, then clasped them tightly together to keep from reaching out to him. A second later she almost laughed at her foolishness in thinking that Lord Ashmore would ever appear uncertain. Or was it wishful thinking on her part that his vivid blue-green eyes seemed to be asking more than his words did? She supposed it was a logical question after what had passed between them that caused her to utter her late husband's name.

"I was fond of him. We grew up together," she said simply, not really knowing what else to say. Some of her happiest memories as a child included Daniel, just as they did Zachary and Ethan. "When we came of age, we married as everyone had planned from the time we were born. His family and mine have been very close, even before our fathers became business partners."

Something flared in his eyes for a moment, but was gone so quickly she knew her imagination was at work again. The smile that played across his wide mouth, however, sent a shiver of reaction down her spine. Gone was his usual cloaked gaze, replaced by something she couldn't quite fathom, but it gave her pleasure.

"Since it seems Foster isn't going to return any time soon, I need your help getting out of this instrument of torture."

She gasped.

"If the request is too much, I—"

"No, Marcus, it's not that. I was concerned for your pain," she answered, closing the space between them. Until now she had forgotten he seemed to anticipate her disgust at his injury.

"That's the damnable part, there is no pain, no feeling at all. I can move the fingers and wrist slowly, but there isn't any strength or sensation," he informed her, still watching her face for any reaction. "My lower arm and hand are now permanently put to sleep, it seems. Too bad the rest of my body isn't so cooperative."

"Tell me what to do to help you."

"Oh, my dear, you are going to be the death of me yet," he murmured, not losing his smile when she frowned at him in confusion. The smile widened as she registered the possible underlying meaning to her innocent words.

She gritted her teeth, hoping to stop the telltale flush that caused his amusement, and asked briskly, "How do I release you from the apparatus? Or would you like me to leave you here with Madison for company until your valet returns?"

"Your lumbering chaperon went back in the bedchamber a few minutes ago." Marcus seemed to find the observation quite satisfying. "We're all alone, my dear."

"And you're still tied to the wall," she shot back, placing her hands on her hips. He raised one eyebrow at her silent challenge that declared either he stop testing her, or she would leave him to his own devices. She didn't trust her voice at that moment, standing so close to his unabashed masculinity. The musky scent of his body seemed to fill her senses, undermining her courage to challenge him.

"All you need to do is unbuckle the straps on my left hand and wrist. The rest I can manage on my own."

She bent to the task, looking only at his hand as she worked. All the while she was conscious of her skirts brushing against the sinew of his thigh. Was it her imagination that the towel over his lap wasn't as large as it appeared from across the room? Suddenly she was all thumbs as she worked on the second strap, fumbling with the simple buckle. After an eternity she was done, and she stepped back to survey her work. Once the harness was released, Marcus lowered his right arm to rest on the crimson damask covering of the bench.

Something pressed against the back of her ankle, knocking her off balance. As she flung out her arm she cursed aloud the miserable animal who was at the root of her current dilemma. A second later the dog was the furthest thought from her mind. She was lying across Marcus's lap, his left arm reaching across her waist to keep her from tumbling onto the floor. Her breath caught in her throat when she looked up to meet his slumberous gaze. Fleetingly she wondered why she ever hated the way he looked at her with his eyelids half-closed.

"It wasn't the dog, sweet Celia," he murmured, moving his arm from her waist to take her hand and press it against his chest. He knew that she couldn't move from her reclining position. "I wanted to reward you for your assistance, so I tripped you."

"Reward me? Do you always have to force your attentions on women?" she asked in a whisper, not sure how she dared. Every inch of her body screamed out for his touch, yet she wouldn't give in to his will without question. "Each time you kiss me you have me at a disadvantage. Have you once considered asking if I want to kiss you?"

His gaze moved to her lips, as if he was willing her to take action. Without speaking he grasped her wrist and directed her hand up to his shoulder, then guided it to curl at the nape of his neck. "What is it about your lustrous emerald eyes that challenges me when more experienced, willing women leave me cold? Will you kiss me, Celia?"

She hesitated. Her first impulse was to run and lock herself safely behind her bedchamber door, then bury her head under the covers until her fascination with this man subsided. The look in his slumberous eyes told her he expected her to run. Marcus was never going to think she lacked courage, she decided, making her decision in a blink of an eye.

Before she could change her mind she used her hand at his neck for leverage, drawing herself upward as she pulled his head down. She smiled at the sound of his breath escaping between his parted lips. Then she pressed her mouth against his in light, teasing movements, first the corner, then his lower lip and on to his upper lip. Each time he tried to deepen the kiss she pulled away slightly. Finally she practiced the lesson he taught so thoroughly in the library, tracing his lower lip with her tongue before seeking the warm cavern of his mouth. Just as he started to parry her movements she slipped from his lap.

"You're welcome, milord," she managed breathlessly

before turning on her heel and fleeing the room. When she reached the relative safety of the bedchamber she called over her shoulder, "I'm sure your valet can help you with any further difficulty. Come, Madison."

She scurried out into the hallway, not sure how long it would take him to release his right hand from the harness. Just as she reached her room, she heard the sound of someone humming from the direction of the stairs. She pushed the bewildered Madison through the door, half lifting him in her haste before jumping across the threshold, unwilling to be caught loitering at this time of night by either her brother or one of the servants.

Once she closed the door behind her she leaned back against the cool wood. Her heart was pounding in her ears as she concentrated on controlling her breathing. She had never done anything so bold and exhilarating as initiating an intimate kiss. Like all her other impulsive acts there would be hell to pay later. Right now she wasn't sure that she cared. She felt excited, alive again, and she liked the feeling. What had she been thinking?

She didn't know what Marcus's game was, now that he knew Ethan actually existed, but she knew that she had the courage and the daring to meet him as an equal. Since she would not be in England much longer, there was little time for shilly-shallying behavior or putting on missish airs. She was dealing with a fascinating, complex man who deserved a worthy opponent.

She smiled and stepped away from the door, taking off her cloak and unbuttoning her gown as she walked across the room. Tonight America had just declared war on England once more, only this time it was going to be a very private battle. The first shot had been fired a few minutes ago. She had made her choice, allowing the sparks of anticipation to tingle through her body. How could she have ever guessed the act of vengeance could be so deliciously wicked?

"I'm sorry to be late, but I slept so heavily last night Tess practically had to drag me from the bed this morning," Celia announced cheerfully the minute she entered the dining room the next morning. As she had anticipated, the three gentleman were seated at the table, but the sight of Sylvia sitting next to Zachary caught her by surprise. Her friend's sheepish smile told Celia there had already been too much conversation on her presence for any further comment. "Did everyone else have a pleasant night? Zachary, Uncle? I hope the unfamiliar surroundings didn't make you restless."

"Must you be so damn chipper at this hour?" her brother grumbled, giving her a sour look. If she didn't miss her guess her brother had been drinking deep the previous night and was what Sylvia would call a bit well to live.

"Oh, I assure you, my dear, the rooms are most satisfactory," Thaddeus said, standing to bow her into her seat despite the footman's attendance. "You know I have trouble sleeping away from home, but his lordship's home is splendid. I wouldn't be so bold to complain that the bed was much softer than my own. After the rigors of the ocean crossing I would settle for a pallet in the most retched hovel as long as it was on dry land."

"Sir, how can you be in shipping if you don't like sailing?" Sylvia inquired, idly playing with the single piece of toast on her plate. She seemed more interested in turning it into crumbs than she did in eating it.

"Oh, Uncle Thaddeus isn't a partner in Tregaron Shipping," Celia explained, pausing a moment to smile at Baskin, who poured out her tea. In her new-found spirit, the imperious butler no longer unnerved her. "He is my mother's brother and has a large horse farm outside the city. When my parents died he joined Uncle Henry, my father's partner, acting as our guardian until we reached our majority. They both made great sacrifices to see that the three of us were brought up properly."

"So, there aren't any other brothers besides Zachary and Ethan?" Marcus's dry tone drew her gaze to the head of the table for the first time. She swallowed a sigh at the sight of his elegant figure in a stark black morning coat, remembering all too well the devastating male physique beneath it. "I won't have to prepare for any other siblings then, just antic-ipate the possibility of another uncle's arrival."

"Good heavens, I don't think Henry will come here," Thaddeus murmured to no one in particular, preoccupied with the mountain of food piled on his plate. "Goodness no, no reason at all."

"Oh, Marcus, how wonderful of you to take this in good humor. I know it wasn't right to disclaim any family, but I was in dire straits alone in a foreign country without anyone to champion me." She aimed a beatific smile in his direction, then took refuge in her teacup. After one look at his wary expression she knew that she had to tread carefully. He might find her intriguing, but he still didn't quite trust her. She would have to convince him that her lie about her family was the only information that she kept from him. "I hadn't realized I was so ravenous until I looked at Uncle Thaddeus's plate. While I make my selection you must tell what you discovered about Ethan. You were both shameless in going off last night without giving us any news. Though I suppose if it were bad news you would have let us know, even if Sylvia and I were in disgrace."

Her babbling was annoying even her, Celia realized as she rose from her seat and crossed the room, so she was sure it was having the desired effect on the two gentlemen. Her brother's groan from behind her made her smile in satisfaction as she made her selection from the chafing dishes along the sideboard. "Was that part of our punishment, to keep us in suspense the whole night long? I'm afraid our little adventure was most tiring, and I had to look after Madison's needs until he settled, so I fell asleep the moment my head hit the pillow," she continued, turning only once to address her brother directly. "Zachary, I instructed Tess to have that wretched animal moved to your room for the duration."

Celia settled once more into her chair and continued. "Now, then, what have you discovered about Ethan? We're dying to know all the details. Aren't we, Sylvia?" She was ready to launch into another endless recitation when Marcus cleared his throat.

"If you'll allow me to speak, Miss Tregaron? I would be more than glad to give you the information and let you rest your vocal chords."

"By all means, milord. Even an untutored Colonial knows better than to talk with her mouth full," she returned, directing a calculating look across the table. "I can't vouch for Zachary, however. His table manners have always been deplorable, probably from so much time spent at sea. Witness his elbows on the table while he is holding his head in his hands."

"*Please,* Miss Tregaron, eat your breakfast," Marcus all but commanded. "I will give you what details I know."

She stuffed a large portion of coddled egg into her mouth to keep from grinning from ear to ear. Lord Ashmore was out of sorts this morning, and she was positive that she was responsible. What a fool she had been not to realize the full potential of a woman's power until last night. It was truly invigorating. How could she have been so ignorant all these years? She really must remember to thank Marcus sometime for broadening her perspective, but only when he was in a receptive mood, which clearly wasn't this morning.

"As usual, those cretinous idiots at Whitehall couldn't immediately put their hands on a list of casualties from the riot at Dartmoor. They didn't report this until we cooled our heels in a drafty anteroom for over an hour," Marcus reported, not hiding his contempt. "They finally informed us that a complete roster wasn't to be found and to come back tomorrow. By then it was too late to stop at the *Morning Post* or *Times* offices to question the publishers about the casualty list. So Zachary and I will be off to obtain confirmation of your brother's well-being right after breakfast."

"Splendid. While you're gone Sylvia and I will begin the plans for our journey," Celia answered, limiting her verbiage for the first time that morning.

"Your journey? Are you going someplace, Miss Tregaron?"

His mild tone didn't fool her one bit, so she didn't bother to prevaricate in her answer. "Yes, milord, we are going with you to the prison after you acquire my brother's pardon. Isn't it nice that I'll be able to see something of the English countryside before I return home?"

"Miss Tregaron, I really don't think that would be advisable. The moors aren't exactly the place to go for a scenic holiday." Marcus made a real effort to keep his tone amicable, but Celia could see the pulse throbbing at the side of his jaw. "Your brother and I can travel much faster on horseback."

"Horseback? Lord Ashmore, it's very likely that poor Ethan is sick, or at least weakened after being imprisoned for so long." Her smile was the pattern card of condescension, or so she hoped. "Surely you aren't going to subject him to a grueling ride on horseback to London in his condition? He'll need nursing and a comfortable ride in a well-sprung coach, which of course you have at your disposal. If not, Zachary can withdraw the remaining funds from our account here and have Mr. Hampton hire us a suitable conveyance."

"Now, Miss Tregaron, though I bow to your suggestion of a comfortable coach, I really don't think it wise for you to accompany us," he tried again, as if he thought she would give in if he repeated himself. "Even if your brother was weak-willed enough to give you permission—"

"Here, now," Zachary broke in.

"Beg pardon, sir. Neither your brother nor I is going to allow two young ladies barely out of the schoolroom to take such a trip." The stern expression on Marcus's face declared that he would brook no argument on the matter.

For a delicious moment Celia wondered what he would do if she left her chair and went to sit on his lap. He had forced her into that position last night, so how would he feel about it in the light of day with an audience present? She resisted the temptation, despite the challenge in his glittering eyes. Instead she would bide her time with several tactics up her sleeve that were less likely to have her brother up in arms.

"I suppose that Tess put our clothing back in the laundry last night, Sylvia. Or do you suppose we might actually purchase something off the rack that would fit us properly? Have you ever worn anything off the rack, Sylvia dear?"

Celia raised her teacup to her lips to hide her smile at the results of her questions. Zachary choked on his coffee, while Uncle Thaddeus stopped eating long enough to begin muttering to himself again. From Marcus there was no overt reaction except that the telltale pulse seemed to be beating faster.

"Ah, there you are, my dears. I was just going to send Baskin in search of you. Are you ready to go shopping this lovely morning?" Lady Knowles blessed the entire company with her gracious smile, regally entering the room as if the atmosphere around her weren't thick enough to be cut with a knife. "After that dreadful rain I really must elevate my lagging spirits with a visit to my modiste. Are you planning anything special today to entertain the gentlemen, Marcus dear? They have come a long way and really should see something of the country while they are here."

"That's exactly what I was saying to his lordship just a moment ago," Celia chimed in, ruthlessly breaking into her hostess's chatter. "Why shouldn't we all accompany him to win my poor brother's release? It would be almost an anticlimax to sit cooling our heels here in London while the men go off alone. Isn't that right, Lady Knowles?"

"How utterly famous! Town is a little flat right now," her hostess responded as anticipated.

Celia continued to watch Marcus's face as his mother countered any opposition on his part. "In fact, I'm becoming decidedly bored with all this talk about Napoleon and where he could be running loose. It really is none of my concern, since my dear boy is home safe and sound. A trip to the country will be just the thing. Celia, you are a miracle. What would we have ever done if you hadn't come searching for your brother?"

"I would have retained a portion of my sanity," Marcus muttered as he rose to his feet.

"What was that, dear? Who did you say was saintly?" his mother inquired while conferring with Baskin by the sideboard. "You know, we really must have a celebration ball for Ethan once we get back from the country. Won't that be delightful?"

"Delightful isn't the word I would use, but I don't think you'd care for my alternative." Though he spoke to his mother, Marcus looked directly at Celia. With a shiver of expectation she could tell he was going to work at discovering her every motive. "Coming, Tregaron? We might as well escape while we can. It is possible we may find ourselves part of a plot to free all your countrymen once we reach Dartmoor. There are many things I'll do for my dear mama, but treason isn't one of them."

"Celia, don't start any more trouble while I'm gone," her brother warned as he stood up. "We're already in deeper here than I anticipated, so please try not to do anything more than plan an itinerary for the trip."

"What, no argument about the trip, Zachary?" she asked, giving him a genuine smile for his capitulation.

Patting her curls unconsciously, she tried to appear as nonchalant as possible.

"My dear little sister, I know better than to argue with you when my head feels like it will split open any minute. We'll discuss the matter later, however. Maybe by then we'll find a place to lock you up while we're gone."

"Zachary!"

He grinned at his ability to shake her. At the doorway he gave his parting shot. "And what have you done to your hair? You look like some street urchin."

"Do you really disapprove of her hair?" Marcus asked as the two men walked out of the room shoulder to shoulder. Though she strained to hear the rest of the discussion their low voices kept her from discerning their words.

While Lady Knowles and Uncle Thaddeus discussed the merits of fresh strawberry preserves, Celia retreated to mull over the morning's events. The only thing that disquieted her was the apparent companionship between her brother and Marcus. She wasn't sure if that was to her advantage or not. The only thing she did know was that she had made the right decision last night. She was going to call the tune of whatever happened between her and one very arrogant earl.

11

"*This is hardly what I envisioned* for my last night in England," Garth commented as he joined Marcus at the edge of the dance floor. He dispassionately eyed the select group of fashionably dressed people milling around the sparse rooms. "Almack's, of all places. The things I do for our friendship, knee breeches and silk stockings along with drinking that foul orgeat. An army bivouac never looked so good."

"We'll find more amusing haunts in a few hours. For now, Mama insisted that I give my support to the presentation of her new barbarians to polite society. I needed an ally in case Tregaron decided to renew hostilities while discussing politics," Marcus said, never letting his attention leave a cluster of young gentlemen across the room. "Or perhaps Abernathy will take exception to the refreshments, since they are far below his epicurean standards."

The thought of the older gentleman's possible

complaints didn't distract Marcus from his observation. Miss Celia Tregaron played the role of centerpiece to a cabal of young men, a vision in silver net over a pomona green satin slip, which seemed to cling much closer to her soft curves than was necessary. As far as he was concerned, the neckline bordered on risqué, leaving too much of her creamy skin bare. She wore no jewels, her only adornment pink rosebuds threaded into her raven curls.

"Well, young Zachary should have his neckcloth in shreds by the time we flee this place, the way he's tugging on it. Although he really should be more concerned with the gleam in Sally Jersey's eyes," Garth remarked. "She looked like she wanted to take him home and mount him on her wall as her next trophy when I spoke to her a few minutes ago."

"Mounting is probably what she does have in mind," his companion returned, his lack of interest in the matter all too clear. He was more occupied with his own amorous pursuit, or rather the lack of any fulfillment in the matter. "I should go and rescue him, I suppose."

"But you would much rather go and knock a few of those young bucks' heads together instead."

Marcus finally turned to regard his friend, his eyes hooded. "Aren't you traveling north before you cross the Channel?"

"Touché, my friend. No, Julia writes that the house is still under quarantine." Garth's brilliant blue eyes flared briefly before he raised his quizzing glass to study his friend's attire. "I want to remember you just this way when I'm huddled around some miserable fire in the wilderness. That, and my waltz with our dear Celia."

If you have a passion for great historical romance, here's an offer you'll love...

Reader Service.

Yes! I want to join the Timeless Romance Reader Service. Please send me my 4 FREE HarperMonogram historical romances. Then each month send me 4 new historical romances to preview without obligation for 10 days. I'll pay the low subscription price of $4.00 for every book I choose to keep--a total savings of at least $2.00 each month--and home delivery is free! I understand that I may return any title within 10 days and receive a full credit. I may cancel this subscription at any time without obligation by simply writing "Canceled" on any invoice and mailing it to Timeless Romance. There is no minimum number of books to purchase.

NAME

ADDRESS

CITY   STATE   ZIP

TELEPHONE

SIGNATURE

(If under 18, parent or guardian must sign. Program, price, terms, and conditions subject to cancellation and change. Orders subject to acceptance by HarperMonogram.)

Marcus smiled. "Since when is Brussels a wilderness? I suppose you'll be doing some traveling south on the Continent as well?"

"I'm not going to be drawn on my activities any more than you are on the subject of a particular young lady."

"By the time you return I promise you that either I will have made love to the chit until we're both senseless," Marcus informed him grandly, grinning at the stunned look on the other man's face, "or I will have given in to my strong impulse to strangle her."

"Well, at least you've found out her secrets. She was hiding the horrible existence of her living and breathing brother and two uncles until two of them had the bad taste to actually appear. Damn shame she turned out to be respectable."

"I'm still not convinced that she isn't hiding something else." Marcus stiffened as one of the young blades had the nerve to touch Celia's arm. The snap of her fan across the idiot's wrist kept him from more serious injury. "She is the most contradictory individual I've yet to meet. Every time I think I have the answer, she changes directions."

"Ah, the lady isn't falling at your feet like so many others in the past. You can't have your way all the time; it would make you complacent."

Garth's chuckle grated on his already strained nerves. If Marcus didn't know better he would think Celia was set on flirting with him, even now giving him a provocative look that dared him to cross the room. Had it been his imagination that her knees kept rubbing against his beneath the dinner table earlier tonight? Was it by accident or design that her hand brushed across his knee during the ride to the assembly, not once but twice? Those thoughts baited him the same way her teasing kisses had the night before.

"You can stand there woolgathering, or you can get yourself over to one of the patronesses before the stampede starts," Garth said, interrupting Marcus's feverish recollections. "Those slobbering dolts over there haven't thought about asking for permission to waltz yet. I know, because I'm the only one who has had the presence of mind to request an introduction to the lady. That means there are only two openings left."

Once the import of his warning sank in, Marcus thrust his glass in Garth's hand. "It looks like I'm going to rescue our bumbling friend from the clutches of Lady Jersey sooner than I thought. Maybe that will put me in a better frame of mind."

An hour later his frame of mind had deteriorated from annoyed to outright foul. The first waltz had come and gone, with Garth as Celia's grinning partner. Since then she passed tirelessly from gentleman to gentleman until Marcus was the only man in the room who hadn't spoken to her or touched her. He had never known such an evening as this. His threat of strangling the chit seemed like more than a possibility with each passing minute. She was enjoying herself while he stood cooling his heels on the fringe of each group.

"Next time you need a dance partner, even for a country dance, look elsewhere," his sister hissed at him as she curtsied to the gentleman opposite her in their set. She stuck her elbow in his side to remind him to bow as the musicians struck the closing chord.

"Escort me over to Mama, then take your dark mood somewhere else, if you please. I want to enjoy the evening, not have you glowering at everyone in sight. You've scared off at least three prospective partners."

"You're welcome, my dear," he murmured, not really paying the least attention to her prattle.

"Really, Marcus, you don't even allow me the satisfaction of a proper set down," Sylvia admonished, grasping his arm and forcing him to look in her direction. He was surprised to see a frown marring her oval face. "Aren't you feeling well?"

"I'm fine. What could make you think I was ill?" he asked, giving her his full attention for the first time. Had all the females in his family taken to acting strangely? Why would his sister think he was ill?

"Nothing, absolutely nothing," she answered, shaking her head as the musicians played a brief melody. "Oh, not another waltz. I haven't had one gentleman ask for permission, so I suppose I'll have to sit this one out. I must find Celia at once. I'm not going to sit aside with just Mama for company this time like some wallflower."

"If I'm not mistaken, Lady Sefton is headed this way with young St. Albane." Marcus didn't wait to hear her reaction, but left her side with more alacrity than he realized. In three strides he was at Lady Jersey's side, interrupting her conversation with a young matron. "I believe you were going to present me for this dance?"

"Ah, yes, the young Colonial's sister. I really should punish you for snatching him away from me earlier," she said in reproof, giving him an arch look before excusing herself from her companion. "I never knew you were this fond of dancing, Ashmore. Unfortunately, your Mr. Tregaron doesn't seem to share your enthusiasm. He prefers talking politics. In fact, he is barely articulate on any other subject."

"You see why I've been recruited to entertain the chit. Tregaron has no social polish, but he amuses my dear mama," he murmured, wondering if he could encourage Lady Jersey to walk any faster. With the thought came the realization that he was acting like some callow youth, and he abruptly narrowed his stride. This whole situation was ridiculous, but he felt a sense of triumph as they stopped in front of his quarry. Celia had played with him half the evening; however, in just a few minutes he would have her where he wanted her—in his arms.

"Miss Tregaron, may I recommend Lord Ashmore as your next partner?" The older woman smiled knowingly as she looked from the young lady to the man bowing in front of her. "He has been most anxious for this dance." With that she nodded and walked away, her attention captured by a young gentleman standing alone near the entrance.

For a moment Marcus thought Celia was going to decline. She stood absolutely still, staring up at him. The sparkling challenge he saw in her eyes whenever their glances met had suddenly vanished. She regarded him gravely now as if she were making a momentous decision. He resisted the temptation to reach out and shake her while cursing her for the unsettling feelings that she caused. No other woman made him so aware of her or his own vulnerability. Until now he could laugh and flirt, then walk away without a second glance as he chose.

"I am honored, milord," she finally murmured, so low he had to bend forward to hear her as she curtsied.

He didn't trust himself to speak as he placed his hands in position. Although he gazed only at his partner's lowered head, he knew that they were being watched by countless curious observers from all sides of the room. He executed the steps of the dance almost mechanically at first, then began to relax into the rhythm of the music. Now that he had her under his hand he felt calmer, more at peace with himself.

For a moment he considered whirling her out of the room to find a secluded place to kiss her senseless. He felt a strong need to assert himself. The warmth of her rose-scented body so close only added to his outlandish reverie. Even as the image formed in his mind he was aware of the sea of interested faces around him. If this had been a private ball, the possibilities for an intimate meeting would have been endless. This was Almack's, however. Even the most profligate gentleman knew he had to be circumspect within these hallowed, austere halls or chance complete social ruin.

"Are you going to stare at the floor all evening?" he asked impatiently after they had circled the floor three times. The look she gave him when she abruptly raised her face to his view almost made him forget his self-imposed restraint. Her emerald green eyes gleamed with mischief.

"I was counting my steps so I wouldn't disgrace you, milord." Her words were demure, but the husky voice was filled with promise, of things past and things yet to be. "I find I have trouble concentrating held so close to you. I begin to think of other circumstances besides dancing."

"You aren't counting now," he said, taking refuge in the mundane conversation. She wasn't the only one who was having trouble concentrating, he decided, his left hand alternately gripping and releasing the sweet curve of her waist.

"But I am. I'm using my fingers to keep the rhythm now." Until she mentioned her fingers, he hadn't noticed the slight pressure against his shoulder. With his attention drawn to the motion he realized she was painting a burning circle on his shoulder with the tip of her finger. He felt like she was branding him, though his clothing and her glove separated her fingers from his skin.

"What is your game, Celia?" He abandoned all subterfuge at that moment. Not for the first time in their acquaintance he stepped from behind the polite facade society established between a gentleman and lady. Was this need for direct talk the influence of the freer society that raised this tempting woman?

"This is no game, milord. If it were, I would be at a loss, because I've never been taught the rules," she returned, her smile beguiling as she lowered her thick lashes. The effect was perfect a moment later as she gave him a sidelong look from beneath the dark brown fringe. "Thus far we've been on unequal terms, always playing to your tune. Not anymore, however. My countrymen have fought yours twice, because they wanted to be treated as equals. So, this isn't a game to me, merely a declaration that we are equals in this game, as you call it."

"Do you really think you can take me on, my dear?" He was intrigued as well as amused by her words. But then, he already admitted that she was the most contradictory woman he had ever met. Last night when she ran from his dressing room he could have sworn it was the action of a nervous young woman.

"Not think, milord."

The simple words shook him to the very core of his being. She was serious, making him want her more now than ever. The situation was impossible, but it didn't keep him from envisioning what it would be like when he finally had her in his bed. It didn't matter that she was a guest in his house, or that she was a properly raised young lady. He knew if it were feasible he would take her directly to bed from the dance floor. America must be a remarkable country, he mused, to have produced this marvelous creature. Why hadn't he realized the wonders of those upstart Colonies before this?

"You're very quiet, milord. Have I offended your sensibilities?" Laughter colored her words, daring him to refuse her. Was that her plan, to have him cry off before she would face the consequences of her challenge?

"I'm silent in awe of your honesty, my sweet. Most women seem to delight in subterfuge and meaningless innuendo." He allowed himself the pleasure of boldly admiring her décolletage. If it was her plan to scare him off by playing at being brazen, she'd misjudged her adversary's will. He fervently hoped she was being truthful for once. Her widening eyes and her small gasp of surprise seemed to be a confirmation of her cunning.

He had no time to pursue the matter as the musicians took the untimely moment to finish the dance. Though Celia and Marcus lingered on the dance floor, they couldn't continue their private conversation without being overheard. As Marcus escorted her back to where his family waited, he wondered just when he could manipulate a private moment alone with Celia. Why had he wasted all those days avoiding her company? Days that might have led to a satisfying result by now.

After bowing to Celia, he went off to fetch the ladies some refreshment. He didn't mind being ordered off like a footman by his mother, as he needed the time to think, to clear his head. Could his distracted mind have imagined the conversation that had just taken place? No other woman of his acquaintance would have dared to speak as Celia had, at least not a respectable lady of the *ton*. Such audacity was common from an opera dancer or a comely phryne in search of a generous protector.

If there was one thing he knew about Miss Celia Tregaron in their short but eventful acquaintance, it was that audacious behavior was a way of life for her. And he didn't mind in the least. Such outrageous deportment from any other lady in his circle would have left him cold, but from Celia it was exciting. He didn't question his reaction, simply accepted it.

"Marcus, old friend, the hour of midnight has come and gone. I have done my duty tenfold tonight, and you promised me a diversion from this bastion of polite behavior." Garth's hearty greeting broke through Marcus's pleasant thoughts like a dash of ice-cold water. The very large and stalwart Zachary Tregaron gave him a friendly smile, clearly as anxious as Garth to quit the place.

With a sigh he signaled the eager St. Albane, hovering nearby, to carry refreshments back to the ladies. Much better to send an emissary than to listen to his mother lecture him on his dereliction of duty. He also didn't want to see what Celia's reaction would be to his departure. Would she think he was bolting rather than face her again, not simply giving in to his friend's entreaty?

He went along with the two gentlemen to collect his cape and *chapeau bras*. Would any of his acquaintances actually believe that he would rather stay at Almack's than venture out to find warmer company in the gaming hells and bawdy houses? He would withstand torture before he spoke of his desires to the two men who accompanied him out the door. Irrationally, he was angered over what Celia would suspect when he couldn't defend his actions.

Garth already harassed him at every turn. It wasn't just for the joy of irritating him, either; Marcus suspected it gave his friend a chance to vent his own frustrations with the fair sex. His Julia was leading him a fair dance, but the man was not even hinting at the cause for dissention with the lady he had known since she was in the schoolroom.

Zachary was an entirely different matter. Their association thus far was based on discovering his brother's fate and on forming an alliance against Celia's impetuous starts. He couldn't very well declare her latest indiscretion—daring him to make advances to her. No man would relate that to the lady's brother, or the fact that he had encouraged her. If Marcus had been so lacking in intelligence, the American's sheer size would have kept him mute— due to a finely honed sense of self-preservation.

As Garth hailed a hackney among the row of waiting coaches, Marcus ruthlessly repressed the thought of what he would do if Sylvia was involved with a man such as himself. He knew that his own behavior was extraordinary, but so was the lady. She was beyond anything he had ever experienced, and no matter what the consequence, he was committed to discovering every nuance of her personality. Just where was this indiscreet attitude going to take him? he wondered with a touch of moroseness, sinking in the corner of the carriage as the other two discussed the evening's amusements.

The gray sky overhead matched Marcus's mood late the next afternoon as he climbed down from his prized high perch phaeton with painstaking care. Though he usually jumped down from the vehicle, today his pounding head dictated cautious movement. As he strolled toward the front door he swore never again to indulge to such excess as he had the previous night. He really wasn't in prime condition to tackle his current mission.

But he was determined to drive Celia in Hyde Park, the only way he could be assured of a private conversation with the lady. Too many people were underfoot at the town house, which now seemed to be bursting at the seams with relatives, his and hers. After last night's amazing discussion on the dance floor he needed to discover if she was serious. If he was going to step over the line of proper behavior with a guest in his house, he wanted to be damn sure she knew what she was doing. This wasn't a game to him, as she claimed.

The front door opened the moment he placed his foot on the top step. One look at Baskin's pained expression made him wary. Something had to be seriously wrong for the butler to show the least touch of emotion. Thus far he had borne up fairly well, his only lapse during the stormy arrival of Celia's relatives, which was perfectly understandable. On the heels of that thought, Marcus heard raised voices coming from the parlor. What disaster had she created now?

With one raised eyebrow as he handed over his hat and walking stick, he asked, "Is there something I should know, Baskin?"

"More relations have arrived, milord." If he wasn't mistaken the man actually sighed to punctuate the announcement.

"More rela—Gad, you don't mean Uncle Henry is here?" he shot out, tempted to laugh out loud, though there was no humor in the situation.

"I don't believe you have an Uncle Henry, milord."

"Not my uncle, Miss Tregaron's uncle," he clarified, smiling in spite of himself as he checked his appearance in the convex mirror. Fortunately his impeccable facade gave no indication he had a splitting headache and his stomach was protesting as well. Or was it merely the distortion of the glass that allowed him that delusion?

"Just so, milord. Will you be stepping into the parlor?" The pleading tone of the question kept Marcus from crying coward and retreating to the sanctuary of his library.

"The sacrifices I make for my family," he muttered. The drive in the park was now impossible due to the arrival of more Americans. Was this the last of them? Could it be that Celia's husband would return from the dead next?

When Baskin opened the double sliding doors the volume of the arguing increased, causing Marcus to wince. The sight of two strangers instead of one made him wonder yet again what else Celia was keeping from him. If the man had been younger, he might have thought both Celia and Zachary had lied to him about the ever-annoying ghost of Daniel.

Once again Celia was toe to toe with a man who towered over her. Dressed in a bronze walking dress with scalloped sleeves and hem, she looked alluring as she fiercely stood up to the stranger's loud demands. Last night he had seen women more amply endowed, not bothering to hide their charms with clothing, but they had left him unmoved. One glimpse of Celia in her glorious anger promised all the passion that he hoped to release. Unfortunately, at the moment, he had to deal with the man who was yelling at his darling.

His resemblance to Zachary, standing at his shoulder, marked him as Uncle Henry immediately. He was slightly heavier in the jowls and had a touch of gray at the temples of his dark brown hair. The second man stood back from the group, seeming somewhat uninterested in the drama being performed a few feet in front of him. First he smoothed back the side of his pale blond hair, then became greatly preoccupied with the condition of his nails. The act irritated Marcus, even if it was a ploy he used himself on occasion. His annoyance increased when the man raised his head and he riveted his gaze on Celia.

"Is this the last of your relatives, Miss Tregaron?" The need to raise his voice only heightened the pain in his head. Either the novelty of a new voice entering the fray or the fact that they ran out of invectives to hurl at each other had the trio turning to face him as one. Almost dispassionately Marcus noted that Thaddeus Abernathy was helping himself to a liberal portion of his best Madeira in the corner of the room, far removed from the conflict.

"I am Henry Tregaron, sir, and I must apologize for my niece inflicting herself on your hospitality in this fashion. The girl never had much sense." The man kept his posture rigid, as if emphasizing his discomfort over the position in which Celia's actions placed him. After a moment's hesitation he gave a curt bow, ignoring the indignant sniff from the furious woman beside him. "I shall take over the responsibility of her lamentable behavior and make reparations for any obligation on your part. Unfortunately, it seems my brother-in-law and nephew have been remiss in their duty, not to mention misplacing their sense of honor."

"There is nothing to repay, sir," Marcus returned, not liking this pompous upstart. The man was condemning everything and everyone in sight without the least explanation. That was undoubtedly what the shouting match had been about, Celia and Zachary attempting to cut through the man's thick skull. "When my mother learned of your niece's plight, there was nothing any of us wouldn't do to help her in her hour of need. No man with any tender feelings at all could do anything less."

Celia's appreciative chuckle over his blatant prevarication was cut short by what could only be called a snort of derision from the gentleman by the fire. Marcus directed his gaze at the tall, thin man, examining his figure as if finding his manner of dress distasteful. He almost smiled when the man unnecessarily tugged on the hem of his embroidered waistcoat. Unlike Zachary and Thaddeus, the new arrivals had apparently taken time to change from their seafaring clothes before landing on his doorstep.

"And you are? I don't remember being introduced," Marcus inquired in his most imperious manner. "Celia does have a lamentably bad memory for details, but I don't believe there are more than two uncles. Of course, it is so easy to forgive lovely women these tiny foibles, isn't it?"

"I am Captain Silas Vanderhoff, sir. Messrs. Henry and Zachary Tregaron are close family friends as well as business partners," the man answered. He seemed to dare Marcus to challenge his presence yet again.

"Ah, you're the gentleman who lost Ethan in the first place. A most unfortunate business, which has obviously plagued your conscience since then." Marcus found that despite his internal discomfort, he was enjoying himself. His unforeseen liking for the brash Zachary and the innocuous Thaddeus had kept him from practicing his sardonic sense of humor; however, Henry and this Vanderhoff practically begged for it. "Just as a matter of information, you should address me as milord or Lord Ashmore, despite your republican leaning. I know it is a quibbling matter, but we English are such sticklers for what is proper."

He turned to Celia. "What was that, my dear? Did you say something?" he inquired in mild interest as she clamped a hand over her mouth. She couldn't hide the laughter in her magnificent eyes, and he almost grinned in response. "Were you going to remind me that you had to be reprimanded over the matter as well? No matter, repetition is never out of place when teaching a lesson, is it?"

Her expression changed from amusement to fiery retribution in a split second. He winked audaciously as he turned to walk toward the bellpull to summon Baskin. She should be reminded that there were more lessons to be learned than the matter of address between them. He intended to repeat the others as well, more intimate lessons, over and over again. The lady was going to learn every nuance of passion that he knew, and he would enjoy the repetition it would take until she was an advanced pupil.

When Baskin entered the room seconds later, Marcus knew the servant had been spying, as he was wont, at the door. "Baskin, send word to Mrs. Wilkins that we need refreshments. Also see if her ladyship is at home. I'm sure she will be in high alt over the arrival of more barbarians from America to add to her collection."

"Really, milord, we can't impose on you any further. We only came today to retrieve the girl and get ready to sail for home." Henry's pronouncement erased all trace of humor from both Celia's and Zachary's faces. "This foolishness has gone on far enough. The sooner we quit England, the better. I need to close our account at the bank and settle with Hampton, but as soon as those matters are completed nothing else can keep us here."

"Gad, haven't they told you yet?" He didn't have to pretend amazement over the matter, however, he couldn't resist a bit of drama that would make Garth proud. With an exaggerated step back he placed his hand over his heart. "Surely by now you've discovered that Ethan is indeed alive and in England."

The statement had a very satisfactory effect. Henry Tregaron opened and shut his mouth without managing a sound, looking as if the news would topple him at any moment. Silas Vanderhoff gave no outward reaction, positive or negative, or so he supposed. But Marcus found his mannerism of calmly adjusting his cuffs and placing a hand at his throat to check his faultlessly tied neckcloth very telling. The man was the coldest fish that he had ever encountered, and as a prominent member of the *ton,* Marcus managed to meet more than his share of unfeeling individuals. What was he to Celia that the man rested his gaze on her whenever he thought no one would notice?

"Please, this isn't a joke, is it?" Henry Tregaron managed in a lower tone than before, busying himself in searching for a handkerchief. After he discovered it in his trouser pocket, he blew his nose vigorously into the linen square. "Apparently Celia's impulsive, feminine conduct has done some good for once. Not before time, I should say. Where is the boy? Why isn't he here now? Zachary, why didn't you tell me at once, instead of carrying on about being capable of handling your sister?"

"That was what we were both trying to tell you," his nephew shot back, his volume at its usual boisterous level to match his uncle's increased magnitude. Apparently only the ladies of London society could subdue the young American, since Marcus noted the man had not been shy or terribly soft-spoken when confronted by Madame Heloise's stable last night. "If you had listened to one word I said, you would have discovered the truth. Instead you were determined to have your own way, without regard to the rest of us."

"Oh, never mind," the elder Tregaron snapped and turned back to Marcus. "Lord Ashmore, would you please tell me where Ethan is now? I've never been able to get a straight answer out of this pair; they always have to argue for a half hour before they can get to the heart of the matter."

"Ethan has been in Dartmoor Prison since last summer," he answered, not bothering to soften the news. "We were able to confirm his location just yesterday. The Whitehall offices are slightly preoccupied with other matters just now."

"Well, milord, what have you done to get him free? What preposterous nonsense must we go through to take the boy back to his own country where this kind of treatment wouldn't be sanctioned?" Tregaron seemed oblivious that he was insulting the only man in the room who could help him. His behavior allowed Marcus to understand some of Celia's actions and look on them a bit more kindly. He was somewhat impressed that she hadn't run away sooner.

"I have my solicitor negotiating his pardon as quickly as possible. When we have that document in hand, a journey to the prison will be necessary," he explained, wondering if the elder Tregaron would call him out if the pardon didn't materialize in the next instant.

"Very well, Vanderhoff and I will return to the hotel. That fool Hampton should have answered my note by now."

"But aren't you going to wait for the refreshments Ashmore ordered, Henry? I can assure you he provides an excellent fare." Thaddeus sounded almost sulky over that matter. Was he worried Marcus wouldn't let him partake if the others left?

"Thaddeus, how did Zachary ever get you away from your own table to come on this venture?" his brother-in-law asked, not bothering to hide his derision. "I never did understand how your sister could be such a charming creature."

"We can discuss the matter over dinner," Zachary put in, directing a glance at Marcus for confirmation. When he nodded Zachary continued, "That should make you both happy."

"Some of you will be happy," Celia muttered, glaring at the five gentlemen around her. Looking Marcus straight in the eye, she announced, "I think I'll go inform Lady Knowles about our new guests. I'm sure she'll have something enlightening to say about the matter. Until later, milord."

Marcus simply inclined his head as she curtsied and left the room without a word to anyone else. He managed not to look after her, torn between anticipation and dread over what scheme she planned to hatch with his mother's aid. He and Zachary continued to maintain that they should travel to the prison alone, unencumbered by female company. Unfortunately, none of the females concerned seemed to take them seriously thus far. At least her second uncle's arrival gained him another ally.

As Zachary and Thaddeus bid farewell to the departing gentlemen, Marcus heaved a sigh of relief. Tregaron and Vanderhoff weren't going to be housed under his roof. Celia had said, *Until later,* which held more than a threat of discussing the journey to free her brother. Her green eyes and slight smile promised a more physical duel between them. It was a promise he was determined she would keep.

12

The loud voices in the hallway told Celia that her uncle and Captain Vanderhoff were leaving. She looked down at the glass of wine in her hand, then took a deep breath. Brandy had given her courage the first night she encountered Marcus, so the extra fortitude offered by a glass of claret wouldn't hurt today. The warm feeling in the pit of her stomach helped buoy her lagging spirits as she began to pace across the middle of the library.

Surely Marcus would come in here as soon as he sent off her relatives. Her only real dread was that Zachary would be on his heels. The unholy alliance between the two gentlemen gave her more than a second's worry. Last night she was sure that she and Marcus understood each other very well. She had all but offered herself to him, which he had seemed to find intriguing. The next moment, however, he'd gone out the door with her brother and Garth Cruthers, off to enjoy the pleasures of some low-class women of easy virtue.

"Ah, my mother's sitting room has changed considerably since I last saw it."

Keeping her reaction neutral, Celia turned to find Marcus watching her from the doorway. He leaned against the doorjamb in his usual manner, one ankle crossed over the other and his left hand cupping his sling-encased elbow. She knew he did it for effect, but she wasn't going to let him know how handsome he looked. For now she needed to keep the upper hand and accomplish her purpose.

"I thought it would be nice to have a few moments to ourselves after that skirmish with my uncle." She smiled sweetly and crossed back to the wine tray on the shelf in front of the bookcase. Pouring the second glass of spirits, she hoped she could keep her hand from shaking. "Sit down and have a glass of port to restore yourself. Uncle Henry can be rather hard to take at first. I wish I could say he improved once you get to know him, but he doesn't."

She turned to find him standing only a foot away. Not knowing what else to do she held out the glass, raising a single eyebrow in imitation of one of his favorite gestures. He mirrored her expression and took the glass before she gave into the urge to throw the contents in his face. How was she going to broach the delicate subject of their intimacy if he was bent on infuriating her? Would he always have this talent for making her burn with both desire and anger?

"Who *is* Silas Vanderhoff?" he asked unexpectedly, sipping at the wine as he waited for her answer.

"Just as he said, an old family friend and a partner in Tregaron Shipping. He bought out the Sloanes' shares after Daniel was killed." She stared down at her feet as she admitted the latter connection. The last person she wanted to discuss was her late husband. Already on precarious emotional ground, she wasn't ready to add her insecurities from the past.

"Daniel was killed? Now I remember. You never told me exactly how your husband died." Despite his words, he really didn't sound like he wanted to know. Celia looked up to see Marcus tossing off the last of his drink.

"He was washed overboard during a hurricane in the tropics," she replied in a monotone. Though she knew he was watching her closely, she couldn't bring herself to meet his regard. "It was a long time ago, or so it seems. But I didn't come here to talk about Daniel."

"You never intend to when his name comes up," he murmured, almost to himself. Celia felt the heat rising to her cheeks, knowing all too well what he meant. "Now is there anything else about Vanderhoff, besides his connection with Ethan's impressment?"

She almost heaved a sigh of relief that he abandoned the hazardous subject of Daniel. This was not the time to confide any more details about her brief marriage. Although she had made the bold decision to encourage his advances, she felt a strong need to shield her innermost feelings.

"I've never particularly liked Vanderhoff, even less after Ethan disappeared. Surely he could have done something to keep your cousin from taking my brother." Was it her imagination, or was Marcus closer than before? She could suddenly feel the warmth of his lean body reaching out to her, the scent of his cologne drugging her senses.

"Finally, you and I agree on something, my sweet," he said softly as he captured her chin between his finger and thumb. She wouldn't allow him to see her expression and resisted his urging. "I find your sudden shyness very tantalizing. What happened to my daring partner from last night? I'm sure you're here for some other reason than discussing that twit with an exaggerated sense of his own importance."

"Yes, as a matter of fact, I do have another purpose." His touch sent tiny sparks racing through her blood as the pad of his thumb caressed her chin. At the same time his teasing roused her anger, prodding her lagging courage.

"In broad daylight, my dear Celia? You take my breath away."

"Not quite yet, but I will," she promised, raising her head and directing her most dazzling smile at him. His sudden stillness told her that she had been able to take him by surprise. That was exactly what she wanted. She wanted him to keep questioning what she was going to do next.

Before he could respond, she reached up and framed his lean face between the palms of her hands. His thumb stilled its provocative caress, but he didn't drop his hand. Very deliberately she wet her lips, staring at his mouth with clear intent as she did so. With her pulse rate accelerating she closed the minimal space between them. Marcus didn't speak or even move, as if he was paralyzed by her actions. As slowly as she could she raised herself up on tiptoe until her lips brushed against his.

For a moment that was all the contact she made, just letting their skin touch. Then she tightened her hold slightly, pulling his head down and increasing the pressure against his mouth as she brought her tongue into play as he had unwittingly taught her.

Threading her fingers through his chestnut curls, she deepened the kiss still further, glorying in the taste and textures of his body beneath her lips and hands. She wanted to be absorbed into the lean hardness of his body, merge with his very soul.

As abruptly as she had started the kiss, she ended it before succumbing to temptation at such an inappropriate time. Her quick step backward surprised Marcus, who didn't have time to clasp her more firmly in his embrace. She was halfway across the room before he realized her intent. At the door she turned, still trying to catch her breath. "That was what I came in here for, Marcus. I just wanted to remind you of what you'll be missing if you leave me here while you go off to Dartmoor."

She didn't wait for his answer, but scurried out the door before he could move to retaliate. His cursing followed her out into the hall before she firmly closed the door behind her. With a sigh of elated contentment she went up to her room for a much-needed rest. She hadn't slept well the night before, wondering what Marcus was doing and with whom. The unforeseen arrival of her uncle Henry with Vanderhoff in tow only added to her fatigue.

When she reached her room she flopped backward onto the mattress in a most unladylike manner, her arms outstretched. She felt wonderful again, even if a little guilty over her parting words in the library. The kiss wasn't intended as a bribe, merely a reminder to Marcus of what was blossoming between them—even if she wasn't exactly sure what it was or where it would lead. There would be so little time for her to explore this new territory once they found Ethan. She had to make sure that every precious moment counted.

Though it was wicked and improper, she looked forward to each clandestine moment she could share with her autocratic host. The look in his eyes just now told her he found her desirable. She wasn't going to fall into his arms like a ripe pigeon, however. After last night she decided that when and where they made the final commitment to passion would be of her choosing. Not that she wasn't adverse to a little sampling here and there beforehand.

Sighing in anticipation of what the days ahead would bring, she closed her eyes and conjured up the dreams of Marcus that so disturbed her when she first arrived. Now she welcomed them, knowing that her subconscious invention was only a prelude to the delicious reality of being held in Marcus's arms.

"What do you mean, we aren't going? Don't be ridiculous, Zachary." Celia glared at her brother on the other side of the dinner table. Everyone turned toward her the moment the harsh words were out of her mouth.

"I think your brother's meaning was very clear, my dear Celia," Silas Vanderhoff stated from his place at the far end of the table, out of Celia's line of vision. Apparently being placed at Lady Knowles's right hand had gone to his head for him to intervene in a family matter. "He and Lord Ashmore don't wish to be encumbered by the trappings necessary if they had to cater to your feminine whims on the journey. Don't you agree, milord?"

Celia turned to look at the man next to her, wishing she could read what was on his mind. He was regarding Vanderhoff with his deceptively indolent expression, which effectively cloaked any emotion he felt. A moment ago she found it frustrating, but now she admired his ability to confound Vanderhoff. The only comfort she had was his words earlier in the library, or had he said he disliked the man merely to humor her? She held her breath waiting for his reply as he signaled the footman to remove his plate.

"I'm not sure that Celia's argument doesn't have some merit," he finally replied, toying with the stem of his wineglass.

"Marcus, are you serious?" Zachary looked thunderstruck at having lost his trusted ally, making Celia want to crow in delight.

"Now, think over the matter, Zachary. Do you really want to play nursemaid to your brother on the return trip?" he inquired, grimacing over the very thought. "I think the boy would appreciate a feminine hand stroking his fevered brow, even if that female is his sister. The ladies were most eloquent on the matter the other day."

"Oh, I would be helping Celia in her nursing duties," Sylvia rushed in to say from her place beside Zachary, directing an entreating smile at her brother on her other side.

"Well, I hadn't really thought over the matter since Celia first broached the subject," the young American admitted, giving the lady next to him a sidelong look. His glance encountered hers, which made both of them look quickly away. Though Celia was intrigued she was much more interested in settling the matter of their journey once and for all.

Zachary cleared his throat, and adjusted his neckcloth before continuing. "If I were in Ethan's place I would much rather have Celia and Miss Knowles taking care of me. I've never been very good in the sickroom, you know."

"Zachary, have you taken leave of your senses?" Henry Tregaron shouted down the table. "Beg pardon, milady," he said abruptly to his hostess, who sat watching the byplay with a tiny frown marring her angelic face. "You can't go gallivanting across the countryside with two unmarried females, even with Lord Ashmore along. Celia will stay in London, and that's final."

Celia wanted to do some shouting herself. What had happened to her lovely evening? Tonight was going to be the next step in her campaign to keep Marcus preoccupied with only her. She began the first foray by removing her slipper to tantalize him beneath the table, caressing his leg with her foot. The prospect of discovery had only heightened her sense of adventure. She knew she was successful from the telltale tightening of his jaw at the lightest touch.

"But Sylvia and Celia won't be going alone. Though why we're still discussing the matter I don't know," Lady Knowles exclaimed, looking from Marcus to Zachary in confusion. "I clearly remember deciding we would all go to free poor Ethan. Has some problem occurred, Marcus, to change our plans? We were going to leave as soon as you procured whatever that document was to release the dear boy, weren't we? You really need to tell me these things, because I've been supervising the packing of the bedlinens and other little necessities for the trip already. I would hate to go through all that bother if you're going to go traipsing off without a by-your-leave."

"No, Mama, you aren't mistaken. We shall leave the day after tomorrow, so you had best see to packing whatever clothing you need for the trip. That should keep you occupied until the hour of departure." Her son gave her an affectionate smile but the pleasant expression was gone a second later as he turned to the gentleman to her right. "Captain Vanderhoff, I learned a long time ago never to argue too much with the fairer sex. If they are determined to get their own way, it will be an uphill battle. Of course, it is always interesting to see what weapons they'll bring into play to change one's mind. They don't fight in the same manner as gentlemen."

"Sylvia, I think we've been insulted," Celia declared, not giving in to the urge to kick Marcus in the shin. It probably would only hurt her toes and not take the smug look off his face. He was up to something, and she couldn't fathom what it could be.

"Not at all, my dear. In fact I think we hapless males should toast the feminine intellect," Marcus replied, then solemnly held up his glass. He waited patiently for the others to join him, though Thaddeus was already drinking deep. When the toast was finished, he turned to Celia and murmured for her ears alone, "I'm always willing to listen to a logical argument without any bribery needed. My mind will rest much easier with you along, and not leave an unsuspecting London at your disposal."

"Milord, don't expect me to be waiting for you in the library in the near future," she returned in a equally low voice. He might not like bribes, but she couldn't resist the statement.

"So, how many carriages shall we need? One for the ladies and another for the luggage, I suppose," Marcus went on as if she hadn't spoken. "You ladies can keep the luggage down to only one carriage?

Good. Zachary and I will ride, of course. What about you other gentlemen?"

"I can't speak for the others, but I have some business in town to complete," Henry Tregaron said, giving his brother-in-law a stern look. "It would be more efficient for me to conclude these matters and be ready to sail when Zachary returns with Ethan. We would look like a confounded parade if all of us went along; however, Thaddeus should probably be present as one of Ethan's legal guardians."

"Now, Henry, the boy's of age by now, isn't he?" Thaddeus managed between bites of his syllabub, the frothy desert decorating his mouth like a moustache. "Zachary will be there as well, so—"

"Thaddeus." The single word was spoken in an ominous tone.

The man blinked rapidly and shivered, staring at his brother-in-law for a moment. He hesitated, then jerked suddenly as if struck by his decision. "Oh, of course, Henry, of course. You and the captain get the ship ready for our departure. Be glad to accompany the ladies, so glad."

"How lovely to have everyone in such accord," Lady Knowles declared, beaming at the gentlemen before signaling to the ladies that it was time to withdraw. "Maybe we should take extra horses along in case Sylvia and Celia would like to ride on occasion. Young girls don't always like to be shut up in the coach for days on end."

"We'll be fine, Lady Knowles. There's no need to strain Lord Ashmore's generosity," Celia put in quickly, glancing over her shoulder at the man in question. "Sylvia and I will be perfectly happy in the coach as long as we are allowed to go along."

When Marcus nodded she relaxed, only then realizing how tense she had become. As she turned to follow her hostess she met Vanderhoff's glance and shivered at his look of pure displeasure. Once she left the room she decided it was her imagination. The man was merely angry that he had been bested; she knew from experience that he liked to have his own way in all matters. She had much more pressing business to worry about.

What had she done in insisting they accompany the gentlemen? She would have more opportunity to be with Marcus, along with everyone else. How was she going to get him alone again? Even her resourcefulness was stretched to the limit as she considered the trip ahead. Somehow, some way, she was going to persevere; she just didn't know how at the moment.

She didn't want or need Marcus Knowles, earl of Ashmore, in her life after all, Celia decided judiciously four days later as the coach lumbered along the highway. She sat snug in the corner of the blue velvet upholstery with her arms crossed over her breasts and stared out at the passing countryside. They hadn't been allowed to stop at any of the interesting locations along the way.

Not even Lady Knowles's entreaty to see the interesting rock formation near Salisbury had been granted. Both Zachary and Marcus were adamant that they weren't on a pleasure trip, which played on the ladies' guilt, as they anticipated. How could they think of their own boredom when Ethan lay wasting away in prison? Celia, for one, thought Marcus almost overplayed his hand in his pitiful portrayal of Ethan's plight at the hands of bullying guards.

Since they had a long distance to travel, she didn't join the argument with the other ladies. Despite her preoccupation with her personal dilemma, she was anxious to see her brother again. As Marcus had warned them the night before, each mile closer found them traveling through bleaker, more inhospitable landscapes. The site for the prison had been selected for just that reason when the French prisoners built their own jail.

She really didn't care about the scenery, wondering yet again if this was some twisted reprisal on Marcus and Zachary's part in allowing the ladies to come along. They knew that the monotony of being in a jolting coach, no matter how well sprung, for days on end would grate on the nerves of the most even-tempered woman. Though Celia had to concede that Lady Knowles still seemed to be enjoying herself, after a few minor setbacks. Perhaps it was because she slept at least half the day.

"Celia, do you think I'm pretty?" Sylvia asked abruptly from where she was wedged in between a snoring Thaddeus and her mother's jewelry case.

"Of course you are," she answered absently, still looking out the window. The scenery had improved considerably as Marcus and Zachary came abreast of the coach and matched their mounts' gaits to the vehicle's speed. Marcus had a superb seat, she noted grudgingly, his back erect while he posted with natural athletic grace. She sighed with regret that their relationship was past before it had a chance to flourish. If she closed her eyes she could imagine the feel of his hard body pressed against hers, his mouth playing against hers, sending a frisson of fiery sensations through her.

"Celia, are you listening to me?"

"Yes, Sylvia. You must know that you are more than pretty," she continued, wondering why her friend would pick this occasion, when her own spirits were at such a low ebb. Apparently she hadn't been attractive enough to hold Marcus's attention as more than a novelty or a plaything to tease. "Haven't all those flowers and young men cluttering up your mother's sitting room during afternoon calls convinced you? You've had more than one proposal, haven't you?"

"Oh, most of them are just family connections making duty calls. None of them are very interesting," Sylvia replied, clearly ready to wallow in her dejection. "None of them are truly in love with me. I would like to be loved."

"Uh-oh." Celia chanced to look in her companion's direction, only then noticing the direction of Sylvia's gaze. "Sylvia, if you're thinking of trying to capture my brother's attention—"

"I know, my dear friend, he isn't going to bother with a child like me, especially an English child." The last was mumbled as Sylvia began to twist the chords of her reticule into knots. For a moment Celia wondered if she actually saw the sheen of tears sparkling in her friend's brown eyes. "Besides, he barely speaks to me. I don't think he likes me very much."

"Zachary is afraid of respectable women. He doesn't plan to marry until he is five-and-thirty, another six years from now," she said quickly, hoping she wasn't causing more harm than good. She rationalized that she simply stated the facts of the matter. Since her own emotional affairs were in such a mess, she couldn't very well be handing out advice. "I don't think he has spoken more than five words to any eligible young lady since he reached his majority. He told me one time that he could resist getting married by avoiding the temptation of suitable ladies until it was time to make his selection."

"He sounds like he plans to make a selection from the market, picking out the proper vegetable or a suitable flower." Sylvia chuckled as she made the observation, watching the subject of their discussion once more.

Celia was glad to see that her friend hadn't lost her sense of humor. She wished that she could do the same with Marcus, but her emotions were too deeply involved. "I'm afraid my brother is rather naive when it comes to matters of the heart, not understanding that feelings can overcome common sense. He had to mature early, taking over his responsibilities at the shipping company as soon as he was eighteen. Sometimes I think he plans to write down the qualifications for his wife, just like he would when writing out the specifications for a ship."

"You're lucky you understand your brother so well. I don't think I'll ever begin to understand Marcus at all. Perhaps it is because he is so much older."

"I don't think Marcus allows very many people to know him." She continued to watch him, luxuriating in the chance to do so without him knowing.

"That is true. Garth is the only person who is truly close to him since father died," Sylvia said. "I know Marcus is worried now that Garth has joined Wellington again, but he hasn't said a word."

"Garth has rejoined the army?" The news shook Celia out of her lethargy. Now she understood the gentleman's sudden absence. She also began to realize something else, or was it wishful thinking on her part? "Did he leave the day after we attended Almack's?"

"Yes, he did. Do you know that he took Marcus and Zachary to every one of his old haunts to say farewell? They didn't come home until six in the morning," Sylvia declared, some of her usual cheerfulness returning. "Foster told Tess all about it, or should I say complained bitterly about the condition of Marcus's clothes."

Celia didn't answer immediately, mulling over the information. Was she wrong in thinking Marcus had lost interest in her? Probably not, she determined grimly, since he hadn't even taken the hint to accompany her for a walk the last two nights to exercise Madison. Instead she had had her brother's company and had lain awake wondering what she could do to confront Marcus about his lack of attention.

Tonight she was going to see to the matter once and for all. If he had lost interest in her, she wanted to know. She wasn't going to sit patiently by and wait for him to crook his finger, expecting her to do his bidding when it was convenient for him. Hadn't she clearly told him that they were to be equal partners in this affair? She had never envisioned herself involved in this situation. What properly brought up young lady could imagine what she would do as a participant in such a relationship?

He had started this unconventional alliance that incredible night in the library. No, before that actually, on the night they first met. Now she was going to finish it, if that was the case.

As she crept slowly down the stairs of the inn Celia marveled at the noise coming from the lower floor. Unlike Marcus's home, which was like a tomb at this hour, the inn was lively and boisterous with numerous candles burning. In fact, she didn't remember the place being this noisy earlier when their party dined in the private parlor that Marcus had secured for them. Just how late did these gentlemen, for want of a better term, stay drinking and carousing?

She hesitated when she reached the bottom step, unsure exactly where she would find her quarry. Marcus hadn't returned upstairs with her brother an hour ago. She listened carefully to each pair of footsteps that echoed along the upper hall. Both Marcus and her uncle Thaddeus remained below, though it was doubtful that the older man was still conscious. He was known for drinking himself into a stupor, even at home, and earlier he had discovered an excellent vintage in the publican's cellar.

"Going out for a breath of fresh air, my dear?" inquired a polite, lazy voice that sent a shiver down her spine. "Or were you planning on a new adventure in visiting the public room of an inn? Another quaint Colonial custom, perhaps?"

"No, milord, I came looking for you," she said evenly, turning to face him. He was partially hidden in the shadows, the light from the open door of the private parlor distinguishing the silhouette of his tall form.

"I see. Are you going to remain hugging that newel post all night? I'm sure our friends in the next room would be delighted to eavesdrop on our conversation, or even invite you to join them." His tone was neutral, so she couldn't gauge his mood, but she noted his speech was not slurred.

"No, I'll join you in the parlor," she replied, stepping down the last stair and walking forward without further hesitation. "What I have to say won't take much of your time, but I didn't think it advisable to wait until morning."

"By all means, my dear. You know that I can hardly refuse you anything."

She didn't bother to answer his provocative statement. With her head held high she walked past him, tightening the hold on her cloak. She was very conscious of her state of dress, her gown half-open down the back.

Not wanting Sylvia or Tess to know of her late-night mission, she had dressed in her nightclothes along with them as usual. When she was sure that Sylvia had drifted off beside her, and Tess was sleeping deeply in the trundle bed, she had quickly dressed in her carriage gown again, but couldn't reach all the buttons. So she had thrown her cloak over her shoulders, determined to have her say tonight.

Once inside the parlor Celia was startled, but not disappointed, to find it empty. Her slumbering uncle was nowhere in sight, though it was hard to tell at first. The only light came from the fireplace and a single candelabra on the small table near the window. At the soft click of the latch behind her she turned slowly to face her companion. His face was devoid of expression as she expected, making her wonder for the first time if she should have stayed upstairs in her room.

She always knew exactly what she needed to do about this man when he was out of her sight. As soon as they were face to face again she began to doubt even her most logical plan. Folding her hands sedately in front of her, she squared her shoulders in preparation for making her speech.

"I don't want your gratitude, Miss Tregaron."

She blinked in confusion for a moment, trying to

fathom his meaning. Then she realized he must think she came to thank him for his help in finding her brother on the eve of freeing him from prison. "I haven't come to give you my gratitude, milord. This has nothing to do with my family. I needed to speak to you on a more personal matter."

She waited for him to comment, but he remained silent. Studying his erect body, she almost sighed with longing over what she was about to denounce. She did have her pride, however. Why should she continue to blatantly offer herself to this man if he wasn't interested in her? Hadn't he made that perfectly clear over the past few days of their journey?

Since he didn't speak, she forged ahead before she lost her nerve. "I seem to have mistaken the intent of some of our conversations during our association and wanted to clear up any misunderstanding." Why did her throat suddenly feel so dry now that the moment was at hand? Why didn't he say something, do something, anything, that would give her an indication of his thoughts? "It has become clear that I foolishly mistook some flirtatious actions on your part for something more. I wanted you to know that I have no hard feelings for you because of my own, shall we say, naïveté. So you needn't worry that I will embarrass you again with any display of physical affection."

"What the blazes are you talking about, Celia? Physical affection?" He looked thunderstruck for a moment, then his eyes narrowed in angry speculation. She got her wish of knowing exactly what he was thinking and wished she hadn't. "Are you talking about kissing? Don't you use that word in your confounded country?"

"Yes, that's what I'm talking about, you ill-mannered

aristocrat." She stressed the last word purposely. Her temper was beginning to simmer. This was his fault for kissing her in the first place. "I was trying to have some shred of dignity left, since you made it perfectly clear that my forward behavior has cooled your ardor."

"What makes you think I disliked your forward behavior?" he asked, throwing her off stride. This wasn't how she imagined the conversation would go.

"You haven't come near me since that afternoon in the library, when I kissed you. That was five days ago, milord," she charged, placing her hands on her hips in annoyance without realizing it. "Of course, I think you dislike my advances. If not, you would have done something about it by now. Well, wouldn't you?"

He smiled, and that worried her. What had she said that would make him smile?

"Don't laugh at me, milord."

"I'm not laughing at you, my dear, but at the situation," he said softly, taking measured steps to close the distance between them. "This whole situation is somewhat amusing. But then, you don't do anything that can be anticipated, do you? Are all the women in your country so unpredictable?"

"I don't know what you mean." Now she was thoroughly confused. "Have you been drinking? That would explain why you aren't making any sense."

"I had two tankards of ale with your brother earlier. That isn't enough to make me incoherent," he replied, stopping directly in front of her. For a moment she considered backing away, but didn't have time before his hand clasped her shoulder. "I shall try to be very clear about this. I haven't done anything about your delightful offer, because I bloody well couldn't figure out what to do with your family constantly underfoot. The one time I thought to get you alone for a drive in the park, your uncle Henry and that snide Vanderhoff showed up on the doorstep. Then my own mother kept you busy packing for this infernal journey. If I could have done it, I would have taken you directly to my bed from the dance floor that night."

"Oh." That was all she could manage as she met his heated look. How could she ever have imagined that he was indifferent to her? "You have been so polite and considerate, not saying one unkind thing to me, since we left London. What was I to think?"

"You might have considered that I would have some difficulty in making love to you with a half dozen people around at all times. I shall be sure to remember to be especially sarcastic tomorrow," he murmured, reaching up to run his fingers through her tousled curls. "You're sharing a room with my sister and her maid, while I have Foster scolding me about the dust on my clothes every waking moment. Not to mention a pair of your male relatives in the room between us. I don't think my mother or your rather large brother would approve of me sharing a room with you."

Encouraged by his actions as well as his lengthy speech, Celia allowed herself to run her palm over the sleek material of his sling. She could feel his heart beating steadily under her hand and was startled when Marcus groaned. "What have I done? Have I hurt you?"

"Oh, I'm in pain all right, and only you can help me. You shouldn't have touched me, my dear. I only have so much willpower."

Before she realized his intent he was kissing her like a man starved for sustenance. Any doubts she had had about his interest in her were quickly dismissed as she gave herself up to the whirlwind of sensations that his touch evoked. Not to be outdone she looped her arms around his neck, eagerly meeting the thrust of his tongue with her own. She trembled with pleasure as he groaned once more, then sighed in satisfaction as his arm circled her waist. The feel of the hard line of his body against her soft curves was what she had been craving.

A second later she gasped in delight as his leg nudged between her thighs. Instinctively she parted her legs, allowing him to thrust his knee between hers. Her gasp turned to a murmur of approval when he pressed against her buttocks, kneading and shaping her to his hand, as he rubbed his arousal against the apex of her thighs. Nothing she had experienced in his embrace prepared her for the ecstatic swirl of desire that shot through her body. Heat seemed to radiate from the center of her body.

Driven by pure, raw sensation she wanted to experience more. Not aware of her movement she grabbed his arm, wanting to show him what she needed. The movement was instinctive, placing his hand against her breast. Soft leather touched her bare skin, and Marcus immediately broke the heated contact of their lips. She didn't hesitate in spite of the anguished look in his eyes. Staring deep into their sea green depths she placed her hand over his gloved hand, pressing it against her skin.

Though she wanted to savor his touch, she knew what she had to do. She raised his right hand to her lips, kissing the palm of his hand so fiercely that he would feel the imprint of her lips through the leather covering. He watched her as one transfixed as she placed his hand against her cheek, rubbing her face against him. "Someday, Marcus, I'm going to do that without the glove in place," she promised, wondering if she had gone too far.

He closed his eyes for a moment, almost as if the pain he spoke of earlier had returned. When he opened them again, he smiled, almost sadly, but she knew that she had done the right thing. "I know I'll regret this in the morning, but I think we need to call it a night," he said softly, his voice filled with tenderness.

Though she wanted to remain in his arms, she knew that he was right. Anything else would take away the meaning of what had just passed between them. She nodded her assent, but found she couldn't move away from him as he allowed his eyes to move over her with a hungry look. Slowly he bent his head, brushing his lips against her exposed breast. Then he pulled the neckline of her dress back in place and stepped back. "Go to bed and dream of me, Celia."

"I promise, Marcus," she whispered in return and fled the room before she begged him to let her stay.

13

When was he going to be able to consummate his relationship with Celia? The thought preoccupied Marcus most of that night and throughout the next day. He couldn't help but smile at the memory of their encounter. What other woman of his acquaintance would give him his *congé* before they had ever made love? In fact, he didn't remember any woman dismissing him from an affair. He had always been the one to break off a relationship, usually from boredom. That would never be an issue with Celia. He knew that she would never bore him.

He was beginning to wonder, however, if they would have an affair after all, proper or improper. Once they had Ethan safely back with his family she would be on her way back to Baltimore with the next tide, if Henry Tregaron had his way. This was why gentlemen didn't have affairs with respectable young ladies, Marcus realized. The logistics defeated them at the onset. They couldn't figure how or where they could spend any time together without having their intimacy interrupted and causing a scandal. Even his outlandish Celia couldn't overcome that obstacle. Not that she wouldn't try if she could. He had been the one to send her to bed alone that night.

"Marcus, I need to talk to you about an ackward situation." Zachary's words startled him, making him stiffen in the saddle and jerk on the reins. Zeus took exception to such treatment and nickered his displeasure. "Seems your mount is somewhat restive. Perhaps we stayed too long over the ladies' afternoon refreshment."

"Just a touch of high spirits to remind me that he is a more superior animal than his rider. What is bothering you?" he asked as casually as possible. Had Zachary seen Celia returning to her room last night? No, if he had he wouldn't have been so affable this morning, though his current expression was as bleak as the landscape around them.

"Well, this is difficult to ask, especially with Uncle Henry ready to ship us all back home as soon as we set foot in London. And I know you've done more than was necessary for us. Lord knows we've disrupted your peace enough with this business, but would it be possible for us to extend our visit?"

"Beg pardon?" Marcus pulled his mount to a standstill, deciding this conversation needed his full attention. Zachary had been quiet most of the day; had he been mulling over this request?

"No, I see that I shouldn't have asked. You've already done enough," Zachary muttered, looking at some distant point on the rolling moors before them. The mottled color of his rugged features told how he hated making the suggestion.

"You just took me by surprise. Don't turn into a hotheaded rebel like your sister," Marcus admonished as good-naturedly as possible. Instead he wanted to toss his hat in the air and give vent to a rousing huzzah. "I can only handle insurrection from one direction at a time."

His companion gave him a sheepish look, then grinned. "The Tregarons aren't the most even-tempered lot at the best of times. I'm afraid Celia's been given her head for far too long. If Daniel hadn't been killed, I think she would have had full charge of that household."

"I thought you told me he used to be your nemesis in the boxing ring? Surely a man like that could hold his own against a fair-sized female." Although Marcus had an unnatural concern over the man who had been Celia's spouse, he never asked questions unless the man's name was mentioned. As usual, Zachary was easily led to talk more of his old friend.

"Oh, he had a neck like a bull, and arms that could crush the life out of a man. Unfortunately, he was afflicted with the same problem that I have," Zachary confided, pausing for breath just at the moment his listener was most interested. Could it be that Celia had never consummated her brief marriage? The thought that his potential ladylove might be a virgin was slightly daunting. He hadn't noticed that Zachary had disappointed any of the lightskirts they'd encountered on their rounds of the city. "Daniel was afraid of respectable women, just like me. I don't know what it is about presentable young ladies, but my brain goes numb the minute I come close to one."

"That, my friend, is sheer self-preservation. Most of the presentable young ladies of my acquaintance seem to have only a single goal from the time they leave the schoolroom," he stated, sure of his subject without a female within hearing distance. "That goal is marriage, a terrifying prospect for any upstanding male of the species. None of us voluntarily place our heads in the parson's noose. You don't seem to have much difficulty in speaking your mind to your sister, so the problem obviously stems from a natural animal ability to sense extreme danger. Consider that after years of living with someone as obstinate as Celia, you should be able to hold your own with a wife."

"There's some sense to that, but I don't think I would want a wife with Celia's temper. A woman like that would never be peaceful."

"That is true, but she wouldn't be boring, either, simply unpredictable at times," Marcus replied, urging Zeus into motion again. Celia would certainly put a man's life into turmoil if she was given a wife's power to dictate to him. The nights in her arms might be able to make up for her clever tongue, dousing her anger or channeling it into passionate response.

"Now you see why I was reluctant to take advantage of your hospitality," Zachary explained, uneasily returning to the subject. "I wouldn't think to ask, except we haven't seen Ethan in over two years now. We need to get him settled somewhat before heading to sea. He was seventeen when he started his maiden voyage, older than he should have been since Celia insisted on keeping him at home. She tended to mother him."

"I think it sounds like a reasonable idea, especially since he'll probably need to regain his strength," Marcus said casually, as if discussing the weather. He did have some concern for the boy, a young man actually, but his real motive was keeping Celia in England longer. The possibility of an extended stay opened all sorts of delightful possibilities, which he contemplated with only a minor twinge of guilt.

"Did you hear that?" Zachary wheeled his horse abruptly and stared intently at the bend in the road behind them. His view was obscured where the hard-packed dirt surface meandered through one of the numerous eroded rock formations that seemed to grow from the moors. The two coaches weren't in sight. A sharp popping noise broke the silence. "Damn, I *did* hear a gunshot."

He dug his heels into his horse's flanks and was off in a cloud of dust before Marcus could turn Zeus. Once he had the animal wheeled in the right direction, he urged the gelding into a full gallop, unmindful of any hazard in the road. His companion wasn't mistaken about the sound of a pistol shot. Surely a highwayman or even a vagrant wouldn't attack a coach in broad daylight? Until he knew for sure, he wasn't going to waste time pondering the issue.

Within four strides Zeus was even with Zachary's mount, and the horses ran neck and neck around the curve in the road. Once they cleared the mound of rocks the road straightened, giving a clear view of what was ahead. Both of Ashmore's vehicles were standing still about a half mile away. Two unfamiliar horses stood beside the first coach that carried Celia and his family. One horse carried a rider, while the other horse grazed by the side of the road. As Zeus closed the distance, Marcus could make out the second figure standing by the coach door, and he seemed to be reaching upward.

He cursed himself for not carrying a weapon just as the report of a pistol sounded beside him. Hardened after years on the Peninsula, neither he nor his mount flinched at the explosive sound so close at hand. The next instant a high-pitched yell from Zachary almost unseated Marcus, however. Once he had Zeus in control again, he acknowledged that cacophonous bellow must be why his countrymen lost the wars to the upstart Colonies. If every Colonial had yelled in that manner, it would have petrified the British into surrendering without a shot fired.

It seemed to do the trick with their unwelcome callers. Both of the horses next to the coach danced nervously as Marcus and Zachary drew steadily closer. The man on the ground seemed to wave off his mounted companion just before Zachary let loose another ear-splitting yell. This time Zeus didn't break stride. They were almost a hundred yards from the lead pair of the coach's team when the man leaped into the saddle.

At this distance Marcus could see that both men wore scarves to conceal their faces, and their wide-brimmed hats were pulled low. Both were of moderate height and weight, dressed in dark, nondescript clothing. They probably could walk into the inn where Marcus' party was staying that night and not worry about being recognized. The pair disappeared into the wooded area near another granite formation.

"Is everyone all right? Did they take anything?" Zachary shouted, practically dismounting before the horse came to a complete stop. He wrenched open the door of the coach and peered inside while trying to catch his breath.

Marcus stepped down from Zeus less hastily, tossing the reins to the waiting postillion. He gaze didn't move from Celia, who was sitting next to the window. She was in full view with the door opened wide. As he drew closer he noticed she was holding her hand in an awkward position against her skirt, almost as if she was holding something in place. He also noted, without surprise, that both of the custom windows on this side of the coach were let down.

"We're fine, Zachary. Nothing happened, so calm yourself," his sister declared as if comforting a distraught child.

"Oh, Marcus, it was the most amazing thing. These two men appeared out of those scrubby-looking woods behind us," Sylvia exclaimed, allowing Zachary to help her out of the coach. Her cheeks were flushed with excitement, her eyes sparkling as she continued the tale. "They fired a shot in the air and when John Coachman protested they fired another."

Marcus only half listened to his sister's recounting of the robbery, if that was what it was. His attention remained focused on Celia. She didn't move from her seat, but that wasn't what aroused his suspicions. Her posture suggested she was waiting for something. The question was, what?

"They would probably have been disappointed in what you had to offer, unless Mama has taken to carrying the family jewels around the countryside," Marcus remarked, still keeping sight of Celia's movements. As he anticipated she moved now that she thought he was addressing his sister and paying her no mind. He was right. Under her hand was a folded piece of paper, which she urgently stuffed into the pocket of her spenser.

"That was the strangest part. He didn't demand any money or jewelry immediately. Instead he asked who we were and where we were heading," Sylvia went on. "I was too horrified to even look at the man, much less speak to him. Not Celia, though, she spoke right up and even let him take her hand when he asked."

"One of our renowned gentle highwaymen, I suppose, which I always thought were more fiction than fact. Didn't he solicit a kiss from your lips as well as your hand, my dear?" The words came out in a much harsher tone than Marcus had intended. But then, hadn't Celia taken him to task for not insulting her more? And he succeeded, judging from her heightened color. What he really wanted to ask was what the man had given her. The whole setup was odd as far as he was concerned. "Apparently Tregaron and I should travel in sight of the coach for the rest of the journey. Princetown isn't that far ahead by my estimation. John, check with Foster in the other coach to see if he and the maids are all right. Then we can set out."

Marcus wondered fleetingly why his mother and Celia's uncle hadn't added to the confusion. Sylvia managed to solve that mystery as Zachary helped her back into the vehicle. "I can't believe that the pair of them managed to sleep through it all, especially that extraordinary yell."

"What was that, dear? No, I'm not asleep," his mother mumbled from the interior, probably not even bothering to open her eyes. "Why would I go to sleep in the middle of the afternoon, for heaven's sake?"

Within ten minutes they were traveling down the road again. Keeping pace with the coach was dashed inconvenient, but it gave him time to think over the strange robbery attempt. Again he questioned if it was a robbery. Thieves would have to be fairly desperate to chance a crime this close to a prison town, as the garrison from Dartmoor undoubtedly frequented this road.

And why would they attempt challenging two coaches without knowing what they would find? A lone coach would have seemed more logical, even though the second one had only a coachman and no outrider.

More troubling was the folded piece of paper that Celia had purposely concealed. She wasn't just hiding it from her brother or him, she was hiding it from the occupants of the coach as well. Did this have anything to do with what she seemed to be holding back? Or was he imagining that she still hadn't told him everything he wanted to know? Tonight he would be sure to keep watch to see if the lady had a desire for a late-night stroll again.

Perhaps this search for her brother had been used to cover her real purpose in coming to England. Celia could have a more personal reason for her secret voyage that her family knew nothing about. He cursed his lack of knowledge over the recent American conflict, though he had been preoccupied with a war of his own. How close had the British come to Baltimore? Was it anywhere near their capital? Marcus knew that British troops had attempted to torch the city in retaliation for the Americans' burning of York. Celia could have met a British soldier any time since her husband died.

He still hadn't come to any satisfactory conclusions by the time Princetown was in sight. The location of the inn outside the city, as far from the prison as possible, gave him some perverse pleasure. If Celia had a contact in the city, he wasn't going to make it easy for her, he determined as he turned Zeus over to the post boys.

As he watched the ladies enter the inn he considered his words to Garth at Almack's only a week before. Would he make love to her before he gave in to the urge to strangle her? Until now Marcus had never been influenced greatly by the women in his life, certainly not by his amorous connections. Celia had changed that, however, almost from the moment he laid eyes on her. Or had it been from that first kiss, which he had intended merely as a jest? She seemed to have colored every aspect of his life in such a short amount of time.

How he wished Garth was here now, for he needed a confidant. The publican scurried to see to his lordship's wishes, but Marcus didn't tarry to see if his instructions were carried out. He left Foster and Zachary to cope with the man, heading straight for the public room, where he demanded a bottle of claret as he threw himself into the nearest chair. He had some serious thinking to do about a man's honor, and what a desirable woman could do to corrode a man's will.

"Well, I'm going to turn in now. Sorry I couldn't have been better company, but I'm feeling preoccupied with our visit to the prison in the morning," Zachary declared as he rose, stretching his long arms over his head. "Though I'm not quite as bad as Uncle Thaddeus, I suppose. At least I stayed upright."

"It appears that he has managed to settle his nerves after that harrowing experience he slept through." Marcus allowed himself a slight smile, nodding at the older gentleman lying across the settle next to the public room fireplace.

Both men chuckled at the sight. Thaddeus was lying on his side with his hands tucked under his head and his knees bent up to his chin. His face looked as innocent as a small child's.

"Are you going to need any help getting him up the stairs?"

"By rights I should leave him there, but he would only come stumbling to bed in the wee hours like last night." Zachary sighed at the memory before walking across the room. "Too bad I can't use my Daddy's yell like this afternoon, but it would bring the entire house down on us."

"What was that horrific sound you made? I've never heard anything like it," Marcus admitted, signaling for another tankard while his companion nudged the older gentleman's shoulder, none too gently.

"Something Daddy picked up when he was fighting against your army in South Carolina and Virginia. It's an old Indian war cry that the woodsmen taught them," Zachary grunted as he hoisted his semiconscious uncle to his feet. Securing his arm around the older man's shoulder, he grinned. "They liked to use it on moonless nights to scare the pants off the redcoat sentries."

"I can imagine. Today's sample was enough to convince me," Marcus admitted, waving his companions off as Zachary led his stumbling uncle out of the room. Once they disappeared from sight he pulled out his pocket watch to check the time.

The time was half past eleven. He tossed some coins on the table, then got up and left the room as well, his tankard of ale in hand. Then, he walked past the stairs, heading for the bench that sat against the back wall. From this vantage point he could see both the front stairs and the door that led to the servants' stairs. It didn't take his experience in the army to make a quick reconnaissance and discover the two routes. He snuffed the candles in the two wall sconces to help conceal his hiding place.

Bracing one foot on the bench he settled against the armrest to wait, sipping the ale that Zachary was so fond of. He found that it left him with a much clearer head than wine. Tonight he wanted to be as alert as possible. Everything was in preparation for what might occur. Zeus was saddled and tied in a stand of trees at the side of the inn, ready to give chase.

As he waited he mused over the lady's intrepidness. He would have to give her a few lessons in covert activities, however. She really should learn that servants and children couldn't always be trusted allies. Though he should be furious over what she was doing, he was elated that Celia wasn't going to meet a lover.

Thanks to his sister's maid, and the post boy, whom Celia had bribed, he knew that she was going to a place called "the pound" to meet her erstwhile highwayman. She had done fairly well in her plan. Under the guise of walking Madison, she had questioned the boy about the location where the man ordered her to meet him. Unfortunately, she had been careless on two counts. First, leaving the note out on the dresser in her room for Tess to retrieve, and then allowing Marcus to observe her talking with the boy.

Now as he waited in the dark he wondered if she was really naive enough to believe the dire wording of the note. The creaking of the stairs didn't allow him to dwell on the matter. As on the night before she was using the main stairway, which was fine with him. He drained the last of his tankard and got to his feet just as she came into sight. As she tiptoed to the front door he slipped out the back, where he could easily

get to Zeus's hiding place while she retrieved her
brother's mount from the stable. She had given the
boy a crown to have the horse saddled and ready.
Marcus wished, not for the first time, that he had
taken that confounded fifty pounds away from her the
moment he knew she had it.

As he mounted, he wondered what she would have
done if mist had already settled on the unpredictable
landscape tonight. The innkeeper had been full of
tales about travelers getting lost in the dense white
stuff, never to be seen again, no doubt falling into one
of the countless bogs and marshes. When Celia
passed him seconds later he was relieved to see that
she was staying on the roadway.

He stayed well behind her, knowing she was going
about four miles down the road before turning off for
her rendezvous. Thanks to the boy's directions to the
walled stone structure the locals called "pounds,"
Marcus knew where to leave the road so he could
head her off. The place had been built in prehistoric
times and seemed the perfect spot for a clandestine
intrigue with a gullible young lady. What he didn't
understand was the purpose of the meeting.

The path the boy had told him about was easy to
find. He reached the point where the tracks crossed
long before Celia was in sight. She was looking over her
shoulder as she came abreast of his hiding place. With
her back to him it was almost too easy, he decided,
moving forward and sweeping her off her horse.

In her surprise, she didn't struggle immediately.
This allowed him to set her feet on the ground and
dismount himself before she reacted. He had her
clamped to his chest with his mouth silencing her
scream before she could expel the sound. For a

moment he allowed himself to the savor the taste of her sweet lips, delving into the honeyed interior of her mouth. Once he released her he wasn't sure if she would let him touch her at all.

He was gratified by her response. She stiffened at the first touch of his lips, then seemed to almost collapse against him. She wiggled against him in the most provocative manner until she managed to work her arms free to clasp them around his neck. He was almost sorry she stopped that particular movement. Then the touch of her restless fingers on his neck and shoulders made him forget his regret.

Reluctantly he raised his head, uncertain about how much time had elapsed. If they continued much longer he would take Celia right here on the woodland trail and be damned to the highwayman. He feathered kisses across her soft cheek until his mouth was level with her delicate earlobe. Nibbling on the tender flesh, he delayed the moment of revelation for a few more precious seconds.

"We are going to keep your secret tryst," he whispered, "then I'm going to take you over my knee and give you the spanking you should have had years ago."

Halfway through his delivery she stiffened and began pushing against his chest. "You arrogant, sneaky, overbearing—"

"Ah, you must care if you're insulting me," he declared, grinning at the outraged look on her face. "We don't have time for any more love words now, sweetheart. Your swain will be with us any minute. I want to observe him before he knows he has more company than a susceptible female."

"Marcus, so help me—"

"My sweet, that is exactly what I'm trying to do.

Your wall of stone is just up ahead." He grasped her shoulder and turned her in the right direction. As he urged her forward, he checked to see if the horses were where he expected.

Both mounts were standing quietly by the trail, waiting patiently for him to come to them as they had been trained on the Peninsula. If only he could do the same with Celia, instruct her not to go more than a foot away if he fell out of the saddle. The image that came to mind at the thought made him groan with need. Then the erotic notion of their coupled bodies was replaced by the more practical wish that just once she would obey a command.

The stone pound was an odd structure, almost like a primitive stock pen of stone slabs. Though it wasn't nearly as imposing as the stone ring near Salisbury, the shadows cast by the dim moonlight where somewhat eerie. He could see why the boy was nervous about his questions concerning the place. The locals probably kept well clear of it at night.

"Marcus, you can't stay here. You'll ruin everything—"

"Do you really think he knows anything at all about Ethan?" he ruthlessly cut into her harried whispering, keeping his voice low. "I don't know his purpose, but I'm damn sure he doesn't know anything about your brother. I do want to know what his game is, however, so listen very closely to what I tell you to do."

Some fifteen minutes later he was satisfied they were ready to receive the gentleman, despite Celia's continued protests. Marcus had an excellent view of Celia's angry pacing while he stood concealed nearby in the shelter of the overgrown thatch of trees, within easy striking distance. He hoped she remembered his instructions to avoid standing between him and the man. All his plans would be useless if the man used her as a hostage.

The noise of the man's approach was very telling: He made no attempt at stealth. When Marcus turned to check what Celia was doing he almost gave himself away with a groan. He should have anticipated that she would embellish his directions for her to distract the man. At the moment she was seated on a large boulder with one shapely leg crossed over the other at the knee. She had pulled up the hem of her skirt and cloak to expose her stocking-clad calves to the night and any curious onlooker. What on earth was she doing?

"Have ya come alone?" the man growled, dismounting in the clearing before Marcus could do anything to deter the dratted female from her wanton posturing. The highwayman still concealed his face with a scarf and the wide-brimmed hat. He fixed his gaze on her clocked embroidered stockings.

"Of course I have. You said I would never hear from Ethan again if I didn't follow your instructions. I couldn't endanger my brother's life, now could I?" She looked up impatiently for a moment, then bent down and reached for her ankle. She seemed more preoccupied with the ribbon lacings of her leather slipper than with her ominous companion. "Don't just stand there, you lout. I've gotten a stone caught in my shoe, and now I've managed to get a knot in the ribbons. This position is so awkward for me."

Marcus watched the man walk forward, licking his lips in anticipation. When Marcus was through with her, he decided she wouldn't be able to sit for a week. Due to his irritation he didn't realize at first that Celia had the man positioned perfectly to be apprehended.

The scoundrel's back was to him as he knelt down to take her foot in his hand.

"What happened to your friend from this afternoon?" she asked, looking over his head directly at Marcus. Her expression was a mixture of outrage and anger, but he wasn't sure who it was directed at. The sudden jerk of her head and her compressed lips quickly told the story. He wasn't the only one who wanted retribution for this little drama.

"He got too drunk ta sit his horse."

In three strides Marcus was behind the brigand, his pistol pressed against his neck. "Now, my friend, why don't you tell us about your interest in Ethan Tregaron."

Celia promptly dropped the hem of her dress and cape, and kicked the man's hands away in one neat movement. She stood up and skipped to Marcus's side while the man kneeling on the ground cursed a blue streak. As Marcus sidestepped in front of her to keep her out of harm's way Celia gave vent to her frustrations. "Couldn't you have moved a little faster? Did you want me to sit and make small talk for an hour or so before you made yourself known?"

"Not now, Celia," he hissed, never taking his gaze from the hunched-over form in front of him. "Place your hands behind your head and move very slowly. Even if you have a weapon, you'll be dead before you can turn around."

The man seemed to respect the authority in the warning. His hands came into view almost immediately, and he followed the instructions to the letter. "I don't know nothin', yer lordship. I jest do whot I been paid ta do."

"You know who my companion is and that I have a title. So who gave you your information and why?"

The latter was the real mystery as far as he was concerned. Why would anyone bother with such nonsense the night before Ethan was to be released? What purpose did it serve? Or, more to the point, what person did it serve? "Someone hired you to lure Miss Tregaron here with that ridiculous but very literate note, which I don't think you wrote."

"He jest told me ta grab the girl. I get the rest of me money after I snatched her."

"Who told you?"

"I don't know, jest a man in a big heavy cloak. He walks up ta me at the Blue Boar and asks iffen I wants ta earn some brass," the man sniveled, half turning to direct a pleading glance at Celia. "I didn't mean ya no harm, miss, jest tryin' ta gets a few coins to rub together."

"Apparently he knows nothing of any value," Marcus said in disgust, relaxing his stance. "Celia, get that rope on Zeus's saddle. We'll tie him up and take him back to the inn."

"Whot ya goin' ta do with me, yer lordship? I didn't do nothin', really." The prisoner became more servile with every syllable. Marcus could almost picture this fool throwing himself at his feet and begging for mercy at any moment. That would be all he needed, a crying petty thief.

"I'm not going to worry over the matter," he replied, stepping back as he heard Celia's approach with the horses. "I'll let the local magistrate deal with the matter of your attempt at kidnapping a respectable—"

The man was on his feet just as Marcus glanced over his shoulder to see what was keeping Celia. Though Marcus was much larger than the underfed thief, the man pushed against him, throwing him off balance and knocking the pistol from his hand in the process. For good measure he grabbed Celia as he ran passed her, pushing her toward Marcus before he sprinted for his horse.

As Marcus tried to untangle himself from Celia he spied the man jumping onto his horse and grabbing the reins of the other two mounts. Just as he considered letting her fall to the ground the highwayman wheeled around and leveled his pistol at them. Acting on reflex Marcus shielded the woman in his arms, but no shot was fired. He realized his mistake too late, looking up to see the man disappear with his horses into the gathering mist.

"Damn, we should have discovered where the rascal was going to meet his employer and apprehended the whole lot of them."

Marcus looked down at Celia's frowning face. He didn't trust himself to dignify her observation with an answer.

14

"Well, I suppose we have a long walk back to the inn," Celia exclaimed in the most cheerful voice she could muster. The muscles of Marcus's arms and shoulders felt like granite under her hands. Even in the dim light she could see the grim lines of his scowl. Just what would he do if he actually lost his temper? What would she do? Her racing heart, still beating rapidly from their encounter with the highwayman, didn't lessen its speed at the thought.

"Do you think we're actually going to venture more than five feet from this spot until daylight?" he asked, each word carefully pronounced. She wasn't sure how he could speak so clearly without moving his lips.

"We're not going back to the inn?" she asked, more to cover her confused emotions than anything else. They were finally alone together with no one likely to interrupt them for hours. What an ideal situation, if only he didn't look as if he detested the very sight of her. She took what comfort she could in the fact that he was still holding her in his embrace. "We can't possibly stay here tonight, milord. We can simply walk along the same road that I followed here. That shouldn't be so—"

"Look behind you, Celia. Tell me what we should do."

Reluctantly she stepped out of his arms, not turning in the direction he ordered. Instead she mutely studied his handsome face, looking for some softening in his demeanor. If she thought she could coax him out of his inflexible attitude they would have a chance for an interesting night. How often in the past had she longed for someone to share her adventures? Not that she ever envisioned one of the dictatorial males in her life being such a companion. Of all men, however, Marcus would be her first choice.

"Celia."

Obediently she turned away and almost gasped at what she discovered. The opening in the dense woods was no longer there. All that remained was a curtain of soft white mist, its opaque depths hiding anything it covered like a moving blanket. In her preoccupation with the highwayman she hadn't noticed the mist rising from the ground to close around them. She had seen the stuff swirling on the road during her journey but didn't think anything about it at the time. Now she understood Marcus's directive. They couldn't possibly find their way back to the inn. With a sigh she let go of the small hope that he had made the choice simply to be alone with her.

"I suppose you're going to rant and rave at me for coming on this foolish trek?" she asked, not wanting to face him yet. Her eyes stung for a moment, a clear indication that she wasn't fully in control of her emotions. She never cried except when she was angry, almost never.

"Will it do any good? I have a feeling you would turn around and do the same if the circumstances presented themselves." His exasperated tone began to give her hope, and Celia smiled softly to herself as he asked, "What possessed you?"

"I know it didn't seem logical, but we're so close to finally finding him, I couldn't take the chance." She turned to face him then, lifting her chin defiantly, waiting for him to begin a litany of her sins. Zachary could go on for an hour without pausing for breath. "If I were a man no one would have questioned my actions. You would have done the same if the message had been about Sylvia, wouldn't you?"

Marcus tilted back his head as if he were deliberating the pros and cons of the problem while studying the sky. When the silence went on for a good three minutes she couldn't stand it any longer. "You would have gone after her. I know you would. She is your only sister, so you wouldn't leave her in the clutches of some villainous knave."

"Villainous knave? Now I know the cause of this disaster," he accused, not concealing the laughter in his voice. "Mama has been feeding you those ridiculous novels of hers. You've cast yourself in the role of the threatened heroine."

"Just how do you know about threatened heroines? I've caught you out, milord, reading your mother's novels on the sly."

"Naturally I've needed to browse through one or two to see if they are fit reading for my impressionable young sister," he explained in a great show of dignity, busily straightening his cloak. "We shouldn't be standing here discussing nonsense. Since we're forced to stay here, I must see what I can forage for our comfort. Unfortunately our light-fingered friend wasn't as dim-witted as I thought. The supplies in Zeus's saddlebags would have been useful about now."

"What do we need?" she asked cautiously, watching with interest as he looked around the clearing. When he took off his cloak she couldn't imagine what he was doing until he began to stack kindling-sized branches in the center. "Are you going to build a fire here?"

"No, we're going to carry this bundle into the center of the pound, once I've determined it isn't inhabited by some other nocturnal wanderers. The stone walls should give us some shelter from the elements and keep whatever livestock nearby from stepping on us in the dark," he related matter-of-factly while covering the branches with the dark cloth. "Now for once please cooperate and don't move until I come back. Here is my pistol. Our one stroke of luck is it didn't misfire when he knocked it out of my hand, even if he took my powder and shot along with the horses. I'll be just on the other side of this wall, so you don't need to shoot anything, just call my name."

Mindful of keeping Marcus in an amenable frame of mind Celia obeyed his orders as best she could after he slipped through the opening between the granite slabs. She moved only a few steps back and forth from her original position to the pile of branches. Movement was necessary because she was nervous. The cause of her nerves wasn't the dastardly felon, who had escaped, but the man just a few feet from her. She was alone with Marcus, and not even the thought of her brother's anger in the morning could dampen her pleasure in the moment.

From the other side of the stone wall she could hear Marcus stomping around, muttering to himself. Was he thinking the same as she was? Would he finish what he had begun that night in the library? She shivered in anticipation at the memory of the feel of his lips brushing across her exposed skin. Would he go beyond a few fervent kisses and a nibble on her earlobe? Would he venture further?

What would it be like to lie in his arms, the barrier of their clothing gone, their warm skin pressed together? Her cheeks burned at the enticing thought, causing her to clench her hands as she longed to feel more than his taut chest muscles beneath her palms. Though her husband had bedded her, she had never been completely naked with a man. Only with Marcus had she been allowed the blissful occupation of running her hands over his hair-roughened chest. Until she had experienced Marcus's drugging kisses she had never once contemplated wanting to do such a thing. Now she longed for it.

"Celia."

She almost screamed at the sound of her own name, jumping in surprise to find Marcus standing directly in front of her. He frowned and seemed about to say something, then changed his mind. Shaking his head, he turned toward the bundle of his cloak and the branches. Almost to himself he muttered, "Now we'll see if I can remember some of my skills from the army. I haven't had to light a fire without a flint in some time, or with one hand."

"Oh, I have a flint with me, or I did." She began looking frantically for her reticule, which she had dropped near the rock where she confronted the highwayman.

The search gave her welcome relief from her wanton thoughts, since it was clear Marcus was far from contemplating a passionate night. "Here it is," she announced a moment later, holding up the satin bag that sagged under the weight of its contents. "I put some things in earlier that I thought I might need."

"I should have known you would come prepared," he returned, giving the pouch a jaundiced look. "What exactly did you think it was necessary to bring along? Perhaps a beaver hat to replace the one now laying mashed beyond recognition by the side of the trail? That was my favorite hat."

She chose to ignore his frivolous request and stuck to far more important matters. "Besides the flint box, I put in two pieces of candle and a packet of bread and cheese. You still have my pistol and my knife is back in Baltimore, but I have my blackjack."

He simply stared at her for a moment, shaking his head in disbelief. His burst of laughter was a surprise and a relief to Celia. Perhaps the night wouldn't be a total waste after all. "Let's get this wood into our chamber so we can get settled," he ordered abruptly, his amusement dying as abruptly as it began. "You'll need to carry one end, since I'm not as adept at this as I used to be."

Pursing her lips to keep from commenting, she bent to the task. Even with both of them working together, maneuvering through the narrow opening of the pound was awkward. Once inside the enclosure the dim light from the half-moon seemed to lessen. Marcus directed her to the center with a series of muttered commands until he was satisfied with the location. She dropped her end with more force than was necessary.

The man seemed much more fascinated with a pile of wood than with her. Once more all her bold planning seemed to evaporate when he was within two feet of her. While she mulled over the problem he opened his cloak and dumped the wood onto the ground. Only then did she notice what he must have done earlier. He had cleaned away the underbrush and debris from a circle of ground, apparently by dragging his feet around the area.

He kicked the branches into a misshapen pile, then held out his hand without saying a word. Celia was tempted to pretend she didn't understand, but thought better of it. She was already in enough trouble without acting like a sulky adolescent, so she handed over the flint box. Marcus knelt on one knee beside his makeshift structure, placing the box on the ground and bracing it with his boot. Resting his sling encased arm on his upraised knee, he struck flint to steel several times before the sparks hit the wood and caught fire.

When the blaze had blossomed to his satisfaction he got to his feet. Celia rubbed her hands over her arms, more to keep from reaching out to help him than from feeling cold. He didn't need her help anyway, she decided with chagrin, entranced by the sheer grace of his every move. What was it about this particular man that appealed to her every sensibility? Even when he angered or annoyed her she still found him attractive.

"Well, fortunately I wasn't as clumsy as I feared." Marcus didn't look her way, seeming preoccupied with shaking out his cloak. The leaves and bark must have stuck tenaciously, because he needed to repeat the motion several times before he was satisfied. "You would have had to display your woodcraft if my injured limb kept me from lighting the fire. Although I'm not sure I won't have to call on you for help later when—"

"Stop it, just stop it right now. I know I'm responsible for this mess we're in. I should have talked over the matter with you, I know, and planned an ambush for the man." The words just came tumbling out one after another, making her wonder if she would be able to stop now that her remorse had taken hold. "Zachary always says I don't think of the consequences until it's much too late. No matter what I should have done, I won't listen to you utter another word about your lack of skill because of your hand. Don't ever make light of your injury to me, as if it is something to be ashamed of. I won't have it, I tell you, not at all."

As abruptly as she had begun her tirade, she ended it. She clamped her hand over her mouth, appalled at what she had just done. Railing at Marcus like some harridan wasn't going to improve the situation. A man wasn't going to feel desire for a woman who screamed at him. Watching him closely, she wasn't sure what he would do in response, so when he stepped around the fire in her direction Celia quickly retreated a step, then another.

His longer stride made up for her faltering retreat, closing the distance between them with little effort. A second later he held her fast against him, his arm like a steel band at her back. She was conscious of holding her breath, waiting to see what would happen next, hoping for a miracle. He simply stared at her for what seemed like an eternity, as if memorizing every feature of her face. Finally he lowered his gaze to her mouth.

"Why don't you ever react like other women? Any other woman in the world would have made polite

comments, ignoring the fact of my worthless arm."
The warmth of his breath tantalized her as he spoke,
his mouth almost touching hers. She was tempted to
move the mere inch that would bring their lips
together, but she also wanted desperately to know
what he would say next.

"I'm not like other women in your world, milord,"
Celia managed to respond, trying not to reveal just
how he was affecting her. She knew in this moment
that the fate of this night rested in her reply, and it
gave her the courage she needed. "I don't think I'm
like any woman you'll ever meet. I rarely notice you
don't have two sound arms, unless you go out of your
way to remind me. Very few men of my acquaintance
have your dignified bearing, milord."

"I can't hold out any longer," he murmured, capturing her lips in a heated kiss. Once again she was
transported to an enchanted world of sensations created solely by his sorcery. It didn't matter that they
were marooned in the middle of the moors, sheltered
in a primitive structure and exposed to the elements.
Her world centered on him.

She knew that she would do whatever he asked of
her and would demand the same in return. If this was
to be the only time for them together, she was going
to make the most of it, she pledged as she threaded
her fingers through his chestnut hair. He was her prisoner as she drank from the intoxication of his mouth,
seeking the moist interior to duel with his tongue.

It wasn't enough anymore. Everything that had
gone between them before was only a prelude to this
moment. She would be satisfied with nothing less
than the total joining of their bodies, complete intimacy. Marcus stiffened slightly as she worked at the

knot of his sling. Then Celia trailed butterfly kisses across his cheek to nip at the lobe of his ear and he relaxed against her. She slipped the black cloth from around his neck and arm, tossing it aside.

He regained the initiative, untying the cord at the neck of her cloak; uncovering new territory to explore, his lips tracing an imaginary pattern on her neck downward to the primly buttoned collar of her slate blue gown. As he fumbled with the four buttons she wanted to tell him to simply rip the material in her impatience to feel his kisses against the skin that lay beneath.

Not to be outdone she began to feverishly work at the fold of his neckcloth, cursing Foster for his talent with the intricately arranged linen. As she labored Marcus teased her by running his finger over the bodice of her dress, though he had already finished unbuttoning it to the tucks just below her breasts. With a murmur of triumph she came to where the starched linen tied at his throat and pulled it apart to set upon the buttons of his shirt.

Only then did she discover she was thwarted by the garment itself, which had to be pulled over his head. In her haste she also forgot his waistcoat and his riding jacket. No wonder clandestine affairs were so difficult, she mused, if just removing clothing was so much trouble.

"Perhaps this will give you a moment to consider." Marcus grasped both her hands in his, holding her still and forcing her to look up. His solemn expression seemed at odds with his passion just the moment before.

Beneath her fingers she could feel the rapid tattoo of his heart. She didn't want to stop with only his neck revealed. "Consider what? That men's shirts should have buttons all the way down so they are easier to remove?"

"No, my sweet, consider what we are doing here. I've been half out of my mind with desire all evening," he murmured, raising her hands to his lips to press soft kisses against each finger. The action robbed her of any capacity to think at all, let alone sensibly as he was insisting. "Despite that, I'm aware that no honorable man deliberately seduces a guest in his house. Unfortunately, I don't want to think of honor when I'm with you."

"I think you gentlemen devise all sorts of strange rules and games to amuse yourselves. Women, on the other hand, know what is important, and that is to be true to oneself." She resisted the need to trace his lips with her fingers. If he was going to come to her it would be of his free will, not because she tricked him. "Though I haven't practiced the art of flirtation like your ladies of the *ton,* I'm not a child. You aren't taking anything that I'm not willing to give. In exchange I want nothing from you that you aren't willing to give."

He went perfectly still, making her heart sink in despair. Had she been too bold, too straightforward? Should she have been coy, playing the winsome maiden overcome by his practiced skill? Celia wanted to protest when he removed her hands from his chest. All her hopes and dreams of Marcus had come to naught on this lonely stretch of desolate land.

"I'll need you're assistance with my shirt, though I'm not allowed to speak of the reason." As he spoke he unbuttoned his waistcoat and stripped it off in one motion with his jacket. Both the soft words and his actions took her by surprise. He wasn't rejecting her as she had feared. Marcus wanted to make love as much as she wanted to.

"Celia, you haven't changed your mind? It still isn't too late."

She smiled to erase the troubled look from his face, an expression of doubt that she would cherish all her life. For once in his life Marcus Knowles, earl of Ashmore, lost the self-assurance that he normally wore like a shield. Her answer wasn't with words. She simply grasped the hem of his shirt and began slowly working the material up the length of his body, making sure she touched him as much as possible with each movement. His sudden intake of breath when her hands grazed his ribs made her prolong the process. Inch by inch she moved the soft linen until she came to his shoulders.

He had patiently allowed her enticing game until that moment. Abruptly his pulled his left arm from the sleeve, then freed the other arm and pulled her against his bare chest. As he pressed her hips into the cradle of his thighs she realized they were positioned as they had been the first night they met. This time the feel of his arousal didn't shock her at all.

"Come lie with me, my sweet," he murmured, trailing kisses down the side of her neck to explore the opening of her bodice. When he stopped just at the valley between her breasts she reached to run her fingers through his hair, almost afraid he would pull back. She was impatient for him to release the rest of the buttons that ran down the front of her dress. "Easy, love, we have all night. I wish this could be perfect with candlelight, a soft bed and a blazing fire to keep us warm. Instead we'll have an illustrious tumble wearing half our clothing."

"We have the fire, at least." Celia began an exploration of her own, following the line of his shoulder with her palm.

"May I escort my lady to her bed?" He didn't wait for her answer, but stooped to pick up first her cloak then his scattered garments. With a sweeping bow he directed her closer to the fire. In another courtly gesture he spread his cloak on the ground, then rolled his jacket into a pillow before taking her hand. As he kissed her hand he knelt at her feet and she quickly sank down beside him on the black superfine material that would serve as their mattress.

Once their lips met in a kiss of promise, their earlier urgency swiftly returned. Celia gloried in the primitive emotions of giving herself to this man and accepting his body into hers in such primeval surroundings. He skillfully removed her dress and chemise from her shoulders almost before she knew it. She cried out at the mere touch of his hand on her breast, his thumb brushing over the engorged peak.

Wanting more of the wild sensations he caused, she took his gloved hand. Though he tensed momentarily, he didn't stop her from removing the leather covering. With her gaze locked with his, she guided his hand to her other breast, pressing his palm to her skin and holding it there.

"Oh, Marcus, I never knew I could feel this way. I think I'm going to burst into flames at any minute."

"And I'll burn along with you."

The next moment they lay full-length on the ground. His lips replaced his hands on her aroused flesh. She cried out his name again as his tongue and lips teased and tasted her, taking her to another level of yearning that she had never imagined. Reaching out desperately to repay such an incredible gift, she stroked the taut length of his back. With restless movements she brought their lower bodies together, moving her hips against his instinctively, wanting to be closer still.

Marcus whispered wild, mysterious promises of what the night would bring as he covered her entire body with feverish kisses. The touch of his hand on the bare flesh of her upper thigh stilled her restive movements. She whimpered her demand when it seemed that he would move no further. His mouth covered her just as his hand delved between her legs, the feel of his fingers stroking her hot core heightening her every sense. She was offering him the very essence of her being from this moment in time. Nothing would ever be the same between them again.

Her hands were clumsy in her impatience as she worked the button of his breeches. Both of them gave a groan of satisfaction as she finally released him, cradling him for a moment in her hands. She knew from the increased pressure of his hand that he was as ready as she was for their joining. Quickly she slipped the material down from his hips.

A moment later he moved over her and slipped deliberately, inexorably, into her body. She arched against him to get closer, to intensify the sensation of being linked to this man. His kisses mirrored the movement of his lower body, taking her on a journey that had her spiraling upward toward the mist-covered sky until she was sure her body couldn't take any more. She begged him for more and pleaded with him to wait, all the while frantically caressing any portion of him her hands could touch.

Finally she gave into his fierce demand to let herself go, allowing the building heat that centered where they were joined to explode throughout her body. He cried out her name just as she called for him to hold her, keep her from falling. Clasped together in the most ancient embrace, they rose to the highest peak of completion, spinning out of control one minute, then slowly descending into a lethargic contentment.

"Sleep, my love," Marcus whispered later, possibly eons later. Celia had no conception of time anymore. All she wanted was to live in the here and now, not worry about the past or future. When Marcus started to move she began to protest, not wanting to release him from her embrace.

"I need to stoke the fire, my sweet," he murmured, brushing the damp tendrils of hair away from her forehead. Kissing her eyes closed, he promised to return as quickly as possible. She smiled contentedly, allowing him to go only after he kissed her.

From under the warmth of the cloak that he spread over her she watched him move around the fire. Once more she was struck by his agile movements, the firelight playing over his naked torso. Seeing him with all the trappings of civilization stripped away, she fancifully imagined him as an ancient warrior preparing for battle, to fiercely defend his home and family from all enemies. Though it was a selfish thought, she was glad he wouldn't be returning to war ever again. This was the man she loved, and she wanted nothing to harm him.

The realization that she loved Marcus didn't truly surprise her. Deep within her she must have always known from the moment he looked directly at her that night in his bedchamber. She never would have acted so boldly to attract his attention if her feelings hadn't been so deep. And nothing could alter them now.

For the first time in her life she was unequivocally in love, and with one of the most obstinate men in the world. She shivered as she remembered Marcus's talk of honor before they made love. What would that honor mean to him? She renewed a pledge she made years before; she would never marry without love again. Mild affection hadn't been enough to weather the problems of her marriage to Daniel. Her pride would keep her from ever making that mistake again. But if she was given the chance, could she turn away from this man?

At that moment Marcus turned and looked directly at her, as if he had sensed the intensity of her thoughts. She smiled and held out her arms. Tomorrow was going to bring back the reality of their lives and the difficulties that could arise between them. Tonight, however, she was going to take advantage of their time together. In the morning she would worry about what she would have to do next.

15

The solitary warble of a bird brought Marcus to consciousness. He continued to lie with his eyes closed, wanting to savor the moment before he acknowledged that it was morning. As the lethargy of sleep left his body he concentrated on the details of his contented position. The faint scent of roses filled his head, and he knew well its source. Nestled against his shoulder were the tousled raven curls of the beguiling female who had kept him awake half the night.

Even in his wildest fantasies he hadn't imagined the sensual journey they had shared in the dark of night. The most astounding discovery was the emotions and sensations that she could arouse merely by touching his right hand. At the moment she held it cradled between her own just beneath her chin. The act was innocent in itself, but far more moving than the fact that his other hand cupped her buttocks. He shouldn't be surprised at this extraordinary circumstance. The lady was unique in everything she did.

Unable to resist temptation any longer he opened his eyes to feast his gaze on the siren who had disrupted his life from the moment she leveled her pistol at him. In sleep she looked so artless that anyone who didn't know her would think she was a demure, guileless woman with the disposition of an angel. Only he knew her fierce, all-encompassing passion, he determined with a smile, remembering her demand that they make love at least once unhindered by their clothing.

She displayed a lack of inhibition that amazed and delighted him. No other woman in his life had such an effect, he thought, then dismissed the comparison, which somehow diminished what he had experienced with Celia. His thoughts wandered once more to the long, torrid night that had just passed. In a very businesslike manner she had tugged off his boots, then succeeded in astonishing him yet again by removing her gown with tortuous, tantalizing slowness. By the time he managed to struggle out his breeches he thought he would go out of his mind. Only sheer strength of will kept him from attacking her like some uncontrolled youth.

The mere thought of their lovemaking was arousing him at the moment. He bent his head and began waking his darling by kissing the half-moons of her thick sable eyelashes. Then he moved on in feather-light touches to her retroussé nose. He felt her stir in his arms, her nose wrinkling slightly as she frowned at his teasing exploration. Finally, as he saw a glimmer of emerald green from her slumberous eyes, he claimed her parted lips, slaking his thirst for her taste.

She pushed against his chest, only to snake her hands around his neck when he loosened his hold on her delicious body. As if he had all the time in the world he concentrated on her soft, full mouth, lazily dueling with her teasing tongue. He felt her smile against his lips as her fingers combed through his hair, setting off a frisson of yearning down his spine. Marcus started to raise his head, but prolonged the contact of their lips as long as possible. She sighed languidly the moment his mouth released hers.

Celia cupped the side of his face in her palm, laughing at the roughness of his skin against hers. "Good morning, milord."

He groaned over her insistence in using the bothersome title, though she had claimed it was an endearment. "Marry me, Celia, my sweet."

Both of them went still in shock at his precipitous words. He hadn't known he was going to utter the impassioned demand. From the stormy look on Celia's face she was more angry than amazed. Though he had spoken without thinking, Marcus knew that it wasn't just an impulse. After the night they spent together, he was honor-bound to marry her, even if he hadn't seduced her. An innocent night stranded on the moors would have had the same result. Their impassioned union sealed the matter.

"No."

All feelings of arousal fled his body to be replaced by outrage. Her unexpected refusal cut through him like the cold hard steel of a sword. She didn't allow him to consider his reaction for she was scrambling to her feet and presenting her naked back to him. The sight of her delicate shiver before she pulled her dress over her head made him aware of the early-morning chill for the first time. Or was the absence of her warm body beside his the cause of the sudden coldness?

"Is that all you have to say?" he finally asked after rising and pulling on his breeches. As he stomped his feet into his boots, undoubtedly ruining the fine leather, he noticed she peeked over her shoulder before turning to face him. Why the maidenly show of modesty now? he wondered, shoving his arms into his shirt.

"What else is there to say, Marcus?" The use of his name made him wince more than her condemning look. Would he ever hear the endearing "milord" again? "You demanded that I marry you, and I declined. That takes care of the matter. What have you done with my other shoe?"

He pointed behind her, allowing his shoulder to sag in defeat the moment she turned away from him. Didn't she know that they must marry? What kind of country was this United States she came from? Had the people there lost all sense of what was fit and proper when they rebelled against their mother country? A man of honor stood up to his responsibilities, he determined, muttering in disgust when he found he had buttoned his waistcoat wrong. As he impatiently rebuttoned it he tried to ignore the warning voice from the back of his mind that whispered an honorable man wouldn't have set out to seduce a guest in his house.

"Aren't you ready yet? I would like to get back to the inn before too many people are about." Celia stood a few feet away from him, impatiently tapping her foot as if they were late for a theater engagement. "Since it seems to be barely past sunrise, we could get back before anyone even knows we were gone."

"Why should that bother you? You don't see any need to conform to proper behavior," he snapped, jerking on the lapels of his coat in a show of temper. Lord help him, he wanted to take her in his arms and not release her until she gave in and accepted his proposal. To curb the feeling his searched out his glove and sling and shoved both into his pocket.

"Now you're going to lecture me on proper behavior. I should have known that you wouldn't let me forget how stupid I was last night," she said, making him wonder if she was talking about her impetuous journey here or their lovemaking. "I just don't want to answer a lot of foolish questions."

With that she began walking toward him, but his spirits plummeted when she stopped to pick up her cloak that lay at his feet. Once she wrapped the garment around her shoulders she walked past him. Snatching up his own cloak, he hastily checked to see if the fire was out, then broke into a trot in order to catch up with her. How did she do this to him? No one in his entire life had made him feel like such a sapscull.

By the time they reached the inn an hour later he was hot, dirty, and very out of sorts. Even the discovery of Zeus and Cronus tied to a tree a mile from the inn didn't lift his spirits. As they crossed the yard he decided once more to talk some sense into the irrational female. She must see that he was in the right. The grim set of her shoulders wasn't very encouraging, but he knew that he must make the effort. His honor was at stake, and perhaps his sanity.

"Celia, you have to listen to reason," he began, catching her arm to make her stop. She shrugged out of his hold, climbing the stone steps to the door without a backward glance. Undeterred, he was a step behind her through the door. The entry hall and stairs were as deserted as the yard, although he could hear noises coming from the kitchen at the back of the building.

"Now, will you marry me?" Marcus demanded, stepping around her to block her way up the stairs. For good measure he put his hand on the bannister as he mounted the first step. "I'm not moving from this spot until you give me a decent answer."

"Decent answer? You mean the answer you want to hear," she shot back, her hushed but indignant tone matching his. He knew if they were back at the pound she would be shouting at the top of her lungs, and so would he. "I will not marry a man just to salve his conscience or some misguided sense of honor. I married once for the wrong reason, but never again."

What could he possibly say to that, for Lord's sake? They would be marrying for perfectly acceptable reasons. He didn't know what else there was to say besides the obvious. "Celia, you have to see that your reputation will be ruined. You're my responsibility as long as you're a guest under my roof. I must do the honorable thing in this matter."

"You arrogant, blind, stupid man!" She gave him a look that he couldn't quite define. How could she be disappointed in his attitude? He was in the right. "I don't give a fig about your fancy friends' opinions. Remember, I'm an American citizen and will probably be long gone before any of the obsequious, groveling idiots of the *ton* even know about this debacle."

"Celia, you aren't being—"

"No one will ever know that we even left the inn if you would just shut your mouth and stop making so much noise. Then you wouldn't have to worry over your silly honor and my nonexistent reputation."

"Too late, I'm afraid."

Marcus dropped his head in defeat and slumped against the wall, a shudder of frustration going through him at Zachary's mocking words. Thanks to Celia's stubborn refusal to accept him she was now going to cause her brother to call him out. When had he lost control of his life to such an extent? Until this moment he hadn't realized what a shambles it had become. Here he was standing on the steps of a strange inn, pleading with the most annoying woman in the world to marry him one minute, then wondering if he could keep from being challenged by her brother in the next.

"Is someone going to explain this interesting exchange to me? I should also like to know why you both look like you've been rolling around in the stable." Zachary's questions finally broke the silence. When Marcus turned to face him, one look at the implacable expression on the other man's angular face made him wish he hadn't. Madison, sitting at his feet, looked equally disapproving.

"Oh, don't be a ninny, Zachary," his sister said, matching his sneering tone. She started up the stairs, pausing as she came abreast of Marcus to give him a scathing look. "Do I look like a woman who has been enjoying herself, frolicking on the moors with wild abandon, perhaps? Don't imagine that I relished being forced to share the company of some pigheaded nobleman for more hours than I would like to count. If he hadn't followed me when I went to meet the highwayman last night, then none of this would have happened."

"Highwayman? What's this?" Zachary caught her arm to hold her in front of him, succeeding where Marcus failed earlier.

From the bottom of the stairs Marcus attempted to speak, but found he couldn't seem to form the words. The whole scene had to be a nightmare. A man who was known for his coolness under fire, his unflappable finesse in any situation, his unperturbed manner couldn't be struck speechless by a chit raised in an uncivilized country. He was nonplussed by the events of the past few hours, or perhaps the past few weeks. They used to set wagers that he could bring a man to his knees with one bone-chilling look.

"It was really nothing, Zachary." Marcus listened as she dismissed the entire episode with her would-be kidnapper in a few airy sentences. From her attitude they might have gone off to a local assembly to dance the night away. Coming out of his dazed reflections he heard her parting words all too clearly. "I will state categorically to you both: I would never marry the earl of Ashmore, even if he had compromised me."

Suppressing the childish urge to fling back an ultimatum of his own, Marcus gathered his shredded dignity and rose stiffly from his reclining position against the wall, straightening his back until it would satisfy a sergeant major's parade-ground standards. Standing at attention, he waited as Zachary and Madison descended the stairs, not able to join in the other man's amusement.

"I suppose I should apologize for Celia once more," Zachary said, finally containing his laughter but smiling ruefully as he reached his side. "Come, I'm sure you need a good hearty breakfast after such an ordeal, if we can get some food at this hour. Speaking from experience, I know how annoying Celia can be in such uncomfortable circumstances. I'm sure she was pestering you every minute to resolve the mess she had created. She is a nuisance at times, but mostly she means well. Though she seems to have outdone herself with this trip to England."

With a firm grip on his self-control, Marcus managed not to flinch over the image of how Celia had pestered him throughout the night. "She just doesn't think before she takes action," he murmured more to himself than to his companion.

"Very true, and I've pretty much given up on counseling her on impulsive behavior," Zachary declared with affectionate malice. "Besides, she is a grown woman, and rarely listens to my advice if she can help it. The galling thing is she usually comes out of each scrap without mishap."

The strain was too much for Marcus. He couldn't stay in Zachary's cheerful presence another minute without blurting out what had really happened. How could such an open, accepting man have such a complex, obstinate sister? Muttering a hasty apology, he turned to go up the stairs and escape to the welcome oblivion of sleep. Maybe then he could deal with the lunatic Americans and the illogical workings of women's minds.

"Well, thankfully neither of you were hurt due to her latest escapade," Zachary called after him. "Once you've had a few hours' sleep everything will look much better. Come, Madison."

Marcus recalled Zachary's bracing words as they were escorted into the prison commander's office at the stroke of ten by the case clock on the stone mantel. Nothing looked any better as far as he was concerned. In fact, his life probably couldn't get much worse, he concluded from the rigid profile of the lady standing next to him. Her demeanor was as grim as the granite fortress that surrounded them. Other than giving him a chilly nod when she stepped out of the inn, she hadn't acknowledged his presence throughout the short drive to the prison.

"Ah, milord, this is an honor." The effusive greeting came from a short, rotund man standing behind a massive desk placed at one end of the tastefully appointed room. They might have been standing in the library of a country estate instead of a prison garrison. Their host, however, was not a country squire, but a prattling fool in an ill-fitting uniform. "Your missive yesterday took us completely by surprise. 'Tis an honor to entertain a heroic veteran of the Peninsular campaign. A noble conflict I wasn't fortunate to participate in, much to my disappointment. So this is quite an event. We don't get many visitors here, as you can imagine."

"The long journey here from America makes it somewhat difficult for the prisoners' families to visit them, I should imagine," Celia put in.

"Major Titus, may I present Miss Tregaron and Mr. Zachary Tregaron of Baltimore, Maryland?" Marcus smiled with what he hoped was a pretentious twist. The ingratiating man in front of him had to be placated until they had Ethan in their hands. Much as he disliked the necessity, he needed to align himself temporarily with the cretin to deflect any damage Celia's righteous anger might do. "I'm sure you understand both my guests are anxious to see their brother again after all this time. You have been more than kind in granting an interview so quickly."

"Yes, yes, I understand. A sorry business, what? Unfortunately we can't just let the rascals go willy-nilly, now can we?" Titus's smile was now so wide the lower half of his face seemed to be all yellowish, crooked teeth. He indicated the only visitor's chair for Celia, then wrung his hands as if he didn't know what to do next. Taking a deep breath he went on. "Would you like some refreshment while we wait for the clerk to bring Tregaron's file? Things have been as sixes and sevens ever since the riot, you know. Bad business, that, very bad business. We can't just let this rabble go, inflicting them on the innocent British population. There are precautions that must be seen to— Ah, Jenkins, there you are."

The opening of the outer door undoubtedly saved the man from grievous bodily harm, Marcus decided. If Titus hadn't stopped his chatter, he wasn't sure which of the three of them would have silenced him first. Even the usually genial Zachary looked as if he wanted to spit nails, though he had the presence of mind to keep a placating hand on his sister's shoulder. If he hadn't, Marcus was sure Celia would have been on her feet by now berating the dolt.

"Oh, dear, no, this is dreadful, simply dreadful. I don't know what to say about this extraordinary problem." Titus looked up from the paper the clerk handed him, starting at the menacing looks that were directed at him from the two Americans. Marcus schooled his features into a bland mask. Didn't the boor realize how his careless mutters were affecting his audience?

"I hope Ethan isn't seriously ill or injured?" Marcus inquired, gripping his cane to restrain his own violent feelings. Where had the army found this toad of a man? he wondered, knowing full well that half the army was populated by numskulls like this.

"No, no, of course not. At least I don't think so," he replied, holding the document in front of him like a shield. His hands were trembling as he looked at the three people before him. "You see, he isn't here any-more."

"*What?*"

Marcus quickly crossed the room to keep Zachary from attacking the hapless major. The look the large man sent him made him hope his companion was never truly angry at him. If providence remained on his side, Zachary wouldn't learn of his relationship with Celia until long after they were married.

"Why isn't my younger brother here, Major Titus?" Celia asked with surprising calm before Marcus could turn to deal with the matter. "And pray tell, where is he?"

"He was paroled last autumn to work on one of the nearby farms," he explained in a rush of speech that was almost incoherent. Warily he kept his eyes focused on Zachary's imposing form as he related the story. "He apparently was an exemplary prisoner, since he was allowed this privilege. The locals are hard to placate at times, you know, so we make special arrangements to keep them in line. We provide labor for the local farmers from a select group of prisoners, if the man is willing to sign his allegiance to the king—"

Marcus wasn't sure if it was Celia's gasp or Zachary's growl that interrupted the man. "Why wasn't any of this reported to the authorities in London?"

"I'm sure it was. I've only been here for a few weeks, so I have no idea what my predecessor did for sure, you understand." He shrugged helplessly, backing away toward his desk. Perhaps he thought it safer to have the bulwark of that piece of furniture between him and the unpredictable Colonials. "Apparently once the peace treaty was announced no one thought it was necessary to bring Tregaron back to prison. He should be grateful that he isn't still locked away with the rest of these miscreants. There's no telling when Whitehall will see fit to allow—"

"Where is Tregaron now?" Marcus didn't bother to soften the question. At the moment he felt like joining his two companions in gagging the cloddish excuse for a human being. He was more than ready to quit the place.

"Oh, here's the direction," the clerk said, scribbling furiously on a piece of paper without looking at his supposedly superior officer. Apparently the man had more sense than his commander, which wasn't unusual, but Marcus wondered if Titus knew how close he had come to having a crushing left delivered to his gaping mouth this morning.

Once the paper was in his hand, he signaled to Zachary with a jerk of his head that he was ready to depart. With no more than a curt nod to Titus he grasped Celia's elbow and guided her out of the room. None of them spoke as they returned to the coach and were driven away from the stone facade of the prison. Marcus remained silent after he gave the direction to the coachman, because there was nothing he could say. Even without Titus's pitiful display of filling the air with ceaseless chatter he would have kept silent.

"How dare they make him sign an oath to the king?" Celia snapped after the coach had barely gone a mile, startling both her companions. "Wasn't it bad enough that he was taken from his own ship, then carted off to prison?"

"Settle down, Celia. I don't like this business any more than you, but I would probably have done it myself to get out of that place." Zachary looked across at Marcus for some kind of support, his expression bleak.

"I would have signed the document declaring your independence from King George if I'd had to listen to the likes of Titus for long," Marcus said. The jest did the trick, although his companions' laughter was short-lived, however, and they soon fell silent again. Marcus knew that their emotions were running high, remembering too well the feel of Celia's trembling arm close to his side as they walked out to the coach. No one had expected the boy to have been released from the prison. Even the anticipation of finding him weak and sick wasn't as terrible as the fact of discovering him gone, just at the moment of the expected reunion.

Though the distance to the farm was short, the journey seemed interminable. None of them spoke again, as if afraid to express their thoughts aloud. What else could be said until they discovered what had befallen Ethan since he left the prison? One curious fact went around in Marcus's mind, a needed distraction from his own problems. The boy had signed his allegiance to the king. Was it more than an expedient way to gain his freedom?

The sudden halt of the coach was a relief, and he jumped to the ground without bothering to kick down the folding steps. His heart sank at the sight of the surrounding landscape. It was clear the stone cottage and the attached barn were abandoned. The door of the house stood at an odd angle while the windows had lost whatever material had covered them. A hole in the roof had been neglected for months.

"Here now, whot ya want?" shouted a surly voice

from behind him. A burly man stood behind a hedgerow that divided the farm yard from the grazing land. Sheep chomped on the sturdy grass without the least interest in their surroundings.

"I'm looking for a man named Holloway. I was told he owned this land and had a worker from the prison." Marcus walked toward him, not sure of the man's reception, but wanting answers quickly. "We're looking for Ethan Tregaron."

"Whot ya want with young Ethan?" the shepherd asked, taking in Marcus's riding attire and not liking what he was seeing.

"Do you know my brother?" Celia's breathless question brought about a marked change in their reluctant host. He snatched the broad-brimmed hat from his head, hastily flattening his hair with his hand. His widened eyes never left her face as he completed his grooming and held his hat over his heart.

"We've come to take him home. Please can you tell us where he is?"

"Oh, milady, I can't rightly say. Me cousin, ol' Holloway, he curled up his toes around Christmastide, it be," the bluff yeoman stuttered, rubbing his free hand against his smock. "Ther widow's been gone these four months or so, and I ain't seen Ethan since then."

At her small sound of distress Marcus wanted desperately to take Celia in his arms, but Zachary was there to perform the service. The other man led her back to the coach as Marcus considered his next move. He wasn't going to be thwarted at this stage of the game. Somehow, some way, he was going to find Ethan for Celia. The Herculean task might just be the key to breaking down the barriers she had erected between them that morning.

*   *   *

"Well, where is he? What have you done with young Ethan?" Lady Knowles demanded the moment they stepped into the private parlor at the inn. She sat in regal splendor at the round table in the center of the room, sharing what appeared to be both breakfast and luncheon with Sylvia and Thaddeus. "Don't tell me you bundled him off to the sickroom without so much as an introduction."

"Celia, what is it? You look so pale," Sylvia said, her perceptions much sharper than her mother's. "Come, sit down and have some wine. You as well, Zachary. You both look in desperate need of a restorative. Now, Marcus, what is amiss?"

He all but fell into the seat next to his mother. Once he sat down he was astonished at how weary he felt, and it wasn't simply reaction from sleeping on the ground the previous night. His spirit was drained as well. "Ethan wasn't at the prison. He was released on parole months ago."

"Good heavens, Mr. Abernathy, have a care. You've spilled mutton stew all down your shirt and almost splattered my best swansdown muff." Lady Knowles sniffed in outrage over the accident as she brushed her linen napkin briskly over the man's shirt. "Now, sir, behave yourself so I can concentrate on what Marcus is saying. It might be important."

His mother's nonsense, accompanied by Abernathy's bewildered look, wrung a smile from Marcus. "We went to the farm where Ethan had been working, only to discover his employer died months ago. The man who took over the property has no idea where Ethan went."

"So, what are you doing here sitting idle? Why aren't you out scouring the countryside?" his mother demanded before nibbling on a jam-laden muffin.

"I haven't been idle at all, Mother. I've already sent John Coachman and Foster off to make inquiries, since we apparently won't be setting out today," Marcus said, looking expectantly at Celia to see what response he would get. His reward was the flash of her emerald eyes directed at him for the first time in hours. "Celia, you must be sure to thank my valet very prettily for his efforts when he returns. Though such menial tasks are beneath him, she felt this was an exception to the rule."

"Well, I refuse sit around this dreary place looking at long faces all day. It simply won't do," Lady Knowles declared. She wagged a slender finger at Celia, who sat directly across from her. "This is only a minor setback, my dear. I demand to see a smile. Ah, that will do for the moment, I suppose. It's disappointing not to have our invalid to nurse— Oh, dear, now I suppose he won't be sickly after all."

"We'll think of something to make up for it, Mama," Sylvia put in with practiced patience. "Perhaps we had better find you a lame horse or a dog about to whelp in the meantime."

"In the meantime is exactly what I'm talking about. Didn't that funny little man in the hallway mention some haunted ruins?"

"Haunted ruins?" Celia exclaimed, giving Marcus an accusing look. He wanted to deny that he knew anything about such foolishness, but his mother forestalled him.

"Don't look so worried, my dear. He assured me that no spirits or ghouls are around in the daytime.

They come out at night with the mist," she continued, unwittingly causing her young guest further discomfort. "Not far from here are some pagan villages and stone circles. Since Marcus refused to let us stop in Salisbury, he can hardly deny us this treat."

"Really, Lady Knowles, I would much rather stay here until Foster and—"

"I won't hear of it. You'll sulk and fret in your room. A good dose of fresh air is what's needed for us all," the lady commanded and rose to her feet. "Now, Marcus, go tell that round little person we want to take the pony cart he offered along with the guide. We leave in twenty minutes, and no excuses from anyone."

"So, the culprits return to the scene of the crime," Marcus murmured, bending as close to Celia's ear as her damned bonnet would allow him. They were standing on a small hill overlooking a dozen or so huts formed in a crescent; beyond them were several stone pounds. If he wasn't mistaken, last night's shelter was the farthermost to their right. Another hundred yards or so last night and they could have sheltered in one of the huts, though half the dwellings were missing large portions of their roofs and walls.

"Hush, someone will hear you. Zachary could be fooled once, but not again if you keep making snide comments." She stared straight ahead, as if he would go away if she didn't look directly at him.

"I'll promise you two things, my dear. First, we are going to find your brother, if I have to bankrupt myself to do it," he stated with conviction, since the search had practically turned into his personal quest. "The second may not be to your liking, but I mean to marry you."

"I told you I'll not marry again. I've discovered that I like my freedom, such as it is with my family always lecturing." He might have been convinced if she hadn't started worrying the seams of her glove with fretful fingers. When Celia fidgeted, she usually wasn't telling the truth. "In just over two years I come into my shares of the company. I won't need any male dictating to me then. I'll set up my own household and do as I see fit without anyone ordering me around."

"I'll make you a wager, my sweet. You have to grant me a single request to keep me from proposing to you every minute we're alone."

"A single request? Probably something so disagreeable that I'll refuse, and you'll still have your way," she charged, finally turning to face him. The shadow of the curved bonnet brim still kept her features partially concealed.

"Just tell me what was so horrible about your marriage that you won't consider trying again." He was going to get to the bottom of this final mystery if it was the last thing he did. Her refusal to take a second husband would make some sense if she had hated her first. By all appearances, however, she held no animosity toward Daniel Sloane, and neither did her brother. What could it be that had made her so adamant?

"It wasn't horrible. I've already told you that there is nothing to tell," she answered, her head lowering so she was looking at his feet. Now he knew that something was amiss. He had noticed her habit of studying the floor whenever she was uncomfortable. "You know that Daniel was the son of my father's partner. He was someone I knew all my life, and when our parents suggested the marriage, I found nothing in him to dislike. We were married on my eighteenth birthday."

He had to resist the temptation to lay his hands on her to prompt the rest of the tale. The rest of the party wasn't far off listening to the innkeeper's son weave some farrago about ancient warriors. "There must be more than that."

She gave a great sigh. Was it in annoyance at him or despair over her memories? "There really isn't much more than that. A few months after the wedding Daniel was given his first ship and headed for the West Indies. On the return trip he was killed during a storm while trying to save the first mate's life. So you see, there isn't anything mysterious or horrible about my brief marriage. Contrary to the masculine opinions in this world, a woman doesn't have to marry to be content."

"I wasn't thinking of contentedness in terms of our marriage," he said, placing his fingers under her chin and stepping closer. With her face tilted upward he could see her expression clearly in the sunlight. "I was thinking more of ecstatic afternoons making love in the woodlands and passionate nights before a blazing fire. Can you have that without marriage?"

"I have already, haven't I?" she shot back, trying to pull out of his grasp. It was too late; he had already seen the darkening of her magnificent eyes in response to his words. "Now I've answered your question, and I demand to ask one of my own."

He quirked one brow as he considered the matter. "Tell me the question with no conditions attached."

"You don't give me the same privilege as you, I see, but such is life." Celia looked squarely into his intense gaze, never blinking as she made her request. "I want to know how you injured your arm."

"I'll be more than glad to tell you, my sweet," he murmured, and after taking a quick look over her shoulder, brushed his lips against hers. "I will tell you on our wedding night."

With that he stepped back, feeling better than he had all day. He still suspected Celia wasn't telling him the true reason she was avoiding another marriage. There was a piece missing in the puzzle, but he was going to find it. He hummed under his breath as he ambled to join the others.

Marcus's good humor had returned the moment Celia began twisting her gloves. As illogical as it seemed, he was delighted that she was still lying to him. If she came out with the complete truth, he would reason that she was totally indifferent to him. Only a woman whose feelings were deeply involved would bother to lie.

He also realized something that she didn't. His promise had only been not to propose. That didn't mean he meant to stop pursuing her.

16

"I wonder what Marcus is plotting."

Sylvia's quiet statement took Celia by surprise after a long interval broken only by the soft mutterings of Lady Knowles and Uncle Thaddeus's gentle, whistling snores. The pair were once more dozing for lack of any other entertainment on the second day of their journey back to London. Since no additional news of Ethan had been unearthed, the travelers agreed that nothing further could be done in Princetown. Once they were back in the city, Marcus proposed hiring a Bow Street Runner to renew the search.

"What makes you think he is plotting something?" Celia asked, wondering if Sylvia could possibly know about her late-night escapade on the moors. Though Zachary made occasional teasing remarks, she was sure none of the others were aware that she had spent the night alone with Marcus.

"He is smiling so frequently, for one thing. Oh,

maybe I'm imagining it, but he has a certain air about him that reminds me of when he and Garth were down from Oxford. They would pull the most dreadful pranks." She nodded out the window to where Marcus and Zachary were riding in erratic circles. "Look at him now in that open field. The pair of them playing with Madison like two schoolboys."

"I suppose they are bored with riding beside the coaches and are taking advantage of the first open ground." Celia kept her gaze directed on the woods in the distance, not wanting to focus on that infuriating man at the moment. She was tempted to reach up to touch her lips, which seemed to still feel the imprint of his possessive kiss not two hours ago. "We've come quite a distance today. Perhaps they're giving the horses their last run before we stop for the night."

"If I never see this coach again it won't be too soon. Thankfully Marcus allowed us to stop more frequently on this leg of the trip."

Celia wasn't sure their additional rest stops were out of consideration for the bored travelers. For the past two days Marcus found every opportunity he could to touch her, steal kisses, even caress her intimately whenever possible. She never knew when or where he was going to strike. Just this morning he had fondled her breast under the guise of helping her with her cloak. He then managed the impassioned kiss at the last stop when she was standing on the far side of the coach, out of sight of the others.

One minute she was bending down to adjust the tie of her slipper, the next she was startled by a familiar hand moving suggestively over her buttocks. When she stood upright she found herself wedged between the side of the coach and Marcus. He didn't say a word, simply yanked off her straw capote. Before she could protest his mouth was on hers, his tongue thrusting within to devastating effect while his body moved suggestively against hers. Though the embrace had taken no more than a minute or two she felt thoroughly ravished when he stepped away with a satisfied smile.

"Are you feeling all right, Celia? You look terribly flushed."

Sylvia's concerned query interrupted Celia's remembrance of how quickly her body had reacted to Marcus's impassioned ambush. "I feel fine. I probably just need some air. Perhaps you can find a fan in your mother's case. The coach can be a little confining at times, but I think we'll be stopping for the night soon."

Marcus's sister thought he was plotting something, but what was it? Celia felt his gaze on every move she made, but the look wasn't of an amorous nature; instead, he seemed to be calculating what she was thinking. Though he bedeviled her with his amorous forays, he kept his word and never once spoke of marriage. In fact, she suddenly realized he had barely spoken to her directly since the afternoon they went to see the primitive ruins. What did it mean?

"Oh, I've just had the most famous idea," Sylvia exclaimed as she burrowed in her mother's traveling case, disturbing Thaddeus in her agitation. "Nothing, sir, just go back to sleep," she said in a soothing voice, stifling a giggle before continuing in a softer tone when he obeyed her command. "I think we're close enough to make King's Rest in a single day from here. Wouldn't it be lovely to spend a few days there and break the journey? Marcus can send a messenger to London for his investigator, and we would be closer to Princetown if it turns out Ethan is still somewhere in the area."

"We'll have to see what your mother and Marcus have to say," Celia answered weakly, not thrilled with the idea. London not only represented another starting point in searching for Ethan, but also a safe haven for her. In the social activity of the season she thought to deflect some of Marcus's allure, but in his own home with so few people around she would be at his mercy.

"You know, I've just noticed something else as well," her companion continued, leaning forward to peer more closely at their escorts. "Marcus isn't wearing his sling and glove today. How extraordinary."

Unable to resist, Celia followed her glance, looking directly at Marcus for the first time since their encounter by the coach. Her heartbeat increased at the magnificent sight he made on the black beast as he gamboled around the field with Zachary and Madison. He moved in perfect union with the horse, the motion emphasizing the grace of his lean, muscular body. She could hear the two men challenging and taunting each other in their sport. Sylvia was right, the sling and glove were gone. Marcus rode with his right hand flat on his strong thigh. She closed her eyes, remembering too clearly their night on the moor and the feel of both his hands pressed intimately against her skin.

She had fallen in love for the first time in her life, but couldn't accept his proposal, not for his reasons. What did she care about honor or other pointless masculine principles? If Marcus would declare one ounce of pure feeling for her, she might be persuaded to give in.

She had her pride, however, and knew how to preserve it when needed. Hadn't she told him the lie about Daniel for just that reason? After so many irrelevant lies about her life, what did another matter, even if it was the most important one? She could explain it easily enough to a man who loved her and no one else.

With a sigh she leaned back against the velvet banquette just as a strange popping noise sounded from nearby. She didn't need Zachary's shout to recognize the discharge after their encounter with the highwayman. As more shouts sounded from the coachman, the vehicle jerked to a stop. By the time she leaned forward, both men were galloping toward the heavily wooded area ahead of them. Absently she noticed that Marcus's beaver hat lay on the ground where he and Zachary had been a moment before.

Lady Knowles gasped, "What's going on? Are we there already?" The others picked up luggage and parcels that fell to the floor during the precipitous stop. "Why are we stopping in the middle of nowhere?"

"There was a shot fired and the gentlemen have gone to investigate," Celia informed her, ready to jump down from the coach just as the two men reappeared from the woods. They were riding slowly, both talking while her brother gestured to emphasize his point. "Here they come now. Zachary, what is going on? Was that a gunshot?"

"Nothing to be alarmed about, ladies," he called back, still several yards from the vehicle, waving in a reassuring manner that set her teeth on edge. He didn't, however, immediately approach. Instead he directed his horse to where Marcus dismounted to retrieve his hat.

"What *are* they doing just standing around out there?" Sylvia asked, craning her neck to get a closer look. Both men had dismounted now and seemed to be discussing the condition of Marcus's hat.

"I can't imagine, but if they don't come to us in a few minutes I'm going to find out for myself."

"Ah, no need, dear Celia. Here they come now, but I wager they aren't going to tell us what they've been talking about so earnestly," Lady Knowles said, busily straightening her bonnet that she just noticed had slipped sideways. "Men are always keeping secrets, whether the information is worth it or not. They do it just to make themselves feel superior."

"What has happened, Marcus? Did someone actually shoot your hat off?" Sylvia asked when the pair finally came close enough for a discussion that didn't need to be shouted.

"Just some hunter with a bad aim. He apparently ran off once he realized what he had done," her brother responded, exchanging glances with Zachary that seemed to confirm his mother's words. They probably weren't telling the whole story. "Coachman, drive on. We're only about ten miles from our destination."

"What did I tell you, my pets? A silly incident, but for some reason known only to themselves, they have to be mysterious about it. Marcus gets that from your father, Sylvia, I'll have you know."

As Lady Knowles continued to prattle about the vagaries of the male species, Celia looked across the coach at Sylvia. Raising her eyebrows in question, she was pleased to see her friend's enthusiastic nod in response. She agreed that this wasn't just some masculine diversion of their brothers. Something was amiss, and the pair of them were going to discover just what the two gentlemen knew.

By the time the coach rumbled to a halt in front of the inn, Celia realized that she was actually looking forward to the evening ahead. In fact, she felt much

better than she had since the moment Marcus had proposed. Whatever this minor intrigue was between
Zachary and Marcus, it gave her something to concentrate on besides her troubled emotions. Her annoyance also gave her a useful weapon to fight against
Marcus's attentions as well.

Celia spooned into her custard and fruit compote
with false enthusiasm, surreptitiously watching the
others around the table as she had throughout dinner.
Even if she hadn't already been suspicious of the two
men's actions earlier, one look at her brother would
have told the tale. Zachary was excited about something, almost brimming over with the need to tell.
Unfortunately, whenever he looked in Marcus's direction he seemed to temper his exhilaration.

"Marcus, you don't suppose that the shot today
could have been the same men who held us up?" Celia's
sally had a very satisfying result as her brother choked
on his ale. "I mean, you said yourself that you didn't
find anyone in the woods. If it had been an accident
wouldn't the man have stayed behind to apologize?"

"I'll put the question to you, my dear," he returned
too smoothly for her peace of mind. "If you were the
culprit, possibly, say, poaching on someone's land,
would you have stayed to make excuses to someone
you accidentally shot? He may not have realized that
he hadn't wounded me, for all we know. So, what is
your verdict?"

"A very interesting description of the events,
milord." Celia smiled, noting with pleasure the flare
of his nostrils as she used the form of address. Two
could play this game of subterfuge with any weapon

at hand. "I would agree I might not have the courage to face such consequences. After all, the king's justice can be very unfair at times, I understand. But the whole thing is still very curious."

"It is amazing what the female mind can conjure up out of nothing," Marcus murmured, idly picking up an apple and giving his whole attention to peeling it. "I suppose those hours with nothing to do in the coach have left you a trifle bored. If you like to make up these charming fantasies, who am I to say nay?"

Celia shot a look across the table at Zachary. She was about to ask his opinion when she caught his look of relief and admiration directed at his fellow conspirator. Her brother couldn't even be roused on the subject of British law. So they thought she could be fobbed off by some droll double-talk. Just for that, if not for a hundred grievances against Marcus, she was going to fight back. She could use persuasion to her advantage in a much more discreet manner, and she had her own allies.

"Lady Knowles, Sylvia was telling me the most delightful stories about your home at King's Rest this afternoon. Wasn't Henry the Eighth supposed to have stayed there at one time?" She smiled sweetly at her hostess before dipping her spoon into her compote again. That should be enough to bait the trap sufficiently, she decided with a sidelong look at Marcus. She needed the quietness of the country house to execute her plan.

"Why, I've had the most marvelous inspiration. I should have thought of this much, much sooner," the lady declared, her eyes sparkling with anticipation. She clapped her hands in delight and graced everyone with a beatific smile. "Marcus, tomorrow we're going to King's Rest instead of London. We'll take a repairing lease in the country for a few days before continuing on to London. 'Tis just the thing to restore our spirits after our recent disappointment. How perfect, how absolutely perfect."

"Just perfect," Marcus murmured, looking at Celia suspiciously. She simply continued to eat her dessert, nodding in agreement as the older woman expounded on how her American guests would adore the country retreat.

A half hour later she excused herself, making sure that Sylvia knew she was to accompany her. While her host may have plans to conceal what occurred that afternoon, she knew the perfect way to get the information she wanted. If Marcus wouldn't tell her, she had another means of finding out that he couldn't even suspect.

"Now, do you think I'm imagining things or not?" Celia asked Sylvia not ten minutes later as they sat before the fire in their small dormer room. "Something is terribly wrong about that incident this afternoon, I just know it. But those stubborn brothers of ours are being all noble and masculine, thinking we're too delicate or feebleminded, I suppose, to be given the truth."

"Without a doubt. Marcus was playing the genial lord of the manor to the hilt tonight," Sylvia said. She stood up, drawing herself to her full height, and lowering her voice to the proper timbre. "Ah, my dear Celia, may I tempt you with a morsel of partridge? Zachary, old man, a touch more ale to wash down that bit of salmon?"

"Oh, stop, please stop." She couldn't believe how exactly Sylvia mimicked Marcus, exaggerating his elegant style to the limit. Tears came to her eyes at the playful caricature.

Sylvia dropped back into her chair, giggling with abandon. "Yes, I told you earlier that he was up to something, and that was before our mysterious shooting. I know that toplofty expression all too well. It usually appears whenever he is telling me something for my own good, or lecturing me. Mostly he does it when I'm not supposed to ask any questions."

"Exactly my point; we have a right to know what is going on. He is playing the same trick he did in London, and I'm not having it," Celia asserted, wiping her eyes with the edge of her handkerchief. In her enthusiasm she leaned forward to take her companion's hands. "Now, I have a plan for these two crafty individuals. If you don't want to participate you don't have to, but I don't think you'll find your assignment too taxing."

"Now you've aroused my curiosity, but I warn you Marcus isn't going to let me cozen him into divulging any of his secrets."

"But it isn't Marcus you're going to question. You remember what I told you about Zachary being afraid of respectable women?"

"Oh, Celia." Sylvia's shining eyes gave her pause for a moment, making her wonder if perhaps her scheming was going to produce some unforeseen results. "This is going to be such fun. I can't believe that I dreaded my second season when we went up to London this year."

Celia relaxed at the show of enthusiasm for the game. Her friend was simply anticipating the adventure. It didn't necessarily follow that Sylvia would become infatuated with Zachary. After all, he was a rather rough-hewn American, who didn't have the polish of the gentlemen that populated the English girl's circle of friends.

"I think all you'll need to do is play on his vanity a little," she instructed, getting to her feet to pace the room while she outlined her plan. "He probably won't last more than a day, but don't overdo the flattery. You don't want to find yourself in the uncomfortable position of rebuking him."

"I don't think that will be a problem."

Celia turned to give her friend a sharp look, but dismissed her suspicions again. She had too much else on her mind at the moment. Sylvia was simply getting into her role with her usual fervor.

"What are you going to do about Marcus? Your brother seemed to be taking direction from him tonight on more than one occasion."

"Yes, I know. You leave Marcus to me," she said thoughtfully, crossing her arms over her breasts as she considered the matter. "Right now, I think I left my reticule downstairs in the parlor."

"But it is right over—Ohh." Sylvia's eyes widened as she understood what Celia intended to do. After a moment her face crinkled into a pretty frown. "Celia, don't underestimate my brother. He can be very dangerous to women, from what I understand. I overheard Mama saying once that he was positively lethal to the ladies when he put his mind to it."

"I don't intend for them to know I'm even there," she said as she headed for the door. As she made her way down the stairs she smiled at the irony of Sylvia's warning, which had come much too late.

Unlike the inn in Princetown, there was little noise coming from the public room, Celia noted when she reached the ground floor. Maybe she should consider writing a narrative for lady travelers about the various inns they had frequented on their journey, she mused as she tiptoed along the corridor to the parlor at the back of the structure. Though she wasn't sure how many of her sisterhood would need instructions on sneaking belowstairs, especially to eavesdrop on private conversations.

The door was ajar, which lessened her chance of discovery. As she moved closer, however, she didn't hear a sound coming from the room, not even her Uncle Thaddeus's distinctive snoring. What could the silence mean?

Had the gentlemen already retired for the evening? Surely not, for the hour was still early by a gentleman's standards. The only reason the ladies were expected to retire so prematurely was so that they might avoid rough company, or so they were told. She always felt it was an excuse used by the gentlemen so they might pursue more earthy entertainment without the encumbrance of respectable women.

Standing motionless by the door, she could hear only the sound of her own breathing. What should she do now—go upstairs and admit defeat, or conceal herself in the shadows of the hall to see what would occur next? Did she really want to know what pursuits Marcus and Zachary were about with their female charges safely off to bed?

"Did you forget something, my dear?" The masculine voice took her by surprise, causing her to whirl around ready to defend herself. "Perhaps this is what you wanted?"

Before she could manage to utter a word Marcus lowered his head, slanting his mouth over her parted lips. Like the kiss that afternoon, he was bent on staking his claim. She sank her fingers into the superfine material of his coat to keep her knees from buckling under at the impact of his need and possession. This was no gentle loving, but hot, burning desire that stormed through her, setting off shock waves of answering passion.

"Gad, Celia, some day you're going to be the death of me," he muttered, raising his head just at the moment she thought she wasn't going to be able to breathe again. Without saying another word he lifted her by a firm arm around her waist and carried her into the parlor. He kicked the door closed behind him, then set her on her feet, only to press her back against the paneled wood.

He stood looming over her, breathing heavily and giving her a guarded look, despite the desire glimmering in his stormy blue-green eyes. Celia waited for what he would do next, rubbing her palms up and down on the soft muslin of her dress.

"You needn't look so frightened. Much as I want you, I have a strong sense of self-preservation as well as a liking for your brother." He groaned when she only frowned at him in response. Shaking his head dolefully, he reached up and rubbed the back of his neck as if to ease some pain. "Although your uncle has been lured away by the rumor of smuggled brandy at a neighboring tavern, Zachary is only as far as the stable walking that hound of his."

"I didn't come down here for an assignation, Marcus," she managed to say calmly. "I thought I'd forgotten my shawl, but remembered I loaned it to your mother when I couldn't find it here."

"Very nicely said, my sweet, but it won't do. Your talents as a cracksman seem to be failing ever since your first effort in breaking into my house." She couldn't move forward or back from where he had her trapped. "Now why don't you trot back up to your room before I forget your oversized brother's imminent return or that there isn't a comfortable piece of furniture in this room? I've had just enough to drink tonight that I might consider making love to you on the table after all. Some day I look forward to the time you choose to visit my bedchamber when we aren't likely to be interrupted. Wouldn't you like to discover what pleasure there would be in making love in a bed?"

She knew a moment of outrage, but then had to smile at the harassed look on his lean face. In her anger over the past two days she had overlooked some very obvious signs. Despite his speeches about nobility and saving her reputation, he still couldn't keep away from her. Even though he promised not to mention marriage, he was still trying to seduce her. She wasn't sure of his purpose, but she suddenly knew what her mission would be during their stay at King's Rest.

She wasn't simply going to find out what he was trying to conceal about this afternoon's misadventure. Whatever had happened really didn't matter; she only wanted to know because she was annoyed he wouldn't tell her. There was something else that was far more important. By fair means or seduction she was going to show him that honor had little to do with their relationship. She was going to show the infuriating man that there was far more between them than a physical attraction.

"What is going on in that beautiful, crafty brain of yours, Celia? Something about that smile makes me very uncomfortable."

She suddenly became aware that she was grinning in anticipation of the coming days. "Marcus, you wound me when you say such things. You make me wonder if you really want me or not," she said softly. Very slowly and with the lightest touch she ran her palms up the front of his waistcoat to the fine lawn of his shirt and upward until she came to his shoulders, then kneaded his tense muscles with exaggerated care. "Just where is your bedchamber at King's Rest? It's not far from the guest rooms, is it? Your nights are much cooler than I'm accustomed to at home, and I wouldn't want to catch cold wandering the halls in a thin nightdress."

On the last whispered word she leaned forward, allowing the weight of her body to rest completely on his. Marcus had to brace his feet apart to keep them both standing. She could feel their heartbeats racing in tandem as she pressed her body provocatively against his, just as he had earlier that day. The proof of his need for her was hard against her abdomen, spreading new warmth through her already overheated body.

With regret she reminded herself of Zachary's proximity, wishing that she could undress for Marcus as she had that night on the moors. Instead she took what pleasure she could at the moment to savor until a more appropriate time presented itself. And it would, she would see to that. "Kiss me again, milord. I need the memory to keep me warm tonight."

She answered his groan with a murmur of approval as their lips met. The taste and feel of him was almost too overwhelming, but she remembered her goal. While she gloried in their physical union, she must teach him that there was more between them. It was difficult to remember that as his hand dipped into the square-cut bodice of her dress. His fingers sought and found her nipple, sending an arrow of heat to the center of her being.

The sharp edge of desire for once brought her to her senses and allowed her to pull away. With only the greatest strength of will she pushed out of his embrace. "Dream of me, milord."

She fled the room before she gave in to the temptation of staying and chance being caught by her brother. As she raced up the stairs she hugged to herself the last glimpse she had of Marcus's face. He looked as stunned as she felt. Perhaps he was going to be a more apt pupil than she anticipated.

When she reached the door of her room, she paused to collect herself before confronting Sylvia. She had to devise a story for her delay, one that didn't include playing seductive games with Marcus. As she thought it over, doubts of her success in winning his love began to overtake her. Was she pursuing a foolish dream? She wasn't going to know unless she tried.

Just a few short weeks ago she had faced him down the barrel of gun, never suspecting where it would lead. Since that first kiss, she knew her life had changed, and she wasn't going to back down now. She would never be able to forgive herself if she didn't at least try to find out if Marcus could love her. A smile crossed her face as she realized she was allowed to enjoy herself while she was making the attempt.

With that thought she opened the door and entered her room. She was going to need a good night's sleep to prepare for the first day of what could prove to be a very exhausting siege.

17

"*She knows, Marcus.* I don't know how, but she knows that the shot wasn't an accident."

Marcus opened his eyes reluctantly at the aggrieved words, focusing on Zachary's back from where he sprawled in his favorite wing chair in front of the study fire at King's Rest. He really wasn't up to the discussion at the moment. The decanter next to him had only an inch of deep red liquid left in it, and an empty glass dangled from his hand. If he had his choice he would probably drift off to sleep from the influence of the spirits he had already consumed, as he had the night before at the inn.

Zachary, however, had a head like a bull and not so much to forget. He seemed determined to figure out if there was a connection between the two strange episodes over the past few days. He didn't have ulterior motives or unfulfilled desires to keep him from that point.

"Zachary, you're letting your imagination run away with you, undoubtedly a family failing," Marcus murmured, still not ready to stir himself. His head lolled to the side of the chair for a better view of the other man's reaction, and when he didn't move, Marcus sighed. He knew he was going to regret this. "How can Celia possibly know what we suspect? We haven't even deduced why someone would want to kill you, if that was what was intended."

"That's the damnedest part. I don't know why anyone would want me dead," Zachary shot back, and began to pace the room. "Or are we imagining that there is some conspiracy? Those incidents in Baltimore I told you about could have been accidents after all. I'm not the most graceful fellow on this earth, so we could be looking for trouble where none exists. They seemed harmless until you started questioning me this afternoon."

"I might tend to agree that the railing on the stairs at the shipyard could give way from age or that stumbling in front a speeding carriage isn't unremarkable," he answered, resigning himself to rehashing their speculation once more. Until now they hadn't been able to fully explore the possibilities, carefully choosing their words in case they were overheard at the inn. Though on their guard while traveling to King's Reach, they had pieced together some startling facts.

"Those events in themselves aren't significant, but during the past six months you were knocked overboard twice and set upon by thieves. On top of this someone hired that idiot to kidnap your sister."

"We do have a problem, don't we?"

Marcus was amazed that a man of such massive proportions could look so defenseless in his bewilderment. Zachary stood in the middle of the room, his shoulders in a dejected slump as he looked to his friend for an answer to the puzzle.

"Celia doesn't know anything, despite your uneasiness, but is simply attempting to wear you down," Marcus reassured him. "That doesn't mean, however, that we shouldn't keep close watch on our two young ladies in case they make matters worse by trying to investigate themselves." He couldn't very well add the most telling point—exactly what occurred after Celia's last attempt to interfere. If she hadn't gone to meet the highwayman, then he wouldn't be brooding over her refusal to marry him. Damn the woman, why didn't she act like she was supposed to just once? Then his conscience, as well as his memories, wouldn't have to be drowned in a bottle, blast her. He also wouldn't be preoccupied with trivial emotional problems when he should be concentrating on the much more dangerous puzzle.

"She hasn't been pestering me at all today," Zachary admitted cautiously, still looking worried as he concentrated on the problem. "Though she didn't act as if she was the least concerned about the shooting today, I know she was suspicious last night at dinner. She has a certain smug look when she is trying to learn something she shouldn't."

"Which is why I am going to keep watch over your sister, and not you. She sees you as an easy target for her maneuvers," Marcus said without malice, still not bothering to move a muscle. Would Zachary question his logic in this? Or was it simply his imagination that his reasoning was somewhat lame? "You can practice your conversational skills on Sylvia, for you know my dear mama has plans to show you off to her friends once we are back in London again."

The large man made a sound that was a cross between a moan and a growl. "Maybe I wasn't so fortunate yesterday that you rode in front of me just as the shot was fired. A nice flesh wound would have put me in bed for a few days."

"Don't delude yourself, sir, you would have been in much worse shape," he returned, smiling at the man's terror over the possibility of talking with such harmless females as his sister and mother. "You would have been flat on your back at the tender mercies of my female relatives as they nursed you back to health. My mother is much more out of sorts that your brother didn't need nursing than she is over his disappearance from the prison. You would have been an admirable substitute."

"You don't suppose someone has done away with him, do you?" He forgot his apprehensions over the gentler sex at the thought. The question was telling, since he hadn't mentioned anything about his brother since they left the inn at Princetown.

"No, I think that we'll find Ethan safe and sound once we run him to ground," Marcus assured him readily. "Though I have no proof, I think the danger only began once you and Celia were both in England. Instinct tells me that your brother is probably the only one who isn't in any jeopardy at the moment."

"It still makes absolutely no sense. Neither Celia nor I have any enemies, especially in England, since we've never set foot in the country before this," the other man continued, beginning his pacing once more. Marcus envisioned a worn strip in the middle of the floor and wondered if he would have to replace another carpet damaged by a member of the Tregaron family. Fortunately Zachary ceased his activity abruptly. "I suppose we aren't going to solve this tonight. Maybe after a good night's sleep I'll think of some reason for these peculiar incidents."

"At least we're in agreement that the less said to your sister the better. The circumstances are bizarre enough without any added complications." Marcus allowed himself to smile at how neatly he had summed up the matter without revealing anything personal. "I doubt she could shed any light on the events, unless she has been receiving anonymous threats."

"Lord knows, I've been tempted to do away with my sister from time to time just from sheer frustration," Zachary acknowledged with a grin. "You have much more self-control than I do, and she hasn't had years of practice trying to wheedle information out of you. That may be why you've been more fortunate in your dealings with her. I wish you luck, Marcus, and good night."

Sheer frustration was as good a motive as any, Marcus decided, thinking over the many times Celia had provoked him into losing control. How would the man react if he knew how little self-restraint Marcus actually had once the tantalizing woman came within his reach? What would Zachary's reaction be if he enlisted his aid in securing Celia's consent to marry him?

He closed his eyes, trying to conjure the picture of a docile, compliant Celia Tregaron. The result caused him to frown. He needed her fire, her determination, and her passion to satisfy him. *Satisfy* was hardly the word for what she brought to him, whether they were arguing or making love. What they had was far more complex than anything he had ever experienced.

Until that moment he had never realized how he had simply been existing since his return from the Peninsula. He went through the motions, dressing as he should, attending the proper—and not-so-proper—

functions that society dictated. His dalliance with the charming Louise had simply been something that was expected of him. All that changed the moment a green-eyed Colonial vixen had leveled her pistol at him.

Damn, it would have been so much simpler if she had been one of his cousin's castoffs. What was he doing becoming involved with a respectable female? That was the rub. She had become his responsibility the moment his mother took her into the household, making him accountable for her well-being. Why didn't the blasted woman understand that it was his duty to marry her now that he had failed in his obligation? Since he had sacrificed his honor to possess her, this was his only path to redemption.

A whisper of sound reached deep into his troubled ramblings. Opening his eyes, he saw a blurry figure in white floating toward him across the room. He dismissed the instant thought that some unknown specter had suddenly taken to haunting the house that had once been part of an abbey. This was no disenfranchised monk that the robust King Henry had cast out in revenge against the church. No one in this world, or the netherworld, could move like his Celia.

It seemed fitting that she pursued him into his dreams. "So, sweet witch, you've come to disturb my sleep once again. Don't you torment me enough during my waking hours?"

The warm touch of her hand surprised him as she removed the glass from his hand and knelt at his side. "You need to come to bed, milord. You need your sleep."

"What an enticing command, my dear, but I doubt I would sleep with you beside me. That last night we spent together was sadly lacking in rest, as I recall."

"I wasn't suggesting that I accompany you. Your

mother would be appalled if she found me warming your bed. I'm sure she has much more ambitious plans for you than a plain American widow."

"Hardly plain, sweet, tormenting Celia. Strange—I think I've become accustomed to the abominable style." He ran his hand through her dark curls, remembering all too well her long tresses. "As for my mother, she knows that I'll marry when and whom I will. Her standards aren't as lofty as you think, since she was a local squire's daughter who married a simple baronet for love, not for position or wealth."

After his observation she went still under his caressing hand. "Perhaps I have misjudged the situation, milord. From what I've seen of the *ton*, love is not much in evidence."

"It's an elusive emotion at best," he replied indifferently, more interested in the soft skin at the base of her neck. "I much prefer you in this mood, Celia my own. Is this the night you'll tell me what you want from me?"

"I don't think you would remember if I did. I'm not sure you'll recall that I was here in the morning."

He thought he heard amusement in her hushed voice. "What about tomorrow, then? Shall I sweeten the request with a reward?"

"Though I shouldn't be tempted by a bribe, I'm not foolish enough to refuse without knowing the prize." She enticed him further by kissing the palm of his hand as he caressed her cheek.

"Ah, if I had the strength tonight to accept your first invitation, my sweet."

"You've strayed from the point at the most interesting moment, milord. What is this reward for my submission?"

"Not submission, never that. I need to know what

keeps you from accepting me." Marcus knew instinctively that she had to understand his meaning. Why, he didn't know, but it must be made clear. "If you grant my wish I will show you a secret place that should be shared only by lovers. There is no submission or surrender between us, my love."

"Yes, that is exactly what I am," she murmured, leaning upward to feather a kiss across his mouth. What did she mean? He wanted desperately to understand, but couldn't seem to gather his thoughts. Suddenly he seemed to be floating, and all his concentration was needed to keep from falling. Celia was there with him, holding him upright one moment, then she seemed to disappear as mysteriously as she had come. When he allowed his body to relax he felt only softness beneath his body and sweet oblivion claimed him.

"So, when do I receive my reward, Marcus?" Celia asked from beside him. Until she had walked up next to him he had been watching poor Zachary being led toward the stables by Sylvia. "Rather an uneven match, isn't it?" Marcus observed. "I don't think Zachary is up to her weight, though, do you?"

"Pardon?" Her confusion was clear as she lowered her parasol and glanced over her shoulder at the couple, who were now almost out of sight. "Are you concerned about my brother's intentions, Marcus?"

"Lord, no. If he even thought Sylvia had a serious interest in him, I think he wouldn't bother to wait for a ship, but run across the ocean to reach the safe shores of home," he returned, not really concerned over the matter. What did pique his interest was the slight frown that marred her oval face. "Don't fret over the matter. Your brother gives her a safe outlet to practice her flirting. He is too terrified of her to do her any harm. Now, what was this about a reward?"

"I knew you would forget. A man can't be trusted when he is in his cups, or was I mistaken that you were a trifle cup-shot last night?" Her smile blossomed the moment his attention was riveted to her face. Dressed in pristine white muslin this afternoon, she didn't look much different from his vision last night.

"Gad, don't tell me that you were real?" He tried to remember what he had said. Could he have given anything away about the incidents that were troubling him and Zachary? Even worse, what had he said about his personal dilemma over his feelings for her?

"You didn't promise to sign away your fortune or forfeit any family possessions," she replied, still giving nothing away. The arch of her brow and the gleam in her emerald eyes told him she was intentionally delaying the telling. "Though there is that Holbein in the sitting room . . ."

"Celia, just tell me straight out. I don't want to play games today." Her tumbled raven curls and inviting lips made him long for other activities, however.

"I suppose I should hide the decanter tonight to improve your disposition," she returned cheerfully as if he weren't scowling at her. "Before you threaten me further, however, I'll confess. You only promised to show me a secret place that should be shared by, er, close friends."

At her hesitation he smiled, knowing immediately what that place was. "It is a place for lovers, my dear, which is much different than friendship."

"Lovers aren't friends?"

"Don't look so innocent, my dear." He linked his

hand with hers. "You know very well that friends can be a world apart from lovers."

"I suppose so."

Her thoughtful answer gave him pause, making him wonder at her interpretation of his careless words. Unwilling to pursue the matter, he remained silent as he led her by the hand across the lawn and into the woods. The old path was still there, though it was overgrown with weeds and fallen branches. Celia didn't comment as they moved deeper into the trees. Enclosed in the woodland with the silver sunlight streaming through the trees, he felt as if they were separated from the rest of the world.

"Marcus, where are we going?" she asked as they walked deeper and deeper into the forest. He only smiled and continued on his way, not bothering to tell her that there was a much more direct route to their destination through the garden. This method played to Celia's love of adventure.

"Here we are, my sweet, a place that holds many family secrets, I suppose," he declared, bowing her forward in a grand flourish. A crescent-shaped clearing curved around the structure he indicated. "An ancestor of mine was interested in antiquities, so he built one of his own, though he apparently liked his creature comforts, as you will see."

Celia didn't say a word, though her eyes sparkled as she took in the mock castle ruin. The front was all tumbled stone and twisting vines at the bottom of the solitary turret, set on a rise above the small lake that bordered the gardens. She wandered up the broad stairs that were flanked by two fierce griffins. He followed her as she explored the narrow terrace that abruptly ended in an artfully arranged pile of debris supporting a fountain.

"This ancestor had rather interesting taste," she managed to say finally, giving him a questioning look. "Is this my only reward?"

"I'm not sure if I should venture further, since I'm still in ignorance of how you won the prize." He could remember very little of their conversation the previous night. What had she done that he had pledged to reward? Nothing about her alluring smile gave him the least hint.

"It wasn't what I did, milord, but what I promised that won your pledge. How lowering that you don't seem to remember."

Though he knew it was dangerous, he responded to her playful pout by taking her hand and pressing it to his lips. "Then I've been very remiss in not showing you the secret of this place at once. We shouldn't be tarrying out here when we could have some privacy."

Without relinquishing her hand he stepped over to the slab wall and pressed his booted foot on the raised stone next to the base of the fountain. When nothing happened immediately he wondered if their sojourn would be in vain, not that he couldn't have devised finding another secluded place to be alone with Celia. Then a grinding noise started directly in front of him. Celia gasped in astonishment as the wall began to move inward laboriously.

"Now we'll see about how you'll reward me for the hidden place I have provided for our tryst."

"Marcus, don't you dare let go of my hand," she warned, her fingers clasping his tightly.

"Don't tell me that I have finally discovered something that intimidates you," he said, stepping into the opening. He was abruptly stopped by the tug of her hand. Looking over his shoulder, he found her expression close to that of a child about to face her worst nightmare. "Celia, my love, there's nothing to be apprehensive about. This place is cleaned out on a regular basis because I like to come here when I want to be alone." When she still mutely refused to move, he added, "Trust me, and I'll guard you against the fierce . . ."

Color flooded her cheeks and she looked down at her feet, seeming to be interested in the stone she fretted with the toe of her kid slipper. Just when he thought he would have to prompt her again she mumbled, "Spiders in closed dark places."

"Ah, come, fair lady, I will vanquish all before me," he exclaimed with gusto, keeping a tight rein on his laughter. Never would he have imagined that the dauntless Celia Tregaron would be afraid of anything, much less something as small as a spider. "Just up these few stairs you'll find your fears are groundless."

"Oh, Marcus, how amazing." Celia released his hand and walked past him to the center of the circular room once they were inside. Her face was filled with astonishment, taking in the lushly decorated boudoir. Though the furnishings were from another century, the room could have graced any of the fashionable homes of the peerage. Two velvet-covered chairs bracketed the marble fireplace, which had wood laid in readiness. Under their feet was a heavily embroidered tapestry of vivid reds, golds, and greens. As Celia turned she let out a gasp of delight.

Raised on a platform at one side was a divan, piled high with pillows of various shades of greens and blues. The wide couch was framed by diaphanous drapery that fell from a golden crown that seemed to be suspended in midair. Through the

partially transparent bed hangings light streamed
into the room from a double lancet window.

"Did you say something about wicked family
secrets?" she asked with a knowing smile. Marcus
cursed his weakness for the enchanting woman as she
walked toward him.

"I didn't bring you here for *that*," he declared with
less conviction than he would have liked. Her hands
were already busy with the sling that he had begun
wearing again. He had only left it off for the last two
days of the journey in hopes of playing on her conscience. He had mistakenly thought she would recon-
sider her refusal, but to no avail.

"What exactly is *that*, milord? Being a poorly edu-
cated female, and an American one at that, I fear I
need to have these matters explained to me." All the
while she spoke she walked backward, leading him to
the raised platform. The sultry look on her face told
him there was very little he needed to explain to her.

What was it about this particular woman that
robbed him of his will? Hadn't he told her brother
just last night that he would see to her, keep her suspicions at bay? Marcus groaned at the trap his
vaulted arrogance had laid for him. The next moment
he shouted her name in surprise, realizing too late
that Celia had taken advantage of his momentary preoccupation. Now he was lying flat on his back in the
soft prison of a dozen pillows. At any other time he
would be overjoyed at his position, with his ladylove
nestling at his side.

"Celia, we have to talk," he said, still trying to save
the situation, though she didn't take any heed.
Instead she began tracing the line of his jaw with butterfly kisses. "We can't, er, go on like this, snatching,

mmm, time together and not facing the reality of what, ohhh, what has to be."

"Yes, Marcus, I agree." Her murmured words against his earlobe sent a shiver of anticipation through his body.

Valiantly he made another attempt, snaring her wandering hand with his before she discovered the advanced state of his arousal. "I won't make love . . . Celia, please . . ." Marcus stopped to swallow heavily, the husky need in his voice giving away his emotional state. Just as her lips brushed against his he gave one last effort. "I won't make love to you until you say you'll marry me. If not, we're leaving immediately."

To his amazement she pulled back, levering herself up with her hands on his shoulders. "Still going to do the honorable thing, Marcus? I told you before, and I'll tell you again, honor has nothing to do with us. I don't want to hear another word about marriage."

"You're letting emotions rule your common sense, as always," he shot back, anger beginning to grow at her obstinate refusal. "Just once, my dear Celia, you need to accept the reality of the situation, not simply do as you please."

"Ah, a foolish female should know to let a smart, strong, brave, *honorable* male take care of her. Is that what you mean?" Her words were direct, but they didn't match the satisfied smile on her face. Marcus frowned trying to understand the incongruity, then he felt her palm against the bare skin of his chest. She had managed to open two buttons without his being aware of it.

"Celia. Stop this." There was little force to the words, since he really didn't want to halt her activities. Taking a deep breath he rolled onto his side and had the satisfaction of hearing her gasp in surprise. He was back in control, he determined with a triumphant smile, propping himself up on his elbow as he anchored her body beneath the weight of his. "Now, young lady, we are going to settle this. I'm not some brute who is going to keep you in a tower and order you around like a servant. I want a wife, not a slave."

"Do you really want a wife, milord? I thought you were looking for a lover," she whispered, reaching up to run her hands over his shoulders. "I have it on good authority that you don't want to marry for years yet, not until it is absolutely necessary. In fact I don't think there is one person in the *ton* who isn't aware of your opinion of marriage."

"That was before I had an aggravating, seductive Colonial vixen come into my life and torment me," he snapped, trying to ward off her treacherous fingers that were working at his cravat. "You've turned me into an idiot who can't think beyond making love to you when there are more important matters that need my attention."

"Oh, milord, what could possibly be more important than what we can feel together? Nothing could be more vital to me than being held in your arms." She moved her hips against his, but he kept himself in rigid control. He closed his eyes briefly as a wave of longing rippled through him.

By holding on to the remnant of his anger he could just resist the insidious need to give in to her. "Damn it, Celia, I can't be playing amorous games while someone could be plotting to kill you. They have already shot at Zachary—"

"That's what you've been keeping from me, then. The shot wasn't some idiot poaching after all." The absolute satisfaction in her words struck him like a crushing left hook. He sprang to his feet and glared down at the woman who was glaring just as fiercely back at him.

"So, the siren's charms were meant to find out what I knew," he said accusingly, taking a cleansing breath to keep from shouting at the top of his lungs. He had never felt so betrayed in his entire life.

"Not exactly," Celia replied, having the grace to look embarrassed. At his skeptical look, she continued, "I can't say I didn't want to know what you and Zachary have been so secretive about. But I had another reason for wanting to seduce you."

"And that is?" he prompted when she didn't speak, but slipped from the divan and busily worked at straightening her dress.

"Ah, there were two reasons, if I must be truthful." She gave him a sidelong glance that he instantly distrusted. Celia took her time, ruffling her fingers through her hair, making him want to do the same. "First, I enjoy making love to you, milord, and the second reason is something you will have to discover for yourself. I can't make all the running, you know."

"Celia, I'm going to—" He broke off at the sound of a horn announcing the arrival of a coach. "Who the devil is making that racket?"

"We had best go see, Marcus. Maybe it will be someone to help solve our mystery," Celia exclaimed, practically running to the stairs. Over her shoulder she called, "Do you suppose the shooting has anything to do with my highwayman?"

Marcus followed her at a slower pace as he adjusted his clothes. How he was going to explain to her brother what he had done? He was supposed to have kept her from even guessing that anything was amiss. Instead he had practically blurted out his suspicions the second they were alone. Even if she had set out to seduce the information from him, he couldn't retain his anger. Almost grudgingly he had to admit that he would have done the same in her place. That is what made her unique, and why he couldn't let her go.

"Look, Marcus, it's Uncle Henry and the horrible captain. Did you know that they were coming?"

"No, I didn't, although I sent a letter to your uncle with the messenger that went to Bow Street," he replied, escorting her down the stone steps of the folly and along the lake path. "They must have set out the moment they had our direction. How very curious."

"Nonsense. Despite his gruff manner, Uncle Henry always had a soft spot for Ethan. He probably wants to help with the search," Celia said with an enthusiasm that made him cringe. Her next words only confirmed his worst fears. "Perhaps we should hold sort of a war council tonight and hash over this entire puzzle."

"Celia, until we know more I think we should concentrate solely on finding Ethan," he cautioned, not really sure why he felt the need for secrecy. The little warning voice that had served him so well on the Peninsula was whispering to him. He had a healthy respect for that warning, since it had saved his life more than once.

Taking a firm grasp on Celia's arm, he turned her to face him. They were hidden from sight by the shrubs of the maze. He was going to have her promise before they went to greet the new arrivals. His life was in enough turmoil now and he knew he couldn't stand it if something happened to the impetuous woman in front of him. Without considering his actions, he pulled her into his embrace, slanting his mouth over hers.

The kiss was a pledge from him to her, promising

his protection for the rest of their lives. Though he still didn't understand her motives for refusing him, Marcus knew that she was his and his alone. No other man was going to taste the sweet honey of her kisses or know the enthralling magic of her touch. As her arms circled his neck he acknowledged that honor had nothing to do with his wish to make her his wife.

18

Why did she have to fall in love with such an infuriating, insufferable man? Celia wondered, directing a glare down the breakfast table at the man in question. Perhaps it was punishment for every one of her transgressions. This was vengeance against her willful nature, loving a man who wasn't about to grovel at her feet or grant her every wish. Unfortunately, her greatest wish was to have him love her.

Instead he had avoided being alone with her since the moment he'd released her from the molten kiss near the tower yesterday. To add insult to injury, after an evening of evading her, he had gone out of his way to place some distance between them at the table this morning. Wasn't it bad enough that everyone in the house seemed to want a morning meal today? He made it apparent he didn't trust her not to play her under-the-table tricks again. Had she finally overplayed her amorous behavior yesterday?

"Well, my dears, how should we occupy ourselves

while we're rusticating?" asked Lady Knowles, who had surprised everyone by appearing at half past ten. She claimed after sleeping so much on the journey to Princetown and back that she had been revitalized. "Of course, once poor, sweet Ethan is found we'll have a celebration ball, but what until then? A picnic, perhaps? A trip into the village to help boost the local revenue? Or a boat race on the lake?"

"You amuse yourself and our guests however you like, Mama. Since I am here, I think Haskell wants a bit of my attention," Marcus said, applying himself to the ham steak on his plate. To everyone but Celia he appeared to have nothing more on his mind than estate matters and conferring with his bailiff. "He plans to go over the needed repairs for the tenant cottages this morning. Thaddeus, would you care to see some of the estate and give me some insight into American farming?"

"I think his insight is more adept at judging your wine collections," Henry Tregaron snapped from beside Celia. He leveled a glare at the subject under discussion. The two men had barely exchanged a civil word since the new arrivals had stepped out of their coach. "How's the head this morning, old boy?"

"Fine, Henry, never better, never better." Thaddeus's bleary-eyed appearance belied his quick assurance. Celia knew by the rigid set of his shoulders and neck that her uncle was feeling the effects of his indulgences, as usual. "Lord Ashmore really doesn't have a suitable mount for me."

"Thaddeus, there isn't a horse in the entire world that you dare ride. Even the gentlest mare makes you quiver in frigh—"

"Uncle Henry, I don't think our friends want to

hear us air our differences, especially on such a lovely day," Celia broke in quickly, knowing all too well that the two men could digress into childish bickering at any time. She noticed that Captain Vanderhoff was watching the exchange with a knowing smile. On more than one occasion she had suspected that he encouraged the animosity between her two uncles, for no other reason than his perverse enjoyment.

She cast a beseeching look across the table at her brother, only to discover he wasn't paying any heed to the squabbling. Though he was holding his fork in one hand, his other hand and half his arm were thrust under the table, causing him to list slightly to the side. When she caught his eye he reddened to his ears and straightened. Celia glanced at Sylvia sitting next to him. Celia wondered what the other girl was playing at.

Why was she still pestering Zachary when they knew what the two men had been hiding from them? Only then did Celia remember that in her annoyance with a certain gentleman she had kept the truth about the shooting to herself last night. She had meant to give Sylvia a full report, but had never had a chance, nor had her friend sought her out.

Shaking her head at her foolishness, she decided that she was imagining things. Marcus hadn't seen anything untoward in the pairs' behavior yesterday and had even commented that it was probably helpful to his sister. Sylvia was simply trying to wear down the man's patience. After the meal Celia would let her know that her help was no longer necessary.

"I'm sure you'll do as you see fit, Mama. Now if you'll excuse me—"

"Pardon, milord," interrupted the butler, clearing his throat nervously. Stokes was a tall, thin man who lacked the authoritative bearing of his counterpart in London. In fact, Celia suspected the man was afraid of everyone in the house, including Meg, her newly appointed maid. Lady Knowles continually bemoaned the fact that most of the staff was green, all hired in the past year. "There is a person at the kitchen door insisting that he see you. I told him you were a busy man, but he threatened me, milord. Most irregular, I must say."

"Stokes, did he say what he wanted?"

"Well, milord, he said you hired him in Princetown." Stokes looked mortified by even the suggestion of an association.

"Then bring him up here at once."

"Oh, but, you can't mean—"

"Stokes, are you questioning me?" Marcus's tone was mild, and Celia thought she detected a hint of a knowing smile, an expression of his she was all too familiar with. Without a reply the manservant stumbled out of the room.

"You don't suppose this could be news about Ethan already?" Her brother asked the question that was trembling on Celia's tongue. She had been too afraid to ask after the letdown, not once but twice, when they thought they were at the end of their search.

"Don't get your hopes up just yet. It could be some good-for-nothing out for the reward," Vanderhoff declared, his tone grating on her nerves.

"Thank you for your sympathy, Captain," she murmured, trying not to look anxiously at the doorway. Though she was beginning to think that she would never see her younger brother again, she couldn't give up hope quite yet. "I know you always thought Ethan was a sniveling brat, but the rest of us are eager to discover his whereabouts."

"That isn't what I meant, Celia," the man returned, sounding as if he were reasoning with a half-witted child. "You always misinterpret my intentions, my dear. I was merely trying to be helpful."

"If you want to be truly helpful—"

The return of Stokes with a rather scrubby-looking individual kept her from completing her unladylike utterance. Celia realized it was the boy from the inn. This was the person who had threatened Stokes? He was the same post boy who had helped her the night of her rendezvous with the highwayman. Before she realized her intent Celia was on her feet and walking toward the incongruous pair.

"You're Jem, aren't you?" she said softly, seeing the look of apprehension in his round blue eyes now that she was a few steps from him. She smiled to ease the boy's nervousness and cast a beseeching look at Marcus, who was also on his feet with Zachary looming behind him. "I remember you from the inn. Have you come all this way on your own?"

"Aye, miss. His lordship he promised a reward, he did. Ther's jest me mum and me, so I needs the blunt." At a derisive sniff from Vanderhoff the boy stopped and wiped his nose with the back of his sleeve. "Mr. Grubbins gave me his ol' plug ta ride, iffen I give him part of ther reward."

"So, you do have news for me, then," Marcus prompted when the boy seemed to be momentarily struck dumb, looking around to discover everyone in the room was watching him. He took an involuntary step back as he gazed up at Zachary's imposing form. "Jem, not only will you have the reward, you'll have a nice meal, and a warm bath and place to sleep tonight."

"Do I have ta take the bath, your lordship, sir?" He looked uncertainly at Celia when he asked the question.

"Not if you don't want to," she assured him, going down on her knees beside him to deflect some of the intimidation. "Do you know what happened to my brother Ethan?"

"He be your brother, then? Well, Mr. Pentalow, the cobbler in Two Bridges, he says the bloke yer looking fer came east ta sell off some of Holloway's stock fer the widow." He paused after this long speech and seemed encouraged to continue by Celia's eager smile. Taking a deep breath he went on. "Mr. Pentalow says Ethan sent the blunt by messenger, but never came back 'cause he took some work fer a farmer named Alsop somewheres near Blanford Forum."

"Jiminy, that's only a few hours' ride from here," Sylvia exclaimed, jumping up from the table to join the others surrounding the thin boy.

Celia almost slumped to the floor at the startling news, light-headed at the discovery that Ethan could be on the other side of the hills after all their travail. A familiar hand grasped her arm to assist her to her feet. When she looked up to thank Marcus, her dizziness returned due to the warm regard in his gaze. At that moment she was almost tempted to ask his true feelings for her. Such an expression couldn't possibly come from a man who felt only passion for her.

"Well, what are we waiting for? Jem wants that meal you promised, Marcus," said Zachary, slapping him on the back with staggering force, "and I want a horse to bring that rascally brother of mine home finally. Ladies, we'll have another gentleman for dinner tonight, so you best begin preparing for the prodigal son while we're gone."

"Zachary," three voices chorused at once, surprising each other in their harmony. Celia and Sylvia looked at each other before turning as one on Marcus, their unwitting third.

"I was merely going to say we might as well take the pair of you along," he said, grinning at their dumbfounded expressions before he ruined his magnanimous gesture. "You'll only trail behind us all the way, so you may as well come with us. Though, my dear Celia, you will use a sidesaddle today, despite your preference for riding astride."

"Come, Sylvia, we'd better change into our riding gear as quickly as possible, in case they decide to renege," Celia managed to say in her most imperious tone, grasping the other girl's arm and pulling her from the room. Behind her she could hear Zachary questioning her tormentor about his last comment. She smiled in satisfaction, glad that his unnecessary reference to their night on the moors was coming down on his head.

While Sylvia chattered about the day's adventure, Celia thought back over what just occurred. Was she finally getting through to Marcus? The look they had exchanged after Jem's disclosure still set her heart racing with expectation. Was she being foolish not to give up hope?

If they found Ethan today, she would have so little time to discover if Marcus could love her. Once again, as she had been almost from the moment she set foot in London, she was torn between the two parts of her life. Her reunion with her brother could be so bittersweet if she had to say farewell to the infuriating, arrogant, and desirable man she had come to love so deeply.

*   *   *

"What do you make of it all, Zachary?" Sylvia inquired over an hour later as the quartet trotted along the road. They were getting closer to their destination by the minute, and despite their conversation, the tension among the group was apparent.

"I don't know. Marcus and I have been over the matter time and again." He took off his hat and settled it on his head again for no apparent reason. "There isn't a logical reason in the world for anyone to want to harm Celia or me. Except for a few mutton-headed British sailors, begging your pardon, I don't have an enemy in the world."

"Then I suppose we need to think of the least logical reason," Celia felt compelled to say. She had to do something or kick her mount into a gallop to race ahead. However, the horses needed some rest, since they had been ridden hard for half the distance already.

"I think that would be right up your alley, wouldn't it?" her brother shot over his shoulder, grinning when she pulled a face at him. Then all humor left his face as they rounded the bend in the road. There on the rise was the thatched cottage, just as the drover they had met about a mile back had said it would be.

Though no one said a word, all four of them reined in their mounts. As they exchanged uncertain looks Celia knew the others were feeling the same sense of unease as she. What if this was another false lead and Jem was only passing along a rumor in hopes of gaining a reward? Her emotions were unsettled enough without having her hopes of finding Ethan dashed once more.

A man stepped out the door of the cottage, and as one the riders nudged their horses into motion. Celia's heart was beating in her throat with each hoofbeat closer. Was the man too tall, too broad-shouldered, his skin too dark? Ethan had been tall but wiry, and his skin as fair as hers, that day she had hugged him in tearful farewell on the wharf. Could he have changed that much in over two years?

When they came abreast of the neat cottage the man didn't say a word. He simply regarded the four travelers with a narrowed, hostile gaze. Celia couldn't move, couldn't make a sound because her throat was too dry. Her gaze locked with the man's hard green eyes, and she swallowed, wondering what to do next. The horse moved restlessly under her, sensing her tension.

"Well, damn it, I see you've found me."

"What kind of greeting is that after all this time, you idiot?" Celia shot back at her brother, his harsh greeting releasing her from her paralysis. "We've traveled all the way across the ocean and half of England, only for you to snarl at us."

"I didn't ask you to come, did I?" he challenged, setting the bucket he had been holding on the ground. Unconsciously he rubbed his hands against the front of his shirt, looking back and forth between his brother and sister. Though he was dressed in a homespun shirt and breeches, the resemblance between them was apparent. He had Celia's black hair and green eyes, and he shared his brother's angular features, right down to the belligerent set of his chin when angered.

"You didn't even write to let us know you survived the war, little brother. Did you expect us, especially Celia, to bury an empty coffin and forget about you?" Zachary's tone was level, a sharp contrast to his siblings' raised voices. "You never did have more than half a brain."

"I didn't want to go back to Baltimore after I got on land again. I never want to see another ship again," he declared, his fists clenching and his chin rising another inch in defiance. "I hate the sea and couldn't care less about Tregaron Shipping. Why should I go back to play second fiddle to you or be a flunky to the uncles? If Henry wasn't yelling at me, Thaddeus was sniveling in his wine and ordering me to fetch him more."

"Ethan, please, we only—"

"No, I'm not going back, so you might as well just go back where you came from with your fancy friends." Stiffening his shoulders, he placed his hands on his hips. "I've got a life here all my own now. I don't need any of you, do you hear me? Just let me be and go back home."

"Why, you are a sniveling brat, aren't you?"

The question took everyone by surprise, and they all turned to stare at Sylvia. She jumped down from her horse and stalked toward him. "You selfish monster, do you know what your brother and sister have been through these past weeks? They didn't know what happened to you until they discovered you had been taken prisoner. And before that, Celia was the only one who thought you were alive. She came all the way here without knowing a soul, just to find you. You stand there and sneer at Zachary, who is twice the man you'll ever be, and would never dare play such a shabby trick on the people who love him."

"Zachary, call off your fancy piece—"

The rest of his words were cut off because his brother was on him a flash. Celia reached out for Marcus without realizing it as Zachary punched his younger brother in the face. Ethan shook his head, slightly dazed, but he recovered quickly and jumped forward to wrap his hands around his brother's throat. The two swayed back and forth, almost evenly matched, though Ethan was a few inches shorter. Sylvia scurried back toward the cottage to stay out of their path as they staggered around the yard.

"Marcus, stop them! Do something before they damage each other." Celia had no idea what she was saying. She felt helpless watching her two brothers take out their anger on each other and nauseous over the bitter words and violence that had erupted between them.

Rescue came from an unexpected source as the cottage door flew open. A young woman staggered out the door, her ungainly walk caused by the roundness of her stomach. She was clearly in the advanced stages of pregnancy. From the way she shouted at Ethan it was clear that she was well acquainted with him. When her words didn't stop the men, she turned on her heel and went back into the cottage.

A minute later she was back, carrying a basin of water. She stood poised for a moment, as if getting her bearings. Then she heaved the contents of the basin at the two men, splashing Sylvia as well, who was also in the line of fire. When she had Ethan's attention, the woman snapped, "I'll not have the father of my child brawling like some looby. You'll not turn my home into a prize fight, do you hear me, Ethan Tregaron?"

"Aye, I hear ya, Bess." He looked like a schoolboy, staring down at his feet, his face as red as a beet.

"And just who are you people to come here like this? Don't the gentry have enough amusement without badgering honest folk?"

"How dare you? Do you know what kind of man you married—"

"Sylvia." Marcus's sharp command was enough to stop both women. Celia wondered if Sylvia and the woman would come to blows. "I think you've said quite enough. Perhaps we should leave before we disgrace ourselves any more."

"Ethan, who are these people?" the woman asked, taking in the resemblance between Ethan and two of the strangers.

"Bess, meet my brother Zachary and my sister Celia," he said reluctantly, moving to stand beside the dumbfounded woman. Her face flushed with color as she gazed back and forth among the three Tregarons. "This is my wife, Bess. We're expecting a child soon."

"I think we all need time to recover from this stimulating reunion. I am Ashmore, sir. Your family are my guests at King's Rest." Marcus's stare was pinned on Ethan. He paused while Zachary assisted Sylvia onto her horse and prepared to mount his own. "If you wish to visit with them, you are welcome at any time. Don't you agree, Zachary?"

"'Tis up to you now, Ethan. You know where to find us, which is more than we could say for you over the past two years." The large man turned his horse without waiting for an answer, though he didn't move any farther than two steps away.

Celia didn't know what to do. After all this, traveling across an ocean, threatening to kill a man—the wrong man at that—making a journey halfway across the country. For what? She hadn't even embraced her brother after two years. It was all so very strange. Not knowing what else to do, she finally managed to say, "Ethan, please come. At least say good-bye to us before we leave for America."

With that she turned away and joined the others for the ride back to King's Rest. The silent group rode away, none of them looking back at the couple standing in front of the cottage. What was she going to do now? Celia wondered, dazed by what had just taken place. Never in her wildest imaginings could she have thought Ethan wouldn't be pleased to see them. What had happened to the boy she had known? Surely his experience at sea and his imprisonment couldn't have changed him that much? Was it possible that she had never known her brother?

She wasn't sure how long or how far they rode as she fretted over the matter. Her horse simply carried her along, just following the lead of the others while their riders were lost in their own thoughts. She surreptitiously looked at Marcus riding easily beside her. As if he sensed her interest he turned. The warm sympathy in his expression was almost her undoing. She looked at her hands clenched around the reins as tears threatened, burning her eyes and throat as she fought for control.

"Marcus, may I pay my addresses to your sister?" Zachary's question was like a rifle shot in the quiet void that had lasted for half the journey back to King's Rest.

"I beg your pardon?" Marcus's voice was strained and he pulled in his mount. His hard stare at the other man didn't make him shrink from his question. He squared his shoulders even more and returned the unflinching look.

"I've fallen in love with your sister and want to marry her." Leaning forward in the saddle, Zachary added, "Is that clear enough to understand?"

"Oh, Zachary, how wonderful." The lady in question cried, tears gathering in her eyes. The look she gave her suitor took Celia by surprise. Was this her doing as well, simply because she had enlisted Sylvia's help in ferreting out information?

"How the devil have you managed to form an attachment in such a short time? It is impossible to fall in love so soon," Marcus said, appearing as dazed over the matter as Celia felt. "You were trembling at the thought of talking to her just yesterday, wasn't it? Celia, say something."

"Sylvia, you were only supposed to question him," she blurted out without thinking, only realizing what she had done when it was too late. "What have you been doing?"

"Exactly what is that supposed to mean?"

"You just don't understand love, Marcus," Zachary cut in, not interested in their exchange since it had nothing to do with his proposal. "Did you see anything more magnificent than my Sylvia defending me against my snot-nosed little brother? How can I not marry the woman?"

"We'll discuss this later, sir. Right now, Celia Tregaron, explain yourself." Marcus grasped her arm to keep her from urging her horse forward. In his preoccupation with her he didn't notice the other couple move away, their hands linked together as their horses walked side by side. "Was that the true purpose of your little performance in the tower yesterday? You were going to wheedle information out of me while you seduced me, nothing more. Not to be outdone in lowering yourself to such behavior, you've instructed my innocent sister in the practice as well."

She jerked her arm out of his grasp and stood her ground, holding the horse in check. "That isn't the reason I tried to seduce you yesterday at all, but you're too stubborn and ignorant to see the real reason. And don't look at me as if I've led your sister into a world of debauchery. I only said she needed to ask Zachary some questions. So perhaps lechery runs in your family. Haven't you used it to keep me from asking questions yourself?"

"Damn it, Celia, come back here. I'm not finished with this discussion," he called after her, but she moved ahead to join the others, belatedly determined to act as chaperone. What else could go amiss today? she thought furiously. Perhaps another attack from their mysterious enemy, which would probably seem tame following a wrestling match and an unexpected proposal.

How had her life gotten so complicated? She had known before she set out that her trip to England might be difficult. But could she have anticipated any of this? With a cautious peek over her shoulder at Marcus, she sighed. How could she ever expect to teach him anything about love when she didn't even realize her closest friend and her brother were falling in love? Not wanting to brood any longer, she gave her horse its head, galloping away from the others as if the wind in her hair could carry away her troubles.

"I can't stand it a moment longer," Sylvia declared, echoing Celia's own thoughts. She didn't stop her pacing in front of the fire, despite the announcement to the others gathered in the drawing room after dinner.

"Please, Sylvia, you're going to exhaust yourself. Sit down and wait until Zachary comes back," Celia urged from the gold and white striped divan. Next to her Lady Knowles sat quietly working on her embroidery as if nothing were amiss. "You're wearing me down just watching you."

"I can't sit still. They've been closeted in Marcus's

study forever now." She never missed a step, and added hand-wringing to her agitated movements.

"They went in the study only ten minutes past," Celia answered, but tempered her words with a sympathetic smile. Her nerves weren't any less settled than her friend's, and not just because of the implacable look on Marcus's face as he called her brother from the room. The outcome of the interview in the library was simply another obstacle in a path strewn with barriers.

How had she ever thought she could merely have Marcus declare his love for her and everything would be right with the world? Nothing had been right from the moment she left Baltimore. If she had stayed at home where she belonged, would she have felt this sense of desolation? Instead of returning her life to a semblance of normalcy, her search for Ethan had changed everything beyond repair.

Ethan wouldn't be returning to Baltimore with them, even if he deigned to speak to them again. He had a wife and the responsibility of a family now. If Zachary could be persuasive enough, she was going to have a new sister. She loved Sylvia and wanted her happiness, but her older brother's marriage was another drastic shift in her neat little world. Her old life was gone forever, and what did she have to show for her adventures?

"I'm not going to stand for this another minute." Sylvia stopped in the center of the room, her hands on her hips as she glared at the company around her. No one but Celia really seemed to notice. Henry and Vanderhoff were playing cards at a table in the corner of the high-ceilinged room while Thaddeus snored in a chair a few feet away.

"That's nice, dear," Lady Knowles commented absently, counting her stitches without looking up. She yawned delicately before reaching for the sherry glass on the marble-topped table next to her.

"Well, it is my future those two are discussing, and I have a right to be present," she went on as if everyone in the room were hanging on her every word. "If I'm going to be an American, I have to start showing I know how to be independent. They can't dictate how my life is going to be without my consent."

Before Celia could utter a word Sylvia turned on her heel and all but ran out of the room. With a melancholy sigh she wondered if she should go after her, but knew that it was useless. Sylvia was as headstrong as her lordly brother. Besides, Celia's motives for interfering were somewhat selfish. She was sure Marcus would blame her influence for Sylvia's interruption of the time-honored male discussion over the marriage portion.

Noting that Lady Knowles was beginning to nod over her fancywork, Celia put aside the book of poetry that hadn't held her interest. She rose to her feet, suddenly needing activity to distract her. Perhaps a walk by the lake would soothe her wounded spirits, she decided, wondering just when she would be leaving this place. She was sure her outrageous behavior had alienated Marcus, despite the passion she could elicit in him.

That was the one fact she was sure of by now. Marcus may desire her at the moment, but it was apparent, even to her stubborn mind and heart, that he would never love her. With the rest of her life in disarray, it was only fitting that she would not attain her heart's desire as well. She slipped through the French doors onto the terrace without a word to the uninterested group behind.

19

"*No matter what you say,* Marcus, I'm going to marry him."

Marcus looked up at his sister in resignation from where he stood next to the large man who would soon be his brother-in-law. Until her entrance, they had been looking over the map spread across the surface of the desk. Turning back to Zachary, he raised his brow in question and was answered by a conspiratorial grin. Hadn't they just been discussing the fact that the women in their respective families tried to direct matters much too often? Sylvia's sudden intrusion into their sanctum was a prime example.

"My dear, I think you should leave this matter to us. When we are ready to discuss this remarkable situation with you, we'll send for you." He studied the contents of his glass rather thoroughly to keep from giving away his enjoyment of her infuriated glare. Didn't he and Zachary deserve a little payment for the scheme the two ladies essayed to discover something that was best left to the gentlemen's tending? "Tregaron has just been trying to justify why he, of all the men that have courted you, should be so fortunate as to become my brother-in-law."

"He is going to be *my* husband, so we really don't need to concern ourselves with his relationship to you. You aren't going to be the one living with him," Sylvia said as she advanced across the room. She skirted the desk to stand close to her beloved's side. "Tell him to be done with this nonsense, Zachary."

"Now, Sylvia dear, your brother is showing good sense. We have to be practical, er, to think of all the, er. . ."

Marcus could see the other man was wavering under the soft, beseeching look of his sister's brown eyes. The agonized look the other man directed at him spoke volumes. "Sylvia, do you want the man to recant already? Your behavior may make him think twice about his offer before I mull over all the ramifications and give my consent."

Zachary reluctantly took his gaze from the woman beside him. His angular face was repentant. "Ah, Marcus, I just can't do this —"

"Oh, Zachary, no, you can't. I'm sorry I intruded on your discourse, but I just couldn't stand the suspense." She grasped his arm, unaware that her impetuous behavior had stopped her betrothed from confessing their game.

"Remember that phrase, 'I just couldn't stand the suspense,' my friend. I fear that will be the watchword of your married life," Marcus said, knowing that the other man would be on his knees begging her forgiveness in another minute. That wouldn't do at all, he decided, after nineteen years of dealing with his sister's caprices. "She will always proclaim that boredom or nerves made her act in this way or that. Although I think you'll find her a relief after the responsibility of Celia. My sister at least listens to reason occasionally. I wish you much happiness."

For once in his life Marcus was able to render his sister speechless. Looking from one man to another, she didn't seem to understand what had just taken place. Then it became apparent that she finally understood that her brother had given his consent. Just as she reached out her hands to her newly declared betrothed, the jest the men had attempted also sunk in. She turned a speaking look on her brother. "Marcus—"

"For God's sake, kiss her, Zachary, before she begins berating us both. That is the best way to keep a woman happy and agreeable," he declared, putting down his glass and heading for the door.

Apparently Zachary was still bemused by the recent winning of his bride, for Sylvia managed one last jibe just as Marcus reached the door. "That was a filthy trick, Marcus. I hope the woman you fall in love with leads you on a merry chase. You deserve to get some of your own odious sense of humor turned back on you."

"Too late, my dear, much too late," he murmured, casting a glance back over his shoulder at the pair. They neither heard his words nor noticed his leave-taking, being much better occupied with their fervent embrace. Zachary was definitely learning how to communicate with a respectable woman after all, he mused, heading for the drawing room. There was a certain respectable woman he needed to converse with at the moment.

She was undoubtedly responsible for his sister's sudden entrance in the study. Though Sylvia had been outspoken prior to the lady's arrival, she had always been overly conscious of the dictates of proper behavior. That wasn't what he planned to discuss, however. Celia had much more to answer for besides teaching his sister her independent, democratic ways. Now that they had solved the riddle of Ethan's whereabouts, he had more important matters to resolve. He didn't have the patience to wait until the emotional issues of the Tregaron family were fully reconciled, because he had a few emotional issues of his own that needed to be faced.

When he discovered the lady wasn't where she was supposed to be, Marcus wasn't surprised. Celia never did what he expected, not from the first moment they met—which was undoubtedly why he found himself so fiercely in love with the infuriating, disrespectful, and totally seductive woman. The emotion he had never expected to feel had caught him unaware, leaving him feeling more vulnerable than he ever had in his entire life. Just when he had lost his heart he wasn't sure, but he now knew that it would never be wholly his ever again.

Glancing idly over the snoozing group in the drawing room, he shook his head and headed for the open doors that led to the terrace. He was cursing a few minutes later when he realized she wasn't to be found. In an uncharacteristic moment of alarm he wondered if she had been spirited away, then called himself a twice-cursed fool. Would the members of their respective families, including Madison, be napping in the room behind him if Celia had been kidnapped? This was what she had done to him, turned him from a rational, reasonable man into an alarmist, jumping to irresponsible conclusions.

He walked down the flagstone steps that led to the gardens and maze, glancing idly toward the tower ruins with a sardonic smile. Their tussle on the divan in the secret room yesterday was an ironic summation of his relationship with Celia. While he had taken her there for a private discussion about their remarkable relationship, the lady had set about seducing him. Had he ever had a clandestine meeting with any woman with such honorable intentions before yesterday?

The moon slipping from behind the clouds confirmed his suspicions. He had seen some movement by the tower and now he could make out the outline of a figure. If he wasn't mistaken he knew the silhouetted form very well, having explored the delightful curves with his hands and lips, though not nearly enough to his satisfaction.

He walked along the gravel pathway, determined to get an answer from the lady once and for all. Though she wasn't as easily handled as his sister, Marcus was going to have her answer tonight, he decided. They had played this guessing game long enough. She was going to be his wife, not because of honor or any responsibility for her well-being. Celia Tregaron was going to be chained to his side by every means possible, legally and emotionally.

She might not be in love with him now, but she would be. He was experienced enough to know he could turn her physical attraction into something more. In fact, he wasn't sure he cared about her feelings at this point as long as she agreed to marry him. She owed him that for charging into his life and demanding his attention. Maybe she had been after his cousin, but she had gotten her vengeance on him, no matter what her intent. She had stolen his peace of mind, his soul, anything that she wanted was hers.

"Celia, are you there?" he called, still a few feet from the crumbling tower.

"Yes, I'm here."

The dispirited tinge of her words changed his resolve into dismay. What turn was this? he wondered at the woeful tone. He rapidly closed the distance between them, not bothering to say another word until he stood before her. The moment she raised her face he could see her clearly in the moonlight. He gathered her close to his chest, offering her comfort for whatever had brought her so low.

As he stroked her soft curls he knew that he wouldn't be making any demands tonight. He simply held her, trying to ease her pain. After endless minutes she sighed heavily, continuing to burrow her face into his shoulder, and he couldn't stand the suspense a moment more. "What is it, my sweet? What has you so melancholy?"

"Oh, Marcus, I'm being a fool, is all. Don't sound so fierce, please," she said, giving him a sad smile as she looked up at him, her hands moving restlessly on his lapels. "I'm being a complete ninny, feeling sorry for myself because I can't control the world." She paused for a minute, fixedly studying the intricate folds of his cravat. "I think I've finally grown up at last and realized that all my adventures aren't going to bring me happiness. I'm going to have to start behaving more circumspectly, and leave my escapades behind. I have to start looking toward my future."

Suddenly he understood what was giving her such a haunted, disheartened look. The startling occurrences of today alone were enough to make her introspective. It wasn't simply Ethan's animosity, but the fact that both her brothers would soon have other commitments that didn't include her. He had felt a similar twinge at the moment he gave his sister's destiny and happiness into a stranger's hand for safekeeping.

"Please don't reform quite so quickly, my love," he murmured, unable to resist the lush invitation of her lips. Bending his head he claimed her mouth, not in passion but in comfort.

He needed to take away the hurt, though he knew that her feelings of dejection would pass. Gently caressing her lips and cheeks, he wanted to take all her pain into himself, tell her that she had nothing to worry about, that he would never leave her.

The moment he felt another sigh shudder through her he knew that he would have to resist the temptation of taking advantage of her weakness. He wanted her more than life itself, but he wanted her to come to him with her natural spirit in place, not because she was feeling sorry for herself.

"Tell me what I can do to help you, love," he commanded softly, pressing her head back into the curve of his shoulder and resting his cheek against the cushion of her raven curls.

"I need a few moments to myself, please." She stepped back from his sheltering embrace, and he let her move back until he held her trembling hand in his.

"Are you sure?"

She hesitated for a moment, her fingers clinging to his, then she took a deep breath and released his hand. "Yes, a half hour to collect myself, then you can come back to escort me through the garden."

Reluctant to leave, he still obeyed, swearing that this was the last time they would part without her pledging her troth to him. He didn't turn away until he was down the steps and could no longer read her expression. The lady wasn't going to get a half hour, he determined, walking aimlessly toward the house, not aware of the direction. In less than half the time he planned to return and take her thoughts from her family once and for all. Lost in his pleasant daydream, he almost didn't hear the voices that seemed to be coming from ahead of him on the pathway.

"Ya dint pay me fer the last job, ya coxcomb," came a familiar snarling voice just off to Marcus's right.

He stopped in his tracks as he recognized exactly where he heard the voice before, on the moors near Princetown. The surly highwayman had the audacity to come on his property. The eventful reunion with Ethan and Zachary's startling proposal had distracted him from the mysterious incidents that had plagued the Tregaron family. What was the felon doing so far from his original crime? Was Celia the purpose of his visit?

"I'll pay you when you accomplish the job and not before," answered a second voice that kept Marcus from racing back to the tower. The second man was Silas Vanderhoff. Rather than act imprudently before he knew what was afoot, Marcus stepped into the shadow of a tree.

"You incompetent fool, you haven't accomplished a thing I hired you to do." Vanderhoff continued to berate the man, apparently feeling secure that no one would overhear him. Marcus realized that the pair were standing not too far from him, but were hidden by the high wall of the maze. "Why did I ever bother bribing Ashmore to impress Ethan into the British

navy, if it was all going to come apart now because of a
two-bit thief? First you make a mess of taking the girl,
and then you can't even manage to make an easy shot.
If I had been there, Zachary Tregaron would be dead.
Instead I have another failed attempt on my hands."

The man's rambling tirade began to neatly fit the
pieces of the puzzle in place. Unbeknownst to the
Tregaron family, they did have an enemy, and right in
their midst. Fortunately, from the sound of it, the man
was surrounded by incompetents, or the Tregarons
had the devil's own luck. The only plan that had succeeded had been Ethan's impressment during the war,
Marcus acknowledged, wondering at his cousin's part
in the matter. He hadn't known Ambrose well, but he
had never suspected that he had such a venal character to be part of such a scheme.

"Don't give me any sorry excuses, you dolt. If you
had kidnapped the girl, I would have been able to find
that sniveling boy before they did," Vanderhoff
snarled, making Marcus realize that he had missed
part of the conversation as he speculated about past
transgressions. "That damn woman, why couldn't she
have stayed home where she belonged? I would have
her married to my nephew by now. Instead she ruined
everything by running away to look for her stupid
brother. How can I gain control of Tregaron Shipping
with so many healthy, living partners?"

Marcus had heard enough, he decided, slipping
away into the darkness. His first concern was Celia's
safety. In her current preoccupied state she could
accidently stumble on the pair and be in Vanderhoff's
hands before she knew what was happening. Moving
as quietly as possible, he stole back to the tower,
cursing the fact that he was being forced to practice

his army skills, not only on English soil but on his own property.

"Marcus? What are you doing?" Celia exclaimed as he rushed up the tower steps onto the terrace. She let out a muffled sound of alarm as he backed her against the granite wall, his hand securely covering her mouth.

"I don't have time to explain now, but we must return to the house as quickly as possible and without making any noise," he commanded, keeping watch over his shoulder to make sure that he wasn't followed. He kept his hand over Celia's mouth, too conscious of the feel of her soft lips against his palm, for he knew how easily sound carried at night. "We have to warn your brother and uncles about Vanderhoff's villainy. Now when I take my hand away, don't utter a sound. I'll explain the rest later."

"Marcus —"

"Not a sound, Celia, or any argument," he hissed sharply, his attention still directed at the garden that seemed to stretch endlessly between them and the house. "As much as I love you I will knock you senseless if you so much as utter a sound."

Not waiting for her agreement, he grasped her hand and began leading her toward the silent garden. The journey seemed to take forever. Every snapping twig or scurrying animal beyond their sight had him tensing, ready to strike. If he had any sense he would have left Celia shut up in the tower room, but somehow he felt safer with her at his side where he could see that she was all right. How Garth would laugh at this exploit when he returned, Marcus decided with grim humor, his former partner in too many dangerous missions sneaking through his own garden.

He gave Celia's hand a reassuring squeeze as his foot landed on the first step of the broad stone stairway to the terrace. Keeping to the shadows, he led her up the steps, then tensed just as he was about to instruct her to go into the house through the study. A shadowy figure was loitering near the drawing room windows. Marcus didn't hesitate but leaped across the flagstones and fell upon the man. His victim didn't put up much of a struggle, except to gasp and sputter in outrage.

"What is going on? Marcus, what are you doing?" Sylvia's voice reached him just as he completely subdued the swearing man.

"Uncle Thaddeus, did you drink the cellars dry? Is that why Marcus is enraged?"

At Zachary's jesting question Marcus released the man, looking down at the pistol that he now held in his hand as he stepped back. What was the old lush doing with a weapon? "I'm sorry, sir, I mistook you for one of the treacherous men I overheard in the garden. Apparently you were on the alert as well. Zachary, fetch my pistols from—"

"That won't be necessary now, Zachary. Just stay where you are for the moment where I can see you."

Marcus turned away from the muttering Thaddeus in time to see Vanderhoff and his henchman striding up the terrace steps. Both men carried two pistols directed straight at him. With a jerk of his head to Celia he motioned her to move closer, not wanting to let Vanderhoff hold her hostage. She readily followed his signal, coming to stand beside him.

"Now, this is how a plan is supposed to work." Vanderhoff's narrow face shone with satisfaction as he looked over the group in front of him. His malevolent form was clearly visible in the dim light coming from the drawing room doors that were flung open to the night. "I would have preferred something less dramatic than this denouement, but it can't be helped, I suppose. Now, if my partner has followed his instructions?"

"Silas, I'm not an idiot," Thaddeus said, snatching the pistol from Marcus's hand at the same moment. He smiled humorlessly at the expressions on his audiences' faces. "Surely you don't think I relished playing nursemaid to you whiny brats and was happy to manage someone else's money without wanting some of it for myself."

"Thaddeus, stand away from them. I don't trust our good host or your lumbering nephew," his fellow conspirator ordered as a malicious grin curled his thin lips. Marcus wondered why he seemed to be addressing most of his attention to him. "I'll let you vent your grievances before we set the fire."

"Fire? What are you going to do? Surely you can't kill us all without someone questioning such a tragedy?" Though he made the charge Marcus knew that desperate men could commit all sorts of unscrupulous crimes. Desperate men could also be careless in their arrogance, which he was hoping would be the case tonight. Keeping a close eye on Vanderhoff's every move he simply waited for the right moment.

"Oh, sweet heaven, where are Lady Knowles and Uncle Henry?" Celia broke into the tense silence, clutching at Marcus's sling covered arm in her distress. "What have you done to them?"

"Nothing much, so far. Your uncle simply drugged their wine, which he would have done to the rest of you, if you had stayed where you were supposed to. This engagement of Zachary's has been somewhat inconvenient."

Vanderhoff's annoyance over the matter gave Marcus an extra measure of hope. He wondered if he could move back closer to Zachary without being detected. In their current position they couldn't make eye contact, which would be necessary in order to overpower their intended murderers. If his judgment was correct, Vanderhoff was the real threat; Thaddeus and the hireling could be easily dealt with, probably by Zachary on his own.

He looked down to see how Celia was faring, just as a rustling of the bushes caught his attention. Though Vanderhoff was watching them closely, he was giving orders to his two confederates, who weren't being obedient. Would he notice that the bushes just to the left of the stairs were now shifting furiously as if buffeted by a high wind or an impatient hand? Cautiously he stepped in front of Celia, hoping to conceal her expressive face from their captors as well as keep her out of harm's way. He knew from her alert posture she was aware of the new arrival, just as he was.

He had no idea who their unexpected ally could be. Vanderhoff would surely have taken care of the servants as well as his mother and Henry Tregaron. He didn't need Celia's gasp a second later to notice the unexpected face that peered up at him through the baluster. The odds were suddenly back in their favor. Vanderhoff wouldn't suspect help from that quarter after tonight's discussion at dinner.

Turning his attention back to the corrupt trio, Marcus recognized that there was no better time to make their move. The three were bickering among themselves over some trivial matter, and Vanderhoff's beady stare wasn't on him for the moment. He looked directly at the moving shrubbery and nodded vigorously. The

result almost put him off stride as a bloodcurdling yell
split through the night. Another yell let loose only a
second later.

Marcus barely had time to see Ethan vault over the
stone railing onto the terrace. He rushed forward,
sensing Zachary at his heels, the element of surprise
satisfyingly clear from the stunned amazement of the
miscreants. Vanderhoff was his, even if he had to
fight off the Tregaron brothers for the privilege. Just
as the man feinted to the side Marcus caught a
glimpse of the two women joining the fray. He continued to stalk his prey as Celia and Sylvia hoisted a
large clay pot between them. A second later the inept
highwayman lay on the flagstones surrounded by
shattered pieces of clay and potting soil.

Ethan's warning cry brought his attention fully back
to Vanderhoff as the man sprang at him. He caught a
glint of metal in the man's hand just a second before
their bodies collided. The impetus of his attack
knocked both men off their feet. Reflex took control as
Marcus felt himself go backward under the other
man's weight, then he began to fall. Aware of their surroundings he turned his body at just the right moment,
knocking the knife from Vanderhoff's hand in the
process before they landed in a tangle of arms and legs
on the stone terrace at the top of the garden stairs.

"Oh, Marcus, my love. You can't be dead, please
not that. You can't die when I love you," he heard
Celia murmur heatedly as he struggled to push
Vanderhoff's unconscious body off his legs. He was
trapped between the man and the stone balustrade.

Not that he minded a moment later when he was
able to prop himself up on his left elbow. Celia was
on her knees beside him, raining kisses on his face

and whispering the most arrant nonsense. He took advantage of every inch of her attention. If it weren't for the interested spectators standing around them, he would allow himself to participate more fully in her love play. Fortunately one of them was thinking clearly, especially about the fact that she had two rather large brothers.

"Oh, no, Marcus, you're bleeding."

Since he was doing no such thing, he resented the intrusion to Celia's amorous litany. With a sigh of regret he sprang to his feet to prove that he wasn't hurt and pulled her up beside him. "That isn't my blood. Vanderhoff grazed his head on the balustrade as we went down. In fact, I made sure he did once I saw how close we were to the edge of the terrace. Now, there was something else I needed to do to prove I'm all in one piece. Ah, I remember."

Grinning in satisfaction, he snaked his arm around Celia's waist, pulling her firmly against his chest. His mouth slanted across hers in a possessive brand, his blood running hot from her kind attentions that had been very sweet, but not terribly gratifying. He took his time claiming his reward, a shudder of desire exploding through him despite the closeness of her oversized relatives. Celia was his.

When he lifted his head his gaze collided with Zachary's. Though the latter's face was stern, his green eyes were filled with amusement. Marcus winked over the top of Celia's head, and the gesture was returned quickly. The other man understood that he had some unfinished business to attend to with the lady who had given both of them so much trouble.

"Marcus, what are we going to do with these bodies?" Sylvia asked with a decided unladylike enthusiasm.

Sharing another look of masculine commiseration with her betrothed, he stepped back from his own lady's clinging hands.

"I, for one, would like some answers before we have them locked up by the local constabulary," he said matter-of-factly, surveying the damage he and his very small army had done. From the corner of his eye he could see Celia frowning at him in confusion. That was a matter he would settle later when they had some privacy.

Now that he knew the impudent lady loved him, he had all the time in the world to explore the possibilities. When he did manage to arrange for a very private interview, their first order of business would be her refusal to marry him. It just didn't make sense when she appeared to be as wildly in love with him as he was with her. Would he ever understand the machinations of the female mind, especially that of this particularly complex female?

"Ethan, make yourself useful once again and help your brother truss up our unwilling guests," he ordered, returning to the task at hand. He wanted everything settled so he could concentrate solely on Miss Celia Tregaron and she on him. "Ladies, I think you had best go check on the others to see if they have survived Thaddeus's doctoring. Gentlemen, we have an interrogation to conduct. Shall we?"

20

"*Now that everyone is here* I suppose we can begin," Marcus stated, his gaze resting thoughtfully on Silas Vanderhoff's slumped figure. The reprobate was tied to a ladderback chair that was placed back to back with the chair of Thaddeus Abernathy, his partner in crime. They were the centerpiece of the drawing room, surrounded by their captors.

Celia sat primly in the armchair by the fire, trying to resist the urge to jump up and demand what was going on. How dare he kiss her like that in front of her brothers and his sister, then act as if nothing had happened? She still squirmed inwardly at all the nonsensical things she blurted out when she thought he was injured. During the past hour she relived the experience over and over again, knowing that she would have done the same under similar circumstances.

"Fortunately, no one was injured, except our prisoners here, by this incredible plot."

He was up to something, but what could it be? Celia knew that lofty expression all too well and exchanged a sympathetic look with Sylvia seated across from her. While they had been attending to Lady Knowles and Uncle Henry she knew that Sylvia was bursting to ask what was between her and Marcus. Thankfully she hadn't been able to voice her questions, first in front of Zachary, or when Ethan had returned with the doctor.

"Which of you would like to tell us the whole tale?" Marcus began walking around the pair, twirling his wineglass negligently in his hand. As he paused and moved slowly past her uncle Celia began to guess his design. He was going to tempt Uncle Thaddeus with wine. "I know part of the conspiracy by now; however, we're going to be here all night, if need be, until you make a clean breast of it."

"I don' know nuffin' about no plot," came a querulous voice from the corner of the room. Chauncey Dalrimple, as the highwayman had identified himself, to everyone's amazement, was laid out on the settee beneath the window with a bandage on his head. "He just wanted me ta hold on ta the girl fer a time."

"Yes, we know, Chauncey. Just lie down and rest. You're going to have a terrible headache for quite some time," Marcus said, giving Celia a speaking look. She wasn't going to let herself be cowed over the matter, however. A woman had as much right as a man to physically defend her family. She didn't have to wait for a man's protection.

"Now, where were we? Oh, yes, we're going to hear a very interesting bedtime story, I believe. Gentlemen, the hour grows late, and my patience grows shorter with every passing minute." Though he didn't raise his voice, a new quality in it sent shivers down Celia's spine. "If necessary, I can have the ladies removed before I show you some interesting techniques in interrogation I learned while I was in Spain."

"I just wanted to live better, that's all," Thaddeus began in a whimper, still looking avidly at Marcus's glass. "I have a certain standard of living to maintain as an important member of the community. That horrible farm barely could make ends meet, even if Father said I was a spendthrift. Henry had to be so scrupulous about the company's accounts and keeps such a close eye on the profits I couldn't skim a little off without someone discovering it."

"Shut up, you fool."

"I'm not going to let you embroil me in this any further than I am, Vanderhoff." His round face was pitiful as tears streamed down his cheeks, yet he hungrily eyed the claret in Marcus's glass. He seemed unaware that every word he spoke implicated him further. "I never thought to kill anyone until you suggested it. I had enough funds from the contraband cargo you handled without killing Daniel Sloane."

"Oh, sweet heaven, Uncle Thaddeus, what are you saying?" Celia was on her feet at the mention of her late husband's name.

"It was *him, he* wanted to buy out the Sloane shares to give him more power," Thaddeus continued, his face eager as he saw her concern. He didn't realize that along with her horror over learning her husband was murdered, she also knew that the truth of his death was finally going to come to light. "*He* arranged it all. Just because I said it would be a pity that the profits would be smaller if you had a child. With Daniel's reputation, Vanderhoff said no one would question that the boy died in a tavern fighting over some whore."

"Oh, Uncle Thaddeus, how could you? Daniel wasn't the best husband in the world, but he never did anything to hurt you," she whispered, finally having her shame out in the open. Until now only Uncle Henry had known the truth. Her sorrow over Daniel's needless death was compounded by the fact that she had never loved him as she should have. The lie about how he died had been meant to save her pride, not to salvage Daniel's wild reputation in any way.

"He isn't worth it." She didn't realize that she was standing in front of Silas Vanderhoff until Ethan's voice came from directly behind her. "If anyone gets another crack at him, it's me. I spent over a year on a British ship thanks to his avarice."

"What? He had you impressed? How could this be?" She clutched at her brother's arms, wanting to take away the pain in his green eyes.

"We each have our disgrace in this business," Marcus explained from across the room. Celia turned to face him, glad for Ethan's supporting arm at the impact of his repentant expression. What was she going to do if he didn't love her? "You were absolutely right to seek vengeance on my family after all, my dear. It seems Vanderhoff bribed my cousin to take Ethan. He was sure that your brother would be killed during his service to His Majesty. I think Ambrose's only saving grace in this disaster is that he didn't murder your brother."

"All this for money and power?" she gasped in wonder. Looking at Vanderhoff's subdued form huddled in the chair in front of her, she couldn't even find it in her to pity him. "And you tried to kill Zachary as well when we were returning from Princetown. That is why you all came to England."

"None of this would have been necessary if you had just stayed put," the man snarled at her with the last remnant of his disdain. "I could have had you married off to my nephew with no one the wiser. Even the disgustingly honest Henry didn't have a clue of what I was planning. He never questioned why I wanted to put up in a hotel for a few days before we showed up on Ashmore's doorstep."

"Thankfully, you Tregarons seem to have the luck of the angels. Ethan also managed to get himself out of prison before the riot, which I'm sure would have found him among the fatalities." Marcus surveyed the culprits in disgust, then straightened his shoulders as if coming to a sudden decision. "Zachary, Ethan, I don't think I can stomach any more of this. I propose we deposit them in the wine cellar until they can be transported to the local gaol in the morning."

"That sounds like an excellent idea. Just think, Uncle Thaddeus, a whole night among the casks and bottles," Zachary stated after his younger brother nodded in agreement. "Ladies, if you'll excuse us we need to clear the room of unwanted debris."

Celia stepped aside as her brothers set to work on releasing the two men from their chairs. Her uncle continued to babble incessantly, begging for just a single glass of wine. She suddenly felt very tired, emotionally and physically. When the three men left the room with their prisoners in tow, she felt let down. Marcus hadn't looked in her direction since his admission that his cousin had helped with Ethan's impressment. Yet she didn't think that was the reason for his withdrawal. He now knew her final lie about Daniel.

"Sylvia, I think we should go and check on our patients. The doctor said they should probably sleep through the night." She was concerned for all the people that her uncle had drugged with laudanum. Fortunately the dose was light, and they had been able to rouse everyone enough to get them to their beds. Only the morning would tell if they were really all right. But what would the morning bring for her after what she knew would be a sleepless night?

She was going back to Baltimore as soon as possible, if she had to swim to do it, Celia decided as she sat beside her uncle the next evening when both families assembled in the drawing room after dinner. If she didn't have to stay for Zachary and Sylvia's wedding, she would leave in the morning. So far she had been able to avoid being alone all day, conveniently finding someone to keep her company at every moment. She wasn't sure how much longer that could continue.

Taking a surreptitious look at the man leaning against the mantel, she knew that she couldn't avoid him forever. The hooded expression on his handsome face was all too familiar, giving nothing away about what was going on inside his head. The last thing she wanted was a private audience with Marcus. It wasn't just her discomfiture over Uncle Thaddeus's shocking revelation about Daniel's death that revealed her final lie. In the middle of the sleepless night she had acknowledged to herself that Marcus would never come to love her.

She discounted his irritated declaration by the tower as the only means to ensure her silence in a moment of crisis. No man declares himself as part of a threat, and his kiss later had simply been part of the exhilaration after his fight with Vanderhoff. She had gambled with her emotions and lost, so she was determined to lose with dignity, not sink into a decline or have a confrontation with the man. That could only lead to an emotional ordeal she wanted to avoid at all cost.

Once Vanderhoff and her uncle had been taken away, the only high point of her day had been Ethan's arrival with his wife for dinner. Otherwise she was miserable, but put on a brave front so no one would guess at her distress, especially her genial host. He was now holding forth, standing in front of the fire as if he didn't have a care in the world. If he did love her, wouldn't he have forced her to face him today?

"I can't thank you enough, Mrs. Tregaron, for making your husband come to make his apologies last night." Marcus smiled down at the blushing Bess in a most ingratiating manner that set Celia's teeth on edge. He could be so charming when he chose, mostly to everyone but her. "The sight of his face peering up at me out of the shrubbery was one of the most incredible moments of my life. Ethan, just how did you know there was trouble?"

"I literally stumbled in at the right moment. When I got here there wasn't a soul around, though the house was ablaze with lights," he replied, tugging at his neckcloth absently until his wife pulled on his sleeve and gave him a reproving look. His tender smile for Bess made Celia envious. "When no one answered my knock on the door, I tried the latch. I knew that there should be servants around, even if the rest of you had gone out. I stepped into the drawing room and discovered Uncle Henry snoring his head off, and Lady

Knowles was out like a light as well. It was apparent something was wrong, then I heard the scuffling out on the porch. Before I could tell anyone I was here, Vanderhoff made his appearance."

"So, my enterprising brother snuck around the side of the house to rescue all the rest of the blind idiots from the dumbest lot of criminals I've yet to see," Zachary finished for him from his seat next to Sylvia. Celia tried not to look at their entwined hands, or her friend's contented smile.

"I still haven't decided if they were so unlucky," Henry put in, most of his bombast gone after his near brush with death, no matter that he slept through the threat. He patted Celia's hand affectionately. "It just seems that the luck was on our side. Not only did we escape the poor efforts of Vanderhoff's plot, we manage to increase the size of the family by two, soon to be three when Bess has her child."

"I'll see to it that we make it four if it takes the rest of the season," Lady Knowles declared from her comfortable chair, not bothering to look up from her embroidery. If she had she would have seen Celia's horrified expression. Celia didn't know where to look, so resigned herself to beginning a study of the floor coverings at King's Rest. "I must have something to show for this adventure. Ethan has been so unobliging as to appear, not only disgustingly healthy, but with a wife in tow. Then, Zachary takes it into his head to steal my only daughter. Celia, my dear, you are my last chance to play matchmaker, since Marcus is a hopeless case. But don't you worry, I shall have every eligible man in London camping on the doorstep in no time."

"But Lady Knowles, I'll be going back to Baltimore

very soon." She rushed in to clarify the matter, not wanting anyone to guess how much she wanted to stay. "We have two ships sitting at anchor with no cargo. As soon as Zachary and Sylvia are married Uncle Henry and I will be sailing home, won't we?"

She carefully avoided looking toward the fireplace as she made her desperate effort to preserve the last of her dignity. After all, she knew that Marcus was undoubtedly tired of the constant unrest she had caused. Every time she turned around she managed only to create trouble for his family. What was supposed to be a simple matter of locating her brother had turned into the near-murder of everyone around her.

Though the danger was gone now that Vanderhoff and her uncle were in custody, she knew she couldn't stand the strain of being with Marcus day in and day out. Not that Marcus hadn't been pleasant to her whenever they chanced to meet during the day. He had made idle chatter while she and Sylvia selected flowers from the garden. She had felt a twinge of guilt at the anxious look in her friend's eyes as she watched the two of them, but she would neither let Sylvia leave her side nor respond to anything that had to do with her brother.

Later, after Sylvia had gone off to walk with Zachary in the garden, Marcus came upon her with his mother as they sorted embroidery silks. Fortunately, he was called away by a message from Haskell. She couldn't fault his behavior at all. In fact, he treated her just as he would any other guest in his house, damn him.

"Now, we can't have you rushing off for at least another month since we have to wait for the banns to be read," Marcus informed her much too amicably for her liking. Perversely, she almost missed his sardonic manner of their early days together. "I want my sister to have a proper wedding, after all."

"Oh, Marcus, we can't possibly be ready in less than two months, even if Sylvia is marrying a Colonial," his mother put in, making Celia want to scream in frustration at how the length of her exile in England was expanding. "Of course, by that time Bess will probably be ready to have the baby, and naturally Ethan will want his family here for that. You will, won't you, dear? You aren't planning on disowning them again, are you?"

"No, milady. I think we've managed to patch up our differences just fine," Ethan said, his discomfort clear over his deception that had unwittingly aided Vanderhoff's insane plans. "In fact, we've managed to come to an agreement about my shares in the business. It seems we need an agent in London, so I can still be part of the family business without going to sea again."

"What happened to Mr. Hampton?" Celia asked in surprise. Though she hadn't like him terribly much, he had been helpful when she first arrived.

"He has decided that he doesn't like working for Americans," her uncle explained, casting a look at the other gentlemen in the room. Celia almost thought she saw Zachary nod before Henry continued. "It seems Mr. Hampton has been helping himself to the Tregaron funds."

"Can we trust anyone anymore?" she wondered, not realizing she spoke aloud until Marcus answered her query.

"Most people can be trusted, my dear; you just have to know when to make a leap of faith and believe in your instincts."

She found she couldn't meet his look and quickly
began a conversation with Bess. Now she knew that
Marcus would never forgive her for her lies, and she
had no one but herself to blame for her unhappiness.
His meaning was all too clear to her. If she truly trusted
him, she would have confided in him from the very
beginning. Instead, she had told one lie after another
until she had been completely unmasked by her family.

The rest of the evening she barely spoke another
word, simply sitting and letting the conversation flow
around her. Whenever she looked across at Ethan and
his wife she experienced a little pleasure. Her adventure had had the most happy result in finding her
younger brother, no matter how much their lives had
changed since his capture. It was a small comfort that
helped ease her heartache.

By the time everyone was saying good night she
was more than ready to retire. She was halfway up
the stairs when Lady Knowles stopped directly in
front of her. "Oh, my dear, could you fetch my shawl
for me? I left it on the chair, and I really must have it
around my shoulders when I sleep."

She turned reluctantly to oblige, keeping a sharp eye
out for Marcus as she walked back to the sitting room.
Stokes was there and smiled at her rather strangely,
she thought, but then decided her imagination was
playing tricks on her. She was being overly suspicious
after so much had taken place in the past few days.

The trip up the stairs to Lady Knowles's room was
uneventful, much to her disappointment. She gave
the maid the shawl and turned listlessly toward her
own room. A small part of her kept hoping she was
wrong about Marcus. As she walked down the hall
Celia decided she had to ask Uncle Henry to rent a

house for them as soon as possible. If she must stay in England for several months, she knew she couldn't possibly stay in Marcus's company, having him so close every day, without giving herself away.

Once inside her sitting room she closed the door and leaned back against it for a moment. Finally she could give in to her feelings of dejection, not having to keep up a pleasant facade. Squaring her shoulders, she straightened, only then noticing that the room was unusually dark. Though the fire was lit, the only candles that seemed to be burning were in the bedroom. Usually Meg had every candle ablaze, an extravagance Celia had become accustomed to during her visit. At home Uncle Henry had always been mindful of the household expenses down to the last candle and lamp.

Then it struck her that Meg wasn't there. In the past few days she could barely step into her rooms without the girl chattering away about what was happening belowstairs, especially if it had to do with the second footman. Shaking her head, she headed for the bedroom. She never made it through the door, frozen on the threshold at the sight before her.

"You needn't look so worried. I haven't brought a pistol with me," Marcus declared dryly, giving her a welcoming smile from where he lay on her bed. "I'm sure that you're as thoroughly tired of people brandishing weapons in your vicinity as I am."

"Wh—what are you doing here?" She could be imagining this, she decided, still not moving away from the door. This could also be a dream. Perhaps she had fallen asleep downstairs and was imagining that Marcus was lying on her bed. She closed her eyes for a moment, thinking that he would be gone when she opened them again. He was still there, and her heart began to beat somewhat erratically, but she couldn't think beyond the moment.

"I'm not going anywhere, my sweet. You see, I've taken quite a lot of trouble to ensure that we won't be disturbed until morning," he continued as if he were relating an amusing piece of gossip. She was having trouble concentrating on his words as her gaze kept straying to his lean body, exactly where she had been imagining it so many nights. "It also cost me a pretty penny to bribe your maid into leaving us here, alone at this unusual hour. Though I think half the household is aware I'm here, including my scheming mama."

"Why are you doing this? Is this some kind of revenge for all the trouble I've caused?" she asked, wondering what to do next. She wasn't sure if she should walk across the room and slap him for his presumption or fling herself at his supine, and very inviting, body. From his dress she knew that his intentions weren't the most honorable. His only apparel was his dressing gown, the same scarlet and indigo garment that had been lying across his bed the first night she met him.

"I'm here to compromise you, of course. Since you kept haring off like a startled rabbit every time I came near you—"

"I did not," she blurted out, then flushed scarlet at his skeptical look. "This is ridiculous, Marcus. You can't stay here."

"Oh, but I can and I will. You see, if you are going to be your usual obstinate self and continue to refuse my proposal, I've seen to it that we'll be found tomorrow morning, in what I hope will be a moment of passion. That would be a nice touch, don't you think?" He smiled at her as if he had accomplished some great feat. The warmth in his eyes was making her believe all sorts of impossible things could be true. "Now are you going to be sensible about this?"

Celia closed her eyes once more, praying fervently that she was making the right decision. What had he said about trust last night? She was going to have to make a leap of faith.

"Yes, I'll marry you." Once the words were out she opened her eyes again to see his reaction and almost groaned in disappointment. Although the desire was clear in his appraising look she couldn't read what was on his mind, or in his heart. "Yes, I'll marry you on certain conditions," she added.

"Ah, I thought there would be a catch. That clever little Colonial mind of yours is always at work. Since this may take some time, would you like some wine?" he asked congenially, dropping his legs over the side of the bed. She tensed in anticipation for a moment, but immediately felt foolish because he was simply pouring himself a glass of wine from the bottle on the night table. Once he finished he carefully plumped the pillows and lay back down again. "Now, what are those conditions, my sweet?"

Clenching her fists at her sides she tried to ignore the way his dressing gown gaped open to expose the hard muscles of his bare chest. She couldn't think of what it was like to run her hands over his hair-roughened skin, not now. Her mind had to keep functioning on a more practical level. "First, I refuse to have any secrets between us. You aren't to keep anything from me, especially if you think it is for my own good."

He lifted an eyebrow when he realized she was waiting for his response. "A hard decision, but I promise. That doesn't count birthdays and Christmas presents, or surprising you with some little trinket now and then, does it?"

She didn't bother to answer the ridiculous question. "Secondly, I won't be treated like an idiot child when I do something you dislike or that you think is unwise. No longwinded, patronizing lectures from you or my brothers, simply a reasonable discussion of the matter."

He grimaced but nodded in agreement.

"Next, I will be in charge of my own money, since I have a full partnership in Tregaron Shipping and have several investments in my name."

For a moment he looked as if he intended to object, taking a sip of wine and looking up at the underside of the tester. She was tempted to pour the decanter of wine on his head. "Done."

"You will also never even think about how attractive another woman looks, since you will only be making love to your wife from this moment on."

"That shouldn't be too difficult. If things go as I envision them, you'll keep me so exhausted I wouldn't care if another woman walked into my bed-chamber stark naked." The lazy way his gaze ran over her made her feel as if her rose-colored gown had suddenly become invisible.

"If you and Garth or any of your friends want to spend the night drinking you can do it in the comfort of your own home."

"You drive a very hard bargain, my sweet. That may open to debate later, I hope."

She nodded and tried not to shift nervously as his interest seemed to linger on the shadowed valley of her breasts, just visible over the top of her dress. Her final demand was going to sacrifice every ounce of pride and courage she possessed.

"And finally, the most important condition of them all, which must be met." She hesitated before making the last demand, uncertain if she was being wise. Then she lifted her chin, and squared her shoulders. She had never backed away from a challenge before this, so she had to take the chance. Marcus had come here of his own free will. "I will not marry again unless my husband loves me."

Before she could decide to stay or flee after her dauntless pronouncement Marcus was on his feet, closing the distance between them in three strides. Then she was locked in his embrace, fervently returning the hot demand of his kiss. The touch of his hands through the thin material of her dress sent fiery sparks through every pore of her body. Celia gloried in his touch and taste, threading her fingers through his chestnut hair to prolong their kiss.

"You've led me a merry chase, sweet witch," he finally murmured against the vulnerable skin just below her ear, his warm breath disturbing a lock of her hair. "Now, I think that one of us is slightly over-dressed for the occasion."

Not letting her demur he spun her around to attack the buttons of her dress. When the second button went flying across the room she tried to protest, but was silenced by the feel of his lips against the nape of her neck. Everywhere he touched her, she burned, and the most exciting caress was the feel of his fingers trembling against the slope of her back. Celia felt that she would melt into the floor at any moment, but one last coherent thought kept chasing through her mind.

Dressed only in her chemise and pink stockings she turned to face him, trapping his hands between hers and holding them against her breast. She had to know before she became totally mindless under his sensuous spell. Leaning forward she placed her lips on his bare chest, exactly over the place his heart beat as rapidly as hers. His groan of response made her smile, and she looked up into his half-closed eyes. "Tell me, please. I want to hear the words without being threatened this once."

He never questioned her meaning. "I love you, Celia Tregaron. You've stolen into my heart and my life would be worthless without you in it to torment me, make me angry, seduce me, make me laugh, and worry me to death about what you'll do next."

Marcus looked down at her with an expression she had never seen before, a mixture of love, need, and laughter all in one. "Now, don't I deserve to hear the words as well? You haven't said anything about your feelings. I only know that you can't resist ravishing me whenever we are alone together."

For a moment she couldn't respond, suddenly shy over her brazen behavior in the past weeks. How had she ever had the nerve to do such things? She caught her breath as his knuckles skimmed over the curves of her breasts, making them feel tight with the need to be touched. Then he raised his hand to tilt her chin up so he could see her face.

"You're not going to become shy on me now, are you? How disappointing," he murmured, his gaze following the path of his hand to her shoulder. In a deft movement he slipped the lace-trimmed strap off her shoulder. "While I was waiting for you I was day-dreaming how exciting it is to have a woman who is so open and honest in her lovemaking. I've never doubted that you desire me, my sweet."

"Honest, Marcus?" she asked, smiling ruefully. "I

began lying to you almost from the moment we met. First about my family, then that fairy tale about Daniel."

Without a word he led her to bed. A moment later she found herself draped across his lap held firmly in his arms. "Tell me what you need to about Daniel and that will finish it. I don't know what troubles you so much, but I want to understand."

"Perhaps I'm being foolish about this," she began reluctantly, allowing him to gently guide her head to the cushion of his shoulder. It was easier not having to look at him and be distracted by his devilish blue-green eyes and beguiling smile. "I was fond of Daniel when we married, but I was young. He had a wild reputation in his youth, and some wondered why he would bother with me. I know he was faithful to me; however, when I found out he was said to be killed fighting over a woman I couldn't face the possible gossip. For years I lied about how he died, not to preserve his reputation, but to save my silly pride."

"I fell off my horse."

"Pardon?" She raised her head, blinking up at him to see what his quiet statement had to do with her confession.

"You wanted to know how I injured my arm. Garth and I were a bit well to live one evening, celebrating a successful mission," he explained, looking like a schoolboy admitting to some minor transgression. "We chanced upon these two, er, young ladies and I was feeling very gallant." He broke off to give her a stern look. "I didn't make rude noises when you were telling your story, did I? We are going to have to discuss these Colonial rag manners of yours sometime, perhaps on our fiftieth anniversary?"

"Sorry, go on." She schooled her features into the

proper expression of fascinated interest. "Marcus, you can't kiss me now, you're confessing."

"Oh, yes. Well, it seems that the *ladies* had some other gentlemen friends and they objected to them expanding their circle of acquaintances," he continued smoothly. "I bowed in farewell, but one of the gentleman took exception to my manners. He pulled me off my horse. In my condition I didn't brace myself for the fall and came down hard, slamming my right arm against an iron trough. Once the swelling and bruising went away, we discovered the real damage. That is how I was wounded in the defense of my country."

"Oh, my dear." She didn't know what to say, and was afraid to open her mouth in case she laughed at his chagrined expression.

"At least you didn't say, 'my hero,'" he returned dryly, which sent her over the edge. Both of them collapsed in laughter, clutching each other until their amusement died. "You see, we all tell little lies to preserve our dignity. I never actually said I was wounded in battle, but everyone assumed that was the case. Of course, Garth holds it over my head whenever he wants anything."

"Have you heard from him?" she inquired, not sure what she should do next, although she knew what she wanted to do. Tracing her initials across Marcus's collarbone seemed to be a good start.

"Yes, he is incredibly bored right now, wishing that the French would either make war or go home." He didn't seem terribly interested in his friend's welfare, however. His fingers were exploring the neckline of her chemise until he reached the second strap. The flimsy piece of silk quickly followed its mate. Then he slipped his finger into the valley between her breasts, moving the pad of his finger downward with excruciating slowness. Celia held her breath as the thin material dragged against her aroused skin, and she couldn't contain her gasp of pleasure when the hem moved over the peaks of her breasts.

Then she didn't have any time to think, only to respond when Marcus bent his head to suckle her. She moved restlessly against him, completely enthralled by his action. Wanting to give him the same tormenting pleasure, she pulled frantically at the lapels of his dressing gown, impatient to feel only his warm flesh against hers.

Marcus groaned low in his throat as her hands moved over him, from his shoulders to his abdomen, pulling the silk away from his body. He moved his attention to her other breast, allowing her to turn in his arms. The hot brand of his arousal throbbed against her hip as she rubbed against him. Impatient with his leisurely caresses Celia wanted to experience the full extent of their passion.

She was almost startled when she found herself astride Marcus, but the dark, hungry look in his eyes spurred her on. Giving him a seduction smile as old as time she rocked her hips against his, glorying in the shudder of response that rippled through his body. His hand at her hip urged her into the unfamiliar movement. All the breath seemed to escape her body at the moment he thrust upward. She closed her eyes to savor the sensation, embracing the incredible feel of his entrance.

At first she moved cautiously, one part of her afraid of hurting her lover, another part wanting their joining to last forever. Marcus took her hands, pulling her gently forward until their lips met. The molten kiss they shared caused both of them to moan with pleasure. He was now fully inside her, causing her to rear back in reaction. The world was spinning out of control, but she didn't care as long as Marcus was holding her. The caressing touch of his hands at her breasts sent her flying into the heavens.

She called out his name, clutching at his shoulders as the climactic force shattered the building tension inside her. A second later Marcus cried out his satisfaction, pulling her down to seal the moment with a kiss. Celia lay on his damp body, wondering if she would ever be able to move again. Though it took some effort she raised her head and smiled. "My hero."

She could feel his laughter vibrating through his body beneath hers. He tumbled her onto her back and loomed over her. "Vixen."

When he raised his head a few minutes later, and she could breathe again, she asked, "Is it always going to be like this?"

"I'm willing to experiment if you are," he mused, outlining the shape of her breast with his finger.

"Oh, good." She sighed and snuggled into his side. "I think I'm going to like being compromised, especially when we're indoors in a nice warm bed."

"And here I thought it was going to take half the night to convince you that being a British countess wasn't going to be so terrible," he murmured against her skin, his lips tracing the slope of her shoulder inward to the base of her neck. "I thought perhaps the thought of joining the peerage was why you were dragging your dainty little democratic feet."

"Oh, sweet heaven." Celia pushed hard against his shoulder with the palm of her hand until he finally pulled back. His face was very solemn as he waited for whatever she was going to say. "Marcus . . ."

"No backing out now that I've met every one of your conditions," he stated in his usual autocratic manner, his back muscles stiffening under her hands.

"A question of honor?" she asked, realizing that Marcus wasn't seeing the humor in the situation at all. "Was there a condition about not behaving like a toplofty aristocrat in bed?"

He smiled at her then before giving her a smacking kiss. "Unlike your brother, we aren't waiting for the banns either, just in case you try to change your mind. I can't think of a more perfect revenge against the audacious woman who threatened me in my own bed-chamber than turning her into a loyal British subject."

"It should be interesting," she murmured, linking her hands at the base of his neck and pulling his weight fully down onto her body. She twisted slowly beneath him, and whispered against his lips. "I'll make sure that all the children will be Whigs."

Author's Note

Celia's search for her brother, Ethan, was already roughed out when I discovered that the American prisoners of war were still being held long after the War of 1812 was over. Somehow it was a fitting footnote to a strange war with great naval victories and disastrous land battles for the Americans. (A war my British grandfather always stated was won by *his* side.) The Battle of New Orleans was fought two weeks after the peace treaty was signed, as news of the treaty—signed on Christmas Eve of 1814— didn't reach the United States until February 1815.

For the curious I've included a brief account of why the Americans were detained. Readers will notice the real prison governor was named Shortland. Since no detailed information was available, I created my own prison commander in the annoying Titus.

Most readers are familiar with Dartmoor Prison in terms of sinister moors in Victorian mysteries such as Sir Arthur Conan Doyle's *The Hound of the Baskervilles*. The prison wasn't used for common criminals until

1850. It was built between 1806 and 1808 to house prisoners of the Napoleonic wars, and by some accounts, the granite fortress was actually built by the French prisoners. The first American prisoners arrived in April of 1813. Most were captured merchantmen and privateers with a small percentage from the American navy.

Before arriving at Dartmoor the American sailors were kept in prison ships at Plymouth, Chatham, and Portsmouth. By March of 1815, 6,500 Americans were incarcerated at the prison. The French prisoners were released in the spring of 1814, but the Americans remained for six months after their war ended. The delay was caused by disagreements between the British and American governments over who was responsible for the expense of transporting the prisoners home.

On April 6, a hole was discovered in one of the inner walls of Dartmoor, leading not to the moors as a possible escape route but to another prison yard. The British troops inexplicably fired on the prisoners in the yards, killing seven men and wounding thirty-one. An investigation of the tragedy by British and American representatives exonerated the prison governor Thomas Shortland and placed the blame on the unidentified troops who fired on the prisoners.

The tragic killings convinced the British authorities that they couldn't wait for American financial help any longer. Any prisoner who could support himself was released immediately. Ships were provided for the others, the cost shared later by the two governments. By the end of June, only 900 prisoners remained, half of them black sailors waiting for ships to northern American ports. (One out of seven prisoners was a free black sailor from the merchant navy.) In mid-July of 1815, the last American left Dartmoor and finally ended the War of 1812.

GLORY IN THE SPLENDOR OF SUMMER WITH

HarperMonogram's
101 Days of Romance

BUY 3 BOOKS, GET 1 FREE!

ake a book to the beach, relax by the pool, or read in the most quiet and romantic spot in your home. You can live through love all summer long when you redeem this exciting offer from HarperMonogram. Buy any three HarperMonogram romances in June, July, or August, and get a fourth book sent to you for FREE. See next page for the list of top-selling novels and romances by your favorite authors that you can choose from for your premium!

101 Days of Romance
BUY 3 BOOKS, GET 1 FREE!

CHOOSE A FREE BOOK FROM THIS OUTSTANDING
LIST OF AUTHORS AND TITLES:

HarperMonogram

____LORD OF THE NIGHT Susan Wiggs 0-06-108052-7

____ORCHIDS IN MOONLIGHT Patricia Hagan 0-06-108038-1

____TEARS OF JADE Leigh Riker 0-06-108047-0

____DIAMOND IN THE ROUGH Millie Criswell 0-06-108093-4

____HIGHLAND LOVE SONG Constance O'Banyon 0-06-108121-3

____CHEYENNE AMBER Catherine Anderson 0-06-108061-6

____OUTRAGEOUS Christina Dodd 0-06-108151-5

____THE COURT OF THREE SISTERS Marianne Willman 0-06-108053-5

____DIAMOND Sharon Sala 0-06-108196-5

____MOMENTS Georgia Bockoven 0-06-108164-7

HarperPaperbacks

____THE SECRET SISTERS Ann Maxwell 0-06-104236-6

____EVERYWHERE THAT MARY WENT Lisa Scottoline 0-06-104293-5

____NOTHING PERSONAL Eileen Dreyer 0-06-104275-7

____OTHER LOVERS Erin Pizzey 0-06-109032-8

____MAGIC HOUR Susan Isaacs 0-06-109948-1

____A WOMAN BETRAYED Barbara Delinsky 0-06-104034-7

____OUTER BANKS Anne Rivers Siddons 0-06-109973-2

____KEEPER OF THE LIGHT Diane Chamberlain 0-06-109040-9

____ALMONDS AND RAISINS Maisie Mosco 0-06-100142-2

____HERE I STAY Barbara Michaels 0-06-100726-9

To receive your free book, simply send in this coupon **and** your store receipt with the purchase prices circled. You may take part in this exclusive offer as many times as you wish, but all qualifying purchases must be made by September 4, 1995, and all requests must be postmarked by October 4, 1995. Please allow 6-8 weeks for delivery.

MAIL TO: HarperPaperbacks, Dept. FC-101
10 East 53rd Street, New York, N.Y. 10022-5299

Name_____

Address_____

City_____State_____Zip_____

Offer is subject to availability. HarperPaperbacks may make substitutions for requested titles.   H09511

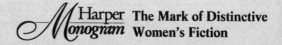

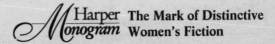